TRADING PLACES

"Let me go over this one last time," Mary Lynn said. "You say that your agent and your mother know, but no one else knows."

"Right."

"I do the publicity for this new movie of yours. I say how great your director is." Mary Lynn consulted her notes. "And I tell cute stories about how much I love camels."

"That's for the animal rights people. I'm famous for my love of animals."

"And meanwhile, you live my life."

"Exactly." Jayne nodded. Two minutes without a cigarette and she was already feeling a little alarm going off inside her head. Could she actually give up smoking? Could she pass herself off as an English professor?

"And for this," Mary Lynn continued, "you pay me a hundred thousand dollars: twenty-five thousand down, and the rest if we can pull this off?"

"Right."

Mary Lynn picked up one of Jayne's Diet Cokes and forced herself to drink it. Diet Cokes were one of Jayne's trademarks. She swallowed with difficulty and put the red-and-silver can back down on the table. "To be honest, Jayne, I don't think this switch has a chance of working, but what do I have to lose?"

"So do we have a deal?"

"We have a deal. . . ."

THE
STAND-IN

Kate Clemens

KENSINGTON BOOKS
Kensington Publishing Corp.
http://www.kensingtonbooks.com

KENSINGTON BOOKS are published by

Kensington Publishing Corp.
850 Third Avenue
New York, NY 10022

First Kensington Mass Market printing: May 2003

10 9 8 7 6 5 4 3 2 1

Printed in the United States of America

One

Jayne Cooper gasped and leaned forward to peer at her own reflection. The face she saw was one of the most famous faces on the planet. At this very moment, it floated on giant billboards above Sunset Boulevard and Times Square and Piccadilly Circus; millions of people knew it better than they knew the faces of their own children. It was the kind of face given to only one actress in each generation: sexy, sweet, vulnerable, kind, and almost angelic in its perfection.

"Oh no!" Jayne moaned. No ordinary mortal could have figured out what she was upset about. The eyes that looked back at her were as blue as cornflowers; the lips were soft and gently curved. Her chin was small but firm, nose straight, and skin flawless as a baby's. Her blond hair (which she always wore long, unless some idiot director forced her to cut it) had natural tints of red and deep gold. Even now, scrunched back in an elastic band to keep it out of the way of the black wig she was about to don, it looked good.

Jayne wrinkled her perfect forehead and opened her pretty mouth. She poked at the mirror with one exquisitely manicured fingernail. "What the hell are those!" she snarled.

"What are what?" asked Clarice calmly.

Jayne again jabbed at her own reflection. "Those!" She turned to her mother. "Those ghastly *things* under my eyes that make me look like Godzilla!"

Clarice cupped Jayne's chin in her hand and turned

Jayne's face toward the lights. Behind them, the makeup trailer had fallen eerily silent.

"I believe those are bags," Clarice said in a measured voice.

"Bags!" Jayne felt the makeup stool slipping out from under her. She felt the kind of dizzy, visceral horror she sometimes felt when she stepped barefoot on a banana slug. "Bags?" Her voice took on an edge that would have reminded her fans of the famous scene in *Queen of Scots* when she ordered the decapitation of the traitor who had betrayed her lover.

"Bags," Clarice repeated mercilessly in a soft, cultured, southern accent that had the cutting power of a straight razor. "You're not sixteen anymore, honey. You can't stay up all night and not expect it to show. How many times have I told you that you have to get your beauty sleep?" Clarice spoke as if she were still running Jayne's life the way she had run it for all the years Jayne was a child star; but the truth was, Jayne intimidated her mother the same way she intimidated everyone else. What Clarice really wanted from her daughter these days was some sign of love and affection, some indication that Jayne realized Clarice had always tried to do what was best for her. But instead, they always ended up spitting at each other like two cats roped together at the neck.

Jayne pointed to the door of the makeup trailer. "Fix these damn bags, Mother, or I'm not going out there. I won't be mocked; I won't be humiliated; I won't be crucified for money. I have my pride. My self-respect."

Clarice relaxed. Everything Jayne had just said beginning with the words "I'm not going out there" were lines from *Bella. Bella,* the story of a woman who kept her self-respect, had been one of Jayne's most popular films. It had grossed $329 million. In other words, this was not a real crisis.

Clarice stared at Jayne and tried to calculate how long it was going to take to coax her out of the trailer. Sometimes she bunkered in for hours, putting on her makeup and taking it off until everyone around her went nuts. As usual, the success or failure of the entire movie was resting on Jayne's shoulders.

She was the only one who could turn this multimillion-dollar turkey into 120 minutes of pure magic; if it bombed at the box office, she would also be the one the studio would blame. But this was no time to panic. The end was in sight. Two more days of shooting left; then they could all fly back to the Coast and check into an air-conditioned hotel, where a person wasn't forced to sit down to a breakfast of weak coffee and skewered goat kidneys.

She reached out and began to massage Jayne's neck and shoulders. "You have to go on," she said. "There are five hundred extras out there being paid union scale. You can't hang them out to dry. This is Salome's big scene, remember? The one where you dance for the king."

"I don't care," Jayne whimpered. "It's too hot."

"You were the one who bullied Bert into dragging all of us to this godforsaken hellhole."

"I wanted authenticity. Is that a crime? Let them wait."

"We're running out of water, Jayne. Even the camels are thirsty."

"I don't care; I hate camels. They spit."

"You were the one who made Bert send a messenger to Paris for your favorite shade of nail polish. That's already delayed shooting for two days."

"I don't care about petty details, Mother. I care about my art. My nails are part of me." Jayne waved her perfectly manicured fingers in Clarice's face. "They're a statement."

Clarice slowly removed her hands from Jayne's neck. "Jayne, let me joggle your memory. Outside that door is a real palace, four hundred transplanted palm trees, forty-two camels, one trained bear, one semitrained python, seventeen priceless oriental carpets, a crew that's sleeping with sand in their sheets, a director who is on the verge of his third heart attack, and one very pissed-off prince who wants his palace back. The rent on the palace alone is a quarter of a million a day. This film is already twenty million over budget, the local newspapers are talking revolution, and there's a sandstorm predicted for tomorrow. So unless you want to be known as the actress who starred in *Ishtar Two,* you've got to walk out of this trailer, hold your chin high, and give it your best shot."

"No!" Jayne shook her head so hard the silk band came off her hair. As it cascaded down over her bare shoulders, it made her look sweeter and more vulnerable than ever. "Not like this. You can't ask this of me. You know how *cruel* the lights are. You know how cameramen talk."

Clarice did know. Although she had never been as beautiful as Jayne, she had been a star in a minor constellation before she married Jayne's father, a high-powered studio exec who had made her his wife on the understanding that she would retire permanently from films. Clarice had made only three movies before her marriage, but one had been with Hitchcock and one with Huston; she knew all about the cruelty of lights, lenses, and cameramen.

Jayne leaned forward, peered into the mirror, and tentatively touched the bags beneath her eyes as if her skin were so fragile it might peel off under her fingers. "They'll say I'm too old for the part of Salome; they'll say I'm over-the-hill." She turned to Clarice and her mouth hardened into a stubborn line. "That's it. I've had it. I'm getting a face-lift." It wasn't a statement; it was an order. And, like all of Jayne's orders, it demanded immediate attention.

"Don't be ridiculous," Clarice snapped. "This is a foreign country where, for all we know, they get blood from camels. You can't have surgery here, and besides, you're only thirty. You start getting face-lifts now, and you won't have any skin left around your eyes by the time you're forty."

"Forty!" Jayne cried. "You may not think I know what you're saying when you mention that despicable age, but I do! You're saying I'm growing old! You're saying my career's over! Well, the hell with you. The hell with everyone. Why don't you just wad me up and recycle me? What am I—a paper cup? No, worse, a Styrofoam cup? Is that what I am to all of you? Toxic waste? Well, then, why don't you just shoot me now and put me out of my pain?"

Clarice ignored Jayne and motioned to Don, a tall man in his early thirties who had stood invisibly in one corner of the trailer like a well-trained dog during the entire conversation. "Don, can you fix these bags under her eyes?"

Don, who was one of the best makeup artists in the industry, ventured a quick smile. "Sure thing. Two little dabs of Preparation H under Miss Cooper's eyes, and those bags will disappear"—he snapped his fingers—"like that."

"It's no use," Jayne wailed. "When you're over-the-hill, you're over-the-hill." But she knew down deep that Don could and would fix her eyes, and that she could and would go on.

As Don tilted back her head to apply the Preparation H, she felt oddly satisfied. She had just given a great performance. What a pity that no one had caught it on film.

Two

"You want what?" Larry Sears leaned forward in his chair and stared at Jayne with the sort of horrified fascination a rabbit might display seconds before it's devoured by a boa constrictor. He sensed his most famous client was up to something that was going to put him back on his blood pressure–lowering medication, but he couldn't figure out what it was. In the six years he had been Jayne's agent, she had come up with any number of strange demands, several of which had driven him to the edge of cashing in his stocks, changing his name, and moving to a country with no extradition treaty with the United States. Was she worth it? Yes, definitely. Was it hell being her agent? Yes, and yes again. He smiled at her weakly. "Explain."

"There's nothing to explain. I want a stand-in. Period. End of discussion." Jayne had known he wouldn't like the idea, but she had thought this over carefully; she wasn't taking "no" for an answer. In fact, she never took "no" for an answer. It was, she thought, one of her virtues.

"But you already have a stand-in."

"Ann Ellis doesn't work in this situation."

"Why not? She's exactly your height; her coloring is the same; she never says a word—which as you will recall was one of the things you stipulated when we hired her; she's about ten times uglier than you—also a plus in your book; and she's willing to stand under hot lights for hours at a time. Ann has the patience of Job. The gaffers call her the human statue. I think you'd be unwise to fire her."

"I don't intend to fire her. What I intend . . ." Jayne stretched out her hand, and her "Personal Assistant" scurried forward to place a Diet Coke in it. Jayne hired and fired her personal assistants so often that she rarely could remember their names. This current one was a mousy little twenty-something with a minuscule nose and watery eyes that were on the verge of being crossed. Some stars liked to surround themselves with youth and beauty. Jayne preferred competent homeliness.

Like all of Jayne's assistants, Irene or Heather or whatever the hell her name was probably had dreams of being in the movies someday. At present, though, her job—the only job in film she was ever likely to get—was to make sure that no matter where in the world Jayne was, her refrigerator was always well stocked with caviar, champagne, Diet Cokes, and microwavable low-calorie meals prepared by the chef at the Blue Azul Spa, plus Jayne's staff of life: Bombay Sapphire gin, tonic, and limes. When Jayne stretched out her hand, the assistant was required to place in it exactly what Jayne wanted without being told, and God help the ones who weren't psychic enough to figure out what that was.

The feel of the cold Diet Coke can coming to rest precisely in the center of her palm reminded Jayne that she and Larry weren't alone. "You can go now," she said. She waited until she heard the sound of her assistant closing the door and then continued.

"I want someone precisely like me in every detail. Call her whatever you like: my double, my twin, Jayne Cooper times two. I want a duplicate of myself. And I don't want her next week—I want her now."

"That's a tall order."

"It can't be that hard. Hundreds of people make their living impersonating me."

"True, but they're mostly gay men."

"Transvestites won't do. They get five o'clock shadows,

and my double has got to look exactly like me from six inches away. She's even got to look like me naked. Which means, of course . . ." Jayne paused. This was hard to say, but she had steeled herself in advance. "She has to be absolutely gorgeous."

"Maybe we should just clone you." He should have known better than to try to joke with Jayne at a time like this. She gave him a blank stare that made him feel like the frog waiting for the princess's kiss. Then she stretched out her hand, but since she had dismissed her assistant, no one put anything into it.

"Cigarette," she said.

Larry took out his gold cigarette case and handed her a cigarette. Jayne looked at it and frowned.

"Not my brand."

"Sorry."

"Light."

He picked up the heavy silver-plated cigarette lighter that graced her coffee table. The thing was covered with flowers, fruit, and some kind of strange animals that resembled writhing griffins. Who'd given it to her? The prince? Or maybe the president of Argentina? There was no telling. Jayne had never had a shortage of admirers.

He flicked the lighter, and Jayne leaned forward and lit her cigarette. Inhaling deeply, she blew the smoke out of her nose and inhaled again.

"I'm serious," she continued. *"Salome* is in the can. Is it good? Does it stink? Who knows? I liked the script. I got to play Salome as a sympathetic character. She's nice. She didn't mean to get John's head chopped off. It just happened. I like nice. My fans like nice. The point is, I've been back from that hideous little hunk of godforsaken desert long enough to recover from the near terminal sunburn I got trying to even up my tan. . . ."

Larry knew exactly what Jayne meant by "evening up her tan." He looked down at his knees and tried his best not to imagine her sunbathing naked and burning her pretty nipples. He had long ago decided that it was best if he never thought of her as a woman.

". . . and, as you know, I'm looking around for my next film. For years"—Jayne went through the complicated inhaling, exhaling, inhaling exercise again—"I've wanted to play more serious parts. Dramatic parts. Roles that show my real range. I've heard rumors that I may be up for the Kleinhaus Award again. This is the fifth time. Will they give it to me? No. I'm not even going to bother to enter the date of the ceremony in my Palm Pilot.

"I'm a talented actress. But the critics"—she stubbed out her cigarette with a quick stab—"never have appreciated my talents." She looked at Larry, and he saw a hint of rising panic in her eyes. "You know what they say. They say I'm shallow. They say I'm all surface. They say I can't do anything but brain-dead blockbusters. My movies make millions, but I've never been nominated for an Oscar."

Larry felt sorry for her, but what could he do? She did big, splashy blockbuster roles better than anyone. Put her in a remake of *Cleopatra* and she'd be right in her element, but if there was an *Erin Brockovich* in her, he'd never seen it— and neither had any director she'd ever auditioned for.

Jayne saw his pity and immediately hardened. She had almost a phobia when it came to intimacy. Thanks to a battalion of therapists (she had once had five at the same time), she knew why. It was simple really: from the day Jayne was born, Clarice had hovered over her, trying to control her every move.

She sat for a moment, smoking, her face an unreadable blank. Inside, she was in turmoil, but she had not been an actress for nearly three decades for nothing. She had to continue. After all, she could hardly expect Larry to get her what she wanted if she didn't tell him what it was.

"I read for Steven the other day." She didn't have to explain that "Steven" was Steven Spielberg. There was only one director Jayne spoke of with that combination of awe, respect, and fear. The sentence, however, seemed to come out of nowhere. Larry once again had the feeling of being stalked by forces he didn't understand.

"Oh," he said cautiously. Jayne wasn't supposed to audition for parts unless he set it up. Technically, he could sue her for breach of contract. Technically, he could also chop off his own head.

"Steven's doing a new film about an ordinary woman who saves a busload of schoolchildren. It's like *Speed* without the bomb, but more serious." She shrugged. "I suppose you could call it a sort of modern *Schindler's List*."

Larry didn't like the sound of this. Spielberg had directed six of the twenty-five highest-grossing films of all time, but *Schindler's List*, although a great critical success, wasn't one of them. Still, he thought warily, it had grossed over $300 million worldwide, which was hardly peanuts. He looked at Jayne with as much enthusiasm as he could muster. "So how'd the audition go?"

"How do *you* think it went?" She stared fixedly at him and then, to his astonishment, leaned forward, took his cigarette out of his hand, put it into her own mouth, and blew smoke out of her nose like an agitated dragon.

"Not so good?"

"That's an understatement. Tell me—am I bankable, Larry?"

"Totally, Jayne."

"Am I one of the hottest properties in the industry? Would any producer in his right mind give his right arm to have me in a film?"

"Absolutely."

"Okay, now tell me why I didn't get the part."

"You're kidding."

"No, I'm not kidding. I didn't get the damn part. Steven's people aren't even going to call you."

"That's insane."

"Insane?" She stubbed out his cigarette, stretched out her hand again, and he obediently placed another cigarette in it. "It's more than insane. It's . . ." Words failed her. She leaned forward and Larry lit her cigarette. When she looked up at him, there was a wounded-tiger look in her eyes that made him want to reach for the phone and dial 911.

"Steven said I'm not ordinary enough. Me! Can you imagine that? He said I'd lived too sheltered a life to play a regular person. He tried to act like it was a kind of compliment."

"Well, you have lived a pretty sheltered life. You've always had a lot of money, Jayne. Take this place, for example: how many other people own a sixteen-bedroom Spanish villa in Malibu on twenty-two and a half acres of prime coastal California real estate with two pools, a formal garden, a guest house, three Italian fountains, a helicopter landing pad, and an unimpeded view of the Pacific Ocean?"

"I don't know. How many?"

He realized that she was really asking. "None," he said. "Almost none. Maybe half a dozen people at most."

"What does that matter? I've been ordinary. Hell, I've been more than ordinary. I've been poor. I've worn rags. I've lived in thatched shacks. I've eaten *gruel!*"

She said the last word with such conviction that it made Larry shudder. She was starting to sound the way Anne Heche sounded when she spoke about her UFO experiences. He hoped she wasn't on the verge of a nervous breakdown.

"Those were parts you played, Jayne. Parts in films."

"That's not ordinary life?"

"No. Afraid not."

"Ask me to describe ordinary life to you, then."

"Okay, describe it."

"Ordinary life is when you can't get into the Sunset Room on Saturday night and sit on the patio in one of those cute little private cabanas with the green canvas curtains and smoke to your heart's content." Ever since the legislature passed tougher no-smoking laws a couple of years ago, Jayne had been obsessed with places she could light up. In the past, she and Larry would have been having this conversation in the Polo Lounge of the Beverly Hills Hotel or the cozy seclusion of the bar at the Bel Air, but she had abandoned all her old haunts in favor of places that provided patio service, heat lamps, and ashtrays.

She paused, took a long drag, and exhaled a smoke ring. "Ordinary life means you can't fly to Saint Martin on the studio jet or drink ice wine in the VIP room at the Ivy. It's when you have to work at some job where you probably don't make more than sixty thousand a year, eat Big Macs all the time, and hang out with terribly dull people who wear pink polyester. There, do I have it right?"

"Of course."

"You're just being kind, but today I don't need kind; I need the truth. I know I don't have it right. I can tell that you're sitting there thinking that I don't have a clue about what it's like to be an ordinary woman. And you know what, Larry? I agree with you. You're absolutely right."

Larry was so shocked he bit his own cigarette in half, nearly inhaled the filter, and went into a terrible coughing fit. In the six years he had been her agent, Jayne Cooper had never once told him he was right about anything.

Jayne never knew what to do when other people got upset. She sat there smoking and watched him struggle for air. Should she throw her arms around him and try the Heimlich maneuver? She liked Larry, but the idea of actually touching him made her feel dizzy with anxiety. She told herself that he'd be okay, and, of course, he was.

When he was breathing again, she continued. "If I'm going to play *serious* roles in *serious* films by *serious* directors like Steven, I need some hands-on experience. Actors don't just sit on their butts these days. They do research. I mean, before Kenneth Branagh could send Ophelia to that nunnery in *Hamlet,* he had to break up with Emma Thompson, if you get my point. And Whippy was practically martyred. Did you know that when he was caught with that Divine Brown person, he was doing research?"

Larry felt his throat seizing up again. "Whippy" was the nickname James Caan had given Hugh Grant when they were making *Mickey Blue Eyes* because, according to Caan, Grant worried about everything like a little whippet dog.

"Fascinating," he said in a choked whisper. "What sort of research do you plan to do?"

"I plan to live an ordinary life for say"—she inhaled slowly—"a week or two."

"Great idea." Larry tried to imagine her doing something normal like shopping at Target, but it was hard going. Jayne had come from a family so rich that Givenchy had designed dresses for her Barbie dolls. She'd made her first million when she was three. The idea of her acting in some artsy low-budget film was ridiculous. She might rent herself an apartment in Santa Monica and order in a few pizzas, but she was never going to be another Susan Sarandon. She would go on making blockbusters. His 10 percent was safe.

He smiled at her. "When do you plan to, uh, go native as it were?"

"Immediately. Which is why I need a double to do the postproduction publicity for *Salome*."

Larry's smile froze. The conversation had finally come full circle. "But the studio . . . your contract. *You* can't be serious."

"To hell with the studio and to hell with my contract. I'm not a talking doll, Larry. I'm an artist. I have needs."

"But they'll sue, Jayne."

"Let them sue. We're only talking about press junkets here. A hundred reporters asking the same idiotic questions over and over. I've always hated publicity. Talking to media about a picture is like being trapped in a sack with a flock of coked-up, brain-damaged parrots. We'll give the double a script. She doesn't have to be much of an actress to bat her eyelashes and say how thrilling it is to work with a great director like Bert. In fact, given what a slime-sucking little Hitler Bert is, it's better for someone who doesn't know him to gush about him to the press. Besides"—she blew a smoke ring and inhaled it through her nose—"she's not going to get within a hundred yards of anyone who actually knows me, so how will the studio find out she's not me unless someone tells them? You wouldn't tell them, Larry. I wouldn't tell them. Mother certainly wouldn't tell them."

"Jayne, for God's sake, you'll never find a double good enough to pull this off."

"Well, then, help me. We've been together a long time. I've made you a lot of money. And we're friends, right?"

"Sure," Larry said. He was surprised to hear that Jayne considered him a friend. He'd always thought their relationship was purely business. Maybe he could talk her out of this crazy scheme without losing her as a client. But was it worth the risk? He did some fast adding and subtracting in his head and decided that he was in no position to argue with her. She was loyal, and he didn't think that under ordinary circumstances she'd desert him for another agent. However, working with Spielberg was clearly important to her, and if he refused to help, she might get mad enough to bail. His whole reputation in the industry was built on being Jayne Cooper's agent. Lose her, and in six months he could be back to booking trick dogs in *Lassie* remakes.

Jayne took his silence for sympathy. She leaned forward and smiled, exposing two rows of perfect teeth. "Great," she said. "I knew you'd see it my way. Here's the bottom line: at the moment, time is on my side. I know for a fact that Steven hasn't found anyone he likes yet, and I also hear he's had to stop auditioning for a few weeks because he's got scheduling conflicts. While he's off working on another film, I am going to learn what it is to be ordinary, and I'm going to learn it fast. Then I'm going back to him and convince him to let me audition again." She sat back, crossed her legs, tapped some ashes into the Diet Coke can, and looked at Larry as if he could conjure her up a double just by snapping his fingers. "So where do we start?"

Finding himself with no choice, Larry made three suggestions in rapid succession. They were all, more or less, Jayne Cooper clones, but even as he spoke, he knew that none of these actresses really looked enough like Jayne to

fool anyone who wasn't legally blind. He drew comfort
from the thought that she wasn't going to be able to get
what she wanted.

Less than an hour after Larry left, Clarice arrived. When
Jayne heard the sound of the helicopter, she stretched out
her hand and her assistant placed a cell phone in it. The
faceplate was a custom-made mirror. Jayne examined her
reflection and reapplied her lipstick. When she was satisfied with the results, she sat back and watched the
helicopter touch down. Clarice leaped out, ducked the
whirling blades, and made for the house, coming straight
across the lawn like a tank.

Jayne speed-dialed and saw Clarice snatch her own
phone off her belt and slap it to her ear.

"Hi, Mom," Jayne said.

"Larry paged me."

"Why am I not surprised?" Jayne stared out the window
at Clarice, who was plowing straight through a freshly
planted bed of *Iris florentina.*

"You can't do this, Jayne."

"Mom, slow down and take a few deep breaths. Repeat
your affirmations. This is going to be okay."

"It is not going to be okay. It's an idiotic plan. It will never
work. You're going to wreck both our lives. Is that what you
want? You know how hard I worked to get you where you are
today. You know how much I sacrificed for you."

"Mom, please. Try to understand. I need to do this. You
know what my therapists said about me living my own life."

"You stay right there. I want to talk to you." Clarice hung
up. Jayne stared at the silent phone for a moment, then put
it aside and stretched out her hand. Her assistant put a glass
of gin and tonic in it.

"Thanks," Jayne said. "That was a good choice. Mom
definitely equals gin and tonic. How much am I paying you
these days?"

"Twelve hundred a week, Miss Cooper."

"Call Charlie Westmore and tell him I just gave you a

hundred-dollar raise. At least someone around here is on the ball."

When Clarice walked in two minutes later, Jayne was sipping her gin and tonic, and her assistant was in her room doing a victory dance.

"Jayne, darling!" Clarice rushed forward to embrace her. "Don't be cross. I'm only thinking of your welfare. That's all I've ever thought of. I know you want serious parts in serious films, but if you go through with this crazy plan and the studio finds out, they'll probably sue you. Even if they don't, you'll get a reputation for being trouble. Trouble costs money. Studio execs have a horror of actors who cost money. Remember what your father always said. . . ."

"Mom," Jayne reminded her, "I can't remember anything Dad said. He died when I was two."

Clarice sighed and lowered her perfectly curled eyelashes like a pair of tiny shades. "Ah, yes," she said softly. "Sometimes I forget that you were, for all intents and purposes, a fatherless child. All that money, and yet there was always something you never had, something I could never give you." She floated across the room and back again in a whirl of pink silk and some exotic perfume Jayne couldn't identify. "If you could only have known Max. He was the best, Jayne. There was no one as good. When I first started working in the industry, I used to hear people saying that Max Korngold could spot talent better than Mayer and Thalberg combined. Of course"—Clarice paused and smiled her best southern belle's smile—"I was much too young to remember either Mayer or Thalberg, but Max . . . Honey, I only wish your daddy were here now. He'd tell you what I'm telling you: don't get into a legal hassle with the studio, or they'll chew you up and spit you out like yesterday's gum."

"I hear you, Mom," Jayne said, taking a sip of her gin and tonic. It was too bad Spielberg couldn't have seen her at that moment. She really was a superb actress.

The sad, brave, resigned look on her pretty face convinced Clarice that she had given in, but Clarice should have known better. As Jayne sat there playing the role of the dutiful daughter, she was secretly planning to make half a dozen phone calls the second her mother walked out the door.

While Clarice congratulated her for finally showing some sense, Jayne licked an ice cube and considered her options. It was odd how much you could miss a father you had never known. And even odder how—despite all the things your mother had just said—you could believe that if Max Korngold had been alive, he would have given his little girl a big hug and told her to go for it.

Three

Late one afternoon, several weeks after Jayne began her search for a double, a checkout clerk named Mary Lynn McLellan stood at Register #15 in the Food Barn Grocery Discount Warehouse thinking about her boyfriend who never called, the funny sound her transmission made when she shifted into third, the rent on her apartment (which was two weeks overdue), and her worthless ex-husband's beautiful new girlfriend, who ran marathons and had a butt so tight you could bounce quarters off it.

She had just gotten to the point of imagining the girlfriend accidentally taking a wrong turn and plunging off a cliff, when a customer set a bottle of gin down in front of her. Without looking up, Mary Lynn automatically seized the bottle with both hands and passed it over the scanner. Mary Lynn was always having to lift things with both hands. The Barn specialized in enormous bales of toilet paper and jars of mustard as big as five-gallon gas cans. The joke in the employees' lounge was that if the management ever decided to sell SUVs, they'd come in blister packs of three.

Mary Lynn heard the little beep that meant the scanner had tallied in the gin. She imagined the girlfriend bouncing a few times as she hit the rocks at the bottom of the cliff; still not looking up, she reached for the limes, which came thirty-five to a bag.

"So have you been working here long?" the customer asked.

Mary Lynn, who was busy tossing the girlfriend in the ocean and strewing it with sharks, hardly heard the question. There was not enough action at the Food Barn to keep the mind of a philodendron alive. Months ago, she had gone on automatic pilot.

"What exactly do you mean by 'long'?" she said. Almost before the words were out of her mouth, she snapped back to reality, but it was too late. Damn! She'd done it again. Mixed up her two jobs. Somewhere outside this concrete mausoleum, the sun was shining, which meant it was daytime. During the day, she slaved away at the Food Barn. Nights, she taught freshman composition at Coast Side Community College. As a part-time member of the Coast Side faculty (no benefits, less pay than she could have made flipping burgers), she was expected to encourage her students to develop their minds by answering every question with a question. But this was the Barn, and as a Barn serf, she was required to extend an almost Jane Austen–like politeness to customers.

"I don't know exactly what I mean by 'long,'" the customer said. "I rarely know exactly what I mean by anything." Her voice took on an alarming intensity. She leaned forward and stared at Mary Lynn as if she were about to grab her, plop her on the conveyor belt, and ring her up.

Mary Lynn resisted an urge to yell for security. Oh no, not another one. What was it about this town? Something in the water? She took a deep breath and smiled her best Food Barn smile. "I'm sorry, ma'am," she said. "Could you please repeat your question?"

To Mary Lynn's relief, the woman made no sudden moves. "I asked if you had been working here a long time."

"Yes, ma'am. I suppose I have." *Go away,* Mary Lynn silently commanded. *Go quietly. Pick up your limes and gin and leave.* But the woman didn't move.

"My God," the woman said. "I don't believe it. Say that again."

"Say what, ma'am?"

"Say anything. Say: 'Bert is simply a fabulous director.'"

"Bert?" Mary Lynn assessed the woman. She was wearing a long black raincoat, a black scarf, and oversize sunglasses that concealed most of her face. That in itself wasn't strange. Many of the Food Barn's customers were recent arrivals to the United States and their customs were different. Mary Lynn had checked out groceries for men in brightly batiked sarongs and Russians who wore wool suit coats when it was 105 degrees out. But the woman could have anything under that raincoat: a knife, an Uzi, a petition to declare Satanism the official religion of California.

"You're too perfect for words," the woman said. "My God, this is a miracle. Wait until I tell Larry. You're a little too heavy and those hideous glasses will definitely have to go, but still, I sense that underneath that smock you're absolutely gorgeous. Am I right?"

Whoa, Mary Lynn thought. *This is getting really strange.*

"Tell me, how do you keep your arms so firm? Do you work out a lot?"

"I lift a lot of heavy stuff." Okay, that explained it. "Black Raincoat" was trying to pick her up. Well, she was out of luck. Mary Lynn didn't have anything against lesbians, but it just wasn't her thing—although given her track record with men, maybe it should have been. She quickly grabbed the bag of limes, passed it over the scanner, waited for the beep, and then scanned the tonic water. "That will be thirteen ninety-five," she said briskly. "Cash or charge?"

"Cash." The customer smiled, flashing the whitest teeth Mary Lynn had ever seen. "What time do you get off work?"

"I get off at five, ma'am." What the hell was she thinking! Why had she told the woman when she got off work? Just because Black Raincoat was smiling didn't mean that she couldn't go totally bonkers at the drop of a hat. They had one or two seriously crazy customers a month: men in pink tights who stood at the meat counter arguing with the hamburger, and old women in curlers who raved about the CIA and kicked over displays of canned tuna.

"Meet me in the parking lot in five minutes." Black Raincoat smiled and slapped a hundred-dollar bill down on the counter. "And keep the change."

Mary Lynn watched her until she was all the way out of the store. Then she grabbed the bill and held it up to the light to look for the watermarks that meant it was real. To her astonishment, it was. Great. She could certainly use the money, but what the hell had she just been paid for? Or more to the point: what did the woman expect her to do in return for a hundred bucks minus $13.95?

Whatever it was, Mary Lynn didn't want to know. She spent the next ten minutes going over a bunch of possible scenarios. By the time her shift ended—ten minutes, two crates of Ziploc bags, and several pallets of dog food later—she had managed to scare herself silly. Usually, she hurried to the employees' lounge, shucked off her red Food Barn smock, and left without a backward glance. Today, however, she stalled as long as she could, wandering down the aisles, picking up remaindered books, and gazing at gigantic bags of frozen lobster tails, which she couldn't afford even at Food Barn prices. Finally she had no choice. She had to leave, and since the Food Barn was built like a box canyon, to prevent shoplifting, she had to leave by the front door. She stepped outside, and as she looked warily to the right, the woman accosted her from the left like a rottweiler.

"Hi there," she said. "I was about to give up on you."

Mary Lynn wheeled around with a yelp of surprise and found herself facing a stretch limo. The thing was black with tinted windows and looked long enough to carry a flagpole; there was actually a chauffeur at the wheel. What in God's name was a woman with a car like that doing shopping at the Food Barn?

The woman seemed to read her mind. "Flat tire," she said. "My driver fixed it. I bet you change your own tires, don't you?" She moved in on Mary Lynn. "Cook your own meals, clean your own house? I bet you have all sorts of skills I've only read about—like baking bread and gutting fish. Get in the car and we'll talk."

"I can't possibly." Mary Lynn plastered a smile on her face and slowly backed away, looking around for help in case Black Raincoat mistook her for a display of canned tuna.

"Please. There's a smog alert today." The woman cast anxious looks in all directions. "I can't stand here and breathe this polluted air." She peered at Mary Lynn and a thought seemed to strike her. "Say, you don't think I'm going to kidnap you, do you?"

"Uh, n-no," Mary Lynn stammered, still smiling. That, of course, was exactly what she had been thinking. She had always had too much imagination for her own good. She could see it all: black hood over head, restraints, box buried in the ground with small breathing tube, ransom notes, parents hysterical, ex-husband's girlfriend elated, brother refusing to pay a dime for her. Mary Lynn took a few more steps backward. "Excuse me," she said firmly, "I have to go now."

"Don't leave. I need you."

"Have a nice day." Mary Lynn turned to flee.

"Wait!" The woman scurried after her. "I don't mean you any harm. I can make life better for you." She cornered Mary Lynn between an SUV and a truck. "You have debts, right?"

"That's none of your business. Go away!"

"All I want to do is talk to you. I'm not asking you to do it for free. I'll pay you."

Mary Lynn came to such a quick stop that she slammed her elbow against a side-view mirror. Had Black Raincoat just said the word "pay"? The buried box with the breathing tube was suddenly replaced by a new transmission. Mary Lynn tried shifting the gears.

"I'll pay you a lot," the woman repeated, "but I really can't stand out here another minute." She looked up at the sky and shuddered. "I'm getting another hellacious sunburn. I can't afford to look like a pigskin wallet." She cast nervous glances toward the shoppers who were streaming out of the Food Barn. "Listen, if we don't get out of here soon, someone is sure to spot me, so how about this: I'll pay you five hundred dollars just to get into the limo and give me five minutes of your time. All I want to do is talk to you about your life." She began to herd Mary Lynn back toward the limo.

Mary Lynn shifted her new transmission again, and then she thought about how she could end up headless in a ditch. "No." She backed away from the woman, who kept edging toward her like a sheepdog. "Good-bye. I really have to go. There are people watching us. Lots of them, so . . ."

"Keys!" the woman cried suddenly.

Thinking that the woman had finally cracked, Mary Lynn gave another muffled scream and scurried backward; but evidently Black Raincoat had been talking to the driver of her limo. The driver snapped to attention. Without a word, he pulled the keys out of the ignition and passed them to the woman, who put them in Mary Lynn's hand and curled Mary Lynn's fingers around them.

"There," she said. "You see? You're perfectly safe. You have the keys. I can't possibly take you hostage, drive off to Tijuana, and sell you into a bordello. Relax. You don't know it yet, but this is the luckiest day of your life. All you have to do is get into the car."

The solid feel of the keys was like a hit of Valium. Mary Lynn calmed down. *Okay,* she thought. *Apparently, she isn't going to cut off my fingers one by one and send them to my closest relatives. What do I do now? She's offering me five hundred dollars to get into her car. Do I take it?*

A person less desperate for money might have said no, but that person probably hadn't recently moved to a strange city. Mary Lynn stood there, mentally spending five hundred dollars on chocolate and wine and a new Mr. Coffee to replace the one she'd broken Friday morning trying to get to the phone machine before Wendell hung up. She added shrimp-flavored Kitty Delight for the cats and a tight red dress with a short skirt that would drive her ex-husband crazy and make him regret he'd ever dumped her.

Not that I want the bastard back, she thought. *But it would be worth it just to see his face.* Clutching the keys, she climbed into the limo.

Black Raincoat climbed in behind her, closed the door, and sat down on the banquette. Mary Lynn checked the place out. A glass partition separated passengers from the driver. The partition had curtains that could be pulled for complete privacy. The woman pulled the curtains, and there they were, the two of them, alone together in a dark, luxurious cave. The seats—which looked as if they might fold out into a bed— were upholstered in crushed velvet the color of Chianti. There was a TV, a makeup mirror, a small refrigerator, and a bar with a silver ice bucket and crystal decanters.

"So," the woman asked, "comfy?"

Mary Lynn eyed her warily. "Yes."

"Good, let's get down to business." The woman took off the black raincoat and draped it over the back of one of the seats. Then she removed her scarf and sunglasses. She looked at Mary Lynn expectantly. "Well?"

"Well, what?"

"Now you know."

"Know what?"

"Who I am. Why I couldn't risk standing around in that godforsaken parking lot."

Mary Lynn stared at her blankly. She looked a hell of a lot better out of that baggy raincoat, but if they'd met before, Mary Lynn couldn't remember the occasion. A blonde. Expensive clothes. Exceptionally pretty. *Hello? Can I have a name, please? No,* said her memory. *No names today.* But wait. Her face was beginning to look vaguely familiar. Where had they met? in Santa Cruz? In Bakersfield? *Is she the cheerleader who sat behind me in fifth-period homeroom? The real estate agent Ron slept with in Cancun?*

"You're speechless?" The woman seemed pleasantly amused. "That's understandable. It's okay. People often react that way when they meet me in person. Don't be afraid. Under all the hype, I'm just an ordinary woman with an ordinary woman's dreams and desires."

Whoever she is, Mary Lynn thought, *she's totally nuts.* She watched in fascination as the woman pulled out a silver case and extracted a long pink cigarette with an eagle embossed on one side. Where did a person buy bright pink cigarettes? Maybe it was filled with dope. Maybe she had just gotten into a car with a junkie.

The woman rolled the cigarette between her fingers and looked at Mary Lynn as if waiting for Mary Lynn to scream out her name and fall over backward. There was an awkward silence.

Finally Mary Lynn couldn't stand it any longer. "I'm sorry," she said cautiously, "but I don't have the faintest idea who you are."

The woman froze, cigarette poised inches from lips. A look of disbelief spread over her face. "Are you serious?"

"Yes."

She let the cigarette fall into her lap. "Oh, my God."

"Beg your pardon?"

"This is the moment I've been dreading. I always knew that sooner or later it would happen. I live in a shark pit. All my life, I've lived in a shark pit."

"You work for Marine World?"

"Marine World?" The woman laughed bitterly. "Oh, if only I did. No, I work in an industry where if your breasts fall a sixteenth of an inch, they replace you with some teenager with legs like a gazelle and tits like tennis balls."

"Teenager? Tennis balls?" Like a good composition teacher, Mary Lynn kept searching for the topic sentence.

"Please tell me you recognize me. Tell me this is all some kind of cruel joke."

"I'm sorry. You do look sort of familiar, but I can't place you. Do you shop at the Food Barn a lot?"

The woman stared at Mary Lynn as if Mary Lynn were a robot who had recently arrived from some distant star cluster and shot her through the heart. "Don't you ever go to the movies?"

"Not too much. I'm on a pretty strict budget. Mostly, I read in the evenings." Movies. The woman had just said something about movies. Maybe she was an actress. But if so, which one? Mary Lynn frantically racked her brain without success—which wasn't surprising, since the only movie she had seen in the last eight months was *Chicken Run*.

"It's so ironic," the woman said. "I search for you everywhere, and when I find you, you announce my demise. 'O Dark Messenger, what paths have you taken to reach me?' Do you understand?"

Mary Lynn might not own a short, tight, red, drive-your-ex-husband-crazy designer dress, but she did understand what "demise" meant, and she didn't like the sound of it. She edged slowly toward the door. "The only thing I understand is that whoever you just quoted is definitely not Shakespeare."

"Right. It's Freddy Weber. Great writer, Freddy, but a total cokehead. 'In five years, Freddy,' I told him, 'you won't have any brain cells left.'" She suddenly leaned forward and stared at Mary Lynn with an intensity that was unnerving. "Let me ask you something: has anyone ever told you that you look like someone famous?"

Mary Lynn shook her head. Actually, she did have a vague memory of being told she resembled someone, but she couldn't remember who. Her mind had gone totally blank. *Calm down,* she told herself. *Nothing really bad is happening here. The woman's probably an actress, and actresses are probably all a little weird.* She felt a name skulking around in the back of her head refusing to come out. Could she be Julia Roberts? No, even she knew what Julia Roberts looked like. *Name,* she thought desperately. *Come on. Name. It begins with a J. I know it begins with a J.*

"Has anyone ever told you that in addition to looking like someone famous," the woman continued, "you *sound* exactly like her?"

"No. Afraid not."

Tears welled up in the woman's lovely blue eyes. "Take a guess who I am," she said. "I'll give you a hint: my first name rhymes with 'rain.'"

"Jayne!" Mary Lynn cried triumphantly. "Jayne Cooper!"

Of course—now it all made sense! The hundred-dollar bill. The limo. The driver. "You're the movie star!" Mary Lynn was suddenly profoundly embarrassed. How could it have taken her so long to recognize someone so famous!

Cooper seemed shaken but relieved. She pulled out a small, lace-bordered handkerchief and dabbed at her eyes. Then she turned to the makeup mirror, switched on the lights, and reapplied her mascara. She spent a long time inspecting the results. Finally she gave herself a brave smile and turned back to Mary Lynn. "I'd be interested to know why you didn't recognize me immediately."

"You were out of context." Mary Lynn wondered if Ms. Cooper was always given to having miniature nervous collapses when people didn't instantly recognize her. She should try teaching freshman English some time. Half the students couldn't find Europe on a blank map.

"Context?" Cooper echoed sadly.

"Yes. You see, I didn't expect someone as famous as you to be shopping in the Food Barn."

Cooper brightened considerably at the word "famous."

"Plus," Mary Lynn continued, "I haven't seen you since you were acting in that sitcom. . . . What was it called?"

"My Familia."

"You look different."

"I was eight when I left the series."

"You're still pretty. . . ."

"Just 'pretty'? Not *beautiful?*"

"Beautiful. Gorgeous. A real knockout."

"You're just saying that to make me feel better."

"No, really. You're stunning."

Jayne was used to compliments, but she never tired of them. She waited for more. When they weren't forthcoming, she gave Mary Lynn a gentle prompt. "So, you don't think I'm over-the-hill?"

"If you're over-the-hill, I want to go over it too. Why, just look at yourself. You've got skin like . . ." Words failed her.

"Yes?" said Jayne brightly.

"The feathers of a dove." It was a horrible metaphor, but it was the only one Mary Lynn could think of.

Jayne glowed. "Ah," she murmured.

"Like I said, I used to watch you on TV when you were a little girl. We're exactly the same age. You were always sweet and pretty. Everyone adored you."

"Everyone?"

"Everyone."

"Ah."

"I had no idea I'd ever get to meet you in person."

"And what about my movies? Millions of people have gone to them. Surely, you've seen me in at least one?"

Mary Lynn racked her brain. Had she seen Jayne Cooper since Cooper was old enough to wear a bra? Suddenly she remembered she had.

"Actually, I once saw you in *The Loves of Leonardo*."

"The one where I played Mona Lisa?" Jayne leaned a little closer, face flushed, eyes glowing with interest. Mary Lynn was only one fan out of millions, but Jayne counted her admirers the way a miser counted pennies.

"Yes, that one."

"What did you like most about my performance?"

"Everything," Mary Lynn lied. "Absolutely everything." The truth was, she'd been trying to see Judi Dench in *Mrs. Brown,* but when she'd arrived at the local art theater, she discovered that it had been torn down and replaced by a nine-screen multiplex.

"Didn't you just love that part where I revealed the secret of my smile?"

"Loved it!" Mary Lynn had no memory of any such moment.

"And the way I nursed Leonardo when he came down with a bad case of bubonic plague? The way I whispered to him when I caught it and was dying: 'Paint on! Paint on! I shall love you forever!' Didn't that just make you cry?"

"Sure," Mary Lynn said. "I went though a whole packet of Kleenex." Now she remembered. The film had been an overblown, splashy mishmash of biography and fiction peppered with hilarious historical errors. She vaguely recalled laughing at the line Cooper had just quoted.

Jayne settled back, satisfied. "*Leonardo* was an amazing film," she said.

"Amazing," Mary Lynn agreed. Amazingly bad, she thought.

Jayne picked up the pink cigarette, slid it between her lips, lit it, and inhaled with a soft sucking sound that reminded Mary Lynn of one of those little vacuum cleaners you could buy to clean the keyboard of your computer. She exhaled and the scent of cloves and something musky filled the limo. Draping her free hand on the back of the banquette, she spread out her perfectly manicured nails like a contented cat. "I think you and I are going to get along beautifully, Ms. . . . but wait. You know my name, but I don't know yours."

"Mary Lynn. Mary Lynn McLellan."

"Mary Lynn." Jayne took another deep drag on her cigarette. "It has a certain music to it. Folk music. When I hear the name 'McLellan,' I imagine fresh-faced Irish peasants dancing in a circle."

And I imagine, Mary Lynn thought, *that I have earned my five hundred dollars and it's time for me to leave.* She started to get up, but Jayne wasn't finished.

"Mary Lynn McLellan, I have a business proposition for you. How would you like to make, say, a hundred thousand dollars?"

Mary Lynn froze. Her mouth went dry and her mind began to squirrel. She must have heard wrong. Cooper couldn't have said a *hundred thousand.* That was more money than Mary Lynn made in . . . She tried to do the math, but her brain was completely paralyzed.

"Joke, right?"

"No joke."

"Whom do I have to kill?"

"No one. It's strictly legit." Jayne blew a lazy smoke ring, which curled into the red velvet banquette and dissolved.

"Ms. Cooper . . ."

"Jayne, please."

"Jayne . . ."

"Don't say 'no' until you've heard me out."

No? Mary Lynn thought. *Who said I was going to say 'no'?* Her heart began to race. "Ms. Cooper . . . that is, Jayne, did I hear you say that you'd pay me a hundred thousand dollars?"

"Yes."

"For what?"

"I'd rather not tell you until I can be sure it's going to work. Let's just say that I want to interview you a bit about your life. If I like what I hear, I'll take you back to my place and give you some new clothes and a new hairdo. You can think of it as a makeover, if you like. Then"—she smoked and surveyed Mary Lynn thoughtfully—"one of two things will happen: I'll either decide not to hire you, in which case I will pay you—what? Say five thousand dollars for your time? Would that be satisfactory?"

Mary Lynn nodded, unable to speak.

"Or I'll hire you and pay twenty-five thousand dollars down, with the rest to come in increments over the next few weeks if you successfully carry out your part of the bargain. In addition, you'll have to sign a nondisclosure statement. That's pretty much routine. All my personal assistants sign them, but if you have any intention of talking to the press, you'd better tell me now."

Mary Lynn opened her mouth, but no sound came out.

"Speechless?"

Mary Lynn nodded.

"It's not surprising under the circumstances." Jayne held out her silver cigarette case. "Here, have a smoke while you think it over."

Dazed, Mary Lynn took one of the pink cigarettes and let Jayne light it for her. She had a sense of having fallen through a rabbit hole into a Looking Glass world where everything was upside down and backward. She was so stunned, that it was only after she inhaled and began to cough herself silly that she remembered she didn't smoke.

Four

You could get to Jayne's compound in Malibu by taking freeways to the Pacific Coast Highway, but Jayne always liked to go surface when she wasn't in a hurry, partly because she thought the air was better and partly because she had a horror of being injured in a high-speed wreck. Surface in this case meant Sunset Boulevard. Sunset connected parts of Los Angeles that were rarely spoken of in the same breath. It ran through Silverlake, the lower-middle-class community where Mary Lynn lived; through the slums of Echo Park, with its barred windows, tattoo parlors, 98¢ Stores, and tortillarias. After a while, if you kept on driving toward the ocean, it became "the Strip," passing nightclubs in West Hollywood where you had to have a famous name or a perfect body to get in the front door. Sunset took you past Beverly Hills, past UCLA and the gates of Bel Air; and before it dumped you out onto the PCH, it even wound you by the Polo Field so you could think about horses and rich playboys, if you were so inclined.

Today the traffic on Sunset was bad enough to make Mr. Rogers go postal, but as usual Jayne hardly noticed. Inside her limo, the only sound was the soft hiss of the air conditioner. Producing a small silver juicer, she squeezed two of the limes she had just purchased and mixed a pair of perfect gin and tonics. Handing one to Mary Lynn, she settled back and stared at her like an eager anthropologist. "So tell me," she said. "What's it like being you?"

Mary Lynn's mind went blank. She couldn't think of anything to say about herself that could possibly interest anyone as famous as Jayne Cooper.

Jayne fluffed her hair with her free hand and flashed Mary Lynn the smile that had earned her millions. "Come on," she urged. "Don't be shy. I'm all ears."

Mary Lynn swallowed some gin and thought again about her transmission and her overdue rent. "What do you want to know?"

"Why don't you start with your job? What exactly do you *do* at the Food Barn?"

"Actually, I have two jobs."

"And?"

"And what?"

Jayne took another sip of her drink and tried to figure out how to move the conversation forward. This was going to be harder than she'd anticipated. She hated ad-libbing. Usually she worked from a script. She automatically looked around for cue cards, but there were none in sight. *I have to make this work,* she thought. For weeks Larry had been parading actresses in front of her, all of them hideously inappropriate: the one who had looked so good, but who had had a voice like Minnie Mouse; the one who spoke like Jayne Cooper and looked like Gary Cooper; the totally crazy one who had told Jayne that *she* was the real Jayne Cooper and that Jayne was an impersonator. Mary Lynn had it all: looks and voice. What were the chances of stumbling on another like her? One in a million? One in ten million?

Jayne took a deep breath and tried again. "Tell me exactly what your two jobs are."

"Well, I check out groceries at the Food Barn. You saw me doing it. There's not much more to know, except that they pay me a dollar-fifty above minimum wage."

Jayne opened her purse and whipped out a pen and a small leather-bound notebook that had cost approximately as much as Mary Lynn made in a week. She was serious about doing research. "What's minimum wage?"

"Five dollars and seventy-five cents an hour," Mary Lynn said, happy to at last be hit with a question she could answer. "Which means I get seven twenty-five."

Jayne looked at her blankly. Obviously, Mary Lynn had not understood her question. She tried again. "No. I mean what *is* 'minimum wage'?"

"It's the smallest hourly wage your employer's allowed to pay you. I thought everyone knew that. Don't you ever hire anybody?"

"No. I have my assistant call an agency and they send someone over." She scribbled some notes.

"If you don't mind me asking, what do you make an hour?"

"I'm not paid by the hour," Jayne said distractedly, examining what she had just written, "but I got twenty-four million for my last movie. That's a million less than Mel Gibson got for *The Patriot*. But the studio hung tough." She looked up and failed to notice that Mary Lynn was gasping at the mention of a sum so preposterous. "Did you really say you're paid seven dollars and twenty-five cents an hour?"

Mary Lynn nodded.

"Fascinating." Jayne had had no idea human life could be sustained on so little. "What's your second job?"

Mary Lynn told her.

"A professor?" Jayne felt as if some clumsy grip had just dropped a rack of klieg lights on her. "I'd hoped for something more ordinary. You know, like a fry cook or a waitress or a grade-school teacher." She nibbled anxiously on the end of her pen. "What ghastly luck. First the camels, then the sunburn, and now this."

Mary Lynn saw her hundred thousand dollars vanishing. Panicking, she began to babble. She explained how her job at the college was part-time, how she wasn't a real professor but only a lecturer who taught a few sections of comp, how her salary was so low she had to work at the Food Barn. As she spoke, a smile began to flicker at the corners of Jayne's lips.

"If I'm hearing you right, you're telling me that you have

two miserable part-time jobs for which you are paid chicken feed, and you get no respect at either of them?"

"None," Mary Lynn said, eager to please. "Particularly at the college. If the college were a food chain, I'd be the green slime on the bottom."

"Excellent." Jayne made a small check mark in the margin and gnawed delicately on the end of her pen. "Now tell me about your family. You know: the traumas, the incest, the petty soul-destroying poverty of your childhood, the divorce that broke your heart."

"My parents have been married for nearly forty years. They're still together."

"A pity," Jayne said, busily taking notes. "Happy families are all alike."

"Why, that's a quote from Tolstoy!"

Jayne stared at her blankly. Her reading consisted mostly of the front page of *Variety*, treatments for films she was considering, and an occasional romance novel. She wrote down the word "Tolstoy" and put a series of little question marks after it, figuring she'd look it up later. "I don't suppose, by any chance, that your father's gay?"

"No." Mary Lynn immediately realized that once again she'd disappointed Jayne. "But on the upside," she added hastily, "he and my mom aren't speaking to each other. Last New Year's Eve, she had a little too much to drink and told him that while he was out selling plumbing supplies, she'd been sleeping with her acupuncturist. Anyway, right now they're acting like idiots. They've divided the house in half. She goes in the front door; he goes in the back. My brother, Wayne . . ."

"'Wayne,'" Jayne murmured. "What a ghastly name. Still, it's perfect." She wrote down the word "Wayne" and made little stars in the margin.

". . . keeps calling from New York to tell me I have to move back to Bakersfield and live with them and act as a mediator; but what's the point? I mean, it's not like they're sick or terribly old or anything. They're just stubborn. The worst of it is,

Wayne keeps calling at six A.M. which is nine his time. He hasn't been back to California for fifteen years, not even at Christmas, but my parents worship the ground he walks on."

"He's the favorite, is he?"

"You bet. As far as Dad and Mom are concerned, the sun rises and sets on Wayne."

"What about friends? Are you in touch with a wide range of ordinary"—Jayne said the word lovingly, as if sucking the pulp out of a ripe apricot—"people?"

"Not really. I just moved to town a few months ago, and I haven't really had time to make friends yet, unless you count the teller at the bank."

Jayne picked a fleck of lime pulp off her lower lip and contemplated Mary Lynn with interest. "You actually walk into banks and speak to tellers?"

"Sure. What do you do when you want money? Somehow I can't see you standing in line at an ATM."

"I call my accountant and he sends it over by messenger. Tell me: are you sleeping with anyone in particular at the moment?"

Mary Lynn's face turned the color of the upholstery. "That's a pretty intimate question."

"Not for me. When I sleep with someone, I hardly get the tangles brushed out of my hair before I read about it in the tabloids."

"I read once that you were gay," Mary Lynn said boldly.

"I read once that I had had a three-way with Prince Charles and an alien. No offense, but we're not discussing my love life here; we're discussing yours. Still, let me rephrase that question." She leaned forward a little, careful not to get too close. "Are you married?"

"Not anymore, thank God."

"Was it as bad as all that?"

"You can't begin to imagine."

"What was the problem?"

"I had to support him because he could never hold down a job."

"Was he disabled?"

"You might say that. Ron always claimed that work messed up his biorhythms. I can still see him lying there on the couch in his jockey shorts watching one football game after another. To tell you the truth, he looked pretty cute with his shirt off, but there's nothing like spilled beer and Cheetos ground into the carpet to put a woman out of the mood."

"How long did you put up with this state of affairs?"

"Longer than you'd believe. No one in my family had ever been divorced, and I kept feeling that I had to make the marriage work. After Ron wrecked my car because he forgot to put antifreeze in it when he drove over to Vegas to gamble during a freak cold snap, we went into couples therapy; we might as well have tossed the money into a shredder. I paid more than three thousand dollars to get in touch with my anger, and just when I was starting to see things from his point of view, he emptied out our joint checking account, killed my cat, and dumped me for a bimbo with thighs so tight she can crack nuts with them."

"He killed your cat!"

"Backed over him in the driveway. Poor Mr. Dickens. Oh, sure, it was an accident, but Ron was always having accidents. You know, when I look back on the whole mess, I think the worst part of that marriage was his rebirthing tapes. Ron listened to the damn things every night." She looked at Jayne grimly. "Tell me, have you ever tried to go to sleep while a voice is saying: 'You are now passing down the birth canal'? Well, then, you must be one of the few women in California who never slept with Ron."

Jayne was fascinated. She sucked on an ice cube and thought about how much the tabloids would have loved these stories if Mary Lynn had been an actress. "So why did you marry him in the first place?"

Mary Lynn shrugged. "I was young and he was a poet. I thought it would be exciting to marry a writer, but it was more like baby-sitting. When I met him, he was a charming child. By the time we split up, he was an angry adolescent.

I figure in forty years or so, he may make it to adulthood, but I'm not holding my breath."

"How ghastly." Jayne silently congratulated herself on having had the good sense never to have gotten married.

"That's not even the worst part," Mary Lynn continued, staring glumly into her glass and then taking a healthy swig.

"How could it get worse?"

"I have to pay him spousal support."

"You're kidding."

"Nope, I'm deadly serious. We were legally married for six years; so under California law, I still owe him most of my income for the next eleven months. That's another reason I have to hold down two jobs. Gotta keep my ex in poker chips, Wild Turkey, and psychic readings."

"I almost got married once," Jayne confided, "but the community-property laws stopped me. Sometimes prenups don't hold up." She lifted her glass in a mock toast. "Date 'em and discard 'em; that's my motto."

"You're a smart woman."

"And yet"—Jayne grew wistful—"sometimes I think that if only I could find the right man: tall, handsome, faithful, sincere, and . . ."

". . . and smart enough to know that Mozart isn't a rock group. Yeah. Me too. But it isn't easy, is it?"

"You can say that again."

They sat for a moment, drinking and contemplating the "Man Problem." When they reached the bottom of their glasses, Jayne made them fresh drinks. Settling back against the cushions, she kicked off her heels and folded her feet up under her legs yoga-style, something she never as a rule did in front of strangers. Thanks to the gin and the peculiarity of the situation, she was starting to feel comfortable around Mary Lynn.

"So what have you been doing since you got out of your marriage?"

Mary Lynn shrugged. "Oh, the usual: the day Ron committed caticide and left me for superwoman, I swore off men forever and ordered my girlfriends to shoot me if I ever mentioned getting intimate with anything larger than a parakeet. Then, naturally, I went right out and got involved in another relationship. This one's name is Wendell. He's a computer programmer, so at least he's got a job."

"How's it working out?"

Mary Lynn frowned and clinked the ice around in her glass. "I guess I'd give Wendell a four out of a possible ten. He's good-looking and a great conversationalist if you like to talk about the difference between PCs and Macs, but he has an annoying habit of answering his cell phone when we're in bed together."

Jayne took an extra-large swig of her drink. "I want you to know that I am trying very hard not to imagine this. The name 'Wendell,' particularly when attached to anyone who has anything to do with computers, makes me want to swear off sex forever." But she wrote the name down anyway and put stars by it.

"He usually comes over the second and fourth Tuesday of every month, but for two Tuesdays in a row, he's canceled at the last minute. Truth is, I think he's got another girlfriend."

"So he's Ron all over again, is he?"

Mary Lynn nodded.

"What first made you suspect Wendell was cheating on you? The strand of hair on the shoulder of his jacket? The scent of an unfamiliar cologne?" This was Jayne's territory. She'd made at least half a dozen movies about women whose lovers had cheated on them, and she figured she knew all the scenarios for discovering infidelity.

Mary Lynn picked a slice of lime out of her drink and began to nibble on the rind. "It's pretty simple," she said between bites. "The last time we had sex, he called me 'Gloria.'"

"He what!"

"Called me 'Gloria.' Of course, it might have been 'Victoria.' " Mary Lynn grew thoughtful. "I couldn't tell exactly because his mouth was full."

"What did you do then? Kick him out of bed?" Jayne leaned forward eagerly. "I had a part in a movie once where I got to guillotine the man who betrayed me."

"I can see how that would be satisfying. But actually, Wendell didn't notice what he'd said, and I didn't mention it to him." She tossed the half-eaten lime rind back in her glass and looked up at Jayne with a twisted smile. "It's not like there are a whole lot of choices out there. I've discovered boyfriends are hard to come by in this town. Don't you find that to be the case?"

"No. Definitely not. They're a dime a dozen."

"Well, I suppose that's one of the best things about being so famous. Men must fall all over you. How many boyfriends do you have at present, if you don't mind me asking?"

Jayne toyed with her rings and took inventory. "Three," she said, "give or take a few."

"So that's where all the spare men go. I've always wondered. Frankly, I'm jealous."

"Don't be." Jayne was seized by a rare urge to be honest. "I've had lovers ever since I was seventeen. They give me flowers, racehorses, diamonds—you know, the usual."

"Nice," Mary Lynn murmured. "Very nice. Ron once gave me a chain saw on our anniversary. Go on."

"They all tell me they love me and swear they'd die for me, but the truth is, every man I go out with wants something from me. Money . . ."

"This is sounding familiar."

"A chance to meet a director or a chance to sell a script. And every one of them—even the rich ones—wants a chance to see a photo of himself with me on his arm." Jayne suddenly felt very sad and sorry for herself. "I'm not a woman; I'm a trophy; I'm a *thing* you put on a shelf. That's the curse of my profession. When you're famous and rich and beautiful, men treat you like you're not a real person. It's what drove Monroe crazy."

"That sucks, Jayne."

"You're right, Mary Lynn. It sucks big time."

She refilled their glasses again, and they sat side by side in companionable silence, getting slightly snockered as the limo rolled on.

Five

"Esther Williams and Elvis," Jayne said as she dismissed the limo driver and strode toward her house. Her four-inch heels clicked on the sidewalk like the hooves of an antelope. She could have played field hockey in them or climbed straight up the side of Mount Everest; even now, slightly tipsy, she walked with the precision of a stamp press.

Mary Lynn found herself looking at a huge white Spanish-style hacienda with a red-tiled roof. To the right lay a formal garden bordered by high hedges of pink and white oleanders; to the left was a vast guitar-shaped swimming pool, landscaped with waterfalls and dazzling clusters of purple orchids. Marble fountains, decorated with lions and nymphs, sent up rainbows of water that cooled the air and made pleasant tinkling sounds. Behind Jayne's compound, the dry hills of Malibu looked fierce and hot, but here everything was green, perfectly manicured, and exquisitely peaceful. Mary Lynn thought of her apartment back in Silverlake: two boxlike stories of chipped gray stucco, a chain-link fence, peeling paint, rooms so small you could almost reach out and touch both sides at once, the ancient tiny shower with the HOT and COLD handles reversed, the moldy rubber mat.

"Elvis and Esther," Jayne repeated. She gestured toward the pool. "They owned this place before I did. It was a ranch in those days, but when I bought the land, I tore down the barn and the original house. That's Elvis's pool. He had it built when he came out here to do *Jailhouse Rock*. I dome it in the winter because of the orchids. Esther's pool is out back. One of those bigger-than-Olympic-size monstrosities that a hundred little starlets can cavort in." She suddenly stopped and stuck out her hand. "Nine-one-one Manicure."

"Nine-one-one what?"

"Nine-one-one Manicure." Jayne pointed her fingernails at Mary Lynn and made them ripple like tiny pink stars. "They provide emergency manicures twenty-four/seven. I have to call them immediately. Your situation is beyond desperate, but don't worry. We're going to get you fixed up in no time." She blew a smoke ring, inhaled it through her nose, and snatched up her cell phone. "This is Jayne Cooper," she said. "Could you send someone over to my place in Malibu as soon as possible?"

Apparently, that was all it took. The manicurist arrived faster than a paramedic. As Mary Lynn sat in Jayne's up-stairs dressing room experiencing the first professional nail-tending of her life, Jayne sipped a Diet Coke and looked out the window at the Pacific Ocean, wondering if it could be rearranged. Finding Mary Lynn had given her a giddy sense of her own power. She had never much liked this particular view. The ocean was too foggy and the pink of the flowering crepe myrtles looked washed out in the fil-tered sunlight. Should she chop down some trees to open things up? Install heat lamps in the backyard? Life was full of a thousand petty decisions that a serious artist should not have to make, and yet there were moments like this: mo-ments when victory was so close, you could almost blow smoke in its face.

When the manicurist was safely out of the way, she rose from her chair and clicked over to Mary Lynn. "Now," she said, "the real fun begins." She gave Mary Lynn a friendly smile. She was actually starting to like her. Looking at Mary Lynn was almost as good as looking into a mirror, but not quite as good. Not yet.

Mary Lynn stared at her nails, which hardly seemed to be

hers anymore. She rippled her fingers as she had seen Jayne do. Little pink plastic shells. Fake, polished, and pretty as a kitten's claws. "So what's next?"

"Patience, darling. That's stage three. We're still in stage two." Jayne strode over to a walk-in closet the size of Mary Lynn's bedroom, and pushed a button: The racks began to rotate. The clothes were all arranged by color and grouped by size. Most of Jayne's wardrobe hung on the racks labeled size 4, but there were several racks of 6s, and even a small collection of 8s that looked as if they'd never been worn. Mary Lynn wondered if Jayne ballooned up and down or if she kept the 8s around in case she needed to gain weight for a role. She stared at the fluttering rainbow of silk, and the cashmere and wool so fine you could almost see through it. *Wooo,* she thought.

"Something casual," Jayne murmured, studying the 6s. "Something simple. Miu Miu? Dolce and Gabbana? Stella McCartney? Or perhaps a classic. Armani? Versace? No. Valentino, perhaps? Yes, definitely Valentino." She seized an outfit, clicked over to a bank of drawers, opened several, and selected a bra, underpants, and stockings. On the way back to Mary Lynn, she grabbed a pair of shoes from one of the shoe racks.

"Voilà," she said, dumping everything into Mary Lynn's arms. The clothes felt light and cool, like the kind of thin, wispy clouds you sometimes see floating overhead on a spring morning. The pants, sleeveless top, and cropped jacket were made of exquisitely cut bright red silk; the stockings were as delicate as cobwebs. Only the bra, underpants, and shoes were substantial. The bra was lacy and slightly padded; the shoes soft red leather with low heels. The underpants, on the other hand, were made of black Lycra and looked hot and uncomfortable. Under ordinary circumstances, Mary Lynn might have objected to the pants, but for a hundred thousand dollars, she would have cheerfully put on iron panty hose if that's what Jayne had wanted.

Ten minutes later, dressed in red silk from head to foot, she was sitting in front of a blank computer screen. Jayne bent over her, swaying gracefully like a benevolent anaconda.

"What do you see?" she crooned.

"Nothing."

"Hold still."

There was a bright flash of light. Mary Lynn jumped. Suddenly the computer screen came to life, and she found herself looking at her own face. It was not, to say the least, a flattering portrait: her mouth was open, and she looked terrified.

"Whoops." Jayne emitted a small noise that sounded very much like a giggle. "If this had been a screen test, you'd be required by law to wear a veil. Try to hold still this time."

Again the camera flashed, and again Mary Lynn's face appeared on the screen. This time she looked more or less normal.

"What do you see?"

"Me."

Jayne grabbed the mouse and moved it around. There were several sharp clicks, and Mary Lynn's image began to change.

"Now what do you see?"

"Me with blond hair."

"And now?"

"Me without my glasses."

"And now?"

Mary Lynn gasped. Jayne had done something to her face, something that had to do with her eyebrows and lips and eyes and skin. Taken by themselves, none of the changes were major, but taken altogether, they had a remarkable effect.

"Why, I'm pretty!" A tingling sensation ran up her spine. She had never thought of herself as pretty. She had always been okay-looking, midrange attractive, five on a scale of ten. Maybe, to be more honest, a four.

"You're not just pretty. You're drop-dead gorgeous. Your hair has style; you weigh less; you're wearing lipstick instead of Chap Stick. In other words, you have the kind of face that turns men's minds to mush, and has exactly the opposite effect on everything below their waists. Meet the new Mary Lynn McLellan, the girl with the I'll-leave-my-wife-and-steal-TVs-to-buy-you-diamonds face." Jayne chuckled wickedly. She loved nothing better than the thought of men crawling, begging, and spending obscene amounts of money.

"Oh." Mary Lynn sighed with delight. "Yes."

Jayne pushed a button and a printer concealed somewhere inside the machine spat out a hard copy of Mary Lynn's new face.

Mary Lynn touched the screen with the tips of her fingers. "I can't believe it. What did you do? I look like . . ."

"Yes, you lucky girl. You really *do* look like me." Jayne picked up her Diet Coke, took a sip, and thoughtfully studied the computer-generated portrait of Mary Lynn. "We're hovering on the edge of stage three. There're only two questions left to answer: is this one of Bill Gates's wicked little tricks, or can I actually make you look like this?"

Mary Lynn sighed and turned away from her prettier self. The answer to Jayne's question was obvious. Short of plastic surgery, you were stuck with the face you were born with.

But Jayne didn't live in a world where faces were permanent. While Mary Lynn was reconciling herself to being a four forever, Jayne was thinking of moisturizing creams that erased wrinkles, tubes of lipstick that cost more per ounce than gold, and sets of fake eyelashes made from real human hair. She was thinking of Michelle Pfeiffer's cheeks and Demi Moore's nose; she was envisioning Sophia Loren, who looked so good at sixty-six that men still ogled her; and remembering a chubby, shy three-year-old with a red face and a shiny nose and the plain name of Jane (the *y* had come later) who had been painted and primped into the most famous child star since Shirley Temple.

Jayne closed her eyes and did her own special form of yoga: she imagined herself in a velvet dress with a stiff lace ruff around her neck and a gold crown on her head. Fawning courtiers in extremely tight pants bowed at her feet, and several producers who had given her trouble hung from the wall in chains begging for mercy. What would Queen Elizabeth have done? Would old Liz have given up at this stage with victory in sight? Of course not. Jayne licked her lips, silently decapitated the CEOs of two major studios, and opened her eyes. "By God and England," she said, "I think I can carry it off!"

"God and England?"

Jayne reached out and touched Mary Lynn's hair gingerly. It was hard for her to touch anyone she wasn't having sex with, but she felt almost drunk with the possibilities.

"I can do it. I'm an absolute genius when it comes to makeup."

"Ah," said Mary Lynn, still trying to puzzle out the God-and-England bit.

"But there's one problem." Jayne paused dramatically. "If I try to cut and dye your hair, you're going to look like Joan of Arc *after* they burned her at the stake." She grabbed her cell phone and speed-dialed. "This is Jayne Cooper," she said. "I have an emergency hair situation. If Vlad is free, tell him I need him to come to my place in Malibu immediately."

The old Mary Lynn looked at the new Mary Lynn and allowed herself a shred of hope. She knew that somewhere, at that very instant, one of Hollywood's finest hairstylists was grabbing his thinning shears and running for his car.

"Bozhe moy!" Vlad moaned. He hovered over Mary Lynn's head like Jackson Pollock trying to decide where to spatter next. "My leetle *kokta,* vot hav you done to your

hair?" He stood five feet four at most: a big-nosed, pale, hyperactive Russian with small, slightly slanted blue eyes that were filling with tears at the sight of Mary Lynn's damaged hair.

"You hav baked it," he said. "You hav dried it with a blower, *da?*"

"Da," Mary Lynn admitted.

"I ham moved to veeping by the sight of so many splitted ends." He turned to Jayne. "I am needing *vodky*."

Vlad's *vodky* of choice was a large bottle of Stoli. He grabbed it from the silver tray and, without bothering to pour it into a glass, chugged about a fourth of it, looked at Mary Lynn's head, and made more sounds of disapproval. He was, Jayne had explained, the best hairstylist in Los Angeles, but he also had a teensy drinking problem. On one hand, this was good, because when Vlad drank, he tended to black out and not remember anything. Privacy, Jayne had informed Mary Lynn, was going to be their first concern. On the downside, every once in a while he had been known to cut off a teensy bit of ear.

"I theenk I start here," he said. There was a sudden flash of surgical steel. Mary Lynn closed her eyes, held her breath, and prayed. The blades brushed her ears, but left them intact. When she opened her eyes, Vlad was whirling above her like a human Cuisinart. Bits of wet hair fell into her lap. Vlad began to hum something that sounded suspiciously like "The Volga Boatman." He took one more dramatic slash at her bangs and suddenly pirouetted to a full stop.

"Vot!" he said. Apparently, it wasn't a question. He stepped back, inspected Mary Lynn's hair, clicked the shears in the air like castanets, and took another long, loving pull on the vodka. "Iz perfect."

"Perfect," Jayne agreed. "Now dye her hair exactly the same color as mine, and I'll have Larry fix that little visa problem of yours." She smiled sweetly. "Of course, if you ever tell anyone about this, Vlad darling, I'll have to have

Larry have a little talk with the INS." She picked up the bottle of Stoli and dangled it just out of his reach.

"I am not talking to nobody." Vlad eyed the vodka hungrily. He draped a fresh cloth over Mary Lynn's shoulders and began to apply something to her hair that smelled like roses and bleach. "I not wanting to go back to Russia. Whole country like Mir. So cold in winter, underwear freezes to balls." He selected little bundles of Mary Lynn's hair, slathered them with some other kind of cream, and began to wrap each packet in aluminum foil. "Vlad not spilling beans."

"Glad to hear it." Jayne put the bottle of vodka back down on the tray. "In that case, when you've finished with her, I want you to do my hair."

Vlad brightened. "Iz honor," he said.

"Specifically, I want you to dye it the color hers was."

"Nyet!" Vlad cried so loudly it made Mary Lynn jump.

"Yes," Jayne went on relentlessly. "And then, Vlad darling, I want you to chop off some hunks of it so I look as much like her as possible." Jayne gave him a grim look. "Maybe you could even manage to split a few ends."

Vlad gave a low moan, picked up the bottle of vodka, and emptied it into his mouth. He was an artist, and he had just been asked to wreck the most fabulous hair on the planet.

A few hours later, two women stood in front of a full-length mirror in Jayne Cooper's dressing room. They were the same height, but one was a bit plumper than the other. The woman on the right (the plumper one) wore red silk and had blond hair with tints of red and gold. Her nails were perfectly manicured; her skin was powdered to pale alabaster. Thanks to a quick visit from an optometrist, her eyes were now the color of blue cornflowers, made more intense by custom-tinted contact lenses. The woman on the left also had cornflower blue eyes, but they were partially obscured by a pair of oversize glasses. Her hair, which was done up in a scraggly knot on the back of her head, was the color of dry grass. She wore a wrinkled green cotton skirt, a white blouse with one button missing, Birkenstocks, and a baggy brown sweater.

For a moment, they stood as if hypnotized. Then one spoke.

"My God," said the woman in red silk. "I don't believe this."

"Hideous, isn't it," said the woman in the glasses. "And yet, perfect in a ghastly sort of way." She put out her hand. Her unpolished nails had been bitten down to the quick. There had been no sacrifice too great. "Keys," she said.

"Keys to what?" said the woman in red.

"To your place, of course." And then she began to explain.

It was late. The remains of dinner littered the room, and the spectacular view of the ocean had disappeared long ago behind a bank of black fog.

Jayne lit a cigarette, blew a bit of smoke at her own reflection, and winced. Her dressing room contained ten mirrors. Not a plus at the moment. "You'll have to lose weight," she told Mary Lynn. She took another drag and rolled the pink tube between her fingers.

"And you'll have to stop smoking."

Jayne bravely stubbed out her cigarette and pulled the baggy sweater tighter. Mary Lynn's clothes were ugly, but amazingly comfortable.

"Let me go over this one last time," Mary Lynn said. "You say that your agent and your mother know, but no one else knows."

"Right."

"I do the publicity for this new movie of yours."

"Salome."

"I say how great your director is." Mary Lynn consulted her notes. "And I tell cute stories about how much I love camels."

"That's for the animal rights people. I'm famous for my love of animals. I donate a quarter of a million dollars a year to the SPCA. The truth is"—Jayne reached for a cigarette and then reconsidered—"I hate anything with fur that hasn't been made into a coat."

"And meanwhile, you live my life."

"Exactly."

"If I have any problems"—Mary Lynn consulted her notes again—"I call Larry Sears, your agent. Ditto if I need spending money."

"Um." Jayne nodded. Two minutes without a cigarette and she was already feeling a little alarm going off inside her head. Could she actually give up smoking? Could she pass herself off as an English professor? She wondered how long it took to cook a potato and what chicken looked like raw. The thought of slimy pink chicken made her feel as if she had just accepted a role in a cheap slasher film. Possibly, she could survive on takeout. She'd never had Kentucky Fried Chicken. Rumor had it that the general public found such food satisfactory.

"And for this," Mary Lynn continued, "you pay me a hundred thousand dollars: twenty-five thousand down, and the rest if we can pull this off?"

"Right."

Mary Lynn picked up one of Jayne's Diet Cokes and forced herself to drink it. The stuff had a hideous chemical flavor that made her want to run to a health food store and gargle wheat grass juice, but Diet Coke was one of Jayne's trademarks. She swallowed with difficulty and put the red-and-silver can back down on the table. "To be honest, Jayne, I don't think this switch has a chance in hell of working, but what do I have to lose?"

"So do we have a deal?"

"We have a deal."

Jayne pushed the contract and the nondisclosure agreement in Mary Lynn's direction. Mary Lynn picked up a small gold pen and signed her name twice with a flourish.

The sight of her signatures scrawled across the bottom of the pages suddenly gave her the same doomed feeling she'd had on the day she married Ron. What had she gotten herself into this time?

The answer was not long in coming.

Jayne folded up the documents and put them into the wall safe. "One final thing," she said. "Be careful."

"Careful?"

Jayne whirled the combination lock. She had saved this part until last—for reasons that were about to become obvious. "I'm famous; I have millions of fans; some of them are—" She stopped, trying to figure out how to put it in a way that wouldn't send Mary Lynn scurrying off in a panic. "A little too devoted."

"You mean stalkers!" Mary Lynn sat up so fast she almost knocked over the can of Diet Coke.

"Well, yes and no."

"What does that mean?"

"Sometimes my fan mail is a bit unusual."

"Meaning what?"

Jayne turned around with a look of perfect innocence. "Well, at present I'm getting about a hundred marriage proposals a week, up ten percent from this time last year."

"I can handle that. Ron proposed to me six times before I was stupid enough to accept."

Jayne sat down and became intensely absorbed in one of the buttons on Mary Lynn's sweater. "There's also some nut who claims to be a Saudi sheikh who's invited me to join his harem, but my security people have tracked his e-mail to Cleveland, so I doubt he's using his real name. Last March I had a kidnapping threat, but the FBI looked into it, and the perp turned out to be a ten-year-old fourth grader from Greenwich, Connecticut, whose parents weren't properly supervising his Internet time. The tipoff came when he demanded a free trip to Disneyland."

Mary Lynn looked at her grimly. "Give me back that contract."

"Don't get upset. It's no big deal. You'll be perfectly safe. If I didn't have crazy fans, I'd have to hire them. A girl is nobody in this town without bodyguards, and I've got the best money can buy. I just fired the firm that used to do my security and hired the geniuses who designed the Popemobile. Remember, except for a few publicity gigs, you're not going out of the house. No one can get in here. I've got state-of-the-art motion detectors and the fence is electrified."

"No moat?"

"No." Irony was lost on Jayne. "I thought about having one installed after I did *The Loves of Robert Bruce,* but my lawyers told me that if anyone fell in, I'd get sued."

Mary Lynn thought about the hundred thousand dollars. She imagined it all in pennies piled up to the ceiling. She would never get another chance like this if she lived to be a hundred. She took a deep breath and forced herself to park her fear of Jayne's fans in the private closet where she kept her fear of spiders, tax audits, and large dogs. "So how real do you think these threats are?"

"I'm not worried." Jayne adjusted Mary Lynn's bra (a horrible harness of limp cotton held up on one side by a safety pin), tugged the cotton skirt into place, and rose to her feet. Her arches, accustomed to high heels, screamed at being forced to pad across the floor in Birkenstocks. "I've gotten crazy fan mail all my life."

"Oh, wonderful. That's really reassuring. And you know what: it also gives us something else in common." Mary Lynn picked up the Diet Coke and took a long pull. "Right now, I have a freshman student named William Hestene. William was recently released from a mental hospital, and I suspect he's been skipping his medication. He's twenty-eight years old, six feet three inches tall, weighs about three hundred fifty pounds, has a pockmarked face, two front teeth the color of old piano keys, and usually wears a black sleeveless T-shirt that reads 'Kill Them All and Let God Sort Them Out.' I strongly suggest that you never give William anything below an A minus."

Jayne went slightly pale. "It will be my pleasure." She picked up her silver cigarette case and flipped it into the ample pocket of Mary Lynn's sweater. "Now that we've got that settled, I'm going out in my garden for one last smoke."

"And I'm going to sit here and think. Look, Jayne, if I really decide I can't do this, will you give me back the contract?"

"Of course. I won't be happy, but if you want to back out, we'll toss that contract in the shredder and I'll have my driver take you back to the Food Barn."

Where, Mary Lynn thought, *if I work really, really hard for the next thirty years, they'll probably up my pay to eight-fifty an hour.*

The garden was dark and silent. On the surface of Elvis's guitar-shaped pool, the water was still; on all sides, the white oleanders gleamed through the fog like tiny moons. Jayne lit her last cigarette and inhaled hungrily. She wished that the idiots who had discovered that smoking was bad for you had never been born. Life had so few real pleasures. She took another voluptuous drag.

"Hey, you!" said a deep male voice. "What the hell do you think you're doing?"

Startled, Jayne whirled around, and a bright light struck her full in the face, temporarily blinding her.

"Freeze, lady!"

She dropped her cigarette. Boots crunched on the gravel. A tall shape loomed up behind the light, and a gloved hand reached out and grabbed her rudely by the arm. She tried to kick her assailant in the shins and missed. "Let go of me!" she snarled. "Who are you? What do you think you're doing?"

"I'm throwing you out of here; that's what I'm doing. This is private property."

"Get your hands off me! Do you have any idea who I am?"

"Yeah, you're one of Miss Cooper's nutso fans."

Jayne suddenly understood: this had to be one of the new security guards she'd just been telling Mary Lynn about. He'd never met her. He had no idea who she was. Well, he was just about to find out.

"Come on." He began to drag her toward the gate. For a moment she was so paralyzed with rage, she couldn't speak. "You people are pathetic," he said. "You need to get a life."

That was too much. "I told you to get your filthy hands off me!" she yelled. "I'm Jayne Cooper!"

"Yeah," he said. "And I'm Batman." He shoved her hard in the small of the back; she stumbled forward, cursing. Behind her she heard the sound of her own front gate slamming shut.

She turned and threw herself against the bars. "You moron!" she yelled. "You've locked me out of my own house! Let me back in! I'll have your job for this!"

"Have a nice day," the guard said. "And stand back. I'm going to turn the electricity on."

Jayne felt a jolt pass through her body. She yelped and let go of the iron bars. Falling to a heap on the neatly raked gravel driveway, she began to sob with rage and frustration.

She promised herself that when she got back inside her house, she'd make that guard sorry he'd ever been born. She didn't have to take this kind of abuse. If this was what it meant to live an ordinary life, she'd already had enough of it. She'd pay Mary Lynn the $5K kill fee and forget about Spielberg. She wanted another cigarette. She wanted decent shoes. She wanted to sleep in her own bed tonight, and when she got up, she wanted to put on underpants that didn't have the days of the week written on them. Most of all, she wanted that security guard's head on a platter.

She wiped her nose on the sleeve of Mary Lynn's sweater, got up, and marched back toward the gate. The roses along the driveway were staked with short wooden poles. She jerked one of the poles out of the ground and banged on the bars.

"Let me in immediately, you varlet!" she yelled. That was a line from one of her most famous films. When she'd said it onscreen, the audience had gone wild; but tonight, for the first time in twenty-seven years, the theater was empty, and her audience had all gone home.

Six

Mary Lynn woke with a start to find her cheek resting in a small puddle of Diet Coke. It was very late, she was still in Jayne's dressing room, and somewhere a cell phone was going off like a demented car alarm. She shuddered as she realized the thing was chirruping out the theme song from *The Loves of Leonardo*. She scrambled around, located the phone, and switched it on.

"Help!" a familiar voice cried.

"Jayne?"

"Make them stop! Make them back off!"

"Jayne, where are you?"

"In your apartment. I . . . Damn it! Here they come again!" There was a scurrying sound, and Mary Lynn heard the crash of crockery hitting the floor.

"Jayne, what's wrong? What are you doing in my apartment? How did you get there?"

"I walked," Jayne yelled. "My back aches; my feet are in shreds. If it hadn't been for a nice man named Carlos who gave me a ride in the back of his pickup, I'd be dead by the side of the road."

"You didn't hitchhike!"

"Of course not. I was raised on *Psycho*. Janet Leigh used to sit in our living room and talk about how she'd never take another shower. An idiot security guard threw me out the front gate. The guy is going to pay big time."

"Jayne . . ."

"So there I was, staggering down the road like an extra in a disaster film, when Carlos stopped for me. I was sure we were headed for the Bates Motel, but I was desperate. It's cold out there; I didn't have on any stockings; I didn't have a cell phone."

"Jayne . . ."

"Carlos was a perfect gentleman. Clean him up and stick him in a velvet doublet, and he could have played Philip of Spain. He told me he had thirteen children and no green card, so I gave him the hundred dollars." Her voice grew shrill. "He saved my life. I didn't even have enough change to make a phone call. It costs thirty-five cents, did you know that?"

Mary Lynn thought of how many phone calls she could have made with a hundred thousand dollars. She took a deep breath and forced herself to accept the fact that Jayne was going to come back and rip their contract into shreds. No surprise, really. The woman had about as much chance of leading an ordinary life as the Queen of England. She had known from the start that this whole wacky deal was too good to be true. Still, the loss of so much money was a major disappointment.

"I had to sit on his lawn mower!" Jayne continued, not pausing for breath. "I've got grass stains on my ass. I look like the Jolly Green Giant. I smell like a crankcase. All I want is a hot bath. But *nooo*. The instant I opened your front door, the fiends started closing in—" She broke off with a shriek.

"Jayne, calm down. What fiends? Are you okay? Should I call nine-one-one?"

"No, no. Just tell me how to stop them."

"Stop whom? What are you talking about?"

"Your cats."

Mary Lynn stared at the phone in disbelief. "My cats?"

"You should have warned me. I'm ailurophobic, and there are five of the little cannibals. They've got claws sharp enough to shred steel, and they're stalking me around your kitchen right now like I'm some kind of giant mouse."

"Jayne, relax. The cats are harmless. They probably just want to be fed. All you have to do is get the can opener out of the drawer under the sink and open a few tins of—"

"I can't talk. They've backed me into a corner! I may have to run for it."

"Jayne, listen . . ."

"Oh, my God! Here they come again! They're charging!" The phone emitted an earsplitting shriek and the connection was severed. Mary Lynn tried to call back, but she kept getting a busy signal. Finally she gave up.

So Jayne had a phobia about cats? Who knew? She'd undoubtedly show up in the morning to announce that the deal was off. Meanwhile, the only danger seemed to be that Austen, Thackeray, Flaubert, Eliot, and Hardy weren't going to get their tuna fish.

Mary Lynn suddenly felt completely exhausted. She picked up the phone and carried it into Jayne's bedroom. If she was going to spend the rest of her life camping out in rented apartments, she might as well get at least one night's sleep in a mansion.

The light provided by the silk-shaded lamps was muted and intimate. The handwoven rug was deep enough to drown in. Jayne's bed, which was the size of a football field, was completely covered in crushed red velvet; and every inch of the mahogany headboard was carved with scenes that, on closer inspection, proved to have been taken from her most famous movies.

Mary Lynn pulled back the covers and gave a small gasp of delight. The sheets were satin. Without a moment's hesitation, she stripped off her clothes and crawled in naked. It was a wonderful sensation, like sliding around on warm ice. She wiggled her way to the right-hand side, flicked off the lamp, and stretched out full length. The satin cupped her flesh more tenderly than Ron or Wen-

dell had ever managed in the uncounted dreary times she'd
made love to them.

Just before dawn, two raccoons dipped their paws in
Jayne's ornamental fishpond and washed half a dozen priceless orchid bulbs, which they ate with relish. By the time
they finished, the eastern sky had started to turn from gray
to bronze. At six-thirty, the automatic sprinklers came on,
and inside Jayne's mansion, the smell of shade-grown organic coffee began to drift up from the kitchen.

Some time around seven A.M., Mary Lynn woke to the
theme song from *Leonardo*. For a moment she had no idea
where she was; then she saw the carved camels on the bed-
post and remembered. She fumbled for the cell phone and
turned it on.

"Jayne?" said a female voice with a soft southern accent.

"Yes." Until Jayne got back to call it quits officially, a
deal was a deal. Mary Lynn waited for the party on the other
end of the line to give her some clue who she was talking
to; but the party didn't cooperate.

"Who am I?"

"Who are you?"

"Yes, who am I? What's my name?"

Mary Lynn stared at the phone. She had no idea and was
afraid to guess.

"You don't know, do you?"

Mary Lynn said nothing. She wondered if she could just
hang up.

"Oh, my dear sweet Jesus!" the woman wailed. "She's actually done it!"

"Done what?"

"You known perfect well what, you impostor. This is
Clarice Cooper Korngold. Ring a bell?"

"Jayne's mother?"

"That's right—Jayne's mother. I booted up my computer
this morning to find a piece of e-mail from Jayne that bor-

dered on insanity. What have you done with my daughter? Where is she?"

Mary Lynn sat up straight and gripped the phone more firmly. Jayne had warned her this might happen. She thought of all the students who had ever asked for extensions on papers, all the grandmothers who died like flies just before finals.

"I can't tell you."

"Oh yes, you can."

"Sorry. I signed a contract, Mrs. Korngold."

The soft southern accent suddenly turned hillbilly. "I don't give a flying cow patty what you signed. This is between Jayne and I, and you're going to give me her phone number right now, or I'm going to come over there and make you sorry you were born."

Mary Lynn took a deep breath. "Sure," she said. "Come on over, Mrs. Korngold. It smells as if the coffee's ready. And by the way, it's 'between Jayne and me,' not 'between Jayne and I.' When the pronoun is the object of a preposition, it takes the objective case."

She punched the POWER button on the phone and cut Clarice off in midsputter. You didn't spend six semesters whipping freshmen into shape without learning how to hold your own.

Ten seconds later, the phone rang again.

"The objective case . . ." Mary Lynn said.

"Whatever are you babbling about?" Jayne said in a dreamy voice.

Mary Lynn took a look around the beautiful bedroom and felt a pang of regret. "I suppose you're calling to say that you've changed your mind."

"Changed my mind? Oh no. On the contrary." Jayne gave what sounded like a sigh of profound contentment. "I just want you to know that I've never been happier in my life. I'm lying here with your cats. They're draped over my body like a fur coat, and they're giving me unconditional love."

"It's not unconditional. It involves tuna fish."

"To think that I feared them. What a fool I was. They purr; they lick my face; they stare at me with total adoration. Have I ever had a lover half so attentive? No. Cats are definitely better than men: sweeter, kinder, more noble."

Mary Lynn resisted a strong urge to tell her to get a grip.

"Your mother just called."

Jayne seemed totally uninterested.

"She's coming over here to grill me."

"What about?"

"She wants to know where you are."

"Don't tell her and I'll give you a thousand-dollar bonus."

"It's a deal. What *should* I tell her?"

"Tell her I love her," Jayne said, and hung up.

"Good morning, Miss Cooper," someone said politely.

Mary Lynn put down the phone and turned to find a young woman standing in the doorway. She had a pretty, round face, short brown hair, and a very small nose that looked a bit like a button. In her arms, she carried a silver tray that held a large silver coffeepot, half a grapefruit, and a china eggcup filled with vitamin pills.

Breakfast, Mary Lynn thought, *and not much by the look of things.* She remembered that Jayne had warned her that she was going to have to lose weight. She thought about scrambled eggs, cheese Danish, and crisp strips of fried bacon. The carcinogenic maraschino cherry in the center of the grapefruit stared back at her accusingly. There was no way out of this.

"Thanks"—she racked her brain for the name of Jayne's personal assistant—"Lois. You can put it down on the table by the window."

Lois put the tray down on the table and broke into tears. "Oh, Miss Cooper," she sobbed, "you called me by my name. You never called me by my name before. You saw me. You actually *saw* me."

"Don't cry," Mary Lynn pleaded. She was stupefied by the girl's reaction. She handed Jayne's assistant a Kleenex and waited while she blew her nose. Then she grabbed the coffeepot and poured Lois a cup of hot coffee.

Mary Lynn pressed the cup into the girl's hands and watched her take a few tremulous sips. The good news was that Lois clearly thought Mary Lynn was Jayne. The bad news was that she looked as if she expected Jayne to boil her in oil.

Seven

Clarice settled back in the red silk armchair, crossed her silk-clad legs with a soft swish, and smiled at Mary Lynn the way a tiger might smile at a gazelle just before it ripped its head off.

"Whoever you are, honey," she said, "you are in deep doo-doo."

Mary Lynn took a deep breath of Clarice's perfume and gagged. She hated perfume. The only thing she'd ever put behind her ears was vanilla extract, and she'd only done that because Wendell had promised to lick it off. She put Wendell out of her mind and summoned up the tone of voice she used at the Food Barn to deal with angry customers. "I understand that you're upset by what Jayne has done, Mrs. Korngold, but—"

"Upset? You bet your sweet little ass I'm upset." Clarice picked up the pot and poured herself a cup of coffee. "Just sitting here looking at you gives me chills. If I didn't know better, I'd think I'd given birth to two Jaynes. That in itself is enough to send me to the loony bin. Jayne times one is like a volcanic eruption—an act of God but survivable. Jayne times two is more like that meteor strike that rubbed out all the dinosaurs. What's your name?"

"Mary Lynn McLellan."

"Well, Ms. McLellan . . ." Clarice took a sip of coffee and paused for a moment to contemplate the pinkish smear her lipstick had left on the rim of the cup. Another mother might have had trouble keeping her temper under control at a time like this, but Clarice was an expert at negotiation. It was she, not Larry Sears, who had gotten Global to agree to pay Jayne twenty-four million for *Salome*. Now, as she faced this thirty-something clone of her own daughter, she almost pitied her.

She slid the cup back onto the saucer. "Let's get right down to business: where's my daughter?"

Mary Lynn said nothing.

"Still not talking?"

"No. Sorry."

"Not half as sorry as you're going to be if you don't tell me while there's still time for her to get back here before the studio finds out what she's done. Look, why don't we save some time here? You need money. I love my daughter and want to save her from her own folly. How much would it cost me to find out where she is?"

"That information isn't for sale, Mrs. Korngold."

Clarice sat back. Fine, if the girl wanted to do it the hard way, she'd oblige her. "You know who you remind me of, besides Jayne?"

Mary Lynn remained stubbornly silent.

"You remind me of Annabel Lee Laveau, a girl I went to Sweet Briar with. The Laveaus were an old southern family. They'd been marrying their own first cousins for generations, and a bigger fool than Annabel Lee never walked the face of the earth. That girl was so dumb, she tried to use Tampax without taking the cardboard off the tube first. Am I making myself clear here?"

"Perfectly," Mary Lynn said through gritted teeth. Jayne had warned her that Clarice was going to be difficult.

"Good. Now let me make myself even clearer. If you don't tell me where Jayne is, you're going to have a major problem on your hands. Have you seen your schedule for today—not the old one, but the update?"

"Not exactly."

"I knew it!" Clarice bent down and retrieved her purse.

"Well, here it is." She pulled out a folded sheet of paper and thrust it in Mary Lynn's direction. "Read it and weep."

Mary Lynn took the schedule with a sense of impending doom. Less than an hour ago, Lois had come in with Jayne's new schedule, which she had transferred from her Palm Pilot to Jayne's using an infrared beam that probably could have hard-boiled an egg. Ever since, Mary Lynn had been trying to read the thing without success. The problem was, she didn't know Jayne's password, and none of the obvious possibilities had worked.

"Jayne's password is mirror—as in 'Mirror, mirror, on the wall, who's the fairest of them all?'" Clarice said. Mind reading was one of her subspecialties. "I'm afraid I read my baby too many fairy tales when she was at an impressionable age. If I had it to do all over again, I'd only read her accounts of horrible accidents suffered by little girls who didn't obey their mamas."

Mary Lynn was no longer listening. Having unfolded the schedule, she was studying it with growing horror.

"This has to be wrong!" she said in a strangled whisper.

"Welcome to the wonderful world of cinematic fame, darlin'. There's no mistake on that schedule. The only mistake around here is the mistake Jayne made when she took off and left an amateur in her place."

Mary Lynn looked up from the schedule. Her eyes had a deer-in-the-headlights glaze that Clarice found immensely satisfying. "It says here that I have an appointment today."

"Well, my, my. So it does."

"At eleven."

"That's right."

"With a group called Animals First."

"Yes, you lucky girl. You have a date."

"But this can't be right. I wasn't supposed to make any public appearances until the publicity campaign for *Salome* began, and every word was supposed to be scripted out in advance. Jayne promised that. . . ."

"Jayne didn't know about this. It just happened. Besides,

she makes a lot of promises. Just count yourself lucky you never bought her an engagement ring. She's got a pile big enough to start her own store." Clarice's voice dropped into a steely purr. "Which, no doubt, is what she is going to have to do for a living when the studio finds out she's using a stand-in instead of fulfilling her contractual obligations. So I'm asking you again, where is she?"

Terrified by the prospect of impersonating Jayne in public without adequate preparation, Mary Lynn briefly considered telling Clarice that Jayne was a few miles away, asleep under a pile of cats. Then she remembered the bonus. "I signed a contract," she said.

"Damn it!" Clarice put down her cup so fast the coffee spilled all over her pink silk trousers. Pulling out a clean hankie, she began to dab at the stains. "There's no contract that can't be broken. You want a lawyer? I'll get you a lawyer. Was there a witness? Did Jayne have this so-called contract notarized? Of course not. Jayne has no sense of what's legally binding and what isn't. When she was nine, she tried to buy herself a castle in Scotland. A nine-year-old can not buy a castle, nor can she buy a stable of racing horses, nor can she legally purchase the Mattel Corporation in order to redesign the Barbie doll in her own image. Half the contracts Jayne has signed haven't been worth the paper they were written on."

Clarice again searched Mary Lynn's face for some sign that she might change her mind, but all she saw was pigheaded stubbornness combined with terror. She cursed her luck and decided that the only option left was damage control.

"So I take it by your silence that you insist on going along with this idiotic masquerade?"

"Yes."

"Well, then, at least do it right. I have no intention of letting Jayne wreck her career. There are a hundred and fifteen million dollars at stake here. The studio lawyers will probably try to take the losses out of Jayne's hide, and, personally, I don't fancy an old age spent dribbling spit in some low-cost senior-care facility."

"A hundred and fifteen million!" Mary Lynn had had no idea the stakes were so high.

"The entire budget of *Salome*. Plus, at least double that if you factor in what the studio expects to recoup in box office receipts the first six months. Animals First is claiming some camels were injured in the making of the movie, and they're threatening to organize a nationwide boycott. If they do that, the studio might as well cut the whole movie up for mandolin picks. You get my drift?"

Mary Lynn nodded. It was all becoming horribly clear.

"Good, because this is where you come in. The studio is sending you to persuade them to back off—not you, actually, but Jayne—because Jayne has a reputation for supporting animal rights. The truth is, Jayne has never loved any living thing that can't legally use a credit card, but on my advice she's been giving a lot of money to the SPCA. It's going to be your job to reassure Animals First that no camels were harmed in the making of *Salome*. You—or rather Jayne—are the only person they'll believe."

Mary Lynn felt as if someone had picked up the entire room and tilted it sideways. She wondered if Jayne had any tranquilizers stashed in her desk.

"Were any camels harmed?"

"Of course not!" Clarice snapped. "Good Lord, do you have any idea how carefully the studio protects every animal that appears on the screen? You can't even kill a spider these days without some nuts staging a funeral for the damn thing."

"Do you think this group will actually go through with the boycott if I don't show up?"

"Oh yes." Clarice smiled grimly. "Animals First are heavy hitters. They once closed Euro Disney down for three weeks because a female tourist from Saudi Arabia walked through the front gate wearing a fox fur *hijab*. And last November, they prevented the distribution of a Thanksgiving movie because they claimed it demeaned turkeys. You want to see a grown man scream and tear out his hair? Well, honey, you just whisper the words Animals First to any studio exec in this town, and then you stand back and wait for the heart attack."

Mary Lynn put down the schedule and tried to do some deep-breathing exercises. "I can't face them, Mrs. Korngold. Not with cameras rolling."

"If you aren't going to tell me where Jayne is, you don't have any choice." Clarice consulted her watch. "One hour and fifteen minutes from now, you're going to climb onto a platform in front of enough cameras to film the Oscars. It's going to be like one of those nature specials on TV: the ones where the cute, fuzzy little bunny gets pounced on by the hawks."

"Tell them I'm sick. Tell them I have a cold or pneumonia. Anything."

"Nice idea. You're a bright girl. But it won't work. You— or rather Jayne—tried that last week, and Carleton Winters himself came over here with a doctor and three lawyers and made her get up out of bed and go give a speech to MAVIC. Carleton's the main honcho at Global Films. He hates to talk to actors. In fact, the last actor Carleton personally deigned to address was Jimmy Stewart; so the fact that he showed up here in person gives you some idea of what kind of hell is going to break loose if you aren't talking to Animals First at eleven."

"What's MAVIC?"

"Mothers Against Violence in the Cinema."

"What did I speak on?"

"You spoke on the topic 'Love Heals All,' and the ladies gave you a standing ovation."

Mary Lynn shuddered but gave no sign of yielding. There was a long pause. Clarice silently counted to twenty just to make sure. Then she spoke.

"Let's move on."

Mary Lynn looked at her warily.

"We both have a lot to gain if you manage to fool everyone until Jayne gets back—and I think I know how to do that." The offer didn't come easily, but one of the secrets of Clarice's success was knowing when to cut her losses.

"I'm not going to lie and tell you I'll do it with a happy heart, but I made Jayne. In some ways, Jayne Cooper is the greatest work of art Clarice Korngold is likely to produce in her lifetime. I crafted the original out of a scared little girl. Now it appears that it's time for me to make a copy out of a grown woman who doesn't have the sense God gave gophers. Like it or not, you're going to be my *Mona Lisa*, and I don't mean the one from *The Loves of Leonardo*." She opened her purse and took out an eyebrow pencil. "Lean forward, honey."

Mary Lynn leaned forward cautiously. She was unnerved by this sudden turn of events. She didn't know what to make of Clarice's offer. Was this some kind of trap?

"Turn your head." Clarice lifted the eyebrow pencil and deftly drew a small, dark mole below Mary Lynn's left eye. "When Jayne taught you to make yourself up like her, she forgot her beauty spot. It's the first thing I noticed when the nurse put her in my arms. And I'll tell you something: Carleton Winters would have noticed that spot was missing. The man has eyes like a fighter pilot."

Clarice tossed the eyebrow pencil back into her purse, fished out a small silver compact, opened it, and handed it to Mary Lynn. "Here, take a look at yourself."

Mary Lynn stared in the mirror, and Jayne's face stared back at her. It was amazing what a simple little spot did to complete the illusion.

She closed the compact and handed it back to Clarice. "Thank you." She was so relieved that she felt like collapsing in a blubbering heap, but she was too proud to cry. She had a feeling some sort of temporary truce had just been signed. Perhaps Clarice felt the same way, because she gave a sigh and settled back in the armchair.

"I swear, I feel like I just baptized you," she said. "I even feel a certain fondness for you, but I imagine that will pass. Meanwhile, don't go thanking me until you hear what I'm going to say next. I've got a list of rules for you. Let's call it 'Clarice's Guide to Surviving in Hollywood Without Getting Totally Screwed.' It's a long list, and I sure hope you got a real good memory, because if you fuck this up, Jayne and I are both going down with you."

At eleven sharp, Mary Lynn stood at a podium facing a dozen reporters, three TV cameras, and approximately two hundred angry vegans. Confronting a hostile audience was an odd sensation: like getting married to the wrong man or standing on the wing of an airplane without a parachute. *I should be scared out of my mind,* Mary Lynn thought, but, to her surprise, she wasn't. There was actually something thrilling about the moment. No matter what happened, talking to a bunch of fanatics who believed squirrels should be able to vote was bound to be more interesting than sitting alone in your apartment drinking peppermint tea and making red circles around misspelled words.

Silently she repeated Clarice's rules: say as little as possible; be nice; deny everything; get out fast.

"Good morning," she said. Her voice came out strong and clear. "Before we get started, I just want to say one thing." She might be a steak-eating, leather-purse-carrying hypocrite, but she'd been teaching persuasion for six years; and she knew the first rule of speechmaking was ethos, which—roughly translated—meant "get the audience on your side." She thrust her fist in the air: "Full civil rights for animals!"

Clarice, who was standing unobtrusively in the back of the crowd, shot her a horrified look, but the crowd loved it. There was a zoolike roar followed by applause.

A tall, extremely thin woman approached the microphone. "Thank you, Ms. Cooper," she said. "You've always been an inspiration to those of us who love animals." The woman paused. Her T-shirt read MEAT IS MURDER, and there was a mildly insane gleam in her eye that Mary Lynn recognized as the look of a true believer.

"I'm Anita Rosetti, president of the L.A. chapter of Animals First."

"Good morning, Ms. Rosetti."

"We have obtained evidence that fourteen camels were killed in cold blood during the making of *Salome*."

"I'm happy to be able to say that the charge is completely false. Global Films is very careful not to harm the animals it employs." Mary Lynn leaned forward slightly. "I never, and I mean *never*, would act in any film where so much as a mosquito was sacrificed." Was she overdoing it? Apparently not. There was another small rustle of approval from the crowd. Ms. Rosetti, however, did not appear convinced.

"Perhaps the camels were killed without your knowledge."

"Ms. Rosetti, I can assure you that—"

"We have pictures."

"Pictures?" Mary Lynn suddenly realized that perhaps Clarice had not been entirely truthful when she said no camels had been harmed.

"Fourteen of them." Ms. Rosetti paused. "One for each camel."

Mary Lynn thought fast. "Those were simulated deaths, Ms. Rosetti. Horribly convincing, yes; but not real. As I said a moment ago, Global never harms the animals it employs." Was she lying? She had no idea. She only knew that Clarice was going to have some explaining to do after this interview.

"Ms. Cooper, if no camels were slaughtered during the making of *Salome*, how do you explain this?" Two members of Animals First suddenly stepped forward and unrolled a large poster. Mary Lynn squinted at the thing. It appeared to be a blowup of a badly focused photo of a bunch of men in striped robes and turbans dipping into a big brass bowl.

"What are they doing?"

"They're eating! Yes, that's right! They're eating the camels!"

Mary Lynn couldn't see how anyone could tell what the men were eating; but this wasn't a comp class. This was a potential lynch mob of enraged vegans who believed that they were holding up proof that someone had been snacking on the stock. *Oh, Lord,* she thought, *how did I ever get myself into this mess? More to the point, how will I ever get out?* Suddenly she had a brilliant idea.

"Ms. Rosetti."

"Yes?" The president of Animals First was looking at her accusingly, and Mary Lynn could feel the crowd beginning to turn nasty.

"I believe I can explain. You say you were told that these men were eating camels? Well, that's a natural mistake. You see, the bedouins of the Great Akmati Desert harvest seeds from the nests of the camel ant. They call these seeds—which are purely vegetable in nature—*chameaux,* which is French for camels. The bedouins use French words because they were once a French colony. The men in this photo are no doubt eating *chameaux.*"

There was a stunned silence. Everyone in the audience, including Clarice and the reporters, looked at Mary Lynn in astonishment.

"Really?" Ms. Rosetti said. For the first time, there was a trace of uncertainty in her voice.

"Really," Mary Lynn said triumphantly. "You can look it up."

Over in the press section, the reporters were grabbing for their Palm Pilots. In seconds they'd searched the Internet and confirmed what Mary Lynn had just said. *Chameaux,* camel ants, the bedouins of the Great Akmati Desert: every word was true.

The reporters stared at each other in amazement as whispers of the confirmation swept through the crowd. Jayne Cooper had just given the most intelligent speech of her career. What had come over her? Had she had a brain transplant?

Mary Lynn gave the crowd one final smile. "I'd like to thank all of you for coming here today," she said. And then, as Clarice had advised, she got offstage as fast as her legs would carry her.

"How the hell did you know about those damn ants!" Clarice demanded as soon as they were alone.

Mary Lynn settled back in the seat of the limo and helped herself to some celery sticks from the low-cal hors d'oeuvre tray Lois had stashed in the refrigerator. "I had a boyfriend in college," she said, taking a bite of celery. "He was majoring in ethnobotany. I wrote all his papers for him."

"You will never do that again. Do you understand? You will never ad-lib in front of a crowd. You will never say a word that I haven't approved in advance."

"It worked," Mary Lynn said stubbornly, "despite the fact that you lied to me about the camels."

"Stop right there. Don't try to spin this so it's my fault."

For a moment, the two women sat glaring at each other. Finally Mary Lynn shrugged and took a bite of celery. "So just for the record, who did eat them?"

"We all did. And they were ghastly."

"What happened? Did you run out of caviar or something?"

"Very funny. No, we ate them because our megalomaniac little director had to go and hire himself a tribe of real live bedouins. The bedouins demanded to be paid in camels. Fine. Bert paid them in camels. How was he to know that they were going to slaughter the flea-bitten beasts and then insist we all join them in a feast?"

"What does camel taste like?"

"Like urine mixed with rubber bands. Don't even mention the word camel to Jayne. She vomited for hours." Clarice shuddered and then took a deep breath. "Okay. I admit it: this time you managed to talk your way out of a difficult situation. It was a very clever move, but don't try it again. I'm going to give you some new rules, and in the future, if you break so much as one of them, I'm going to make your life a living hell."

She held up her hand and began to count on her fingers. "First, you are not to get near the director of *Salome*, the producer, the head of the studio, Jayne's usual makeup person, Jayne's usual hairdresser, or anyone else who might know Jayne intimately enough to suspect that you aren't her. If, by some horrible quirk of fate, you run into some-one who actually knows Jayne well, you are to pretend to have laryngitis and get away as soon as possible."

"Seems reasonable." Mary Lynn reached for another stick of celery.

"Second, the people who are handling the publicity for the film don't actually know Jayne, so you can go ahead with the public appearances, provided you never utter a word I haven't—"

"Approved in advance. Yes, I know."

"And you agree?"

Mary Lynn took a bite of celery and waved the remains at Clarice. "I'm not making any promises."

Clarice moaned. "What did I do to deserve this? You're starting to act exactly like Jayne."

Mary Lynn kicked off her heels and curled her feet under her yoga-style, just as she'd seen Jayne do. "You have my sympathies. A mother's life is often thankless. Now that we've got that settled, would you please open the fridge and get me a Diet Coke?" She smiled wickedly. "You know, I think I'm actually starting to like them."

Eight

Earlier that same morning, Jayne had awakened in a state of manic optimism. Rolling off Mary Lynn's futon, she scattered cats in all directions, dropped to the floor, and did fifty push-ups. Then she rolled over on her back and did a hundred crunchies. As the cats mewed for food and made swipes at her hair, she bicycled her million-dollar legs toward a pitted ceiling that looked like gray cottage cheese.

When she'd finished riding her phantom Exercycle, she did ten sets of yoga stretches at five times the speed a person was supposed to do yoga, finished up with the Breath of Fire, and spent a few giddy moments admiring her toenails, which were the only part of her body still perfectly groomed. Then she bounded to her feet, plunged into the horror of Mary Lynn's bathroom, and took a shower in a stall so small a person practically had to be oiled to turn around. The showerhead was a demonic contraption attached to a pink rubber hose that kept leaping out of her hand and thrashing around like a snake, but even that didn't bother her. The water was hot, Mary Lynn's vanilla-scented soap smelled passably good, and she felt as if she were on the brink of a great adventure.

By the time she finished, sunlight was streaming through the windows, while samba music was floating up from somewhere down below. Jayne sambaed into the kitchen and began to search for something to eat. She was a very good sambista: fluid in the hips, graceful as a wave. When she flew down to Rio two years ago to preside over carnival and have her well-publicized affair with a handsome government official who owned a sugar plantation the size of Florida, the Brazilian press called her *Senhorita Sexy,* which didn't need any translation. Too bad, she thought as she sambaed toward the refrigerator, that all this talent was being wasted on a roomful of cats.

As she sambaed past them, the cats butted her legs, mewed piteously, and stared at her like starving children on posters about African famines. Jayne was seized by an urge to pick up the phone and order them catnip mice and little beds, play equipment, gallons of cream, fresh salmon, matching sweaters, and diamond collars. Didn't Mary Lynn ever feed the poor things?

"Hush, my darlings," she cooed.

In Mary Lynn's meat keeper, she located a piece of sirloin, which bore a yellow sticky note reading: FOR WENDELL. Wendell be damned. Extracting the steak from its plastic wrapper, she took it over to the counter, hacked it into neat cubes, and fed it to the cats, cooing and stroking them and whispering endearments.

When they finished eating, she gave a sigh of satisfaction and stood up. Now all she needed was coffee—lots of it—hot, strong, and preferably cappuccino. Still in samba mode, she danced over to the kitchen counter and opened a promising-looking canister. The smell of peppermint drifted out. Jayne sneezed and made a face. She hated peppermint tea. She grabbed another canister and discovered it contained chamomile.

Five minutes later, she stood over a pile of organic rubble, swearing and on the verge of desperation. Various hideously healthy herbal mixtures were heaped on the counter, some identifiable, some mysterious. She planted her hands on her hips and surveyed the kitchen. There had to be coffee somewhere. No one lived without coffee. On the door of the refrigerator, Mary Lynn had stuck a magnet that said: GIVE ME COFFEE AND NO ONE GETS HURT. That proved she drank the stuff. But where the hell did she keep it?

Suddenly Jayne had a burst of inspiration. She had once read a script in which spies hid atomic secrets in ice cubes. Striding over to the refrigerator, she opened the freezer and smiled triumphantly. There, sitting in lonely splendor, was a can of coffee. Orange and red and ridiculously large, it bore the logo FOOD BARN, which no doubt meant it contained the sweepings from some grimy Colombian warehouse. However, she wasn't in a mood to be picky. A splitting headache was inching its way toward the front of her skull, and she knew if she didn't have coffee in the next five minutes, she would become dangerous.

She seized the can, pried off the lid, and gave a yelp of disappointment. The stuff was ground! She had no idea how to turn ground coffee into something drinkable. Coffee always came in a pot, borne on a tray by Lois or someone like her. *I'm perfectly capable of making coffee,* she told herself. *I shall boil water.*

And boil water she did. When it was roiling, she dumped in the coffee and watched the little black grounds dance on the bubbles. The water turned brown and then nearly black; the sweet aroma of coffee filled the kitchen. Satisfied, she turned off the burner, poured some into one of Mary Lynn's mugs, and blew on the surface to cool it. The coffee looked strange. She had thought the grounds would dissolve, but they hadn't. She lifted the mug to her lips, took a cautious sip, and gagged. It was horrible—record-breakingly horrible—perhaps the worst coffee ever made by any human being in recorded history. She spat a gritty mouthful into Mary Lynn's sink and decided that death would be preferable to drinking the stuff.

Rinsing her mouth out with cold water, she faced the fact that the time had come for her to take her first plunge into the real world. Outside somewhere, the samba music was still playing. Where there was music, there would be other human beings; and at this time of morning, where there were other human beings, there would be someone who could lead her to coffee.

She pulled Mary Lynn's ratty pink terry cloth bathrobe tighter, secured the sash with a double knot, started for the door, and then hesitated. Last night no one had recognized her, but today might be different. Fans might flock to get a look at her. She might even end up having to sign autographs, a task she detested since it always ruined her manicure.

"Courage," she whispered. Bracing herself, she opened the sliding door and stepped out onto the balcony. For a moment, she felt totally disoriented. The backyard of Mary Lynn's apartment building was unusually large. Most of the space was bare, but someone had planted flowers along the fence—a whole row of bright orange California poppies that nodded in the breeze. There were some purple plants that looked like wild vetch, a few geraniums in tin cans, and a patch of feathery fennel. None of them could compare with the plants she grew in her own gardens, but there was something lovely about the way the flowers and weeds were mixed.

In addition to the flowers, the yard was filled with mobiles that hung from a dozen or so metal poles clustered together like flocks of small, brightly colored birds. The dangling metal pieces came in every shape and size, and as the wind blew, they clinked together making sweet, bell-like sounds. Jayne stared at the mobiles in disbelief. They were works of art. They should have been in a museum. What the hell were they doing in the backyard of a low-rent apartment building?

At the exact center of the yard sat a short, squat, crazy-looking birdbath cobbled together out of red, blue, green, purple, and orange scraps of steel. A radio sat on the birdbath blaring out a samba. Around the birdbath, a tall man and two little girls were dancing. The little girls, who looked as if they were about four and five, were wearing two-piece bathing suits; the man had on work boots, jeans, and a white T-shirt. Jayne stood for a moment watching them samba. The little girls were good, and the man was passable.

"You could model," she said.

The three started at the sound of her voice and stopped dancing. They turned and looked up at her, and the man reached out and switched off the radio.

"Beg pardon?"

"I said your daughters could model. They are your daughters, aren't they?"

The man nodded.

"There's a lot of money in modeling children's clothing. I should know. It was one of my first gigs before I started doing films."

"Films? I thought you taught at the college?"

"Oh." Jayne realized with a start that in her desperation to find a decent cup of coffee, she had forgotten who she was supposed to be. "Sure, I teach. But a long time ago, I was in a little commercial for"—she scrambled desperately for some neutral topic—"cat food."

"No kidding."

"No kidding." She had the feeling she hadn't been very convincing. She wondered if she should go into more detail. "Organic cat food," she added.

"I like kitty cats," one of the little girls said.

"Me too." Jayne could have kissed the kid for changing the subject. "You know, you dance the samba really well."

The little girl giggled, stood on one foot, and said something Jayne couldn't understand.

"She just said 'thank you' to you in Portuguese," the man said. "My girls were born in Brazil. That's why they do the samba so well. Their mother was from Bahia. Bahia's the capital of samba. It's in their blood." He paused. "You know, we've seen each other around a few times, but I don't think we've ever really met. I'm Joe Porter, and these little charmers are Lisa and Janeira. Say 'hi' to the nice lady, girls."

"Hi," the girls said, and giggled.

"Hi," Jayne said. "My name is Mary Lynn McLellan." She felt a little guilty about lying to the children. She turned to the man, and for the first time, she took a really good look at him. He was about six feet three with a high fore-

head, dark brown eyes, and medium-length dark brown—
almost black—hair. The guy was well built, a fact that did
not escape her, and he had a kind of smoldering, sexy bad-
boy quality that might have gotten him some attention if
he'd been an actor. He looked as if he worked out a lot, or
maybe he did physical labor. Jayne felt a stab of curiosity.
She couldn't recall ever having met a man who had gotten
his muscles by working.

"You know who you remind me of?" she said before
she could stop herself. "Hugh Jackman. Did you see him
in *X-Men*?"

"No." Joe Porter looked slightly startled. Apparently, he
was not accustomed to his neighbors telling him he looked
like a movie star.

"Jackman played a character called Wolverine. Even
under all that fake hair, you could tell he was a hunk. *X-
Men*'s not my kind of movie—too much violence, too little
romance—but it grossed 57.3 million the first weekend it
opened. The execs at Fox danced in the studio parking lot
when they heard the news. Meanwhile, the boys at Global
are eating their hearts out. They could have had Jackman;
maybe they could even have had *X-Men* if they'd played
their cards right. Of course, if you wanted to do the kind of
stuff Jackman does, you'd have to get a nose job."

Joe turned to the girls. "What language is this lady speaking?" he asked them. The girls giggled.

"Ingles?" Janeira said in what Mary Lynn took to be
Portuguese.

"Yes, English," Joe said. "And yet, I'm not following her.
She doesn't seem to like my nose. Do you girls like my
nose?"

"We love it, Daddy," they chorused in unison.

Joe turned back to Jayne. "There, you have it. It's settled.
My daughters love my nose. I'm not changing it."

Jayne went red. "I didn't mean to imply that there was
anything wrong with your nose."

"No offense," Joe said. "It's okay."

"It's just that when I see people, I automatically cast them in films."

"Kind of a strange habit."

"Yes." Jayne decided that she'd better get off the topic of films while the getting was good. "Look, Mr. Porter."

" 'Joe,' please."

"Look, Joe, I was wondering if you could spare me a cup of coffee."

"Coffee?"

"Yes. I'm all out."

"I smell coffee coming from her apartment," Lisa said. "How can the *senhora* be out of coffee if I smell coffee?"

"Hush." Joe drew the little girl close. "The nice lady is our neighbor. She wants coffee, and we have coffee." He looked up at Jayne and smiled. "Will instant do?"

"Instant will be fine." Jayne was tempted to ask him how one went about making instant coffee, a substance she had never to her knowledge tasted. She vaguely recalled that one mixed the stuff with hot water. But then what did one do?

"I'll have Janeira bring it up to you."

"Thanks."

"Don't mention it." He went back inside and the two girls followed him. Jayne stood on the balcony and watched the mobiles flutter in the wind. A few minutes later, she heard a knock at the front door. Janeira stood in the hallway holding a glass jar of instant coffee. Jayne thanked her, took the coffee, and unscrewed the lid. The stuff looked like crystallized gravel. She remembered the fiasco that had taken place when she boiled the ground coffee. She did not intend to make the same mistake twice.

"Daddy," Janeira said in Portuguese when she returned to the kitchen of her father's apartment a few moments later, "the *senhora* upstairs is doing something really funny."

"What would that be?" Joe put two ham sandwiches in his lunch box and snapped the lid.

"She's eating instant coffee with a spoon."

"Sounds icky."

"Is icky." Janeira gave her father a sharp look. "You aren't going to marry her, are you?"

Joe sat down, picked her up, and put her on his knee. "Honey, I know you miss your mom, but you have to stop asking me if I'm going to marry every woman we meet. I am not going to marry Senhora McLellan. I hardly know Senhora McLellan."

"She's pretty," Janeira said stubbornly. "But she doesn't speak Portuguese." Since their mother's death, Joe Porter's daughters had been mother hungry. They were always trying to match him up, but any woman who didn't speak Portuguese was automatically disqualified.

Nine

At ten-thirty A.M., fortified with instant coffee, Jayne arrived at the Food Barn ready to throw herself into Mary Lynn's job with all the enthusiasm of Tom Cruise heading out on another *Mission Impossible*. As she clicked her way across the vast cement wasteland of the parking lot in Mary Lynn's only pair of high heels (a pathetic pair of clunky black horrors that looked as if they had started out as hiking boots), she felt happier than she'd felt in years.

Even the bus ride had been thrilling. First she'd had to figure out how much it cost, a feat she had accomplished by simply tripping downstairs and knocking on Joe Porter's door. Then she'd had to smash Mary Lynn's piggy bank with a skillet and dig out exactly $1.35, a sum so minuscule that at first she had thought there must be some mistake. At that point, having forgotten to ask Joe which bus to take, she'd returned to his apartment, only to find him gone and a woman of Hispanic extraction taking care of the girls.

"Are you the nanny?" she'd asked, which had turned out to be a faux pas. The woman had introduced herself as Carmen, Joe's ex-mother-in-law and the little girls' grandmother. Fortunately, Carmen had no idea what the word "nanny" meant, and in a mixture of broken English and Portuguese, she explained which bus Jayne needed to catch and where she'd find it.

From there on, the day had only gotten better. While standing at the bus stop in Mary Lynn's ghastly heels and a baggy blue cotton skirt, which appeared to have been purchased from the Goodwill, she had received admiring glances from a number of male passersby, including several muscular men in bright orange hard hats, one of whom had actually whistled at her. On the bus, a short man carrying a lunch pail had called her a "fine-lookin' lady," an old man with a cane had asked for her phone number, and a boy with a large metal ring in his nose had winked and made playful sucking noises at her.

Possibly, she had received all these compliments because she had sliced six inches off the hem of Mary Lynn's skirt with a pair of pinking shears and had put on a tiny tank top that clung to her like glue. But Jayne preferred to think it was because—even disguised as an ordinary woman—she still had that special star quality that brought in the big bucks.

Jayne's first order of business this morning was to find Mary Lynn's car, a vehicle that Mary Lynn had described as a "sort of blue '86 Toyota Camry." After wandering around the Food Barn parking lot for what seemed like hours, she finally stumbled on it, crouched like a geriatric mouse between two immense SUVs. The car, which appeared to have survived some sort of catastrophe, was indeed "sort of blue"—the "sort of" being a hard gray paste that had been slopped into several unsightly dents. Jayne put Mary Lynn's key in the lock and gave a small squeal of pleasure as it turned. So what if the Camry was rusty, battered, and so dirty she could have written her lines from *Salome* on the hood? She had wheels!

She slipped inside and sat for a moment, enjoying the sensation of total privacy. The seat covers, which had been ripped and then neatly mended with duct tape, gave off an earthy smell that reminded her of a puppy she had once been given when she was four. Her mother, she thought grimly, had not let her keep that puppy, thus fostering her lifelong mistrust of animals.

She took a deep breath, closed her eyes, and put Clarice out of her mind. If she was going to work for Spielberg, she could not simply imitate Mary Lynn: she would have to become her. She tried to remember everything her acting coaches had taught her about inhabiting a character.

My name is Mary Lynn McLellan, she told herself. *I was raised in a town called Red Bluff. My parents now live in Bakersfield. I am an ordinary woman who is about to go to work at an ordinary job among ordinary people. And I wish to hell I had a cigarette.*

When she opened her eyes, she still craved a cigarette, but she felt ten pounds lighter. Method acting, she decided, was not only better than therapy; it was faster. She yawned, glanced down, and saw a pile of papers on the floor on the passenger's side of the car. She reached over and picked one up. It was entitled: "Pursuasion Assignment." The first sentence read: "Genetic altar stuff are not good as to crops corn and maybe soy bees I think my uncle growed them wons before he went to prisin butt know doesn't."

For a moment, she wasn't sure she was reading English. Then she noticed that Mary Lynn had circled several of the words in red ink and had written "Your spellchecker is not your friend!" in the margin. The paper had been written by a student named William Hestene, who had received an A-.

Jayne threw the paper back onto the pile, twisted the rearview mirror around so she could get a clear view of her face, frowned, and reapplied her lipstick. "William Hestene" rang a bell. She remembered that he was one of Mary Lynn's students, but she couldn't recall what Mary Lynn had said about him.

A few moments later, having fluffed her hair and applied a bit of powder to her cheeks from a compact so caked it should have been declared a public health hazard, she strolled into the Food Barn. Although it was still indecently early in the morning, the air-conditioning was already going full blast. Jayne stood for a moment taking in the hopelessly ugly cement walls, long lines, and screaming children. What little light there was came from flickering fluorescent tubes. Jayne knew that kind of light. She had been ambushed by it in rest rooms. Green, ugly, and merciless, it made your pores look like potholes and gave your skin a rotting, undersea look.

She shuddered. This wasn't going to be easy. She had always been exquisitely sensitive to her surroundings. She wondered if the fluorescent lights were going to give her migraines. Well, if they did, there was no help for it. An actress had to be prepared to make sacrifices. This was ordinary life, not Rodeo Drive.

She steeled herself, plunged into the mob, and headed toward a door marked EMPLOYEES ONLY. She had not gone more than five steps before a large middle-aged woman in a red apron bore down on her. Jayne watched her approach, not knowing whether to run in the other direction or offer her help. The woman was a walking fashion disaster. She had slathered so many layers of purple shadow on her eyelids, it was a wonder she could keep them open. Her lips were the color of carrots, and she had a head of hair so big, so black that if Vlad could have seen it, the poor man would have immediately given up all hope and impaled himself on his own shears.

"Honey," the woman said in a theatrical whisper, "where you been? You got any idea what time it is?"

"No," Jayne said, still mesmerized by the hair. "Not the faintest."

"It's ten-thirty." The woman gave Jayne—whom she obviously took to be Mary Lynn—a conspiratorial look. "You know how that little rat-faced bastard of a supervisor freaks out when you're late."

"I'm late?"

"Sure, you're late. You were due in at eight."

Jayne started to protest. What was the problem here? The difference between eight and ten-thirty was trivial; before she could even open her mouth, the woman slung a meaty arm around her shoulder and began to hustle her off between the aisles as if they were spies trying to escape aerial surveillance.

"Don't worry," she whispered, briskly snapping her gum in Jayne's ear. "It's okay. I covered for you, but I was beginin' to wonder if you'd been crushed by a truck."

"Covered for me?" Jayne noticed that the woman had a name tag on her apron that read VANDA.

"Punched in for you. Put your card in the time clock and put my ass on the line. What's the matter with you this morning? You're acting just like Travis does when he's been huffin' glue. Arisa covered for you too. Worked your shift at the cash register and pretended to be you on the electric leash."

"Leash?"

"The damn cell phone." Vanda pointed to her head, and Jayne saw that a telephone headset was buried in her hair between layers two and three. "Arisa does a great imitation of you, by the way. Born actress, that girl. Should be on TV." Vanda gave her gum another decisive crack.

Jayne came to an abrupt halt in front of a shelf displaying mammoth tubes of toothpaste. "Wait a minute. Are you saying two people risked their jobs to keep me from losing mine?"

"Sure, honey." Vanda attempted to propel Jayne into motion again, but Jayne was too stunned to move. She stood there staring at the toothpaste and tried to think of a single person in Hollywood—except her mother—who would risk his or her career to cover for her. There wasn't one. Tears sprang to her eyes. The sweetness of it, the charity, the generosity! When she was no longer living the life of an ordinary woman, she would reward these people.

Vanda tugged at her arm more insistently. "Look, honey, don't start crying. Everything's okay. Just don't get into the habit of being late, because sooner or later that little twerp will catch you."

"What little twerp?" demanded a high-pitched voice.

Vanda's face collapsed and a look of terror came into her eyes. "Good morning, Mr. Bently," she said in a tone Jayne generally associated with defeated Scottish chieftains pleading not to be drawn and quartered.

Jayne turned to locate the source of Vanda's anxiety and found herself face-to-face with what appeared to be an angry child with extremely bad acne. The kid was short and scrawny with a caved-in chest and arms like sticks. His hair, which was pale as mold, was cut short in front and long in back—a style that she thought had mercifully disappeared years ago. Jayne met his eyes, which were small, close together, colorless, and rather cruel-looking; to her surprise, he winked at her.

"That skirt's not regulation," he said. "I could dock you, but you're lookin' too good, baby."

Baby? Jayne thought. *Did this kid just call me baby?* Behind her she heard Vanda laughing shrilly as if this were the greatest comedy line in human history.

He winked again. "Where you been all morning?"

Vanda stopped laughing. "Mary Lynn's been workin' real hard, Mr. Bently," she said in a voice so convincing that Jayne half believed it herself. "Just a little while ago, she almost got a pallet of frozen corn dogs dropped on her. It's a wonder she's not posttraumatic."

The kid wheeled on Jayne. "Don't go reporting that," he snarled. "I got two hundred forty days now with no reported accidents on my shifts; I'm up for a merit raise. I don't want you or anyone else screwing it up, unless you lose so much blood we have to take you out in a body bag and hose down the aisle." He pointed to the far end of the store. "Speaking of hosing, we got a cleanup on aisle twenty-four. Hop, hop, ladies."

Suddenly Jayne understood: Mr. Bently was the supervisor Mary Lynn had warned her about, the one she had described as an ambitious and ruthless slave driver. Jayne studied him with curiosity. So this was her boss. She'd certainly expected someone a lot older. What made him tick? Why was he so rude? How did an arrogant, sawed-off teenager with bad hair become the supervisor of people twice his age? She wondered if this Mr. Bently was related to someone important.

Fifteen minutes later, as they were mopping up the last of a forty-gallon maple syrup spill, she asked Vanda this question, and Vanda confirmed that Mr. Bently (or "Peckerface," as everyone called him behind his back) was the manager's nephew.

When Jayne heard the news, she felt relieved. She was on familiar ground. Despite the fact that two wonderful people had risked their jobs for her, the Food Barn was basically just a low-rent version of Hollywood.

Her confident mood lasted for nearly half an hour, during which time she bought a carton of cigarettes with some of the leftover change from Mary Lynn's piggy bank, and then—realizing that she got an employee's discount—topped the purchase off with a case of Diet Cokes. Taking a fifteen-minute break (which Vanda informed her she was entitled to by law), she stashed the soft drinks in the trunk of Mary Lynn's car, smoked two cigarettes, promised herself she would smoke no more, smoked a third cigarette just to say good-bye to smoking, threw the rest of the carton in a Dumpster as a pledge of her sincerity, and reentered the Food Barn precisely on time.

Five minutes later, she was standing at Register #15 staring at it as if it contained Ebola. Mary Lynn had spent a good fifteen minutes explaining how a cash register worked, and Jayne had faithfully written down every step. Now, as she consulted the little crib sheet in her pocket, the directions made no sense.

She closed her eyes and summoned all her strength. *I can do this,* she told herself. *I have spent my entire life shopping.* When she opened her eyes, a heavyset elderly man in a bright orange polo shirt was staring at her suspiciously.

"Well?" he said.

"Well, what?" Jayne gave him her most winning smile.

"You gonna check me out; or you gonna just stand there?"

Jayne looked down and saw there were fifteen large cans of some kind of herbal supplement on the conveyor belt.

She picked up one of the cans. The label read: FOR MALE IMPOTENCY.

"Looks like you've got a hot date."

The man glared at her. "Mind your own damn business."

Deciding that further conversation would be unwise, Jayne passed the can quickly over the scanner and waited for something to happen. Nothing did.

"Try scanning the bar code," the man snarled.

Jayne gave a nervous laugh, turned the bar code down, and passed it over the red beam. There was a little beep and the cash register window displayed the sum of $29.99.

"That will be twenty-nine ninety-nine," she said brightly.

The man's face softened. He handed her a twenty and a ten, picked up all fifteen cans, stashed them in a cardboard box, and hurried away so fast she didn't even get a chance to give him his change.

Turning back to the register, she carefully keyed in the thirty dollars, pushed ENTER, and was rewarded with immediate results: the cash drawer popped open, and a penny came sliding down the automatic change chute. Lifting the change tray, she placed the twenty under it as she had seen clerks do on the occasions when she herself had used cash instead of a credit card. Then she put the ten in the ten tray, pocketed the penny, and turned to the next customer. This was easy. Everything was automated. She decided that she'd worried unnecessarily. Any idiot could work a cash register.

For the better part of an hour, she scanned purchases, took credit cards, and invited the customers to sign their names on the proper line. She didn't check their IDs because they all looked honest. When someone offered her cash, she counted it, put the twenties (and occasional fifties) under the change tray, and punched the little button that automatically spat out the change. She even remembered to say, "Thank you for shopping at the Food Barn," as if she really meant it. Once or twice, if someone looked really strapped—like an old lady in a hair net or a mother with five children in tow—she only rang up part of the groceries.

After a while, she grew reckless and a little drunk with her own power. In the course of twenty minutes, she gave away a carton of frozen steaks, six boxes of Fudgsicles, and an entire pallet of disposable diapers. She caught herself getting envious glances from the other checkers, and began to regret that she hadn't hired a video crew to tape her unobtrusively.

If only Spielberg could have seen her. This was an Oscar-winning performance. Her impersonation of Mary Lynn was so good it almost brought tears to her eyes. Everything was perfect, right down to the red apron with the little name tag that read MARY LYNN. As always, she drew a bigger crowd than anyone else. As word of her talents spread, the customers refused to let anyone else check out their groceries; the line to her cash register grew so long it doubled back on itself.

Jayne hummed happily, scanned groceries, raked in cash, dispensed presents, and congratulated herself. She was clearly the best checker the Food Barn had ever hired.

The initial clue that something had gone wrong was a loud sirenlike noise that made the hair on the back of her arms stand up on end. Somewhere far above her, a poorly balanced speaker system had been broadcasting musical drivel. As soon as the siren stopped, Wayne Newton broke off in midcroon and gave a cough as if he had been throttled; a high-pitched voice, which could only have belonged to Bently, squeaked: "Security! Front entrance! *Now!*"

As a small explosion of blue-uniformed security guards rushed toward the front doors, a great silence descended on the Barn, and the customers froze like mice about to be taken out by a flock of eagles. The only people who moved were the cashiers, who just went on ringing up purchases as if nothing had happened.

Jayne waved at Vanda, who was standing at the register next to hers trying to wrestle a very large bag of frozen chicken breasts across the scanner. "What's up?"

"They must have caught them one," Vanda yelled as she

dragged the chicken over the laser beam, pushed the bag into the customer's cart, and turned to the next item without breaking stride.

"Who are 'they'?"

"You know: the exit checkers."

"Oh, sure." Jayne tried to sound as if she understood. The truth was, she had no idea what the hell "the exit checkers" were, not to mention what "they'd caught"; but being resourceful, she knew whom to ask. She turned to the customer in front of her. "What's an exit checker?"

The man looked at her as if she were slightly demented, but he was in a good mood because she had just given him forty-five pounds of apples because it was too much trouble to figure out how to punch in the numbers on the little sticky tags.

"The guys at the front doors, the ones that check the receipts."

"Fascinating." Jayne leaned closer so he could get a better view of her cleavage and spent an enjoyable moment watching his face turn bright red. Then she noticed that the woman in the blue polyester shorts and Hawaiian shirt standing behind him looked like a rattlesnake about to strike. She straightened up and became all business. "Why do the exit checkers check the receipts?"

"Because, you little bimbo," the woman snarled, "they're lookin' for people what have things in their damn basket they didn't pay for."

"Shoplifters, that is," the man said apologetically. He pointed to a large billboard hanging from the rafters behind Jayne that read: WE PROSECUTE SHOPLIFTERS TO THE FULL EXTENT OF THE LAW.

"Security!" Bently squeaked again from on high. "Entrance! *Now!*"

"Well, ain't this their lucky day," the woman said. "Two in two minutes. I think that's a record, Norman." She wheeled on Jayne. "I think you better ring up them apples.

We got things to do today besides standing around here listening to the Barn arresting shoplifters."

Under normal circumstances, Jayne would already have ripped the woman's heart out for calling her a "little bimbo," but she watched the woman's lips move without hearing a word she was saying. So receipts were checked against purchases. She hadn't known that. She wondered if by any chance . . .

"Security!" Bently's voice screamed again. "Security! Security!"

Now even the cashiers had stopped working. Vanda locked her register and wandered over to Jayne as if in a dream. "I make that five," she said. Another cashier joined them.

"Security! Security!"

"Seven," said Vanda, and a look of awe spread over her face. "Maybe it's one of them gangs."

"Pretty dumb gang," said the other cashier. "Must have rocks for brains to all get caught like that."

Jayne began to slowly back away from the counter. All through the store, she could see people frantically pulling things out of their carts. Their faces were ominously familiar.

"Where you going?" Vanda asked.

"Out for a smoke."

"Ain't your break time, honey. Besides, you gotta stick around and see them haul the perps to the manager's office."

"Yeah," the second cashier said, popping her gum. "The rent-a-cops always hold 'em there until the real cops come. I don't know how they keep 'em from making a run for it. I don't think Barn security is allowed to shoot shoplifters."

"Seein' the perps is the best part of this job," Vanda said cheerfully. "Last year we had a famous criminal in here. He'd stuck up a bank and was on the way to Tijuana, when he decided to stop off at the Barn and shoplift some chips. Dumbest thing you ever saw. Man had fifteen thousand dollars on him and three strikes. Got twenty-five years for a bag of Ruffles." She put her hand on Jayne's shoulder and brought her to a stop. "You got to see them; it's better than them real-crime shows on TV."

"I have the feeling I've already seen them."

Vanda gave Jayne a blank look.

"Security! Security!" Bently screeched hysterically. The loudspeaker gave a burp of static as if it were about to lose it too.

"Jesus H. Christ," said the woman in the Hawaiian shirt.

Jayne untied her red apron and tossed it to Vanda. "Thanks for everything," she said, and turned and ran for the exit. In retrospect, running in Mary Lynn's heels was a bad decision, but she was having the worst attack of panic she'd experienced since a very large black spider climbed inside her wig during the filming of *Madame de Pompadour.*

She took a fast turn around a stack of videotapes. Up ahead, she could see sunlight pouring in through the big doors that led out of the Barn. For a few seconds, she thought she was home free. Then she saw the shoplifters and security guards coming toward her.

The whole scene was like a dream sequence from a Fellini film. Jayne recognized every face. There was the old man in the Lakers cap who had carted off the steaks; the expectant mother whom she'd presented with free diapers; the lady with the cute kids who had hauled away the complimentary Fudgsicles.

At the sight of nearly half a dozen of her former customers advancing on her, Jayne lost it completely; she tried to make a sharp turn in the other direction, slipped, and fell. When she looked up, Bently was standing over her. Behind him stood Vanda, Arisa, and a crowd of customers and cashiers with awestruck expressions on their faces.

"You been giving merchandise away, haven't you!" Bently screamed.

Jayne stood up, straightened her skirt, and fluffed her hair. She wondered if there was still some way she could talk herself out of this situation. Instinctively, she looked around for cue cards.

Bently drew back his thin lips in a snarl. "What the hell were you thinking?"

Jayne wished she had a great line to deliver, but she needed a good screenwriter to feed one to her, and there were none in sight. "I got confused."

"Confused? You got *confused!*" Bently went red, then white, then red again. He opened his mouth and waved his arms as if he were directing traffic. "You always said you was a professor, but that's a lie: you're dumber than a bag of rocks, and now you've gone and wrecked my chances for advancement to a high-paying managerial position."

He stuck his face close to hers. "I'm not only gonna fire you for this. I'm gonna have you arrested. You just committed larceny and maybe grand theft when we add up all them Fudgsicles."

"I don't think so," said a familiar voice.

Jayne turned and saw that Vanda had moved out of the crowd and was now standing beside her.

"You butt out of this!" Bently snarled. "Or I'll have your job too."

Vanda lowered her head and narrowed her eyes, and her hair seemed to puff up to twice its normal size. "I'm not butting out. You can fire Mary Lynn, Mr. Bently, but you aren't gonna have her arrested while I'm alive and draw breath. Do the words 'sexual hairassment' mean anything to you? 'Cause thems words you're gonna be hearing a lot from the lawyer I'm gonna hire."

"Damn straight," Arisa said, moving up on Mary Lynn's left. "Everybody knows you been creatin' a climate of fear around the Barn by coppin' feels off all the female employees' butts, and you can't legally do that. I know; I saw a two-hour TV special on 'Inappropriate Sex in the Workplace.'"

"And then there's that cute little sixteen-year-old you was bangin' after hours in the stockroom," one of the male clerks said, joining the lineup. "I know Jeseree got her job with a fake ID, and we all thought she was legal, but the law's the law."

"Don't forget the peat moss he's been letting that worthless landscaping brother-in-law of his have on the employee discount," another voice said.

"All of you, shut up!" Bently screamed. He wheeled on Jayne. "You're fired. Now get the hell out of here!"

"Just a moment," Jayne said. "I still have a line to deliver." She pulled out her compact and freshened up her lipstick. Then she turned to the crowd, waved, smiled, and blew them kisses. "Thanks," she yelled, "for shopping at the Food Barn!"

Vanda walked her to the parking lot. When they got there, Jayne thanked her again, then asked her for a favor. It wasn't easy to ask, because Vanda was sobbing at the thought of never seeing Mary Lynn again, and somehow that made Jayne feel like sobbing too.

"Could you give me a boost?" she said as she and Vanda drew near the big orange Food Barn Dumpster.

"Sure." Vanda folded her hands into a step and Jayne hopped up on them, flung the upper half of her body over the rim of the Dumpster, and retrieved her carton of cigarettes. Once again, she wished Spielberg had been there to see her. If Dumpster diving wasn't real life, what was?

Ten

Mary Lynn was getting a massage when the cell phone rang. Without opening her eyes, she stretched out one exquisitely relaxed arm and retrieved the chiming receiver from beneath a pile of fluffy white towels. Sick of the theme song from *The Loves of Leonardo*, she had reprogrammed it to play "Take Me Out to the Ball Game."

"Bad news," said a familiar voice. "I got us fired from the Barn."

Mary Lynn sat up so fast she knocked over a bottle of massage oil. The delicious odor of ylang-ylang and cedarwood spiraled up from the carpet, but she didn't notice. Her body had gone from rubber to barbwire. Little shards of panic caught in the back of her throat. Without her job at the Barn, she'd never make it to the end of the month. She wouldn't be able to pay her rent or buy gas for her car. She'd have to move to a residence hotel with vomit-green walls and a view of the freeway. She saw herself sitting in the lobby on a ratty sofa watching a black-and-white TV. Would the old winos in undershirts let her watch *Larry King Live*, or would she spend the rest of her life as an involuntary fan of World Wide Wrestling?

Just as she was coming to the part where she was thrown out of the hotel and became a bag lady, she suddenly remembered that Jayne was paying her so much she didn't need to work two jobs. A warm sensation flooded her body.

Her spine relaxed; her shoulders went slack; she could have cried with relief.

"I'm sorry," Jayne was saying. "I thought it was going to be so easy, but things kept happening. I know I could do the whole thing perfectly if I had another chance; I feel that in some ways I was born to check out groceries. But the problem with real life is that there are no retakes."

"It's okay. It's no big deal." Mary Lynn swung her legs over the edge of the massage table and admired the sheen of oil on her kneecaps. Everything in the room smelled delightfully of ylang-ylang. It was a golden afternoon, there was a box of Godiva chocolates within reach, and she would never have to see Peter Bently's ratty little face again.

"I feel like such a failure. I could hardly face the cats. What kind of person can't work a cash register?"

"It's not as easy as it looks."

"You're being very nice about this."

Mary Lynn stared at the receiver. "Are you sure you're okay? You don't sound like yourself."

"I'm having revelations. I'm learning about ordinary people. I always thought of them as extras. I saw myself in the starring role; everyone else had bit parts. But it's a lot more complicated than that. Vanda may have bad hair, but she's nearly a saint. Are you alone?"

"No. Moonflower's here."

"You better tell her she can go. We've got some business to take care of."

Mary Lynn dismissed the masseuse, who glided out the door as if she were on wheels. Mary Lynn strongly suspected Moonflower's real name was something normal, like "Sarah." But when you had magic hands, you could call yourself anything you pleased.

"Is Moon gone?"

"Yes."

Jayne gave a deep sigh. "That woman's a genius. An hour with Moon is better than a week at my ranch in Belize. Did she do your feet yet?"

"Yes."

"Including your toes?"

"Particularly my toes."

"Did she use that little twisting motion that sends exquisite shudders up your leg?"

"Probably. I've never had a professional massage before, so I'm not sure about the details."

Jayne sighed again. "You have no idea how much I need a massage right now. It's been three entire days since I let Moon work me over. I wish I was stretched out on that table right now. I miss my flower garden, my gin, my little white room."

"It's not really a little room, Jayne. It's twenty by twenty and has a full view of the Pacific."

"Your life is so hard."

"You have my sympathies."

"Standing at your cash register all morning was ghastly. I don't see how you've managed to survive. My feet hurt so much I could cry. Whatever possessed you to buy heels two sizes too small? No, don't answer that. I understand perfectly. That's why I have Moon." She paused, and Mary Lynn heard the distinct sound of smoke being inhaled. "Say, I don't suppose living your life could include having Moon come over here and work the knots out of my shoulders?"

"I'm afraid not. The only massage I've ever had besides this one was with an electric toothbrush I bought on sale at the Barn. Darn thing broke after only one use, and you can't take back personal-hygiene products."

"How'd it break? I mean, as an ex–Barn checkout clerk, I have a personal interest in Barn products."

"Wendell."

"Wendell?"

"He insisted on using it as a sex toy. Believe me, you don't want to know the details."

There was a brief silence on the other end of the line as Jayne digested this information. "Okay," she said briskly. "Let's just move on. I forgot your credit cards were completely maxed out and tried to buy a tank of gas with your

Visa. A big tattooed guy with gold teeth threatened to put me under citizen's arrest when it wouldn't go through. Fortunately, I was able to sweet-talk him out of it by claiming I loved men who have 666 inscribed on their biceps, but I don't want to get in the habit of being dependent on the kindness of Hell's Angels. Do you happen to know where my purse is?"

"Yes."

"I don't mean to sound bitter here, but if you could ooze off my massage table, wrap yourself in one of my lovely thick towels, amble over to it, find my wallet, pull out my credit cards, and read me the numbers, I'd be grateful."

Slightly taken aback by the notion of a grateful Jayne, Mary Lynn slid off the massage table, padded over to the other side of the room, and did as Jayne requested.

"Thanks," Jayne said between puffs. "Of course, this will only work when I order things by phone. What I really need is cash. I could get my accountant to send a courier over with a couple of thousand, but I don't want to blow my cover; so instead, I'm going to send my special assistant by to pick up my credit cards and my ATM card so I can get a cash advance. You need to remember that he'll have no idea you're not me. Believe me, he won't notice unless you slip up. He just does what I tell him to do and doesn't ask questions."

"Are you absolutely sure you can trust him? Clarice is offering big money to anyone who will tell her where you're hiding."

"I've been in the movie business too long to trust anyone, particularly Gino." Another puff. "Actually, he never gives me trouble because I've got something on him."

"Like what?"

"I'd tell you, but then I'd have to kill you." Jayne laughed wildly. Mary Lynn wondered if experiencing real life was causing her to become a bit unhinged. "Seriously, you don't want to know. Of course, I'd never actually *use* the information. I'm too softhearted. But Gino doesn't know that. So every once in a while, I threaten him a teensy bit. Works wonders."

Mary Lynn bet it did. "How will I recognize him?"

"Think Andy Garcia in *Godfather Three*. Gino's a little shorter than Garcia, more square-chinned, and has a broken nose. He wanted to be an actor, but looking so much like Garcia kept him from getting parts, and then the nose happened and he had to go into another line of work. Anyway, the bottom line is, I've paged him, but I'm not sure when he'll show up. Maybe today. Maybe tomorrow. You never know when he's out of the country for a few days."

"Anything else?"

"No. That should do it."

Mary Lynn studied the phone for a moment, wondering if she was about to get herself arrested as an accessory to something. She decided if she got busted, she could probably hire a lawyer to get off on the grounds of mistaken identity.

"Okay," she said, not without misgivings. Since there seemed to be nothing more to discuss, she was preparing to say good-bye, when she glanced down and caught sight of her—or rather Jayne's—watch lying where she'd tossed it at the start of the massage. The watch was a delicate gold circle with rosettes of tiny diamonds clustered around the dial, but the diamonds weren't what attracted her attention. "Hey!" she cried. "Do you realize it's after five o'clock! You're supposed to be on your way to the college right now to teach my evening class."

"Don't worry. We called in sick."

"What do you mean *we* called in sick? Part-time instructors don't get sick days."

"Part-time instructors with brain tumors do."

"You told the college I had a brain tumor!"

"Relax. I was very convincing. I was all Bette Davis and *Dark Victory*. I even told your secretary that I had an appointment with a Dr. Frederick Steele—that was the name of the character who became Davis's lover after he diagnosed her. I recited some of Davis's best lines. I have an incredible memory."

"Jayne! You can't do this!"

"Is there a problem?"

"There sure is. I don't give a rat's ass about working at the Barn, but I love teaching. I've been thinking about getting a Ph.D. so I can land a job at a real university. To do that, I'm going to need a letter of recommendation from Professor Nelson C. Whitney, Chair of the Coast Side Community College English Department, the very same Nelson C. Whitney—let me emphasize this—who is going to fire me when he finds out that I don't have a brain tumor." Mary Lynn reached into the gold Godiva box and crammed a handful of chocolates into her mouth.

"Don't you know anything about life besides what you see in the movies?" She swallowed the chocolate and helped herself to another handful with the desperation of a woman downing straight martinis. "This is a complete disaster. I should have known you weren't capable of impersonating a professor, but the hundred thousand fogged my judgment. I've been in denial, and now I'm totally screwed. No one's going to believe these stories of yours."

"Calm down, take a few deep breaths. If you want some tranquilizers—"

"I don't want tranquilizers! I want an academic career with dental benefits, a lighter course load, and sabbaticals every seven years!"

"You'll get all that and more. Everything is under control. Trust me: you're wrong about my stories. Audiences always adore tragedies. That's why my movies make so much money. Besides, I gave an absolutely brilliant performance. Your department secretary not only hung on my every word, she actually wept. I had no idea you were such a popular instructor."

Mary Lynn moaned. "Jayne, listen; you can't do this. We're going to get caught. . . ."

"No, we won't. I'll just call them back tomorrow and say the tumor tests came back negative. So do you want to hear some good news?"

"I'm not sure I'm up to any more news right now, good or bad."

"Now don't go all negative on me. Guess what?" Jayne paused dramatically.

"Okay, I surrender. What?"

"Your landlord came by this afternoon and demanded the rent. He pointed out that it was several weeks overdue, and he wasn't very pleasant about it either. So guess what I did."

"You paid him in diamonds."

"No. But you're close. I bought your building."

"Jesus." Mary Lynn felt like pounding her head against something.

"No, his name was Bob. Anyway, he was so rude that I slammed the door in his face and called Harry, my wonderful real estate agent—I own a lot of property in this town, by the way—and I said, 'Harry, I want you to buy me a building right now.' Then I gave him your address. A couple of seconds later, I hear your landlord's pager go off; then I hear him on his cell phone; then I hear him having a near cardiac arrest when he finds out what I'm offering for this dump you live in. No offense."

Mary Lynn tried to say something, but she couldn't make her lips form words.

"So pretty soon I hear him scurrying off to Harry's office to sign the papers. Of course, escrow won't close for a while, but I've made it a condition of sale that he not set foot on the property again. So no more landlord, unless you count me; and I'm not evicting you, or that nice man downstairs with the two little girls, or anyone else in this building."

Mary Lynn took a deep breath, got a better grip on the phone, and tried on the feeling of not having a landlord. It felt great. She decided she'd been too hasty. Jayne meant well. It was just that her approach to life had all the subtlety of a buffalo stampede. "Jayne, thanks. You're an angel."

"Make that an avenging angel. Nobody calls me a 'dirty little deadbeat' and gets away with it. Your landlord's lucky

I didn't have my lawyers hand him his head on a platter. After all, the last part I played *was* Salome."

"I'm grateful. I really am, but . . ."

"But what?"

"I have to level with you. You're not leading an ordinary life here. Ordinary people don't just *buy* buildings. They have budgets. If you really want to live like me, you're going to have to stop throwing money at problems to make them go away."

There was a long silence on the other end of the line.

"Jayne, are you still there?"

"How much?"

"Are you asking me how much you get to spend per month to live like a part-time college instructor who moonlights as a cashier?"

"Yes."

"You aren't going to like it."

"I'm bracing myself."

"I take home about fourteen hundred dollars after taxes. After I pay my rent and my bills and send Ron his spousal support, I have about eight hundred left for food, clothes, and entertainment."

"You have to be joking. I spend more than that a month on perfume."

"Eight hundred. Not a penny more."

"I'm thinking Peace Corps here. I'm thinking houses constructed of tin cans and cardboard, sandals made out of tires, and a family of six poor but noble people huddled around a fire sharing one small bowl of rice."

"Cut! You're running a film again. It's not like that."

Jayne wasn't listening. "Yes," she said. Her voice trembled slightly. "I can do it. For the sake of my art, I can deprive myself of those little luxuries that make life bearable. I can live on scraps. I can chip my nail polish and never look back. I can buy ghastly pink-and-orange skirts at Target. On the other hand"—her voice suddenly became

brisk and businesslike—"make sure I get those credit cards.
I might have a hair emergency or something."

"Sure." Mary Lynn gave up. This was clearly a lost cause.

"I want to thank you for being so honest with me. No one
except my mother ever tells me the truth. I have the feeling
that you and I are becoming—how shall I put it? A team.
Frankly, I've never been a team player. In Hollywood it's always competition, competition, competition. But this feels
different. You're helping me advance my career, and I'm res-
cuing you from . . . I'm not sure how to describe your
situation."

"Try hideous poverty."

"Exactly." Jayne grew thoughtful. "Actually, your life—
although unspeakably poor—isn't all that hideous. To tell
the truth, I'm rather enjoying being you."

Mary Lynn was so touched that she didn't bother repeating the obvious: that when you could buy your building
instead of paying your rent, you weren't living an ordinary
life in any sense of the word.

After she and Jayne finished talking, Mary Lynn called
Moonflower back and enjoyed the rest of her massage. Then
she showered, climbed into one of Jayne's bikinis, and took
a leisurely swim in the Elvis pool. When she felt like she'd
had enough exercise for one day, she dried her hair, put on
a pair of white silk lounging pajamas, located a book, and
settled down to read. The book—one of the few Jayne appeared to own—turned out to be a historical romance about
the loves of Cleopatra. Jayne must have been considering
doing a film based on it, because inside the front cover, she
had scrawled, "Elizabeth Taylor, eat your heart out."

Although the plot was a little silly, the novel was well written, and Mary Lynn soon found herself lost in ancient Egypt
among handsome young slaves with well-oiled bodies and
hunky priests of Isis who stripped off their tunics and declared
undying love at the slightest nod of the royal head.

It was a lovely, quiet afternoon, filled only with the hum
of distant lawn mowers and the twittering of birds. At four

o'clock, Lois appeared with jasmine tea and low-fat muffins, which Mary Lynn had ordered after discovering Jayne's standard teatime snack was gin and tonic.

By the time she crawled into bed some seven hours later, she was beginning to believe that she and Jayne might actually be able to carry off the switch without being discovered. Plumping the pillows, she stretched out on the silk sheets, wiggled into a comfortable position, and put herself to sleep by counting Cleopatra's lovers.

"Jayne," a voice said.

Mary Lynn suddenly snapped wide awake.

"Jayne?" the voice repeated.

Mary Lynn froze. It was late. She was in Jayne's bed, and a stranger was staggering around the room, muttering and knocking into things.

"Who the hell are you?" she hissed.

The stranger stumbled in her direction and encountered a patch of moonlight. He was stark naked, male, and definitely in a mood to party. Every slasher movie Mary Lynn had ever seen flashed through her mind. She screamed, and then, for good measure, she screamed again. Evidently taking her cries for encouragement, the man lurched forward and fell on her, muttering endearments.

"Help! Go away! Get off me!" she cried, beating at him with her fists. And then she did what her mother had always told her to do in such circumstances: kneed him in the balls. The second her knee connected with his scrotum, he gave a screech of agony and flopped to one side, writhing. Mary Lynn sat up, snapped on the light, and gave a screech of her own. There, lying not more than six inches from her, was Edward Surrey, the most famous British actor since Richard Burton. Surrey was smarter than Kenneth Branagh, cuter than Hugh Grant, and had more sex-crazed fans than Brad Pitt.

"Oops," she said.

Surrey stared at her like a wounded bull elephant. His eyes

were bloodshot and blank, and his famous jaw was slack with pain or maybe bourbon. He made a clumsy gesture of apology and smiled that brave smile that made women want to throw themselves into his arms like lemmings.

"Jayne, darling," he mumbled, "so veddy sorry."

Suddenly Mary Lynn understood: Surrey thought she was Jayne. Which meant Jayne must be sleeping with Surrey. That explained how he had gotten into the house without setting off the alarms.

She got out of bed, put on some clothes, went back, and tugged him into an upright position. God, she thought as she propped him up against the headboard, even drunk he looked beautiful. She stood there admiring his green eyes, strong mouth, high cheekbones, perfect nose. The guy had shoulders like a Greek god and a butt to die for. All she had to do was roll him over on his back like a turtle, and she could have her way with him. The best part of it was, there'd be no hell to pay the next day because Surrey would think he'd slept with Jayne.

For a moment, she was sorely tempted. Then she got a grip on herself. He was drunk—and she'd never liked making it with drunks no matter how handsome they were. Also, she'd never had sex with a stranger, and this didn't seem like a good time to start. "Ed," she said, "you have to leave."

He looked at her adoringly. "Darling," he mumbled.

"Now, Ed. I mean it. I'm not in the mood tonight, and I want you out of here."

"But, darling . . ."

"Enough with the 'darling' bit." She grabbed him by the arms and pulled him toward the edge of the bed and onto his feet. "Put on your clothes."

"Darling," he said, and toppled over on top of her. Fortunately, the carpet was soft. Mary Lynn crawled out from under him, checked herself for bruises, and found none. On the floor, Edward Surrey lay out cold, naked, and snoring like a drunken walrus.

Okay, she thought. *There's only one way to go about this.*

I'll have to dress him. She located his pants and slipped them over his legs with a twinge of regret. Heaving him into a sitting position, she wrestled him into his shirt, buttoned it, and stuck his loafers on his feet. At that point, she would have preferred if Surrey had stood and walked out of the room, but he was clearly out for the night. Since he outweighed her, she only had one choice.

Rolling his limp body onto a small carpet, she opened the sliding doors to Jayne's bedroom and dragged him out onto the deck. From there she took him down the steps, one thump at a time, being careful to keep his head elevated so he wouldn't get a concussion. When she finally got him down to ground level, she picked up one edge of the carpet and dumped him onto the grass. The lawn slanted a bit and he began to roll, picking up momentum. Giving him a gentle kick every now and then, she kept him going until he took off at a good clip, tumbled down the hill on his own, and landed spread-eagle on his back in one of Jayne's flower beds, where—with a little luck—the security guards would find him in the morning and escort him off the premises. Jayne must have ordered the guards to let him come and go as he pleased. Orders she would immediately cancel.

Meanwhile. Ah, meanwhile.

She stood over him for a moment, thinking what an incredible body he had. She wondered if, when he was sober, he had a personality to match. Something told her he didn't. Still, it seemed like such a waste.

"I don't imagine I'm ever going to get another chance to sleep with anyone as famous and handsome as you," she whispered. Impulsively she bent down and kissed him on his bourbon-soaked lips.

" 'Good night, sweet prince.' " That was her favorite line from *Hamlet*. She remembered Surrey in the screen version. He'd been absolutely dazzling. "If you ever want to sleep with Mary Lynn McLellan instead of Jayne Cooper, give me a call and I'll be there faster than a pizza delivery guy."

With that, she left him snoring among the iris and went back to lock the bedroom doors.

"Oh, my God," Jayne said groggily when Mary Lynn woke her out of a sound sleep to tell her the news. "Eddie was supposed to be in London. Listen, I'm really sorry he ended up in bed with you. What did you do with him?"

Mary Lynn thought of Edward Surrey, drunk and snoring his beautiful head off in the iris bed. "I didn't have any use for him," she said, "so I composted him."

After she and Jayne had spent a few moments sharing their mutual admiration of Edward Surrey's buns, Mary Lynn hung up and went back to sleep. Her plan was not to open her eyes until well past lunchtime, but almost as soon as she closed them, the phone rang again.

"It's nine-one-one time again," said Clarice. *"Auugha, auugha.* This is not a test, honey. This is real. I am sitting here looking at my e-mail."

"At this hour?"

"I'm an early riser, and you're Carleton Winters's fair-haired girl."

"Carleton Winters? The head of Global?"

"The man adores you. He's written what practically amounts to a love letter. Thanks to that little act you put on for the benefit of Animals First, you're walking on water at Global. That's the good news."

"And the bad news?"

"Carleton's invited you to his place in Bel Air tonight for a kiss-and-make-up party."

"Clarice, this is crazy. You know I can't go."

"I'm glad to hear you say that, because it must mean you're ready to tell me where my daughter is." Clarice paused for a reply, but Mary Lynn said nothing. She just sat there staring stubbornly at the alarm clock. It was four forty-five in the morning, she was tired and cranky, and if the entire Spanish Inquisition had shown up to roast her over hot coals, she wouldn't have given Jayne's phone number to Clarice.

"Silence?" Clarice said. "Is that silence I hear? Well, then, I guess you have yourself another problem, darlin'. If you're not ready to tell me where Jayne is, then not going to Carleton's little soiree isn't an option. When the head of Global summons actors into his royal presence, everybody scrambles, even Jayne. And that's not all. It gets worse. Carleton 'invites'—which translated means *orders*—you to show up with your current flame. It seems he's going to include some of those dreary people who make a living leaking celebrity gossip to the press. He wants you and your beau photographed together. I've got to hand it to the man: he never passes up a chance to stir up interest in one of his stars, particularly when she's about to start doing the prerelease publicity on a big film."

Mary Lynn seized a blanket and pulled it around her shoulders. "You can't want me to do this, Clarice. Think of the trouble it will make for Jayne. I won't know who anyone is. I won't know what to say. And if Edward Surrey remembers anything after he sobers up, he sure won't want to take me to a party."

"Edward Surrey? What's Eddie Surrey got to do with this?"

"He's Jayne's boyfriend, right?"

"Wrong. According to the tabloids, Jayne's current lover is an Italian count. She's supposed to be the reason the count and his wife aren't living in marital bliss. The count is actually in the U.S. at the moment, and Carleton was hoping to persuade him to show up with Jayne. That would have been perfect because he and Jayne hardly know each other, so he wouldn't have realized you weren't who you were pretending to be. But, of course, the studio couldn't get him. So that leaves us with the task of finding you a suitable boyfriend between now and eight-thirty this evening."

Clarice grew thoughtful. "Did you say Jayne was sleeping with Surrey? I had no idea. But then a mother is always the last to know. I swear, sometimes I think the girl should put out a program so I can keep track of the players."

"Clarice, it doesn't matter who I show up with. It won't take five minutes for Mr. Winters to figure out I'm not Jayne."

"Five minutes is optimistic. I'd put it at under two. And by the way, you always call the son of a bitch 'Carl' and kiss him on both cheeks whenever you meet him. That's your perk as a big star. If your films ever stop doing major box, then it will be back to 'Mr. Winters' so fast you'll get rope burn."

"This is a nightmare."

"Quiet. I'm thinking." There was a long pause during which Mary Lynn tried to come up with some kind of plan that didn't involve scaling the electrified fence and hitch-hiking to Bakersfield.

"Are you allergic to anything?"

"Yes, walnuts."

"What happens when you eat them? You don't go into shock and stop breathing, do you?" Clarice sounded mildly hopeful.

"No, my throat swells up, I lose my voice, and I break out in hives."

"Perfect!"

"The way you said that makes me nervous." Mary Lynn stared at the phone suspiciously. "Exactly what do you have in mind?"

Eleven

At ten A.M. Arnie Levine was sitting in the Global Films commissary, drinking black coffee and trying to make sense out of the screenplay he'd been flown out from New York to rewrite. The film—which had the working title *Star Whale*—was going into production in less than three weeks. As far as Arnie could see, it was going to be a disaster. It was a science fiction adaptation of Melville's *Moby Dick*. On the way to the screen, Melville's whale had become an alien spaceship. The ocean, of course, was space. All that worked pretty well, but the plot and dialogue sucked big time.

Arnie took a sip of coffee, which was laced with some kind of horrible nutty flavor only found west of New Jersey, and asked himself a few questions. What the hell had possessed the original scriptwriters to make Ishmael female? That one was easy. Melville hadn't written for the masses, and as far as Arnie knew, Global had never put out a film without sex scenes. So Ishmael, now known as a hot little number named Ilanda, was having an affair with handsome, thirtyish Starship Captain Ahab. Okay, okay, maybe he could buy that.

But the dialogue was unbelievably bad. Because Global was afraid of offending the disabled, the producers had nixed Ahab's missing leg. Somewhere in the process of developing the script, some writer, who had probably done too much ecstasy the night before, had had the bright idea of making up for this by having him speak like a cheery combination of Long John Silver and Popeye.

As Arnie read on, a feeling of dread spread over him. This script was beyond terrible. He'd never be able to fix it in time. What was he doing here, anyway? He was a serious playwright with four off-Broadway productions to his name, one of which had been a modest success. The successful play had been a one-man show about the life of Herman Melville, full of Melville's angst, depression, and sexual ambivalence. In the two weeks he had spent in California, Arnie had yet to meet anyone at Global who had actually seen a performance of his play or had even read the script. All they knew was that the title was *Melville*, which presumably made Arnie an expert on zero-gravity sex and interstellar whaling.

He took another sip of coffee and told himself that even though he was at Global under false pretenses, it wasn't his fault. He'd had a hard eight months since he walked into his rent-controlled apartment and found Teresa in bed with a second-rate actor who had a day job delivering singing telegrams. In the subsequent split-up, Teresa had gotten the apartment, the cat, and the opportunity to listen to her lover sing an off-key rendition of "Happy Birthday" anytime she wanted. Arnie had gotten a chance to find himself a new apartment in a city that had some of the highest rents in the known universe. Under the circumstances, the phone call from his agent offering him this gig in California had been a godsend.

Giving up on the script, he stared through the glass partition that separated the commissary from the executive dining room, but there was something mildly depressing about watching studio execs in expensive suits sitting at linen-covered tables eating Caesar salads. He turned his attention to the posters of famous Global films and then to the front window and the pathologically green lawn that spread out in front of the commissary like an ad for AstroTurf. A row of bushes along the sidewalk was flaunting big pink tropical-looking flowers the size of saucers; in the distance, he could see palm trees, just like in Florida.

Just as he was wondering if the sun ever stopped shining in L.A., he noticed a middle-aged woman making her way across the room. She didn't look like the other people in the commissary, which was strictly an eating place for the small fry. Arnie, who had a good eye for character, could tell from the brisk way she walked that she was used to being obeyed. He watched her approach with curiosity. She was dressed in a fashionable white linen suit accented with heavy gold jewelry, pale cream-colored stockings, and the highest heels he'd seen since he'd left Manhattan. Her hair was auburn, stylishly short, highlighted with blond overtones; and her face had the impeccable tone and smoothness that was either the result of incredible genes or fabulously expensive plastic surgery.

She must be an actress, Arnie thought.

To his surprise, the woman kept on coming in his direction. When she reached his table, she pulled out a chair and sat down.

"Hello," she said in a soft southern accent, "I'm Clarice Korngold."

Arnie frantically searched his memory for an actress by that name and came up blank, but he had been in the theater business too long and known too many actresses to let on that he didn't recognize her. He arranged his face in an expression of surprised delight. "Clarice Korngold!"

"You're good. Very good. But there's no use pretending that you recognize me. I haven't been in a film for over thirty years." She leaned forward and stared at him intently. "You're new in town, aren't you?"

"Yes." Arnie was totally nonplussed by the attention she was giving him. He wondered if she was trying to pick him up. Back in New York, the only actresses who had ever been attracted to him were the young, ambitious ones who thought they might be able to snag a part in one of his plays if they got him into bed. But out here, the rules were differ-

ent. A guy who wrote film scripts had less clout than the
gaffers and electricians. And a guy who had only been hired
to do rewrites was so low in the pecking order that even the
cute would-be starlets, who would sleep with anyone, only
noticed him if they bumped into him on their way to get
coffee for the more important guys.

Clarice Korngold leaned closer, and he smelled expensive perfume. He was seized with an almost overwhelming
urge to sneeze. "New York, right?" she said.

He nodded, furiously trying to repress the explosion that
was building up inside his nose. She was definitely trying
to pick him up. By some chance, he had encountered the
one actress—make that the one *former* actress—in L.A.
who wanted a short, out-of-shape, goateed scriptwriter for
a boy toy. The urge to sneeze vanished, leaving him slightly
light-headed. "How did you know I was from New York?"

"Simple." Clarice settled back in the chair and gave him
a dazzling smile. "You're wearing black, honey. Black shirt,
black pants, black shoes, black socks." She laughed a soft,
rippling laugh that had a cutting edge to it. "For all I know,
you're wearing black underwear. Of course, you didn't have
to be from New York. Black's been all the rage out here for
years, but you're also as pale as the underbelly of a lizard."
She made a sweeping gesture at the window. "No one lives
under this sun and stays that color for more than a few
weeks. What's your name?" He told her. "Do you know
many people in this town?"

"No."

"I take it you're working for Global?" He nodded. "That's
a filmscript in front of you, so I assume you're a writer,
right?"

He confirmed her guess and told her about being hired to
rewrite *Star Whale*. As he spoke, he began to panic. Her
next question would undoubtedly contain a proposition of
some kind: a request that he take her to dinner, or perhaps
a straightforward invitation to come back to her mansion in
Beverly Hills and rub her from head to foot with edible oil.

He couldn't do it. He'd never in his life been able to take sex casually. As a result, he knew almost all there was to know about the fury of women scorned. Whoever Clarice Korngold was, she didn't look like the kind of female who would ever forgive a man who turned her down. There was no knowing whom she knew in the industry or whom she'd been sleeping with before she decided to troll the Global commissary. One word from her, and he'd probably be out of a job. *Star Whale* might be dreck, but he needed the money if he wasn't going to end up living at the Y.

She leaned even closer, and Arnie felt his ordinary level of anxiety reach new heights.

"How would you like to meet the head of Global?"

He blinked, unable to take in what she had just said. "Head of Global?" he echoed idiotically.

"Carleton Winters. At a party, at his house, tonight."

"What do I have to do?" He could have slammed himself in the head with the flat of his hand for saying that. Was he crazy? He'd just given her an opening.

"Escort my daughter."

"Miss Korngold?" Once again, the name rang no bells.

"That's the name on her birth certificate." Clarice sat back and looked at him as if she'd just bought him by the pound and were trying to decide how to carve him up. "But you probably know her by her screen name: Jayne Cooper."

Arnie suddenly understood. This was a practical joke. Someone had bet this woman that if she came over and offered the poor schlemiel who'd been hired to rewrite *Star Whale* a date with one of the most famous stars in Hollywood, he'd snap at it. Well, she should think again. He hadn't spent a lifetime riding the subways without learning how to tell a fake watch from a Rolex.

"Sorry. I can't do it. I've already got a hot date with Cameron Diaz." He could hear the anger in his voice and he hoped she heard it too. "Cameron and I are planning to go back to her place and lick milk chocolate off each other."

"This is no joke," she hissed in a steely whisper. "This is

the chance of a lifetime; you've just won the lottery. If you're too stupid to pick up the prize money, then I guess I'll just have to find my little girl a beau with more brains."

Sometime around four that afternoon, Mary Lynn sat at the dining-room table sipping a gin and tonic and studying a pile of photographs of people she might meet at Carleton Winter's party: producers, directors, studio execs, and even a chubby man in a pink turban who, Clarice had assured her, gave astrological readings to half of Global. There were no photos of stars, because Winters loathed actors—although no doubt he'd fake it nicely tonight when she made her entrance. She was just studying a candid shot of James Cameron in a baseball cap when Clarice glided into the room. She was carrying a white cardboard box tied up with a silver ribbon.

Clarice placed the box in front of Mary Lynn and gave it a little shove in her direction. "A present," she said.

Mary Lynn inspected the box suspiciously. The lid bore a small sticker that read: ATHENOS BAKERY.

"What's in it? A bomb?"

"Don't get melodramatic," Clarice snapped. "Just open it."

Mary Lynn untied the ribbon and lifted the lid. Inside were a dozen pieces of freshly baked baklava swimming in a pool of honey. They smelled wonderful. When you had ordered someone to lose weight, did you give her baklava? Mary Lynn didn't think so. She closed the box and shoved it back toward Clarice.

"Forget it. I'm not eating these."

"Don't be ridiculous. They're absolutely delicious. Alexandros made them just for you."

"I bet he did. They're filled with walnuts, aren't they?"

Clarice picked an invisible speck of lint off the sleeve of her linen jacket and looked out the window as if admiring the iris. "I cannot tell a lie," she said. "Lord knows I'd like to, but I can't."

She turned toward Mary Lynn and her eyes went hard. "Yes, they are filled with walnuts. And yes—don't interrupt me here—you *are* going to eat them. It's not going to be enough for you to pretend to have lost your voice; you actually need to lose it. Otherwise, Carleton will figure out you aren't Jayne, cut you up in small pieces, and strew you from here to Catalina. Carleton is merciless. He never forgives an attempt to deceive him, and he keeps an entire law firm on retainer."

She reached into the box and extracted a square of baklava. "Open wide."

"Forget it. My face will swell up. I'll break out in hives and itch."

"So much the better. A puffy face will be a plus. Carleton has a sentimental streak. He'll be touched by the notion that Jayne came to his party when she wasn't feeling well; and if he notices that you don't look exactly like her, he'll chalk it up to the hives. Of course, he'll be annoyed that his photo opportunity has been ruined; but, all in all, I think you'll gain Jayne points." She paused. "Or we can stop all this foolishness, and you can tell me where Jayne is. There's still time for her to get ready if we call in Vlad for an emergency comb out."

"Sit down!" Mary Lynn said in the tone of voice she sometimes used to deal with unruly students. Shocked, Clarice sat.

Mary Lynn got up, strode over to the sideboard, seized a glass, carried it back to the table, made another gin and tonic, and placed it in front of Clarice. "You and I have to talk."

"Don't you dare use that tone with me."

"Clarice, I'm a grown woman with a master's degree, cellulite, and an ex-husband who's spending his spousal support on a bimbo with abdominal muscles like Arnold Schwarzenegger's. But more to the point, I'm not, and never have been, your daughter. You may be able to pull Jayne's strings, but you have no control over me."

"I don't treat Jayne like a puppet. I love her. . . ."

"I'm not saying you don't love her. That's not what we're talking about. I'm saying: I may look like her, I may talk like her, but I'm not her. So back off."

They glared at each other. Clarice picked up her gin and tonic and took a long, slow sip. "Are you quite finished?" She was exquisitely polite, which is to say bordering on homicidal.

"No. We have to get something else straight: I am not eating walnuts in any form."

"Fine. Then suppose you tell me just exactly how you plan to attend Carleton's party."

"Simple. I *pretend* to have lost my voice, and you make me up to look like I have hives. You're an expert with makeup. I can tell." Mary Lynn pointed to the large mirror over the sideboard. "Look at yourself. You're what? Fifty? And you look a good ten, maybe fifteen, years younger."

Clarice was blindsided by the compliment. In all the years she had argued with Jayne, Jayne had never used this tactic. Her face softened. She put down her glass and looked at Mary Lynn in a way that could only be described as suspicious but hopeful. "Do you really think I could pass for thirty-five?"

"Yes." Mary Lynn decided there was no harm in stretching the truth a little.

"That's one of the nicest things anyone has said to me in years."

"It's time we stopped fighting, Clarice. You need me; I need you. Let's work together."

Clarice took another sip of her drink. There was a long silence as she thought it over. "You're pigheaded," she said. "Yet, as much as I hate to admit it, you have guts. You're starting to remind me of my great-great-grandmother Ida Belle Monfort who buried the family silver in her daddy's grave and lied her pretty little head off to the Yankees.

Frankly, I didn't think you had it in you to defy me. I admire that quality. Jayne has it too from time to time. It's as annoying as hell, but it's one of the things I love about her."

She put down her glass. "Okay, you have a deal. I'll do your makeup for Carleton's party. Hell, honey, I'll make you look so blotchy the man will be tempted to scream when he catches sight of you. I only have one condition."

"What's that?"

Clarice turned to examine herself in the mirror. "At least once a day, I want you to tell me I look thirty-five. I know it's a lie, but it's such a nice one."

One of the first rules of "Clarice's Guide to Surviving Hollywood Without Getting Totally Screwed" was that you never arrived on time for a party unless you wanted people to think your career was on the skids; so at nine-thirty, exactly one and a half hours late, Mary Lynn and Arnie drove through the east gate of Bel Air and up the road that led to Carleton Winters's estate.

Just to make sure you didn't mistake Bel Air for some kind of ordinary subdivision rather than an incorporated city filled with multimillion-dollar homes, the gate was a massive pile of gray limestone and wrought iron that looked as if it had been built by a Roman general to withstand a siege of spear-wielding barbarians—a powerful effect almost completely ruined by the cheerful blue-neon Bel Air sign that served as an electronic welcome mat.

The car Arnie and Mary Lynn rode in was a beautifully restored 1955 two-tone baby-blue-and-white Chevy convertible, leased from a very discreet company that specialized in providing impressive cars for people who wanted to look like they were pulling down big bucks. Clarice, whose taste was flawless, had selected the Chevy because it had just the right touch of eccentricity for a successful screenwriter. In L.A. there was nothing more important than your wheels. Arrive at a party in the wrong car, she had warned, and you might as well not arrive at all.

She had also picked out Arnie's clothes as well as Mary Lynn's. Arnie was wearing what Clarice called "the screen-writer's uniform": faded jeans, a black T-shirt, running shoes, and a black blazer that looked casual but screamed money. Mary Lynn had on one of Jayne's informal party outfits: dove-colored slacks, a perfectly cut white silk blouse, open-toed sandals, and enough gold chains to hold down the T. rex in *Jurassic Park*. Mary Lynn had objected that wearing so many gold chains looked tacky, but Clarice had stood her ground. "Hollywood," she had insisted, "is all about illusion, and tonight you're the main attraction."

Thanks to the strange car, the strange clothes, the impending party, and the fact that they were both on the strangest blind date of their lives, Mary Lynn and Arnie were about as cheerful as two people on their way to get their teeth drilled. As they drove along the winding road, they sat in total silence, darting occasional, anxious glances in each other's direction and wondering how the hell they had gotten themselves into this situation.

Arnie figured he had probably been asked to escort Jayne Cooper to this party because she'd broken out in hives and didn't want any of her usual boyfriends to see her with spots all over her face. Even hived up and spotty, she still intimidated him so much he could hardly keep his mind on his driving. He kept thinking that he, Arnie Levine, was actually sitting next to a woman who used to date Tom Cruise. If only his buddies back in New York could see him now. No, maybe better they couldn't. They'd probably laugh themselves sick. "Arnie, you *putz,*" they'd jeer, "you're not on a *date* with Jayne Cooper. You're her chauffeur."

Mary Lynn seemed calm, but that was also an illusion. The effort of trying to remember all those names and faces had put her smack in the middle of the kind of panic attack that made her want to crawl into bed, pull the covers over her head, and never come out. She was already regretting that she hadn't taken the Valium Clarice had offered her.

Breathe, she commanded herself. But she couldn't. Her mind was racing like a squirrel on speed. She was having regrets, second thoughts, deep desires to leap out of the convertible and flee across the immaculately landscaped lawns like a psychotic deer. Who was she really underneath all this makeup? What was she doing in a rented convertible on her way to a party where she might have to make croaking sounds at James Cameron? Where was she going in the ultimate, existential sense?

Don't ask yourself those questions. Think of seascapes, butterflies, Zen gardens; think of the poor guy who is sitting next to you who doesn't have any idea what he's gotten himself into.

She really wished she could talk to Arnie; however, since she supposedly couldn't speak above a whisper, any kind of normal conversation was out. She closed her eyes and tried to concentrate on this little problem instead of the big ones lying in wait for her. The car suddenly took a sharp turn. Mary Lynn slid toward Arnie and felt her body hit his with a soft thump. *Excuse me,* she mimed.

"No problem," Arnie said. He kept his eyes straight ahead, although he could no longer see the road. He could feel his face going red. He had just been touched by Jayne Cooper's left breast. Instantly he got the kind of erection that doesn't go away no matter how much you plead with it. *I'm going to make a total fool of myself tonight,* he thought.

Sliding as far to the right as possible, Mary Lynn clung to the door handle and pretended to admire the view. *Everything is going to be just fine*, she told herself. And then, just like Arnie, in exactly the same words, she thought: *Who am I kidding? I'm going to make a total fool of myself tonight.*

Twelve

Carleton Winters hurried in Mary Lynn's direction with outstretched arms. "Jayne, welcome!" he said. Carleton jogged, he watched his cholesterol, he played a ruthless game of tennis, he cut his hair short, he wore expensive casual clothing, and he would live forever because a greater health nut had never been born. In the forty-some years he had worked in Hollywood, the head of Global had never willingly shaken hands with any man or woman; so the fact that he was preparing to embrace Jayne Cooper said more about her position at the studio than a full-page ad in *Variety*. Carleton fully expected *Salome* to open at $42.3 million, and for that much money he was willing to allow her a two-cheek air kiss, provided that afterward he could beat a quick retreat to the bathroom and disinfect his body with Betadine like a returning space capsule.

Behind him, Darcy, his fifth wife, trailed like an afterthought. Darcy wore a low-cut white silk outfit that clung to her like a second skin, gold flats, and a diamond ring so large it was a wonder her left arm wasn't longer than her right. Darcy was very pretty, very blond, very thin, and very young. Although she had a reputation for being one of the most merciless gossips in town, she always maintained a sweet, near-total silence in Carleton's presence, a ploy that had trapped more than one unwary guest into mistaking her for his daughter.

Mary Lynn smiled at Carleton and Darcy, held out her

arms, and—as Clarice had ordered—made a small croaking sound that might have been taken either for delight or the word "Carl." At that precise moment, she stepped into the light and Carleton saw her face.

He froze.

"Don't worry," Arnie said. "It's not infectious. Jayne just had an allergic reaction to walnuts."

Carleton stared at Mary Lynn the way a man might stare at a carrier of bubonic plague and quickly gestured for Darcy to stand back. He wasn't buying the allergy theory—at least not entirely—and it was clear that no matter what happened for the rest of the evening, he was not going to get any closer. Everything was going exactly as Clarice had predicted.

"Walnuts?" he said as if he had never heard the word before, and suspected it of having some dark meaning that would result in instant contagion. On all sides, the party went on. It was taking place outdoors around a swimming pool that had been landscaped to look as if it sprang naturally from the rocks of the mountain. There were torches; long tables set with shrimp, caviar, and platters of fruit; waiters in black silently circulating with twelve superb French wines, eight varieties of martinis, sixteen different kinds of bottled water, pink Cosmopolitans, and trays of Bloody Marys adorned with celery sticks. Although Bloody Marys had been out of fashion for years, Carleton always plied his guests with them because tomato juice was acidic enough to prevent botulism.

The rich, the famous, and the powerful were there: faces Mary Lynn had only seen in documentaries or in the pile of photos Clarice had handed her. These were the people behind the scenes who really made films happen. They worked together; they lunched together; they slept together; they made multimillion-dollar deals together. And, whenever necessary, they ate one another like demented guppies. Right now, they were all pretending not to notice that Jayne Cooper had arrived with a face that looked as if it were in the initial stages of chicken pox. And being eager to end the evening with their careers and major body parts intact, they were also pretending not to notice that Carleton was having another attack of his most famous phobia.

"Jayne ate some baklava," Arnie said. "The stuff is usually made with pistachio nuts, but this time they put walnuts in it. She'd love to tell you about it herself, but her throat closed up and she lost her voice."

Mary Lynn smiled, opened her mouth, and produced another cheerful croaking sound that made Carleton shudder. Darcy, always obedient to her husband's whims, rapidly scuttled away toward the buffet so as not to become an unwitting vector.

"Who baked the baklava?" Carleton demanded.

"A place in West Hollywood called the Athenos Bakery."

Carleton knew it well. The Athenos was famous for its pastries, but he had never tried them. He had always suspected the cream puffs of harboring salmonella. He made a mental note to get the place closed down and the owner deported back to Greece, where he couldn't poison people who had multimillion-dollar contracts with Global.

"Jayne wants me to tell you that she's sorry she looks this way," Arnie continued, "but she wouldn't have missed one of your parties for anything." Arnie was very convincing, which wasn't surprising—not being in on the deception, he believed what he was saying.

Carleton softened. "It was very loyal of you to come, Jayne." He liked loyalty in his actors—expected it, actually. He was particularly impressed that Jayne had shown up with hives, because she was famous for her vanity. On the other hand, this had better not be part of a downhill slide. Thirty wasn't all that young for a female star, and she had clearly put on weight since the last time he saw her. With a monumental effort of will, he forced himself to stop thinking about how much he stood to lose if she let herself go to seed. Giving her a warm smile, he turned to Arnie. "I don't think we've met," he said.

"I'm Arnie Levine. In fact"—Arnie laughed nervously,

and then could have kicked himself—"I'm the guy you hired to rewrite *Star Whale*."

"Ah," Carleton said enigmatically. *Star Whale* was not going well. He had a vague memory of having ordered the producer to hire a playwright from New York to do rewrites. This must be the playwright. Out of long habit, Carleton tried to assess how much power, if any, Arnie Levine had, and if he was likely to cause Global trouble, embarrassment, or money. He clearly had something going for him, because he had walked in the door with Jayne Cooper; that must mean he was either sleeping with her or about to do so—but what was a star like Cooper doing with a writer?

Carleton decided that tonight would not be grist for the tabloids after all. The moment he walked away from Jayne and her new lover (what *was* the attraction?), he would hunt down the people he had invited to leak the story to the press and make it clear to them that if he saw so much as a word of this in print, the only employees at Global they would get to talk to in the future would be the workers who cleaned out the portable toilets.

After a few more polite interchanges, during which he complimented Jayne on the "superb way" she had handled Animals First and Arnie on the "superb way" he was rewriting *Star Whale*, Carleton excused himself and fled shuddering into the nearest bathroom to douse himself with disinfectant.

Still following Clarice's orders, Mary Lynn sat down at the nearest table and let people come to her, which they did, rather like the subjects of the queens in some of Jayne's most popular films. Arnie sat beside her and, as instructed, threw one arm casually around her shoulder as if they had been sharing a toothbrush for several weeks. He was surprised to discover she was trembling.

"Are you okay?" he whispered. He wondered if her allergic reaction had taken a turn for the worse. He hoped she wouldn't end up stretched out on the tiled patio fighting for breath while some amateur tried to give her CPR. He suspected from the envious glances he was getting that there'd be no lack of volunteers.

She put her face very close to his ear and he felt his entire body quiver as though he had grabbed a live electric wire. "Thanks," she whispered in a hoarse croak. "I'm fine. Just a little nervous."

He was amazed that Jayne Cooper could be nervous at a party given in her honor. He gave her an encouraging smile. "No need to be nervous. You look great, even with all those zits." Zits! He'd just told Jayne Cooper she had zits! Maybe he should just drown himself in Carleton's tastefully landscaped pool now and get it over with.

Instead of smacking him senseless with her purse, she leaned over again and put her mouth to his ear. "I could use a drink."

"You want a drink? You got it!" Anxious to do something to make up for insulting her, he leaped to his feet with the intention of bringing her a drink. Behind him, just out of his range of vision, a waiter had been approaching with an entire tray of Bloody Marys balanced on the palm of his hand. As Arnie rose, one of his arms connected with the tray and it went airborne, spiraling across the patio like a demonic Frisbee. Drinks flew in all directions. There was a series of crashes as the glasses hit the tiles, and then a stunned silence.

Arnie stared in horror at what he had done. Some of the tomato juice had fallen into Jayne Cooper's lap, staining her slacks. But most of the drinks—eight to be precise—had pelted down on Darcy Winters, who stood beside the pool dripping and sobbing. Darcy's hair was a matted mess; her white silk outfit was ruined beyond repair; a stick of celery poked out of her cleavage. She looked like a cat that had been doused in tomato juice to get rid of the smell of skunk.

"I'm sorry!" Arnie cried. Unfortunately, Clarice hadn't anticipated the possibility of airborne Bloody Marys; she hadn't scripted this. "I'm sorry" was exactly the wrong thing to say. You never apologized in Hollywood. *Never.*

Apologies meant you were the one who had screwed up. They meant you were history.

Darcy gave Arnie a look of hatred so intense it could have turned the water in the pool to steam. Then she wheeled around and fled toward the house. For a second, the only sound was the squishing of her little gold shoes on the tiles.

When she was gone, conversation resumed. No one looked at Arnie. For all practical purposes, he had ceased to exist.

Mary Lynn saw that they had written him off, and it made her furious. Who the hell were they to judge Arnie Levine? He was a nice guy. Was it his fault he didn't have eyes in the back of his head?

It's time to be Jayne, she thought. *Really be Jayne.* Standing up, she slid her arm around his waist so everyone could see that Jayne Cooper was still nuts about Arnie Levine. She smiled adoringly, drew him close, and put her mouth to his ear. "My slacks are stained, so I've got a good excuse to leave," she whispered. "Let's get the hell out of here."

Fifteen minutes later, they were parked at an overlook in the Hollywood Hills laughing themselves sick. To the right, Santa Monica glittered against the blank darkness of the ocean. In the center, the skyscrapers of Century City rose like illuminated chimneys dwarfing the cakelike dome of the Mormon Temple. If you looked south, you could see the planes circling LAX; if you looked straight down, you could see the cars on Sunset Boulevard dancing like a conga line of fireflies.

But neither Arnie nor Mary Lynn noticed the spectacular view. They were making up for lost time. Mary Lynn had miraculously gotten her voice back, and as they chatted, they discovered that they had a mutual love of live theater, small bookstores, beaches, dogs, pastrami, and an up-and-coming young jazz saxophonist named David Sanchez.

About the time a silver-tipped crescent moon was starting a long slide into the Pacific, Arnie put the Chevy in gear and drove back down the hill and over to Santa Monica where he was staying in an old Spanish-style hotel frequented by screenwriters. For an hour or so, they strolled barefoot along the edge of the ocean, watching the moonlight play on the water and talking about Arnie's childhood in Brooklyn and Mary Lynn's imaginary childhood as an infant prodigy in the world of film. Mary Lynn felt bad about lying to him, but she found that with a few twists, she could insert a lot of her own life into Jayne's. After all, even a famous little girl could have loved the Oz books, or sprained her ankle on a hike with her Girl Scout troupe, or owned a golden retriever named Charlie.

They were so absorbed in the pleasure of getting to know each other that they didn't notice the tide was coming in. Just before midnight, a big wave sneaked up on them and splattered them both to their waists with salty water and liquid sand. They retreated to Arnie's hotel room to dry off and continue their conversation over cups of hot tea, which he made by immersing a little wire coil in two mugs of water.

"I know it's not what you're used to," he apologized, kicking his underwear under the bed and straightening the spread like a nervous housewife.

"It's fine," Mary Lynn reassured him. His hotel room, in fact, was larger than her living room. She sat down on the bed, accepted the mug of tea, and sipped it slowly. "Tell me more about yourself. What's it like living on the East Coast?"

"You probably wouldn't find it very interesting."

"Oh, I think I would." She had never been east of Denver; but, of course, he thought she'd been all over the world. It was hard for her to keep remembering that.

Encouraged, Arnie talked on. After a while, he forgot to be nervous and began to discuss the technical structure of his plays and the problem of writing for a live audience. At one point, she stunned him by quoting a long passage from *King Lear*. He had always thought actresses were, for the most part, poorly educated and shallow; but this woman had depth, wit, and intelligence. And she was no snob. She'd grown up beautiful, famous, and fabulously wealthy, yet there wasn't an ounce of arrogance in her.

Arnie registered all this with a combination of delight and growing despair. Jayne Cooper was exactly the kind of woman he'd been looking for since he was sixteen, and after this evening, he didn't have a chance in hell of ever seeing her again, at least not in the flesh. A woman like her belonged with a man who was her equal. The best he could hope for was that every once in a while she'd remember the weird little writer she'd spent an evening with.

He fell silent.

"What's wrong?" Mary Lynn asked. Jayne, of course, could have told her in an instant.

Arnie shrugged. "Nothing."

"You seem sad all of a sudden."

"No, really. I'm fine." He cleared his throat. "So, I suppose you must be getting sleepy. Maybe you'd like to be getting home?"

Was it the question? The look of longing on his face? The fact that she liked him more than any man she'd ever been out with in months? Who knew? Mary Lynn suddenly leaned over and kissed him with no more forethought than a heat-seeking missile. It was a great kiss, an electric kiss, a kiss that deserved its own case in the Museum of Erotic Kisses.

"Whew," Arnie gasped. He came up for air, took her in his arms, and kissed her again. Their second kiss was even better than their first. Somewhere in the middle of it, he forgot she was Jayne Cooper, and she forgot that she was pretending to be someone else.

They kissed some more, and before they knew it, they were under the bedspread instead of on it. Mary's Lynn's designer slacks and frilly underthings were on the floor in a heap getting to know Arnie's jeans and black blazer. They both felt a shock of pleasure as their bodies touched. And then, just as quickly as it had begun, it was all over.

Arnie suddenly remembered he was making love to a famous movie star who had made love to Tom Cruise and

Russell Crowe. *Who am I,* he thought, *to go where those guys have gone?* His enthusiasm withered. He pulled away from her and sat up.

"Sorry," he mumbled. He couldn't even look at her. He felt like a total *putz.* He expected her to be furious. There was a moment of ominous silence, and then, to his surprise, he felt her gently kissing his cheek.

"It doesn't matter," she murmured. "I'm pretty nervous too. Only with me, it's not as obvious. I think it's too soon."

"Yeah." Arnie shot a glance in her direction and discovered she was looking at him in a friendly way. Encouraged, he managed a smile. "Isn't this where I'm supposed to say this has never happened to me before?"

She smiled back. "How about just cuddling?"

"Sure. Sounds like a plan." He took her in his arms, and they lay there for a while. She felt nice and warm and friendly; he really liked the way her breasts pressed against his chest. She weighed a little more than he thought she would, and he liked that too. He'd always been attracted to women with hips and curves and cute little bellies, soft women whose bones didn't jab at a man like sticks.

"We'll wait," she whispered.

"Right."

"Until we get to know each other better."

"Absolutely."

He gave her a friendly kiss. "No reason we can't do this while we're waiting, is there?"

"No reason at all."

They kissed again and then again. On the third kiss, something irrational seized them, spilling out of nowhere and making them forget all about being friendly and prudent. All at once, they were kissing, touching, making love: swimming naked together straight out toward the horizon.

Thirteen

On Wednesday morning, Joe Porter got up late. The day before he had worked fourteen hours patching the hull of a tanker so it wouldn't spew oil all over the beaches of southern California. Welding tankers paid big bucks, but it was an exhausting, dangerous job. Joe had only been at it eleven months and was already seriously thinking about getting into another line of work. The best thing about slaving away at the shipyard was that he sometimes got days off in the middle of the week, which, in theory, allowed him to spend more time with his girls. But lately, all they had gotten to do was listen to their daddy snore, which was hardly a definition of quality time.

Joe yawned, strolled over to the window, and opened the blinds. The weather was sunny as usual, and out in the backyard, his mobiles were spinning in a stiff breeze that had blown in off the Pacific, removing the smog and scrubbing L.A. as clean as it had been in the thirties before freeways and fourteen million people turned the basin into a swamp.

He stood for a moment admiring his handiwork and listening to the clink of metal hitting metal. The apartment had the quiet hollowness that meant his mother-in-law had taken the girls to the park so they wouldn't wake him up. Overhead, he could hear his neighbor walking around. He wondered if her schedule had changed. She had a long commute and was usually gone by seven.

Today, he decided, he'd go out to the shed and weld another mobile, a small, pretty one that would ride the wind like a feather. He grinned and scratched his chest. What would the boys at the shipyard say if they knew Joe Porter spent his spare time welding scraps of junk together? He tried to imagine himself explaining that his mobiles were works of art. "Art?" he imagined them saying. They'd give him blank looks and go back to talking about football and women; and when he sat down to have lunch, there'd be a little space around him the way there was always a space around guys who liked to pick fights or talk nonstop.

Pulling on an old pair of jeans and a T-shirt, he strolled into the kitchen and made himself a no-nonsense breakfast of bacon, eggs, toast, sliced mangoes, and coffee. The mangoes were a special treat his mother-in-law had bought for him at the Mexican produce store down the block, but they didn't remind him of Mexico; they reminded him of Brazil and Claudia and the lazy, love-dazed breakfasts they had shared in a little white stucco house built so close to the beach they could sit on the front porch and wiggle their toes in the sand.

He forced his mind back to the present. The pain of losing Claudia was still there, but after three years, it no longer filled his every waking moment. He ate the mangoes, ate his bacon and eggs, put jelly on his toast, and ate that too. Then he reached for the illustrated biography of Alexander Calder he had been reading last night and began to page through it as he sipped his coffee.

Calder had been one of the most innovative sculptors in America. He had made witty portraits in wire, bizarre and playful jewelry, and miniature zoos, but his enduring fame had come from his mobiles. Joe had actually met Calder when the artist was an old man and Joe was seven. His parents had been wealthy enough to collect the best contemporary art for their apartment on Fifth Avenue, and his father, who specialized in the legal aspects of the art world, had briefly had Calder as a client.

Joe sipped his coffee and admired a glossy print of one of Calder's mobiles that now hung in the Guggenheim. He had always wondered if his parents regretted introducing their youngest son to the sculptor. On the evening Calder came to dinner at the Porters', he had presented Joe with a small mobile and then smiled as Joe—to his parents' horror—proceeded to take it apart and try to put it back together again.

At that moment, Joe had known he would never grow up to be a lawyer like his father; but it had taken him four years at Harvard, one semester at Harvard Law, and six years of bumming around to get it straight that building kinetic sculptures wasn't his hobby but his calling. It hadn't been an easy decision. Since the day he told them he was dropping out of law school, his parents had refused to speak to him. Joe didn't mind being disowned; he'd always been proud of being able to support himself. But he often thought it was a pity his mom and dad had never met their grandchildren.

He closed the book and put it up on the top shelf of the kitchen cabinet, where Lisa wouldn't be tempted to scrawl on it with her new crayons. Then he went over to the sink to wash his breakfast dishes.

He was standing up to his elbows in soapy water, lost in thought, when he smelled smoke. The acrid plastic odor grew stronger. Suddenly he heard a piercing shriek.

"Help!" a female voice cried. "Fire!"

Joe recognized the voice as that of his upstairs neighbor. Dashing across the room, he grabbed a fire extinguisher and ran up the stairs to her apartment. Evil-smelling black smoke was streaming into the hall through her open door. Joe followed the smoke to her kitchen and saw her approaching a flaming toaster with a dishpan of soapy water.

"Stop!" he yelled. "You're going to fry yourself!"

She froze and gave him a look of pure panic. Her hair was sticking up in little tufts and she was wearing an enormous pink terry cloth bathrobe that made her look both beautiful and silly. If there hadn't been an electrical fire in progress, Joe might have taken time to admire the combination, but the flames were edging perilously close to the kitchen curtains.

"Stand back!"

She threw herself back against the refrigerator, spilling the water on the floor. Joe charged past her and began to spray foam on the toaster. In a few seconds, the fire was under control, and all that was left of the toaster was a smoldering mess of charred metal.

Joe went over to the double doors that led out on the balcony and slid them open to get rid of the fumes. When he turned around, she was still standing against the refrigerator with the empty dishpan clutched to her chest and her eyes firmly shut.

"It's okay now," he said. "You can open your eyes now."

She opened her eyes and he noticed for the first time that they were the vivid tropical blue called cerulean. "Is it out?"

"Yes." He smiled at her, partly to encourage her and partly because close-up she was one of the most beautiful women he'd seen in a long time. He wondered why, in the months she had been living above him, he had never noticed this. "What happened?"

"I don't have any idea." She pointed at what remained of the toaster. "I was just trying to cook myself some breakfast, and the thing went up like a prop from *Backdraft*."

Joe approached the toaster and batted what was left of the plug out of the wall with the handle of a wooden spoon. Then he turned the spoon around and probed the interior. "It looks like you put something plastic in here." He noticed an empty box lying on the counter. It was charred, but some of the label had survived. He picked up the box and inspected it with disbelief. "Is this what you were toasting?" She nodded. "But this is a Boil-in-Bag meal."

"And your point is?" she said in a faint voice, approaching the toaster with the wariness of a woman who expected it to charge her at any moment.

"You can't toast these things." He held the box out to her. "Look." He pointed to the directions. "You have to put the plastic pouch in boiling water."

"Who knew?"

"Don't you ever read directions?"

"I've never been a detail person. I only read my part of the script."

"Script?"

"Whoops!" She flashed him a smile so disarming that he felt as if floodlights had been turned on. "Let's not go there." She took the box out of his hands and tossed it into the wastebasket. "You must think I'm a complete idiot."

"Well, actually, I do." He smiled at her. She was hard not to smile at. "But I imagine after I get to know you better, I'll learn that you have a deeply complex mind. After all, you're a professor, aren't you? And professors are expected to be absentminded. One thing you should remember, though: never throw water on an electrical fire or you can get electrocuted."

"I'll file that away." She flashed him that amazing smile again. "It should come in handy the next time I try to toast something that should be boiled. How did you happen to have a fire extinguisher?"

"I do welding." She didn't look impressed. He stood for a moment staring at her, trying to think of what to say next. He was in no mood to rush away. There had been no professors like her at Harvard. He wondered what her male students thought of her, if they could think at all in her presence. *I'm a sexist dog,* he thought, and was amused at himself.

"Joe. . . It is Joe, isn't it?"

He nodded.

"Do you know anything about plumbing? I'm having a problem with the garbage disposal. . . ."

A few seconds later, he was again up to his elbows in

soapy water and had found the source of her problem. He began to laugh. Pulling his arms out of the sink, he dried them on a towel, sat down on one of the kitchen chairs, and kept on laughing.

She looked at him warily. "What's so funny?"

"The reason your garbage disposal isn't working is"— he paused for effect—"that you don't *have* a garbage disposal."

She looked annoyed, and then she saw the ridiculousness of the situation and started laughing too. Joe felt their laughter fill the kitchen and spill out into the backyard, where it jangled the mobiles. He felt irrationally happy.

Jayne also felt happy, but not for the same reason. She had just made a stupid mistake, but no one had yelled "Cut," no one had lectured her, and no one had demanded a retake. She felt a deep sense of relief. She might have clogged up the sink with bread crusts and banana peels and nearly burned down the apartment, but this man sitting on her kitchen chair clearly didn't give a damn.

The sense of being able to screw up at will was intoxicating. She picked up a saucepan, shoved it under the kitchen faucet, and turned on the water. "Let me make you a cup of coffee," she said. And striding over to the stove, she slammed the pan down on the burner with reckless abandon.

Her second try at coffee making was no better than her first, but Joe gamely drank the stuff and told her about his mobiles. Jayne enjoyed the conversation, but she found it strange. It was odd to talk with a man who treated her so casually. For thirty years, she had moved through the world like Cleopatra sailing down the Nile. On the distant banks, her fans trampled one another for a chance to catch sight of her; while in the royal barge itself, anything male flattered her shamelessly.

Joe seemed to belong to a different species. He didn't stammer, didn't flatter, and wasn't intimidated. He just sat there with his elbows on the kitchen table being friendly, and soon she found herself talking about nothing in particular in an easy way that was more relaxing than a full-body massage. She was actually sorry when he said he had to leave to go work on his mobiles.

After he left, she found herself at loose ends. Having been fired from the Barn, she had no job to go to until late afternoon. After a few failed attempts to read one of Mary Lynn's academic journals, she did what she always did when she was bored: she shopped.

Although she couldn't deal with toaster ovens and coffeemakers, Jayne had put in a lot of time surfing on-line stores, so she had no trouble using computers. Mary Lynn's should have been on display in a Museum of Obsolete Technology, but after a bit of trial and error, she managed to get it connected to the Internet. At first she just ordered a few things to make life more comfortable: five pounds of gourmet coffee, an automatic coffeemaker, several sets of towels, a new toaster, and some body oil. But then she began to branch out.

Watching Mary Lynn's ancient browser download Web pages was about as interesting as watching paint dry, but still, within less than half an hour, she managed to buy six ounces of beluga caviar, new drapes (Mary Lynn's old ones appeared to have been made from brown burlap), and two hundred dollars' worth of cat toys.

Having met her immediate needs, she turned off the computer and smoked a cigarette. Then she wandered into the kitchen, tossed the remains of Mary Lynn's toaster into the trash, sponged up the mess, and made herself a ham sandwich.

As she sat at the kitchen table eating the sandwich and drinking one of the Diet Cokes she'd salvaged from the Food Barn, she began to feel guilty. She had no idea how much she'd just spent, but the caviar alone had cost nearly eight hundred. Perhaps she should cancel everything. But no. The cats were horribly bored and needed some amusement, and Mary Lynn would love the new drapes. She promised herself that she'd be more careful in the future to live within her supposed means.

She blew a smoke ring and watched it drift out the door onto the balcony like a little inner tube. Suddenly she was seized by a wild idea. She knew she'd have trouble keeping her vow to live on Mary Lynn's income. She loved to shop, and as long as there was an Internet, she'd be tempted to log on and buy oriental rugs, small fountains, personal saunas, and God knew what else. The only way to make sure she didn't spend more money was to cancel her credit cards.

She tapped a few ashes into a saucer and gave a little shudder. The thought of having no credit cards was terrifying and, at the same time, thrilling. It would be like going into a tiger-infested jungle armed only with a pointed stick.

Hurrying into the living room, she seized the phone and dialed the credit card companies before she lost her nerve. It only took her a few minutes to cancel her cards. When she hung up, she was breathing heavily. She'd actually done it. There was no going back. She was desperately, hideously poor.

She lit another cigarette and smoked it, her fingers trembling. How long could she afford even generic brands? What would it be like to go off tobacco cold turkey? She felt drunk with possibilities. Never had her future seemed so unpredictable.

Putting the cigarette out, she carefully saved the half that was left so she could smoke it later and went into the bedroom to take a complete inventory of the clothes in Mary Lynn's closet. The moment she saw the skirts and blouses lined up in a neat row, she realized she had acted too hastily. She should have remembered how much trouble it had been to find anything to wear to the Barn.

Mary Lynn's wardrobe wasn't horrible. You wouldn't expect to see anyone dressed in those blouses stumbling down the street pushing a shopping cart and raving. But evidently, she'd spent years carefully purchasing the kind of outfits you'd wear if you were smuggling cocaine and didn't want to attract the attention of the dope-sniffing dogs. Where in God's name had she found this stuff? Was there some vast Food Barn–like store that only sold practical skirts guaranteed not to show dirt?

Jayne pulled out a navy blue suit, a long-sleeved white blouse, and a narrow navy blue belt with a brass buckle. She hung them on a nail that, for some mysterious reason, was sticking out of the wall next to the dresser. She stood back and contemplated the combination with growing despair. She'd look like a nun in that outfit, and a baggy nun at that. She'd totally forgotten Mary Lynn weighed more than she did.

Plopping down on the futon, she picked up one of the cats and tried to figure out what to do next. Gino, her special assistant, still hadn't come back from wherever the hell he'd gone, so she wouldn't be getting an infusion of cash any time in the near future. Without cash or credit cards, she couldn't shop. In a few hours, she was scheduled to appear before an entire classroom of students.

This was an emergency situation. As far as she could see, she only had one option. She'd promised herself she'd stop buying things, but surely living an ordinary life didn't mean you couldn't call in a few favors. Putting the cat aside, she picked up the phone and punched in an unlisted number that was almost as hard to get as an Oscar.

"Disguises and Surprises," a gravelly voice said.

"Eva, this is Jayne."

"What is it this time?"

"Professor."

"Era?"

"Contemporary."

"Impression?"

Jayne thought for a moment. "Smart and sexy." She paused. "I realize that real professors wear all sorts of ghastly things, but let's not go there. Think glamorous, fantastically intelligent woman with her own special sense of style."

"You want glasses?"

"No, I already have a pair." Jayne never ceased to be amazed by Eva's attention to details.

"When do you want the outfit delivered?"

"Today."

"Four hours do?"

Jayne consulted Mary Lynn's clunky Timex. "Make it three."

"You got it. So where does the courier drop it off?"

Jayne gave her Mary Lynn's name and address without hesitation. Actors called Eva when they didn't like the costume they had been handed, when they needed to venture out incognito, or—for all Jayne knew—when they wanted to rob a bank. You could ask her to run up a size 4 wolf costume and the only thing she would ask you was what color you wanted the fur. Eva was the soul of discretion. If she hadn't been, she would have been out of business in twenty-four hours.

Having solved her wardrobe problem, Jayne curled up in a deck chair on the balcony and tried to make sense of a composition text she had found in Mary Lynn's briefcase. From a dramatic point of view, the text was a real turkey. It had no screen potential, not to mention that it was so boring that she felt as if someone were pouring sawdust into her head every time she turned a page. Still, she soldiered on diligently, ignoring all the terms she didn't understand. In some ways, reading the damn thing was like skimming a script. Of course, if the textbook had been a script, she would have been counting her lines. Larry had standing orders not to bother showing her a screenplay unless the heroine had a three-page monologue somewhere in the second act where she poured out her heart and brought the audience to the verge of tears.

As she read on, she grew more confident. Despite all the technical gobbledygook about thesis statements and exposition, the basic principles of composition were so easy any idiot could grasp them.

1. *You had to have something to say.*
2. *You had to say it in a way that made the reader want to go on reading.*

In other words, writers were more or less like actors: they all had an audience to please.

She stopped reading, jotted down a few notes, and tossed the text onto the deck. Leaning back, she put her feet up on the railing and lit her carefully saved half cigarette. So what was the big deal? She'd been pleasing audiences since she was old enough to walk.

Section 17 of "Introduction to College Composition" had an official enrollment of twenty-five students. On most days, fewer than half showed up, but on Wednesday afternoon, every seat was taken ten minutes before class was scheduled to begin. Since yesterday, rumors had been flying that Professor McLellan had called the English-department secretary to say she'd been diagnosed with a brain tumor; there wasn't an eighteen-year-old at Coast Side Community College who'd miss a show like that.

Partly their interest came from real concern. Professor McLellan was well liked by the majority of her students, and it made them sad to think that she might be on the verge of a tragic death. Others saw her illness as a first-hand chance to watch a soap opera live; while still others—who were distinctly the minority—had already started placing bets on how long she would last. The bet placers were without exception the same students who never turned in their papers on time, talked on their cell phones in class, hated to read, and loathed Mary Lynn because she insisted on talking about grammar and topic sentences. They were a hard lot who figured she deserved what she was getting for boring them all semester with dumb stuff they'd never have to use in their whole lives even if they lived to be a hundred.

And then there was William Hestene. William, who never missed a class and who always sat in the back row, did not simply like Professor McLellan; he loved her the way Romeo had loved Juliet. William knew Professor McLellan loved him too because she was nice to him and gave him good grades. No other woman had ever been nice to him: not his other professors, not the nurses at the psychiatric hospital, not the few women he'd gone out with, and certainly not his own mother, who had thrown him out of the house just for trying to build a flying saucer out of bicycle parts.

But mostly, William knew Professor McLellan loved him because she told him so, right in front of the whole class, but without moving her lips. She'd look at him, and he'd hear her voice in his head saying: "William, I return your affection." Or "William, some day we will marry." She couldn't say it out loud, of course, because he was her student; but when the semester was over, she'd invite him into her office and they'd make wedding plans. This was their secret. William was already making payments on the ring.

So when he heard she had a brain tumor, he was devastated. At first he blamed her for not telling him. But then he realized she had wanted to spare him for as long as possible because she had known the news would break his heart. Today he had come to class with a plan. After she announced that she would no longer be returning to Coast Side, he would stand up and tell everyone that he and Professor McLellan were going to drive to Las Vegas that very afternoon to be married. Their secret would be a secret no longer. He would take care of her and they would be together for whatever time she had left.

He was just trying to decide if they should have a civil ceremony in the courthouse or pay for a wedding chapel, when Jayne walked through the door wearing four-inch heels and a white suit with a softly pleated skirt so short she couldn't have bent over without a cabaret permit. At the last minute, worried about looking sufficiently professorial, she had tossed aside the lacy tank top Eva had provided and put on one of Mary Lynn's blouses and a rather dismal ethnic necklace that looked as if it might have escaped from Morocco in a rubber raft. She had also pinned her hair into a bun, but tiny wisps had escaped giving her that soft I-just-got-out-of-bed look that had been the delight of every hairstylist who had ever worked her over.

"Hi," she said, flashing her audience a smile. Besides the composition text, she was carrying an armload of books that she had plucked at random from Mary Lynn's bookcase. Had any of her students been in the mood to notice the titles, they might have wondered what Professor McLellan was planning to do with *Protein Power* and *A Week in the Zone*. But no one saw the books. They only saw her. For a full ten seconds, there was a silence so complete that you could hear the professor in the next room droning on about Milton.

The male students were, to a man, paralyzed by a rush of testosterone so strong it gave lust a new name. They were eighteen, it was spring, and at the sight of their professor in a white miniskirt, their brains—which focused on sex even when they were getting their teeth cleaned—simply stopped as if their transmissions had dropped out. The female students were equally paralyzed. What had happened to Professor McLellan? Had she won a free makeover from *Fashion Emergency*? Where had she bought that rad jacket, and did those cool heels come in a size 9?

"I said 'hi,'" Jayne repeated. When she made an entrance, she expected a reaction. "What the hell's wrong with you people? Have you all had lobotomies?"

There was a startled gasp, followed by nervous laughter. The professor had just said "hell." Whoa. She must have a brain tumor. There was no other explanation. In the back row, William Hestene stared at Jayne intently, and then shook his head as if trying to re-sort his brains.

Jayne opened Mary Lynn's briefcase, extracted the old compositions, and handed them to a tall boy with stylishly spiked purple hair. "Spread these around," she commanded.

The boy obediently passed out the compositions. As the students turned to the final page, they gave little shrieks of joy. Jayne had crossed out Mary Lynn's grades and given everyone an A+. As far as she could tell, these people were basically fans, and you didn't earn millions by making your fans feel stupid.

As the students leafed through their papers, she picked up a piece of chalk, went to the board, and began to scribble down a few terms from the textbook. She drew a bunch of arrows from one word to another for no particular reason except that they looked nice, and finished by drawing a couple of interlocked circles about the size of her compact.

She was doing just fine until she turned around and saw all twenty-five of them staring at her expectantly. My God, she was going to have to perform. This time there would be no trailer to bunker up in, no Clarice to argue with, no director willing to beg and flatter her into stepping in front of the cameras. She hadn't had a single rehearsal, and she was going to have to make up her own lines. For a moment she was so terrified, she couldn't speak. This was even worse than live theater. *Help!* she thought. *Somebody get me out of here!*

"Yo, Professor," a lanky, athletic-looking boy said. "You okay?"

"I'm perfectly fine," Jayne said in a weak voice. She made a heroic effort and got a grip on her panic. These people had already paid to hear her. Even if she turned in a terrible performance, they weren't going to get their tuition back. Also, for possibly the first time in her life, it didn't matter if she had runs in her stockings or pimples the size of bottle caps.

She took a deep breath and approached the board again. "Okay, here's the deal. A composition is basically like a movie. You have your topic sentence." She slapped the

words with the chalk. "That's the preview of coming at-
tractions, otherwise known as the 'trailer.' You don't want to
give away too much in the trailer; you want to leave your
audience panting for more. Think *Broken Arrow*, one of the
best trailers of all time, fast action and music by White
Zombie. Does it get any better than that? I don't think so.
Or think *Dirty Rotten Scoundrels,* when Michael Caine all
at once reaches out and pushes Steve Martin off the dock.
That scene didn't even appear in the film. Was it a winner?
You bet. I'm talking Frank Oz here. I'm talking genius."

She began to feel more confident. She was on a roll. The
students were scribbling furiously.

"Then you have the rest of the composition. Once
you've sucked your audience in with a great trailer, the
rest pretty much writes itself. All you have to remember
is that you need to use a lot of participles and gerunds."
Again she tapped the board with the chalk. "And never
use a sentence fragment because that's like guaranteed
total box office poison."

The students looked at her with awe. Composition had
never been so interesting. Why hadn't someone told them
this stuff before?

"Any questions?"

A pasty-faced girl with a pierced nose who looked much
too smart for her own good raised her hand. "What's a
gerund?" she asked.

Jayne's mind suddenly froze. She had memorized that
term less than two hours ago. She knew she knew what it
meant. Gerund? Gerund? She was going to have to fake it.
"A gerund," she said, "is a small animal. Very cute. You
can buy them in the better pet stores. Unlike ferrets, they
aren't illegal in California, but I'm sure we all want to love
and protect them as we want to love and protect all of God's
animals." No, no! She shouldn't have said that! She was
supposed to be talking about composition, not animal
rights.

In front of her, the students were bent over their notebooks, taking notes at a mile a minute. My God, they hadn't noticed. Were they even listening to what she was saying? What would happen if she told them the earth was flat, chewing gum caused venereal disease, and Elvis was the first president of the United States? Would they just write it down?

She realized that one student in the back row was looking at her suspiciously. *Busted,* she thought.

The student rose slowly to his feet. "No!" he cried so loudly that several students uttered small screams and dropped their pens.

"Good morning," Jayne said brightly. "May I help you?" Whoops, that was a line from the Food Barn. She tried again. "Do you have a question . . . ?" Out of the corner of her eye, she noticed that the rest of the class was in motion. It was well past the middle of the semester, and knowing William Hestene well by now, they were scrambling for cover.

William's face turned bright red; he rocked back and forth as if he'd been caught in an earthquake without a bolted foundation. *"You* never read 'Fluffy'!" he yelled. "Fluffy" was a poem he had written about his dearly beloved cat. It went: "Fluffy is white/Fluffy is mine/Fluffy is dead." Every time he read it, he broke down at the word "dead" and started screaming. He had read it in class once, and Professor McLellan hadn't called security the way the other professors had. Instead, she had waited until he had finished, and then given him an A-, even though, strictly speaking, it wasn't a composition. That had been the moment he'd first known she loved him.

" 'Fluffy'?" Jayne had no idea what this student was upset about, but she knew she couldn't afford to lose control of the class so early in the game. Having never actually been in a college classroom before (she had always had private tutors), she fell back on the only form of discipline she knew.

"Sit!" she commanded. When she had delivered that line

in *My Heart Is in the Heather*, the beautifully trained Scottish wolfhound had obediently fallen to his haunches, but William Hestene was no wolfhound. He was a six-three, 350-pound man with the temperament of a pit bull.

He pointed his index finger at Jayne and jabbed at the air. "What have you done with Professor McLellan?" he demanded.

My God! He'd seen through her disguise! He knew!

"I'm on to you! You're an alien! You snatched Professor McLellan's body just like in that movie about the big green pods! You've got her in your basement, and you're performing sexual experiments on her!"

When most people were yelled at, they fell apart; Jayne, however, drove people crazy on a regular basis. Directors screamed at her. Producers screamed at her. Sometimes even makeup people cracked and screamed at her (even though they got fired so fast they didn't have time to pack up their powder puffs). Over the years, she had perfected a reaction that made all screaming stop. She turned to ice. Calm ice. Very dangerous ice.

She relaxed. This student was clearly crazy; so even though he was right about her not being Mary Lynn, no one was going to believe him. She decided to give him her sternest, coldest line: the one she had used in *Queen of Scots* just before she sent her own lover to the block.

" 'You have betrayed me and all of Scotland,' " she said. " 'Go now, my lord, and let me see you no more!' " As soon as she said the words, she realized they didn't sound like anything Mary Lynn would have come up with, but it was too late to backtrack. She wheeled around and confronted the rest of the class.

"Can anybody identify that quote?"

"Shakespeare?" said the pasty-faced girl with the nose ring.

"Right. It's from"—she thought fast—"*Romeo and Juliet,* with Claire Danes and Leonardo DiCaprio, one of the twenty-five top-grossing films of 1996."

The students dutifully wrote this down. Meanwhile, William Hestene had fallen silent. Jayne had been lucky. Anyone else would have wondered why the hell she was babbling on about Scotland and Shakespeare, but in William's world, everything she had just said made perfect sense.

Tears filled his eyes. "You don't love me anymore," he whispered. Suddenly he cracked and began to scream. "That's what always happens! The aliens come for everyone else, but they never come for *me!*" On the word "me," he bent down, seized his desk, and lifted it over his head.

Jayne whirled on him. "Don't you dare!" she snarled.

Jayne Cooper was more than a match for William Hestene any day. He froze, and then, with a bellow of despair, hurled the desk to the floor, and ran out of the room.

There was a stunned silence. Jayne cleared her throat. "Okay," she said briskly. "Where were we?"

The students resumed their seats. They looked like the survivors of a train crash.

"Oh, I remember. I was about to give you your next assignment." She consulted Mary Lynn's syllabus. "Today we're scheduled to have in-class writing. Everybody got pens and paper?"

The students nodded nervously, all except the girl with the nose ring who was sobbing convulsively. Not knowing what to do about the sobber, Jayne ignored her. Opening her purse, she extracted a sheet of paper that contained the essay assignments she had thought up while waiting for her suit to arrive. Should she ask them to write on the topic: "Would you want to date the president?" No. She'd go for the gold.

She cleared her throat and gave them her most professorial stare: "Write a two-page essay on your favorite female movie star."

The students seized their pens, bent over their notebooks, and began to write. Jayne stood for a moment watching them. Then she turned to the board, erased it thoroughly—

paying special attention to the word "gerund"—sat down at
the desk, opened *Protein Power*, and pretended to be absorbed in a recipe for meringue tart shells. From time to
time, she darted furtive glances at the students. How many
would pick her as their favorite star? She liked her popu-
larity polls to come out at 100 percent, but unfortunately,
even among eighteen-year-olds, there were always a few
clueless holdouts who thought "star" automatically meant
Julia Roberts.

Fourteen

Clarice walked into Jayne's dining room unannounced and found Mary Lynn seated at the table, picking at half a grapefruit and scowling at Jayne's cell phone, which lay belly-up in front of her like a turtle. It was nearly noon, but Mary Lynn was still wearing one of Jayne's nightgowns. Her hair looked as if she hadn't bothered to comb it; her eyes were red and swollen. Mary Lynn gave Clarice a grim nod and then jabbed at the cell phone with the tines of her fork. "I want a hammer," she said bitterly. "I want to smash this damn thing to bits."

"What's the problem?"

"Arnie."

"Don't tell me; let me guess: you slept with him last night and, so far this morning, he hasn't called you?"

"How did you know?"

Clarice sat down beside Mary Lynn and crossed her legs with a silken swishing sound. "I have my little ways." Today she had dressed in pale lavender right down to her amethyst bracelets. Amethysts were a love charm, but she decided Mary Lynn was in no mood to appreciate this. "Perhaps Jayne's cell phone's broken," she suggested.

"I thought of that hours ago, so I called Time. Since then, I've called the Weather Report; the Audubon Society; and Dial-A-Prayer. Do you realize that someone may have spotted a blue-footed booby on Catalina? The Audubon Society people are delirious with joy." Mary Lynn put down the fork. "He promised to call me this morning, damn it."

Clarice helped herself to an English muffin and spread a nice, thick smear of butter over one half. "Honey, they always promise."

"Arnie and I had such a great time the other night. I thought he—"

"Loved you?" Clarice prompted, taking a large bite of buttered muffin and washing it down with coffee. Mary Lynn had ordered a full breakfast. There was no use letting it go to waste.

"No, I wasn't to the love stage yet. I'm not that crazy. But I thought he at least liked me enough to call." She gave Clarice a suspicious look. "You don't, by any chance, have something to do with this, do you? For example, is there any possibility that you had Arnie deported back to the East Coast because you disapproved of Jayne being seen in public with him?"

"I plead innocent." Clarice took another bite of muffin. "I picked him for you, remember? Besides, Jayne can be seen in public with anyone she wants. Think Jennifer Lopez and Ojani Noa or Mel B and Jimmy Gulzar." She took another sip of coffee. "So, have you tried calling his hotel?"

"Repeatedly." Mary Lynn continued to look at Clarice with suspicion. "He doesn't answer. I just get voice mail. So I—"

"Hang up without leaving a message?"

"Exactly."

Clarice seized one of the napkins and wiped the butter off her lips with a dainty swoop that left her lipstick perfectly intact. Placing her purse on the table, she delved into it and brought up a small box wrapped in gold foil. She slapped the box down on the table in front of Mary Lynn. "Eat this," she commanded.

"What is it? More walnuts?" Mary Lynn laughed bitterly. "Great idea. Suicide by walnuts. I should have thought of that myself."

"It's emergency chocolate." Clarice opened the box and

pressed a chocolate-coated caramel into Mary Lynn's hand. "I carry it at all times. Lois told me you'd already eaten all of Jayne's stash, and chocolate is the only solution for what you're going through. Trust me. I've been there."

Mary Lynn inspected the chocolate warily. "Why are you being so supportive all of a sudden?"

Clarice shrugged. "There are several reasons, some of which I'm not quite ready to tell you. For the moment, let's just say that, as you pointed out, we have to work together. So instead of fighting you, I've decided to mother you. You look as if you could use some mothering. Plus, to be brutally honest, it's in my best interests to persuade you to snap out of this dark little mood you're in. I need you in shape to do the publicity for *Salome*. Here, eat."

Mary Lynn accepted the caramel, took a tentative nibble, then stuffed the entire piece into her mouth and went for more. "It's the story of my life," she said thickly between bites. "I meet a great man, we have fabulous sex, and then he goes into a Federal Witness Protection Program and I never hear from him again. You know what happened this morning? I got five dozen long-stemmed red roses. Lois brought them to me while I was brushing my teeth. I screamed with joy. I thought Arnie had sent them."

Clarice made a sympathetic clicking sound and buttered the other half of the muffin. "Let me guess. The roses were from Carleton Winters."

"Close." Mary Lynn stuffed a piece of chocolate into her mouth and munched on it glumly. "That teenage wife of his sent them along with a note that said: 'I hope you're feeling better.' Better? Oh yeah, I'm feeling just great, Darcy. Thanks."

"So, at this particular moment in time, you don't have any idea why Arnie hasn't called you?"

"No, except that all of Western literature tells me that when a man gets a woman into bed on the first date, he's going to lose interest in her. I feel like a total idiot. I knew I should have played hard to get, but I followed my heart."

"In other words, as we used to say in my day, you were 'easy.'"

"Easy? Let's put it this way: even Lady Chatterley held out longer than I did. And I'm not alone. I bet at this very moment there are thousands of us out there—women who followed their hearts and ended up crying into their grapefruits and trying to figure out if their cell phones have gone dead. You know, I think Hallmark should put out special sympathy cards for us. It's quite a niche market. They could call it their 'Slam-Bam-Thank-you-Ma'am' line."

Clarice finished her muffin and gave Mary Lynn's arm a reassuring pat. "You need to calm down, gather your forces, and steel yourself for the next stage."

"What next stage? Surely, it doesn't get any worse than this."

Clarice cleared her throat and developed a sudden interest in the tablecloth. "Oh yes, it does."

Mary Lynn froze with her hand poised over a caramel.

"Brace yourself, honey." Clarice produced a rolled-up newspaper from her purse and slid it in Mary Lynn's direction.

"What's this?"

"It's *Hollywood Comet,* one of the most popular daily tabloids in America. Circulation 2.2 million nosy idiots who don't have lives of their own. Take a deep breath, count to ten, and open it."

Ignoring her advice, Mary Lynn seized the paper, unrolled it, and gave a screech of horror. The headline read: COMET UNCOVERS THE NEW MAN IN JAYNE COOPER'S LIFE. Under it was a photo of Mary Lynn and Arnie walking on the beach with their arms around each other. Mary Lynn remembered the moment perfectly: just after dawn, reluctant to say good-bye, she and Arnie had taken another barefoot stroll in the surf and then bought cappuccinos at a little stand.

"Who in God's name took this!"

"Antonio Malfredi. His style's unmistakable. Malfredi is one of the paparazzi who follows Jayne around night and day.

We've gotten half a dozen restraining orders on him and had him arrested for trespassing and harassment more times than I can count; but he keeps coming after Jayne like Hannibal Lecter stalking a free lunch. Malfredi gets about ten thousand dollars for a candid photo like this one. He's taken pictures of Jayne from the air using Web cams attached to balloons; he invaded her twelfth birthday party disguised as a clown. He once caught her topless on her private beach in Belize; he's even gotten shots of her at night using infrared film. As much as I hate to admit it, it's my fault this happened. I knew Malfredi was out there; I should have warned you."

"Ten thousand dollars for a photo of two people walking on a beach! Why, that nasty, sneaking little creep . . ."

"Not just two people: Jayne Cooper and a *writer*. I said Jayne could date anyone she wanted without losing status; I didn't say it wasn't news. Everyone knows Jayne sleeps with sheikhs, dukes, heirs to thrones, billionaires, powerful political figures, and famous actors. On very rare occasions, she sleeps with a major director, but he has to be foreign, preferably Italian. So Malfredi catches you being intimate with an ordinary guy like Arnie, snaps this, and sells it to the *Comet* for enough money to replace the cameras Jayne's bodyguards are going to break the next time the little bastard tries to get within a hundred yards of her. It's like the time the Duchess of York got caught sucking her accountant's toes."

Mary Lynn picked up the last piece of chocolate, put it into her mouth, and stared at the photo. She no longer needed to wonder why Arnie hadn't called. The reason was sitting right in front of her.

"At least this Malfredi character didn't get a photo of us in bed."

"Think so?" Clarice flung open the newspaper and spread it out over Mary Lynn's plate. "Try page four."

Arnie was scheduled to show up at Global for a script conference, but he wasn't going to make it. He was on the run and had been ever since he stepped outside of his hotel and found a dozen photographers lying in wait for him. As he dashed down a side street and veered into a park, the paparazzi followed him, braying like a pack of hounds.

"Hey, Arnie," one yelled, "what was it like to sleep with Jayne Cooper?"

"Go away!" Arnie begged. He sprinted around a swing set, took a wrong turn, and found himself backed up against a brick wall. The paparazzi closed in, snapping photos.

"How'd you get to be the secret man in Jayne Cooper's life, Arnie?"

"Are you going to get a development deal at Global?"

"I hear you slugged Edward Surrey when you found him in bed with her. Care to comment?"

Arnie put his hands in front of his face. "Go away!" he pleaded.

"Did you have to fake an orgasm, Arnie? Or did you really have a good time?"

Arnie took his hands away from his face and found himself staring at a short, dark-haired man with a pocked face.

"Who the hell are you?"

"Antonio Malfredi. Jayne and I go way back. Talk to me, Arnie. Tell me what she looks like when she comes."

"You schmuck!" Arnie advanced on Malfredi with his fists clenched.

"Hit me," Malfredi taunted. "Break my camera, Arnie, and I'll sell the story for a hundred thousand. Does she quiver? Does she moan?"

Arnie slugged him hard. As Malfredi went down, the rest of the paparazzi closed in, their cameras clicking like demented crickets.

Mary Lynn was spread out on Jayne's bed, staring blankly at the wall. "Arnie was the nicest guy I ever met. I knew someday after this was all over, I was going to have to admit to him that I wasn't Jayne, but I had this fantasy that he'd understand and we'd keep seeing each other. I was sure he liked me, the real me."

"Try to pull yourself together." Clarice couldn't help but think that the conversation she was having with Mary Lynn was eerily like a hundred similar conversations she'd had with Jayne. The only things lacking were a wardrobe trailer, a director, and a bunch of extras waiting for the cameras to roll.

"Why?" Mary Lynn said. "What's the point? All I've got ahead of me is a future filled with Wendells."

"You've got to do publicity for *Salome* in less than an hour."

"No way. I can't face people who've seen photos of me having sex."

"It's not like you've been on the Playboy Channel. The editor of the *Comet* had the decency to make Malfredi Photoshop out the details. It was all"—Clarice made a dismissive motion—"very fuzzy."

"Fuzzy! Two million people now know that my belly button goes in instead of out."

"Granted. But nevertheless . . ."

"How does Jayne live in this fishbowl?"

"Short attention span."

Mary Lynn made a grumbling sound and turned to face the wall. Judging from her experiences with Jayne, Clarice decided it was time to take things in hand. She sat down on the edge of the bed and began to give Mary Lynn a back rub mixed with a little shiatsu. Back rubs always cheered Jayne up.

"I'm being perfectly serious." Clarice pressed her thumbs into Mary Lynn's shoulders to relieve some of the stress. "You see, honey, what you don't realize is that Jayne's fans all have the attention spans of mayflies. Their short-term memories are bulk erased weekly. Six months from now, unless *Comet* runs another front-page story, no one will remember your romp with Arnie Levine. And even if they do, you won't have to live with the scandal. Remember, you're going back to your own life. You're going to be Professor McLellan again. And Jayne won't care, I promise. We'll just claim those photos of you and Arnie having sex were faked. Maybe we'll even sue the *Comet*. Jayne always enjoys suing the *Comet*. It's one of her hobbies."

Mary Lynn took a deep breath and relaxed a little. "I see your point. I'm not Jayne. . . ."

"No."

"And although it's probably too late for me to patch things up with Arnie, the public is going to forget about those photos, so I won't have to wear a scarlet letter for the rest of my life."

"I can guarantee it."

"How can you be so sure?"

Clarice kneaded the tension out of Mary Lynn's shoulders and then moved on to her neck. "If I tell you, do you promise to get up, take a shower, put on your makeup, and go out there and do the publicity for *Salome*?"

Mary Lynn made a noise that Clarice decided to interpret as a yes.

"Fine, then. It's true-confession time." Clarice cleared her throat. "Over thirty years ago, I was involved in a scandal. You see, when I met Max Korngold, he was married." Clarice began to work her way down Mary Lynn's spine, gently pushing her vertebrae into alignment. "Never mind that Max and his wife had been separated for three years and hadn't slept together for ten. I was young, I was pretty, and I was an aspiring star with a couple of good roles to her credit."

She reached the small of Mary Lynn's back and began to work her way up again. Mary Lynn gave a small contented sigh. "When Max started appearing in public with me, the gossip columnists labeled me a home wrecker. In those days, that's what they called a woman who took up with a married man."

"That sounds nasty."

Encouraged by the fact that Mary Lynn seemed interested, Clarice continued. "It got a lot worse."

Mary Lynn rolled over and sat up. "How?"

"They dug up things about my past."

"You had things to hide?"

Clarice shook her hands to remove the stress she'd accumulated. Then she extracted her compact from her purse and reapplied her lipstick. "Honey, we all have things to hide." She paused and contemplated herself in the mirror. "You hear this lovely southern accent of mine? This upper-class Tidewater Virginia drawl?"

Mary Lynn nodded.

Clarice snapped her compact closed. "Well, it's all fake. I learned to talk like this the way people learn to speak French or German. I had to, because at the start of my career, the studio had put out the story that I was from an old southern family. Supposedly, my parents had an estate bigger than Tara before they were killed in a tragic plane crash when I was fifteen. The truth is, I was born in a shack in a little shit hole of a town called Obediah, West Virginia. My daddy was a coal miner, who died of black lung when I was five; my mama worked as a waitress in a local diner. For the first sixteen years of my life, I never had a new dress or a pair of shoes that hadn't belonged to one of my older sisters."

"So when you started going out with Max, the tabloids dug all that up?" Mary Lynn had started to show real interest. She brushed her hair out of her eyes and a little color drifted into her cheeks.

"That and more. The *National Enquirer* found out that I had gotten to California by hitchhiking across country. *Confidential* tracked down a long-haul trucker who claimed I'd traded sex for rides—which was a lie. Then they came up with the owner of a club in Houston who swore I'd worked for six weeks as a stripper under the name 'Bubbles Galore.' The Bubbles story was true, but fortunately the club owner backed off and denied everything when he realized that I'd been underage."

"Bubbles Galore?" For the first time in hours, Mary Lynn smiled.

"I had a great ass in those days, if I do say so myself, and

I've always had a superb sense of showmanship." Clarice held up her compact. "I used to take out a great big fluffy purple powder puff and let the cowboys dust my bottom. Bubbles, needless to say, was a big hit. Those cowboys stuck so many twenties in my G-string that I was able to show up in L.A. looking like my rich daddy had given me a charge card for Christmas."

"And now no one remembers?"

"Oh, probably someone remembers, but not even the *Hollywood Comet* thinks the story's worth rehashing."

"So how did Max react to all this?"

"Max was a gentleman. He pretended not to notice. He loved me, and he didn't care what other people said about me." Clarice looked thoughtful. "Of course, he did give me a great big purple powder puff for my twenty-first birthday, but that's another story. In any case, if you ask me, that's the way Arnie should react. He should have a sense of humor about this whole thing. If he lets that spread in the *Comet* scare him off, he's not man enough for you."

She took Mary Lynn by the hands and gently tugged her to her feet. "Come on, honey. It's time to get up, get your makeup on, and quit fretting. Arnie will either call you or he won't. Take it from me, there are a lot of men in the world who'd hold up liquor stores and steal TV sets just to get next to a girl as good-looking as you. Plus, as my mama always used to say: 'If a man can't take the heat, you don't want him stokin' your stove.' "

Half an hour later, just as Clarice was applying the last of the makeup that transformed Mary Lynn into Jayne, the phone rang. Mary Lynn jumped for it so fast she knocked over the chair she'd been sitting in.

"Hello?" she said. "Hello, Arnie? Is that you?" She stood frozen in place waiting for him to answer for a full three seconds before she realized that there was nothing on the other end of the line but a dial tone.

On the other side of the room, Clarice was talking into

her pink Nokia. Gradually it dawned on Mary Lynn that it was Clarice's phone that had rung.

"When?" Clarice asked. There was a long pause. "Of course. Of course, Jayne will pay all the expenses. Tell Carl we're delighted the studio has decided to spin it this way. Yes, I agree. It's brilliant. Humanizes her." Clarice hung up and stared at the phone with an odd expression.

"What was all that about?" Mary Lynn asked.

Clarice stopped staring at the phone and stowed it away in her purse with a decisive motion that set the amethysts in her bracelets knocking together. "I have some good news for you, honey: Arnie wants to call you, but his lawyers don't think it's a good idea right now."

"His lawyers?"

"Actually, they're the studio's lawyers. That was Ray Hester on the phone, head of Global's publicity department. The whole studio is in crisis mode. It seems Arnie got himself arrested for assault this morning. The judge is going to set his bail in about an hour. After that, Global will chauffeur him over here so you and he can have a little talk."

"Arnie got arrested!"

Clarice righted Mary Lynn's chair, sat down on it, and crossed her legs. "This could be fabulous."

"Clarice, you're not making any sense! How can Arnie being arrested be 'fabulous'?"

"The man he assaulted was Antonio Malfredi. There are a dozen witnesses who say Malfredi was making obscene comments about you when Arnie decked him. Don't you see: an ordinary guy defends Jayne Cooper's honor from a slimeball photographer who has a long history of harassing her. Jayne pays the ordinary guy's bail; she tells the world that she'll stand by him during the trial, which will never happen because Global will buy Malfredi off. Jayne publicly declares her gratitude to Arnie and says something about how glad she is that there's at least one man left in America who can act like a gentleman; then she makes an impassioned plea for more laws guaranteeing celebrities privacy. Every word she says is perfect, because the Global publicity spin team writes the script. Which is a good thing for you, because you'll be the one actually delivering her lines.

"Result: Jayne's fans eat up every little detail and flock to *Salome,* which makes millions. Jayne becomes the most bankable star since Elizabeth Taylor, and I buy that darling little island off the shore of Greece that I've had my eye on. And you"—Clarice smiled at Mary Lynn benevolently— "take home a nice bonus."

Mary Lynn moaned. "This is a complete nightmare. Arnie and I never had a chance."

Clarice's smile froze. "Before you make that dreary sound again, Professor McLellan, you might try to remember that *Notting Hill*, a film based on more or less the same plot, grossed nearly seventy-two million dollars the first month it was released."

Fifteen

About the time Mary Lynn had been calling Dial-A-Prayer, Jayne had been sound asleep under a delicate mobile that danced and turned above her like a miniature rainbow. Jayne had found the mobile hanging on the doorknob when she returned from teaching what she was convinced would soon become the most popular composition class ever offered at Coast Side Community College. Along with the mobile, Joe had left a note containing his phone number and an invitation for her to give him a call if she had any more problems with her garbage disposal.

Jayne had been pleased with the mobile. Besides being a cute little thing, it was definitely a work of art; plus, it did not escape her that Joe had made the pieces cornflower blue to match her eyes. She had immediately hung it over her bed with a piece of Mary Lynn's sewing thread so it would be the first thing she noticed when she woke up in the morning. Instead, she woke to the sound of a ringing phone.

Snapping bolt upright, she scattered the cats in all directions and grabbed the receiver. "Who is it?" she snarled. She hated to be called in the mornings. Whenever someone woke her up by accident, heads rolled.

"Hi," a male voice said.

"Who the hell is this?"

"It's Wayne."

"Who the hell is Wayne?"

There was a puzzled silence on the other end of the line.

"I'm trying to call my sister, Mary Lynn McLellan. Do I have a wrong number?"

Sister. Wayne. Suddenly Jayne snapped into waking reality. In the confusion of being jerked out of a perfectly lovely dream, she had forgotten who she was supposed to be.

"No, Wayne. It's me, Mary Lynn. You called the right number." Jayne glanced at the clock. "Do you know what time it is?"

"It's nine."

"No, it's six. Six in the morning, California time, Wayne. What the fuck are you doing calling me at six in the morning?"

"Are you okay?"

"Sure, I'm okay. I'm thrilled, Wayne. I'm dancing across my bedroom naked, tossing flowers at the cats, and singing 'Oh, What a Beautiful Morning.'"

"You sound drunk, sis. Sober up. You have to drive to Bakersfield this morning. Mom's car broke down and Dad won't take her to her acupuncture appointment."

Jayne gripped the receiver and her face took on an expression that sent the cats fleeing into the other room. "Let our dear old mom rent a car, Wayne. Or better yet, since she's screwing her acupuncturist, let him come to *her.*"

He started to protest, but she cut him off. "And don't ever call me this early again, or I'll personally hire two guys I know in Jersey to take you for a drive and recycle you as toxic waste." Jayne had never acted in a movie about the mob, but she was a devoted fan of *The Sopranos*. *"Capisce?"*

There was a gasping noise on the other end of the line. Wayne sounded as if he were choking, a prospect Jayne greeted with grim satisfaction. She slammed down the receiver, stared at the phone for a minute, then picked it up again and dialed her own wake-up service. Mary Lynn had caller ID; there was no use letting it go to waste.

"Sammy, I want you to call me every night for the next two weeks at the following number sometime around midnight." She read him Wayne's number.

"But two-one-two is a Manhattan area code, Miss Cooper. Are you sure you want to do this? It's going to be three A.M. there."

"Do it. Put it on one of those automatic machines that calls back six times if it gets a hang-up." She reached for a cigarette, lit it, and sat for a moment thinking, while Sammy waited patiently. No one ever ended a call with Jayne Cooper until she decided it was over. "I've changed my mind. Don't call at three A.M. eastern time. Program the computer so the calls are spread between two and five in the morning, including weekends. And don't call every night for two weeks. Call twice a week for two months, and vary the days." There was no use letting Wayne think he could escape by simply unplugging his phones.

She put out her cigarette, drew the covers up over her head, and fell back to sleep until nine A.M. when the phone rang again.

"Who the fuck is this!" This time she was not merely angry. Two unscheduled wake-ups turned her into a dangerous beast.

"Good heavens," a shocked female voice said. "This is Rana Dowd. I was calling Professor McLellan, but obviously I have the wrong number."

Whoops, Jayne thought. She recognized the name as that of the secretary of the English department. Slamming down the receiver, she sat up, lit another cigarette, and started counting. On ten the phone rang again.

"Good morning," she said sweetly.

"Oh, good morning, Professor McLellan. This is Rana Dowd."

"And how are you this lovely morning, Rana?" Jayne's voice was so cheerful it almost made her sick. She took another puff on her cigarette and reminded herself that she didn't have to smile since the woman couldn't see her face.

"I'm fine, Professor McLellan, but I was a little worried about you." For a moment, Jayne was puzzled. Then she remembered the brain tumor. Evidently, she had forgotten to call Rana and tell her that the "tests" had come back negative.

"False alarm," she said, blowing a smoke ring at the alarm clock. "I'm in perfect health."

"Oh, good." Jayne noted with interest that Rana actually sounded relieved. "When you didn't pick up your paycheck yesterday, I thought—"

"I have a paycheck?"

"Of course."

"Where?"

"Why, in your mailbox."

Jayne had never had an actual paycheck before, at least not one she'd seen. When you got millions of dollars per film, the funds were transferred electronically. "Hang on to it," she said. She jumped out of bed and grabbed Mary Lynn's robe. "I'll be right over."

Jayne's enthusiasm about receiving her first real paycheck lasted until she opened the envelope. She was standing in the miserable little closet that passed for the English department mail room, surrounded by small cubbyholes that looked as if they might have once housed rats. To her right, Rana was laboring away on a computer so old it looked as if it had been picked up from a recycling dump. Rana was somewhere in her mid-thirties, tiny, and dark-haired, with a patient, long-suffering smile that didn't crack when harried professors popped their heads in the door and demanded things in loud, panicked voices. She was the kind of woman who put calendars of puppies on the wall, and would have been very pretty if she hadn't been one of the many contenders in what appeared to be the ongoing Coast Side Community College Disastrously Dressed Contest.

Jayne bore down on her, waving her paycheck. "This has to be wrong." She tossed the check on Rana's desk. "Look."

Rana picked up the check, examined it, and gave Jayne a rerun of the long-suffering smile. "It looks okay to me, Professor McLellan." She pointed to the signature. "Your pay rate is the same as the rate for all the other part-time faculty; the State Controller of California signed it, so it's good."

"Good isn't the problem." Jayne pulled out a cigarette and started to light it; then she saw the look of horror on Rana's face and remembered that the entire university was a smoke-free zone. "The problem is that it's ridiculously small. Look at how much was taken out for federal and state taxes. And what the hell is 'Soc Sec'?"

Rana gave her a puzzled look. "That's Social Security."

Jayne ran her fingernail down the list. "Dues?"

"Those are your union dues."

"I belong to a union?"

"Yes."

"What do I get for it? I don't see any benefits here."

"Well, like I said, you aren't full-time, Professor McLellan. Only full-time faculty get health care, vision care, dental, things like that."

Jayne's eyes narrowed dangerously. "Interesting." She jabbed at another incomprehensible combination of letters. "And C-H-T-B-L C-N-T-R-B, what's that? The cable charges for my TV? No, of course not. I, Mary Lynn McLellan, obviously can't afford cable."

"That's your charitable contribution, Professor McLellan."

"I make this pathetic salary and I still give some of it away? What the hell am I thinking of? I should be *getting* charity."

Rana had fallen silent, but Jayne didn't notice. She was angry, and when she got angry, someone paid. "Where's the boss's office?"

"Boss?"

"You know. The whatchamacallit? The chair guy?"

"Dr. Whitney's office is right where it's always been," Rana said gently. She pointed to the door across the hallway. On it was a large sign: NELSON C. WHITNEY, ENGLISH DEPARTMENT CHAIR. Poor Professor McLellan was clearly losing it. She couldn't remember anything. The story about the brain tumor must be true after all.

Jayne snatched up her paycheck and started toward Whitney's door.

"You can't go in there!" Rana cried. "Dr. Whitney is writing a speech that he's scheduled to present to the Renaissance Society."

"Well, then, this is his lucky day. After he gives me a raise, I can tell him all the dirt on Leonardo da Vinci." And with that, Jayne strode across the hall, threw open Whitney's door, barged in, and kicked it closed behind her.

The chair's office was a lot larger than the mail room. There was a hideous green carpet on the floor, a couple of thousand books, and a large gunmetal-colored desk. At the desk, half buried in a pile of papers, a potbellied man in a short-sleeved white shirt and bolo tie was enjoying a mid-morning nap.

"Wake up!" Jayne yelled.

Nelson Whitney, Chair of the Coast Side English Department, opened his eyes and stared at Jayne in confusion. He vaguely recalled that the woman standing in front of him was a member of the part-time faculty. He fumbled for a name. "Ms. McLellan?"

Jayne lunged forward and stuck her paycheck in his face. "Look at this!"

Whitney went pale and suppressed an urge to bolt for cover. Last year a depressed food service employee had climbed onto the roof of the library and refused to come down for three hours. The man hadn't had a weapon, but no one had known that for sure, and the SWAT team had nearly shot him before a police negotiator had persuaded him to surrender. Because of this incident, every department chair in the college had been forced to take five weeks of training in "How to Deal with Workplace Violence." Whitney had emerged from these classes hoping to God that he would retire before he encountered a dangerous nutcase. Evidently, that was not to be his fate.

Very, very slowly, he sat up and reached for his glasses. *Make no sudden moves,* the violence management instructor had warned. Very slowly, he put on his glasses and stared at the strip of paper McLellan was holding two inches from his nose.

"What appears to be the problem?" he said. This was it; McLellan had snapped. He remembered the professor at Stanford who had been hammered to death by a graduate student for criticizing the student's shoes. Had he ever said anything unkind to this woman? For that matter, had he ever spoken to her since the day he hired her?

"The problem is that you aren't paying me enough to live on. In fact, it seems you aren't paying any of your part-time people enough." Her face was only inches from his, and she had a look in her eyes Whitney had never seen before in the eyes of any of his part-time faculty. It was the look of a woman used to getting her own way.

He cleared his throat. "I appreciate your concerns," he said. *No matter what your real feeling is, always appear to be sympathetic and helpful. The point is to convince the potentially dangerous employee that you are on his or her side.* "Let's make an appointment to discuss your salary, and I'll see what I can do." *Stall. Try to get the employee to leave the room so you can summon help.* He smiled benevolently. What he really was thinking was: *Help! I've got a crazy woman in here!*

Jayne knew bad acting when she saw it. Whitney was so unconvincing he couldn't have gotten a job narrating an instructional film about athlete's foot. "Raise my salary now," she said.

"I'd love to, but . . ."

"You can't?"

"Not at the moment. But perhaps if we were to meet later and discuss your situation . . ."

"Fine," Jayne said softly. "You want to play games? Then we'll play games. Tag!" She reached up, grabbed her blouse, and tore it open, exposing her bra. "You're It!"

"Ms. McLellan!"

"Help!" Jayne screamed. She threw herself at Whitney and

pressed her lips to his, smearing her lipstick and leaving a big red blotch on his mouth. "Help! Rape! Somebody help me!"

The door crashed open. Rana had come, just as Jayne had known she would. With her were two young men dressed in blue jeans who were probably students. Jayne saw all of this with perfect calm despite the fact that she appeared to be hysterical. She had never really been a method actress; when the occasion demanded she could easily separate herself from a role.

Sobbing, she fell into Rana's arms. "He—he tried to—" She broke off as if filled with horror and stared at Whitney with big, lovely, frightened eyes. "He—he wanted to . . ." It was a stunning performance. She was so vulnerable, so upset, so clearly the injured party.

Vanda and Arisa had taught Jayne about sexual harassment (or "hairassment" as Vanda had termed it) on the afternoon she lost her job at the Food Barn. Jayne had always been a fast study. She figured a harassment suit could cost the university hundreds of thousands of dollars. Particularly when there were witnesses. Particularly when the harasser was the boss of the department. She pressed her face into Rana's shoulder and sobbed harder.

"Whoa," exclaimed one of the students. "This is so totally whack." He looked at Jayne's open blouse and turned red from the tip of his nose to the tips of his ears.

Jayne gave the boy a tearful smile, which nearly fried his brains. Then she turned to Whitney. "I'd like to think this was all a horrible misunderstanding, but . . ." There was a little catch in her voice. She was utterly credible.

An hour later, Jayne emerged from the English building in one of those delightful moods that always came over her when she had successfully trampled all opposition into the dust. She had discovered many interesting things during those sixty minutes, including the fact that every department chair at Coast Side had a discretionary fund composed of California Lottery money that was earmarked for "faculty development." Prior to his encounter with Jayne, Dr.

Whitney had erroneously interpreted this to mean "full-time faculty."

After their little conversation, he had realized that part-time faculty were the ones who most needed "development." As a result, Mary Lynn and every other part-time instructor in the English department had immediately been given a three-hundred-dollar bonus. In her purse, Jayne also had a private note from Whitney promising that in return for forgetting their "misfortunate misunderstanding," he would personally work to see that part-time faculty salaries were increased.

All in all, Jayne was very satisfied with the way she was reorganizing Mary Lynn's life. As she drove away from the college, she wondered if she should try writing her own scripts. The world of ordinary people was remarkably inspiring.

Sixteen

"Bert is a marvelous director. Words can't express what a marvelous experience it was to work with Bert on *Salome*. Bert was simply marvelous."

All afternoon Mary Lynn had repeated the word "marvelous" like a parrot. In Jayne's living room, the studio had set up two video cameras, one that faced Mary Lynn and one that faced whoever was interviewing her. Forty-eight television reporters had responded to Global's invitation. They had been given five minutes apiece to ask about *Salome*, and so far, forty-seven of them had asked exactly the same questions. Every seven minutes a new interviewer was herded into the room, and the old one was herded out. Before she left, each female reporter was given three videocassette copies of the interview, a press kit, and a filmy black scarf that bore the logo SALOME. Male reporters got the press kit and the videocassettes, but instead of one of Salome's seven veils, Global gave them oversize black T-shirts.

Forty-seven times in less than six hours, Mary Lynn swore that *Salome* was a marvelous film filled with marvelous scenes and marvelous dialogue. The crew was marvelous; the host country—a godforsaken hellhole that seethed with snakes and scorpions—was marvelous. She'd had a marvelous time in heat measuring 120 degrees. The camels hadn't spit or stunk or tried to trample anyone to death. In fact, the dear things had been simply marvelous.

If Global's canned promo speech had been a composition, she would have taken a red pencil to it. "Word variety!" she would have written in the margins. "Increase your vocabulary! Please go to the Tutoring Center and get some help!" Not to mention that if she'd been in an ordinary state of mind, she would have vomited after the tenth "marvelous" and refused to go on. But she wasn't in an ordinary state of mind. All she could think of as she sat under the hot lights smiling like a demented Cheshire Cat were those photos of her and Arnie. The interviewers—who had obviously been warned to stay off the subject—were pretending they had never heard of the *Hollywood Comet*, but Mary Lynn could feel them undressing her.

"So, Miss Cooper, what do you think of the work of Elizabeth Taylor?"

"Miss Taylor is one of my idols. She's simply marvelous." *Blouse. Skirt.*

"Do you think *Salome* will revive the biblical epic?"

"Oh yes. Biblical epics are marvelous."

Bra. Panties.

"The studio says this role was written specifically for you."

"Yes. The writers gave me marvelous lines."

Mercifully, this nightmarish publicity junket was coming to an end. Interviewer number forty-eight, a brisk young woman whose name had slipped out of Mary Lynn's mind like a wet Gummi Bear, leaned forward and gave Mary Lynn a probing look. "How did you *really* feel about playing Salome?"

"Simply marvelous."

"How did you feel about the fact that John the Baptist was Jesus' cousin?"

Mary Lynn stared at the reporter blankly. None of the other reporters had asked this question. It must not be on Global's approved list. "Marvelous?" she said tentatively.

"You felt marvelous about getting an innocent man beheaded? A saint? A man whom millions of Catholics around the world pray to. . . ."

Clarice, who had been sitting silently beside Mary Lynn all afternoon just out of camera range, abruptly rose to her feet. "Thank you so much, Ms. Chalmers. I'm sure Miss Cooper has had a simply . . ."

" . . . marvelous . . ." Mary Lynn supplied.

". . . time chatting with you about her latest film. But I'm afraid she's tiring, and she still has a long day ahead of her."

The woman stood and offered Mary Lynn her hand. "Thank you, Miss Cooper." She started toward the door. Then, apparently deciding she had nothing to lose, she turned around.

"Miss Cooper, is it true that you and Arnie Levine—"

"Out!" Clarice snarled.

The reporter's mouth snapped shut as if it were on springs. Clutching her press kit, she turned and fled without looking back.

Clarice walked up to the cameramen. "Give me those tapes."

The men pulled the cassettes out of the cameras and handed them to her without a word. Clarice stripped the tapes out of the cassettes, pulled out a tiny pair of silver nail scissors, and cut them free.

"I'm shredding these." She handed the empty cassettes back to the men. "You didn't see this; you didn't hear this. Remember that and you'll spend the rest of your career in L.A. working for Global. You mention what just happened to anyone—your bosses, your union shop steward, your girlfriends—and you'll both get reassigned to South America to tape documentaries on dengue, cholera, and Bolivian hemorrhagic fever." Clarice turned to the rest of the publicity team. "That goes for all of you. Not a word of what just happened goes outside these walls. You get my drift, ladies and gentlemen?"

They all nodded.

"Good," Clarice said. "Now, everyone, get out."

Clarice waited until the lights had been taken down and the last of the publicity team had left. When she heard

Jayne's front door slam for the final time, she sat down on the couch, kicked off her high heels, leaned back, and began to massage her feet. After a while, she looked up and noticed that Mary Lynn was still sitting bolt upright.

"You can relax now, honey. That was a close call, but you handled it like a pro. Jayne herself couldn't have done better. So how do you feel?"

"Marvelous, of course." Mary Lynn poured herself a glass of ice water and chugged it. She felt hot, sweaty, anxious, and exhausted, which was no doubt how Jayne felt most of the time. No wonder Jayne was sometimes hard to get along with. She had been at this sort of thing since she was a kid.

She wondered what the Global publicity department had said to forty-eight interviewers that had made forty-seven of them steer clear of the subject of Arnie. Should she ask Clarice? No, better *not* to know, just in case Ms. Chalmers turned up floating facedown in the harbor. Refilling the glass with ice water, she dipped a tissue in it and dabbed at her wrists.

Clarice retrieved her shoes and stood up. "It's time for me to start making sure that someone puts Ms. Chalmers on the next plane to Outer Mongolia. You might want to freshen up a little. By my calculations, Global's legal team will be springing Arnie out of jail in less than half an hour. After that, he'll be coming over here for that little chat we talked about."

"How can I face Arnie? What am I going to say to him?"

Clarice stuffed the crumpled videotapes into her purse and started toward the door. "Just follow your heart. Say what needs to be said." She paused and looked thoughtful. "But whatever you do, honey, don't tell him the truth."

After Clarice left, Mary Lynn called Lois and told her to let Arnie in as soon as he arrived. Then, carefully protecting her hair with one of Jayne's fancy French shower caps, she took a cool bath in the big marble tub and changed into a simple white T-shirt and a pair of tastefully ripped designer jeans. Pouring herself a glass of wine, she settled back to worry. She hadn't been at it long when the cell phone rang.

"Hi," Jayne said with near-pathological cheerfulness. "I have some wonderful news for you. I convinced your department chair to give you a three-hundred-dollar bonus."

"Great," Mary Lynn said in a tone of voice usually reserved for speaking of the dead.

"Try saying 'thank you.'" There was a small sucking sound as Jayne inhaled cigarette smoke. "I thought you'd be thrilled. Or have you spent so much time living my life that three hundred dollars sounds like chump change? Let me tell you, it doesn't sound like an insignificant sum to me at the moment. I've been having a serious cash-flow problem since I canceled my credit cards. Right now, there's nothing in your kitchen cabinet except a bottle of tarragon vinegar, a box of stale Triscuits, and three cans of Food Barn tuna that I'm saving for the cats. All this, despite the fact that I was able to forge your signature on the back of both checks. I was even able to deposit them in your bank account by means I'd rather not go into, except to say that it involved a male teller and a very short skirt. So, imagine my surprise when I tried to withdraw the funds and found that the bank had put a three-day hold on them."

Jayne made the sucking sound again. "They'd only let me take out twenty dollars. Frankly, I'm starting to suspect that your credit rating must fall somewhere below Argentina's. Don't you ever pay your bills on time?"

Mary Lynn stared at the phone glumly and took a sip of wine. "I take it you haven't seen today's issue of the *Hollywood Comet*."

"No. Like I said, I've had to feed and clothe myself using the change I pilfered from your piggy bank. I can't even afford a copy of *Variety*. I'm totally isolated here. It's like *Survivor,* with a cast of one. So tell me: what has the *Comet* come up with this time?"

Mary Lynn told her, and to her surprise, Jayne reacted

with what sounded like real sympathy. "Sex! They published photos of you having sex!"

"Yes." Mary Lynn felt somewhat comforted by Jayne's reaction. "The only good thing about it was that they Photoshopped in some shadows. You couldn't exactly *see* what Arnie and I were doing. Except for the lack of a referee, I suppose we could have been wrestling."

"How did my ass look?"

"Your ass!"

"Well, technically it's your ass, but everyone is going to think it's mine. I mean, it didn't appear to sag or anything, did it?"

"No," Mary Lynn said grimly. "It didn't."

"You should have pulled the curtains."

"I realize that now, but it's no longer relevant. It's all asses under the bridge." Mary Lynn drained her glass and reached for the bottle.

"Malfredi's stalked me for so long I don't even go to the bathroom to powder my nose without checking for his shoes under the stalls."

"Thanks. I'll keep that in mind."

"I suppose you think I'm being unsympathetic."

"It has crossed my mind."

"I keep forgetting you're not used to this. I've never known privacy. Everything I've ever done has been done in public. Once, when I was five, I wet my pants on the set of *My Familia*. Five is pretty old to wet your pants in public under even the best of circumstances. The photo of me crying made the front page of one of the tabloids." Jayne paused. "Look, if all this is driving you completely crazy, I can come back."

"Come back where?"

"Back home. We can call the whole thing quits. I've only been living your life a few days, but I already know things I'd have never learned in a million years any other way. Like, for example, did you know that without cable you only get eleven channels, two of which are in Spanish? Or that rat poison in your local Korean market comes in four pleasant scents, including pine and tutti-frutti? Information like that is priceless; but I've gotten most of what I need to audition for Spielberg, not to mention that I'm tired of wearing panty hose that comes in plastic eggs."

"Are you serious?"

"Totally."

"And you'd still pay me?"

"Of course."

Mary Lynn was seriously tempted. A few words spoken now and she'd be able to return to her old life with a hundred thousand dollars in her pocket. The only catch was that she'd probably never see Arnie again.

"Are you still there?"

"I'm still here."

"So what's your decision?"

"What do you want to do, Jayne?"

"Personally, I'm in no hurry to wrap this up. Despite the hideous hardships of your life, I'm having a fascinating time. Besides, the cats have bonded with me, and I'd hate to traumatize them by vanishing before their toys arrive."

"Their toys?"

"It's a long story. So which is it: do you want to go or stay?"

Mary Lynn closed her eyes and took a deep breath. "Stay." She couldn't leave before she worked things out with Arnie. She owed him that for getting him on the front page of the *Comet*. Maybe if she told him who she really was, there'd be something left between them. On the other hand, if she told Arnie the truth, Jayne would probably sue her for breach of contract. Was being honest with Arnie worth a hundred thousand dollars? Who the hell knew? They'd only slept together once. If he had only been interested in her because he thought she was Jayne, that was going to be the world's most expensive blind date.

"I admire you for hanging tough," Jayne said. "Call me crazy, but I'm even starting to trust you. It's a heady experience. I've never trusted anyone but my mother before, and sometimes I'm not even sure about her."

Mary Lynn put down the wineglass and stared at it glumly. She felt about as guilty as she'd ever felt in her life. "Thanks."

"No problem," Jayne said, and hung up.

Thirty seconds later, she called back.

"I forgot to ask you if you know anyone who drives a white car."

"I know a lot of people who drive white cars." Mary Lynn reached for the wine again and decided against it. It wouldn't do to be drunk when Arnie arrived. "Could you be more specific? What make is it?"

"I haven't the slightest idea. The only kind of vehicle I recognize with any reliability is a Jaguar. Anyway, I have the distinct impression that a white car has been following me. Every time I look in the rearview mirror, it's there."

"There are millions of people in California with white cars, Jayne. It's the most common color. Are you sure these aren't different cars you're seeing?"

"You're right. I'm probably just being paranoid. Like I told you, I've been stalked my whole life. But since we're on the subject of paranoia, let me pass something else by you: do you happen to know anyone who looks like a serial killer?"

"A what?"

"A serial killer. You know: one of those tall, thin, blond, baby-faced guys who commit ghastly murders. The kind who chops old ladies up and stores them in his freezer; the kind the neighbors always swear was 'such a nice, quiet boy.'"

"Not offhand. Why do you ask?"

"Because a guy like that showed up at your front door this afternoon. I'd ordered a pizza by phone—a wonderful, nearly transcendental experience involving a request for anchovies and extra mushrooms—when your doorbell rang. Of course I answered it with a few pathetic bills clutched in my hand, and there they were."

"They?"

"The serial killer and his girlfriend."

"Oh no!"

" 'Oh no' what?"

"What did the woman look like?"

There was a brief silence while Jayne considered this. "She was—how shall I put it?—beautiful in a hideous early-twenty-something sort of way. She had good hair: wavy, brown, and lots of it. But her eyes were too close together, and she had the kind of chin that only gets you bit parts."

"Was she in great shape? Really buffed-out? And was the guy with her really sensitive-looking?"

"If you mean by 'sensitive' that he looked like he'd never held down a steady job, I'd have to say yes."

"It must have been my ex-husband, Ron, and his girlfriend. My God, don't tell me you didn't recognize him!"

"How could I recognize him? The only photos in this apartment are of your cats." Jayne paused. "Actually, I did find an album of what I presume to be your wedding pictures, but that was no help because the groom looked exactly like Keanu Reeves."

Mary Lynn grabbed the wine bottle and refilled her glass. "It was Keanu Reeves. I was very depressed after my divorce, so I took my wedding photos to a lab called Second Chances and had Ron digitalized out and Keanu put in his place. It was only a holding action. I figured when I finally found the right man, I'd go back to Second Chances and get him put in Keanu's place. What did you say to Ron?"

"I said, 'Where's my pizza?' "

"And what did Ron say?"

"He said, 'Where's my check?' "

"Ron hasn't gotten his spousal support check this month. Well, that's no surprise. I haven't written him one. You know what shape my bank account is in. So what did you do then?"

"I went back inside and wrote him a check for forty dollars, which was the cost of the pizza plus a thirty-dollar tip. Since I was forging your signature, I didn't see any need to be stingy. Anyway, when I went back, the two of them were gone. About ten minutes later, a pimply-faced teenager arrived with my pizza, and everything went downhill from there."

"Downhill?"

"Pizza World had forgotten the anchovies. My first independently ordered pizza ever, and they had forgotten to put on the anchovies. I hardly need to tell you that it was a bitter disappointment. Think the *Titanic* going down. Think Mel Gibson being drawn and quartered in *Braveheart*."

"I feel your pain." Mary Lynn took a large sip of wine. "Look, do you think there's any possibility Ron realized you weren't me?"

"Not a chance. I was wearing your bathrobe, and my hair looked absolutely hideous."

"Jayne, make a note somewhere that you're never to accept a position as a diplomat."

"Why?"

"Trust me on this one," Mary Lynn said, and hung up.

For the next half hour, she divided her time between worrying about Ron and worrying about Arnie. In the end, Arnie won out. Ron had no reason to think there was anyone else in the world who looked like her. Arnie, on the other hand, had every reason to be sorry he'd ever met "Jayne Cooper."

As time passed, her anxiety grew. Every few minutes, she glanced out the window in the hope of seeing Arnie arrive, even though her view of the driveway was blocked by a hedge of oleanders. Finally she heard the crunch of tires on gravel. The doorbell rang. There were muted voices, followed by the sound of footsteps.

"Miss Cooper?" Lois stood in the doorway looking uncertain. "It's . . ."

"For God's sake, Lois, just show him in!"

As Lois scuttled away, Mary Lynn had a sinking feeling that she had never sounded more like Jayne. She had to get a grip on herself before she turned into a monster. When

Arnie walked through that door, was he going to find Jayne
Cooper waiting for him, or was he going to find a part-time
professor dressed in borrowed clothes? Was she willing to
gamble a hundred thousand dollars on the possibility he
might forgive her if he knew the truth? And even if he
didn't, wasn't she morally obligated to be honest with him?
Morally obligated? In Hollywood? Was she crazy?

Yes, she was crazy, okay? Crazy and maybe a teensy, tiny
bit drunk. But she could do this. She'd done harder things
in her life. She couldn't remember what they were at the
moment, but she knew she'd done them.

The door opened, and . . .

"Arnie . . . " Mary Lynn stopped in midsentence, and
her mind froze as if her brains had been superglued to the
inside of her skull. The man who had just walked into the
room wasn't Arnie. He wasn't even remotely like Arnie. He
was tall; he was dark; he was even handsome in a rough sort
of way; And he was a total stranger.

"Hi, baby," the man said. "I got you the stuff." He held out
what appeared to be a small bottle of white pills, and for a
split second, Mary Lynn had the insane thought that he was
a doctor making a house call. Maybe big stars like Jayne got
that kind of service. Maybe they didn't belong to HMOs.

"Real quality," he said, giving the bottle a little twirl. "No
plastic garbage cans. No cheap chemicals from the former
Soviet U. Only the finest for my baby." The man tossed the
bottle of pills onto Jayne's coffee table and approached
Mary Lynn. "Hey, aren't you even going to say thanks?"

"Thanks." Mary Lynn took a few steps backward. Who
the hell was he, and what the hell was in that bottle? He
clearly thought she was Jayne, and Jayne must know him
pretty well since he was calling her "baby." Was he supply-
ing Jayne with drugs? Was he her dealer?

The man looked confused. Apparently, she hadn't reacted
the way he'd expected. "Aren't you happy to see me, baby?"

"I'm delighted." Mary Lynn stalled for time. Who could
he be? Maybe he was an actor. She had a sense she'd seen

him somewhere before. Dark hair, tall, a pretty face except for a crooked nose that looked as if it might have once been broken. Broken nose! That was it! The guy looked like Andy Garcia with a broken nose!

"Gino?" she said.

"Yeah, baby?"

So he *was* Gino, Jayne's special assistant, the one who was supposed to bring Jayne her ATM card so she could get a cash advance. Mary Lynn felt relieved. She'd figured it out. All she had to do now was give Jayne's card to Gino and get rid of him before Arnie showed up.

Gino took a few steps toward her, and she took a few more steps back. He frowned. "You're acting sort of whacked today, baby. You aren't doing the hard stuff, are you? You know you can't get away with it. You're too high profile. Besides, unless you buy from me, there's a quality-control issue."

"I'm not doing the hard stuff." *He's definitely a drug dealer,* she thought. *Wait until I get Jayne on the phone. She's got some heavy explaining to do.* Thank God whatever Jayne was into wasn't "the hard stuff." On the other hand, there was clearly something besides aspirin in that bottle.

Gino looked puzzled; then he shrugged. "Then maybe you should cut back on the coffee. Maybe you got a bean on your back, baby. Get it? That's a joke. Coffee. The Colombian connection."

Mary Lynn forced herself to smile. "Very funny."

Apparently taking this as an encouraging sign, Gino drew closer. "So how about that little thank-you kiss?"

"I don't think so." Mary Lynn moved swiftly to put the sofa between them.

To her surprise, he seemed amused. "Oh, so you want to play."

"No." She had to stop scampering away from him like a deranged mouse. After all, she was supposed to know this guy. In fact, by the look of things, he and Jayne were inti-

mately acquainted. "Actually, all I want to do is give you an
ATM card."

"Baby, sweetheart." Gino shook his head. "No, no, no.
You don't have to pay. Only the ugly girls have to pay."

"Gino, I think we're having a serious misunderstanding
here. I just want you to take an ATM card to—"

"So what is it today?" He continued moving around the
end of the sofa. "Am I the chauffeur or the gardener?" He
suddenly made a grab for Mary Lynn, who ducked under
his arm and scrambled to the front side of the sofa. He came
after her. All at once, they were circling the sofa like a relay
team, Mary Lynn out in front, Gino gaining.

"It's *Burglar!*" he cried triumphantly. "Hey, that's one of
my favorites! I'm the big bad second-story man, aren't I?"
He lunged for her again and missed.

"No," she yelled. "Stop! I don't want to play!" He tripped
her, and she fell to the carpet. In a second, he was on top of
her. "So here's the scene," he said. "You're all alone, and I
just broke in and entered. I was taking the silver when I
found you all horny with no one to protect you."

Mary Lynn thrashed around, trying to break his grip.
"Stop! You're making a big mistake. I don't know you. I'm
not even Jayne!"

"Sure you aren't, baby. You're the countess. Or maybe the
queen whose big, bad bodyguard just got a little out of
hand. I know the drill. Just remember, if you really want me
to stop, you have to say your code word."

"Code word? What code word? I don't know what the
hell you're talking about!"

"That's the spirit, baby." He leaned toward her.

"Help!" Mary Lynn yelled and tried to bite his nose.

"That's it. Struggle. It always makes it a lot more fun."
Gino pressed his mouth to hers and kissed her. There was a
moment of silence punctuated only by Mary Lynn's muffled
squeaks of protest.

"Jayne?" said an all-too-familiar voice.

Mary Lynn looked to her left, and to her horror, she saw

Arnie standing in the doorway. "Arnie!" she cried, only since Gino's lips were still on hers, it came out more like "Arffnee!"

Gino turned his head. "Shit," he said as he caught sight of Arnie. "Things were just getting hot." He released his grip on Mary Lynn, who immediately scrambled out from under him. Stumbling to her feet, she pulled down her T-shirt.

"Arnie, this isn't what it looks like."

Arnie looked at her and then he looked at Gino. "I can't deal with this, Jayne," he said sadly. "This just isn't my world. Plus, it's a rerun of a very bad personal movie."

"It's not my world either. It's just a big misunderstanding. You see, Gino just came by to get an ATM card, and . . ."

"I'm tempted to make a pun here," Arnie said. "A really bad pun. That's what happens when minor playwrights walk in and find their women in the arms of other guys. They say something really stupid. Like when I found Teresa humping the singing-telegram employee, I said: 'So what is this, a Western Union?' "

"This dude isn't making any sense," Gino said. "You want me to pop him for you?"

Mary Lynn turned on him. "No! Just get out of here and never come back!"

Gino shrugged. "Hey, baby, no problem." He nodded to Arnie. "Have a nice day, you whacked-out nutcase. And do the *Gardener* with her. It's a lot more fun."

"Arnie," Mary Lynn said as soon as Gino was out of earshot, "I can explain. . . ."

"No, Jayne. You don't owe me an explanation. I understand. You're famous and rich, and you can do whatever you want. But I can do whatever I want too; and right now, all I want to do is get out of here."

"Arnie . . ."

"Thanks for going my bail."

"Arnie, please. . . ."

"You know, I thought you really liked me." He shook his head. "I'm such a schmuck."

"I'm not Jayne!" Mary Lynn cried. "I'm Mary Lynn

McLellan. Listen, Arnie, it's the truth. I've never been in a film in my life. I'm a nobody. I teach composition at a community college. I—"

"Sure," Arnie said. "Great. You're a comp teacher. And I guess that makes me what? The gardener?"

"Jayne," Mary Lynn snarled, "what is your code word?"

"My code word?"

"Don't play dumb. You know exactly what I mean. When you and Gino play your little fantasy sex games, what's the word you use to tell him to stop."

"My God," Jayne said, "don't tell me Gino—"

"Yes, he did. On your rug. In front of Arnie. It was horrible. Or to use one of your favorite words, 'ghastly.' No, it was beyond ghastly. It was one of the worst moments of my life."

"But Gino and I haven't done that for months. Did you, by any chance, say anything to encourage him?"

"What are we playing here!" Mary Lynn yelled. "Blame the victim? Gino jumped me under the mistaken impression that I—or rather you—wanted to play a little game you two apparently call 'the burglar.' I couldn't stop him, because I didn't know your damn code word. I was like Mickey Mouse in *Fantasia* when all the brooms are marching toward him with the buckets of water. So what's the magic word, Jayne?"

Jayne mumbled something.

"Speak up. I need to commit this to memory in case your boyfriend comes back."

"Oscar," Jayne said sheepishly.

"Your goddamn code word is 'Oscar'?"

"Yes."

"That's pathetic, Jayne."

"Gino's not my boyfriend."

"My mistake. He's your drug dealer. Don't bother to deny it. At this moment, I am holding in my hand a bottle of white tablets that he left compliments of the house. Or does he always take his payment in sex?"

"Don't you dare talk to me that way."

"I'll talk to you any way I want. I had to get this straight with your mother, and now I'm going to get it straight with you. Being rich and famous doesn't give you the right to treat people like dirt. You can't bully me, so stop trying. My heart is broken. Sound melodramatic? Sound like a line from one of your cheesy, romantic blockbusters? Well, then, let me put it the way a professor of composition would say it: Jayne Cooper, you are in deep shit. I'm furious with you. I've lost any chance of ever patching things up with Arnie. I'm so mad I don't care about the hundred grand, or about your career, or about keeping your damned secrets. In fact, I am strongly tempted to take this bottle directly to the police. I like the idea of you spending court-ordered time in rehab. Maybe if you passed a few months in group therapy, you might actually become a real human being. No, scratch that last comment. It's foolish optimism."

There was a long silence on the other end of the line. When at last Jayne spoke, her voice seemed small and very far away. "That wasn't very nice," she said.

"I know," Mary Lynn said. "I'm actually somewhat ashamed of myself. But damn it, you deserved it."

"You know that bottle Gino brought me . . . ?"

"I've got it right here in my hand. Is it crack? Is it speed? Is it ecstasy? Listen, Jayne, if you're using drugs, you need help. This stuff can fry your brains; it can even kill you. Think of Robert Downey Junior, Kurt Cobain, River Phoenix. To be honest, after a week of living your life, I can see why you might want to medicate yourself to the edge of oblivion, but you don't want to go that way."

"Why should you care?"

"I care because, against my better judgment and despite the fact that I'm mad at you, I've actually grown fond of you. Okay, I know. I'm a fool. But I like you, Jayne, even though you're a bitch on wheels sometimes, and if you need help, I want to see that you get it."

There was a muffled sob on the other end of the line. "That's the nicest thing anyone's ever said to me."

"I'm sorry to hear that. You deserve better."

"L-tryptophan."

"What?"

"There's just L-tryptophan in that bottle. It's an amino acid. It helps me sleep. Gino gets me some every time he travels. You can't get it in the U.S. without a doctor's prescription, so technically it's illegal to import it, but not very illegal, sort of like bringing in a bag of apples without a permit."

"Are you telling me the truth?"

"Yes, I swear. Take one of those pills if you don't believe me. L-tryptophan occurs naturally in turkey. You'll just feel drowsy like you ate a big Thanksgiving dinner." There was another long pause. "Listen, I'm really, really sorry this happened."

Mary Lynn stared at the phone in amazement. "Did I hear you right?"

"Yes."

"You're actually apologizing to me?"

"Yes. I'm going to make this up to you, I promise. How does an extra fifty thousand sound?"

Mary Lynn gave a small gasp.

"I know money won't make things right with Andy, but—"

"Arnie," Mary Lynn said. "His name is Arnie. Thanks. An extra fifty thousand will make a lot of difference in my life. It's always a lot better to be brokenhearted and rich than brokenhearted and poor. I accept your apology, and, by the way, I'm sorry I called you a 'bitch on wheels.'"

"Don't be," Jayne said. "I've been called worse things. Besides, it's true enough, except for the wheels part."

Seventeen

At Coast Side Community College, the story of Professor McLellan's short skirt and whacked-out lecture style spread faster than free pizza. On Friday afternoon, the twenty-five students in section 17 were joined by fifty refugees from miserably boring classes about famous dead white guys. In the adjoining room, Professor Lawrence Stidger looked glumly at the empty desks and wondered if, after thirty years, it might be time to update his lectures on the "Great Poems of Milton." Two doors down, Elizabeth Perry, the incredibly sensitive poet-in-residence who had been lured from her Vermont retreat for one semester to bring culture to the masses, took a look at the three students who had shown up, swore like a marine sergeant, and stormed off to the chair's office to demand an explanation.

In room 203 of Thackeray Hall, Jayne was putting on a fabulous performance, if she did say so herself. Her stage fright was gone, and as she faced the class, she felt that pleasant sense of accomplishment she always felt when her adoring fans nearly trampled one another to get a glimpse of her.

"You were supposed to write on this today," she said, holding up a copy of *Hamlet*. "Well, I've got news for you. Unless you're Kenneth Branagh, it's impossible to understand Shakespeare. I know, because last night I tried. I mean, this play has got words like 'fardels' and 'bodkin' in it; plus what is Hamlet's problem, anyway? Is he the only guy ever to have a stepfather he didn't like? I don't think so."

She slapped the play down on the desk. "Bottom line: this whole script needs a rewrite. Try to imagine it as a karate film with Bruce Lee. In the new version, Hamlet kicks ass every fifteen minutes. In between, we put in a couple of be-headings, some car crashes, and a few steamy sex scenes with what's-her-name."

"Ophelia," supplied the girl with the nose ring.

Jayne beamed at her. "Yes, Ophelia. My point exactly. We're going to have to change that name. So what do you want to call her?"

"Tiffany," a girl perched on the windowsill volunteered.

"Amber."

"Charmon."

"Desiree."

"Good, good. You're on a roll. Keep it coming." Jayne sat down on the edge of the desk and crossed her legs, and twenty-eight young male students moaned.

Jayne's problem was that she was hungry and short on cash. With Gino out of the picture, she had no prospect of getting any money until Mary Lynn's bank opened Monday morning, and she wasn't about to waste the little she had on lunch. As she continued the group rewrite of *Hamlet*, she assessed the male students. By the end of the hour, *Hamlet* had been transformed into an action-adventure film set in South Central, and she had picked her victim.

"Martin," she said as the class filed out, "I'd like to see you for a moment." The boy stopped abruptly and stiffened as if his spine had been plugged into a 220-volt outlet. His mouth fell open so far Jayne could see his tongue ring, and his eyes went crazy with something between hope and fear. He had "extra" written all over him, but he'd do. Tall, skinny, and better dressed than most, he wore a gold chain around his neck that suggested he had cash in his wallet.

Jayne walked up close enough to smell his aftershave lotion. She stood for a moment staring at him. If he had had the courage to stare back, he would have seen desire in her eyes. The desire was for a cheeseburger.

"You're taking me to lunch," she told him.

Martin turned bright red and made a small choking sound. "No problem, Professor."

Twenty minutes later, Jayne had eaten two double cheeseburgers and an order of fries, washing it all down with a chocolate malt so thick she had to eat it with a spoon. Martin had paid for it all without a murmur, and then had the guts to ask her if it was true that she had a brain tumor. Not wanting to disappoint him, and feeling a bit on the frisky side, Jayne had told him that she'd be dead within weeks.

She returned to Mary Lynn's apartment in a particularly good mood and knocked on Joe's door. Joe's mother-in-law, dressed in an apron, answered. The smell of something wonderful wafted out into the hall. Behind Carmen, Jayne could see Lisa and Janeira sitting on the couch watching TV.

"Hi," Jayne said.

"Hi, *senhora*," said Carmen.

"So I was wondering if you got my note."

"I get it," Carmen said; then she made a face and shook her head and said something in Portuguese that made the girls swivel around and stare at Jayne.

Carmen threw open the door. "Come in," she commanded. She led Jayne into the kitchen and motioned for her to sit down at the table. There was a pile of shredded coconut on the cutting board, and in a skillet on the stove, something was stewing in a bright orange sauce.

"What's that?"

"Moqueca de peche."

"What makes it so orange?"

"Palm oil." There was a long silence.

"Look," Jayne said, "do we have a problem here or something? I mean, did my FedEx packages come or didn't they?"

"They come," Carmen said. "So you buy with what? You win the lottery?"

Jayne stiffened. The woman was leaning too close to her. She seemed almost to be about to touch her. "I don't think how I pay for things is any of your business."

THE STAND-IN   197

Carmen sat back. "Janeira!" she cried. Janeira suddenly
appeared in the doorway. There was a quick exchange in
Portuguese; then to Jayne's intense surprise, the little girl
crawled up in her lap. Janeira's body was warm and soft and
smelled like caramel corn. Jayne didn't know what to do.
She had never held a child before.

"Janeira gonna translate," said Carmen. Once again, the
rapid exchange of Portuguese commenced.

"Gramma says you're a nice woman." Janeira looked
at Jayne thoughtfully. "But you don't know how to be a
neighbor."

"What!"

"She says you shouldn't have given her a check to take in
your packages. She says neighbors don't pay each other to
do things."

"They don't?" Jayne was surprised. If anyone had done
anything for her without being paid for it, it had been so
long ago she couldn't remember.

The little girl shook her head. "For a grown-up, you don't
know much, do you?"

"Insulto," said Carmen, looking at Jayne sadly.

"Did she just say paying her was an insult?"

Janeira nodded. "Gramma said you treated her like a ser-
vant. She wants you to know she went to school and was a
dancer on her toes in front of very important people."

"She was a ballerina?"

"She danced in Heyu."

"Heyu?"

"That's the way we say 'Rio' in Brazil. I like Brazil. I like
America too. But in Brazil, kids can run around after dark and
no one makes them come inside and the candy is better."
Janeira grew thoughtful. "Also, there you can have a puppy."

"Tell your grandmother I didn't mean to insult her."

"You better say more than that," Janeira warned. "In
Brazil people say, 'I'm sorry, I'm sorry, I'm sorry' when
they've done something wrong. And they sort of look like
they're going to cry. Can you look like you're going to cry?"

"I'll try," Jayne said. "Meanwhile, tell your grandmother I said I was sorry, sorry, sorry."

An hour later, Joe came home from work to find his upstairs neighbor sitting on the couch with one arm around Lisa and the other around Janeira. The three were watching a tape of *Sesame Street* together, and the girls were laughing like crazy.

"Daddy," Lisa cried, "the *senhora* says she danced with Big Bird."

"No kidding." Joe smiled at Jayne. "How did that happen?"

Jayne waved her hands vaguely. "Oh, it just happened."

"She was on *Sesame Street* when she was a little girl," Janeira said. "She was on with a man named Yo-Yo, who played the cellar."

"Cello," Jayne said, and smiled sheepishly.

"And she knew Bert and Ernie too! She knew their 'handlers.'"

"Handlers?"

"The people who work the Muppets." Jayne looked uncomfortable. "You know, the ones you can't see because they're offscreen."

"Is this true?" Joe said. "Were you really on *Sesame Street*?"

Jayne looked from Janeira to Lisa, and decided she'd better cover her tracks. "Of course not," she said. "I made it all up."

The little girls groaned with disappointment.

"We thought you knew Big Bird," Janeira said. "But it was a nice story. I liked the part about Miss Piggy saying she was a bigger star than you were."

Carmen appeared in the doorway and said something to Joe that made him laugh. He turned back to Jayne. "Carmen says you're full of stories. She says she and you surfed over to E Television while the girls were outside playing, and you told her the dirt on all the celebrities. Like which famous star showed off her new swimming pool without mentioning that her husband had tried to drown her in it, plus some other things she doesn't want to repeat in front of the girls."

"I hope I didn't insult her again." Jayne looked at Carmen nervously.

"No, no, she loved it so much she says you have to stay to dinner. She says even though her English isn't very good, your stories were better than *Pedra Sobre Pedra,* her favorite soap opera of all time."

Jayne was always pleased by compliments. She leaned back, put her feet up, hugged the girls closer, and thought about the three cans of tuna fish and the box of stale Triscuits waiting for her upstairs. She had never felt so at ease. Nothing was going on, but for some reason the whole scene—the children, the grandmother, the father coming home from work—made her feel warm and safe. She had spent most of her childhood in a TV family where everyone always said something witty and the parents were so perfect they regularly got fan mail from real parents asking how they could raise children as polite as little Jayne. But *My Familia* hadn't been a real family. It had been a bunch of actors with agents, a set with no ceiling. Joe's family was real. For the first time, Jayne had the sense that she'd missed out on something.

"I'd love to stay for dinner," she said.

"Yippee!" the girls squealed.

Jayne suddenly had a burst of inspiration. "I can cook biscuits." She turned to Joe. "They're a lot better than my coffee, I promise. Biscuits are the only thing I know how to cook. My mother taught me one week when I was home sick with measles." She smiled shyly, and for an instant, her face relaxed and she looked very young and vulnerable. "I'll feed you biscuits with honey, and you'll love me."

"Yes!" the little girls cried. "We'll love you!"

Carmen said something, and Joe laughed and translated.

"Carmen says: 'Of course we will love you. What choice do we have?'"

Dinner was perfect in a messy, wonderful, noisy way that made Jayne feel as if she'd known all of them for years.

They sat around the kitchen table drinking cold milk and iced tea and eating Jayne's biscuits and Carmen's *moqueca de peche,* a spicy stew of fish and green peppers bathed in orange palm oil. Everyone talked at once, and Janeira and Lisa kept trying to sprinkle something called *farofa* on Jayne's food. At first she rejected the stuff, which looked exactly like sawdust, but after a while, she gave in to the girls, who kept smiling at her irresistibly.

Actually, the *farofa* didn't taste bad, and it sopped up some of the oil. Once, when the others temporarily lapsed into Portuguese, she looked down at her plate and realized that, counting the two cheeseburgers, the French fries, and the malt she'd had for lunch, she had probably consumed more calories in the past six hours than she usually ate in six weeks. Then she decided she didn't give a damn, and, leaning over, she helped herself to two more biscuits and another serving of *moqueca.*

Dinner ended with a killer coconut flan, mugs of peppermint tea for the kids, and tiny cups of strong, sweet coffee for the adults. After Jayne had drunk four or five thimble-size cups of the coffee, she realized that everyone else had gotten up to do the dishes, so she got up, grabbed an apron, and joined them. Apparently, this was just what she had been expected to do, since no one commented on it or even thanked her.

Her fear that she would break everything in sight proved to be groundless, and to her surprise, she found it oddly soothing to immerse her hands in warm soapy water while everyone went on chatting in a mix of English and Portuguese. She decided that when she returned to her own house, she would have a small state-of-the-art kitchen built next to her study so she could wash dishes from time to time. She might even . . .

"Hello? You still with us?"

Jayne looked up and saw Joe staring at her with curiosity. The dishpan was empty; the kitchen was clean; Carmen was nowhere in sight; and the girls, who had been standing on chairs to dry the dishes, had climbed down, hung up their towels, and gone back into the living room to play some kind of board game that involved a lot of laughter and shrieking.

"Uh, yes," she said, quickly pulling her hands out of the water. "I was just thinking about how I like doing dishes."

"That's a rare trait. You should cultivate it. It'll make you welcome anywhere." He paused. "What next?"

Jayne was thrown for a loop. She had no idea if she was supposed to stay after dinner, or if they'd be more comfortable if she left. She wondered if they would expect her to write them a thank-you note. She always sent thank-you notes after she was invited to dine at a private home. Of course, her assistant actually wrote the notes, but she signed each one personally.

"I've had a perfectly marvelous time," she said stiffly.

"Glad to hear it."

"I'd like to thank you and your family for a fabulous bit of insight into the lives of ordinary people. I'd like to repay you in some way. Perhaps a small contribution to the girls' education . . ."

Joe held up his hand. "Hold it. You aren't offering us money again, are you?"

"Uh, no," Jayne said, backpedaling rapidly.

"Because we aren't in the habit of charging our guests for dinner." He smiled, and there was a brief but not entirely uncomfortable pause. "So how are you at Run Bunny Run?"

"What's that?"

"It's like poker, except that it involves plastic bunnies, a deck of cards, and fake carrots. You draw a card, try to get enough points to outrun the fox, and pile up the carrots until you can yell, 'Run, Bunny, Run!'"

"Do you play it often?"

"Every night. The girls are crazy about it. Before that, they were obsessed with *Mary Poppins*. Carmen figures we watched the video at least a hundred times. So how about it? Want to join us in a no-holds-barred session of Run

Bunny Run? An extra bunny is always welcome. Makes the competition for carrots more fierce."

"Thanks, but I don't play board games." Jayne was suddenly seized by an urge to be honest. "I'm very competitive. I have to win. If I started getting low on carrots, I'd probably cheat."

Joe laughed. "No problem. The girls love cheating. Last night I caught Janeira with a Farmer McGregor card up her sleeve."

Jayne untied her apron and tossed it on the counter with a flourish. "In that case, lead me to the board. You just got yourself a bunny who's going to kick some ass."

By the time Jayne went back upstairs to her own apartment, she was the uncrowned Run Bunny Run champion of greater Los Angeles. She'd wheeled and dealed, negotiated with Joe and Carmen, formed alliances with the girls, stacked up carrots as if they were gross points in a five-picture contract, outcheated everyone at the table, and screamed, "Run, Bunny, Run!" until she was hoarse.

As she crawled onto Mary Lynn's futon and settled down among the cats, she decided that the whole evening had been surprisingly entertaining. She'd particularly enjoyed the moment when she'd caught Lisa trying to mark the fox card by biting off the bottom corner.

She closed her eyes. Outside, a car passed, and then the street fell silent again. Somewhere very far away, a siren wailed. The cats moved closer, curling against her in soft warm balls and purring contentedly like small motors.

Sometime after midnight, she woke with an overwhelming urge for a cigarette. Switching on the light, she stumbled out of bed, threw on Mary Lynn's robe, and launched an all-out search. After ten minutes of frantically looking in every place she could think of, she had to admit defeat. How could she have managed to smoke so many cigarettes in such a short period of time? More to the point, why hadn't she thought to put two or three aside for late-night emergencies?

Shaking the last flecks of tobacco out of one of the crumpled packs, she dumped them into the palm of her hand and ate them; but it didn't do any good. Inside her head, a voice kept saying: *Smoke another cigarette now!*

Go away, she commanded the voice. *I don't need to smoke. In fact, starting now, I'll never smoke again.* Bravely, she endured the next five minutes; then the voice spoke again and she cracked. She suddenly remembered that there was an all-night market around the corner. She decided she'd walk to it and buy some cigarettes.

Throwing on a pair of pants and a sweatshirt, she slipped into Mary Lynn's sweater, dumped some change in her pocket, and made her way downstairs.

Almost as soon as she walked out of the building, she knew she'd picked a bad time to go on an errand. It was late, most of the streetlights were broken, and there wasn't another human being in sight. She felt a ripple of fear move up her spine. The whole damn street looked like a set from a low-budget horror movie. She was about to turn around and go back upstairs when the voice went off in her head again. It was frantic, insistent, and getting nasty. *What are you waiting for?* it said. *SMOKE ANOTHER CIGARETTE NOW!*

Damn it, if she didn't get some cigarettes, she was never going to be able to get back to sleep. Lowering her head, she charged forward, ignoring the hollow sound her shoes made on the pavement. She had almost reached the corner, when she heard a car coming up behind her very slowly. As it passed, the car suddenly sped up, and she saw that it was white. She opened her mouth to scream and then snapped it shut; she continued to walk toward the market. What the hell was the matter with her tonight? She was not Jodie Foster, this was not *Silence of the Lambs,* and as Mary Lynn had pointed out, there were millions of white cars in L.A.

Nevertheless, when she saw the blue-green fluorescence of the market spilling out onto the sidewalk, she breathed a sigh of relief. Walking inside, she ordered the skinny kid behind the counter to get her a pack of cigarettes.

"What brand?" he asked.

"I'd prefer Nuit de Istanbul, but since they cost fifteen dollars a pack, some cheap scrapings from the floor will do."

"How about a pack of Waves? They don't come much cheaper than that."

"Perfect," Jayne said, and went off to see if the market offered anything else worth having. She wandered up and down the aisles, but it was hopeless. The chocolate consisted of very old-looking peanut butter cups in orange wrappers; the wine was sweet and had a large bird on the label; the bread appeared to be made out of slightly soiled Styrofoam. Turning a corner, she came upon a miserable display of produce: some sprouting onions in a bin, some withered lettuce, a bunch of half-rotten bananas, and a few pathetic grapes that looked as if they might have been prestomped. She picked up a couple of the grapes and ate them and nearly choked. They were sour, seedy, and tasted like mold.

This was the last straw. She simply couldn't take this life any longer. She would walk back to the apartment, call Mary Lynn, and tell her the game was over. Then she would call a taxi and go back to her flower gardens, her wine cellar, and the cartons of Nuit de Istanbul tossed carelessly on a shelf in her closet. She'd done enough research; it was definitely time to . . .

"Hold it right there, lady," a voice said.

Jayne turned around and saw the skinny kid behind the counter pointing an accusing finger at her. "I seen you eating them grapes."

"What?"

"You was shoplifting."

Jayne stared at him in amazement. "You can't be serious! You're accusing *me* of shoplifting some of those miserable grapes!"

"I don't give a damn about the grapes, but how do I know what else you took while I wasn't looking? We get a lot of people comin' in here lookin' for a five-finger discount. You walk out with a box of Pop-Tarts or something, and management docks my pay."

"I hate Pop-Tarts," Jayne snarled. "I would never put one of the loathsome things in my mouth!" Forget the cigarettes. It just wasn't worth it. She wheeled around with the intention of leaving the store and collided with a rack of candy, scattering it all over the floor.

"Take off that crummy-lookin' sweater!" the kid yelled. "I know you got a bottle of wine or something under there!"

"Oh, get over it!" Jayne yelled in return. "There's nothing in this pathetic excuse for a store worth taking!"

"What did you steal?"

"Nothing, you idiot!"

The kid vaulted over the counter, trotted forward, put his face close to hers, and hopped up and down like a small, excited chihuahua. "Who you callin' an idjet!"

"You!"

He made a grab for her sweater. "I'm no idjet! I know you got stolen merchandise in there! Hand it over!"

"Get back, you little rat-faced bastard! Don't you dare touch me!" Sidestepping him, she seized a package of cupcakes and was just about to throw them, when the door of the market suddenly burst open, and a large man charged in, yelling at the top of his lungs, "Get away from Professor McLellan!"

Jayne and the clerk both froze.

"Don't touch her! She teaches *Hamlot*! She's read Fluffy! She's mine!"

"Hey," the clerk said, backing up. "No problem. I—"

"Did you hurt her?" The man stuck his face in the clerk's face and screamed so hard, spit came out of the side of his mouth.

"No, sir," the clerk whimpered in a terrified little squeak.

Jayne knew she should run, but there was a crazy man between her and the door. Although she didn't know his name, she remembered him well, which was hardly surprising since the last time she'd seen him he'd tried to throw a desk at her.

"You scared her!" the crazy man screamed. He grabbed the clerk by the shirt collar and began to shake him like a rag doll. "You scared my fiancée! She's sick! She has a brain tumor!"

"Whoa!" The clerk gasped for breath and his face turned the color of a cherry Slurpee. "Like, I'm totally sorry. Like, I didn't know the lady was sick."

"I'm going to beat the shit out of you." The crazy man suddenly whirled on Jayne, still carrying the clerk. "Excuse the cussword, Professor." He lifted the clerk off his feet and shook him harder. "And then I'm going to feed you to the space aliens who live in my backyard! Get the picture!"

"Help!" wheezed the clerk.

"Nobody scares my fiancée!" the crazy man screamed. He slammed the clerk down on the floor so hard, the pickled eggs and beef jerky sticks in the plastic jars quivered. "I love her! I drive by her house ten times a night! I watch over her to make sure she's safe! No one fucks with the professor!" He turned to Jayne again. "Excuse the cussword, ma'am." Then he turned back to the clerk and began to kick him.

Seeing her chance, Jayne bolted toward the door. Just as she went running out, two policemen came running in.

"Hold it right there!" one of the cops said, grabbing her by the arm.

"Thank God!" Jayne cried. She slumped up against the officer's chest and buried her face in his uniform. She felt weak with relief. The LAPD had arrived; everything was going to be okay.

Eighteen

The lights in the police station were sickly green, and the counters were made of gray metal. Everything smelled of boiled coffee, Lysol, and some kind of hideous cherry air freshener; and no one was listening to Jayne, who kept trying to tell them the biggest secret in Hollywood.

"I'm Jayne Cooper!" she kept repeating.

"Right," said a storm trooper with pink plastic Hello Kitty barrettes in her hair. "And I'm Oprah Winfrey. I'll book you on my show as soon as I finish booking you into jail." The Hello Kitty Nazi seized Jayne's wrists and slapped the palms of her hands down on a gray pad. The pad was cold and slimy, as if a million other hands had been forcibly pressed against it. Jayne shuddered and tried without success to break the woman's grip.

"Let go! I'm not going to let you fingerprint me! I hate getting ink on my fingers. It runs into my cuticles and stains horribly."

"Too late. I just took your prints. Computer. We don't use ink anymore."

"I'm not going to submit to this! I've seen it on TV. I know how it works. You shave off all my hair, you spray me with disinfectant, you make me wear orange—which is not my color—and then you beat and molest me!"

The woman released her grip on Jayne's wrists and sighed. "Well, it sounds like fun, but I got news for you: we don't do it that way in real life. Now hold still so I can take

your mug shot or I'll have to call the guards to restrain you."
She pointed toward the corner; on the floor was a piece of
dirty white tape. "Over there," she ordered. "Face forward;
toes on the line; no smiling unless you want to look like
you're on drugs."

"You can't photograph me! I'm not wearing any makeup;
the lighting in here is horrible. I never permit myself to be
filmed in fluorescent light. It's in all my contracts! Please.
I'm begging you. As one woman to another. Don't take a
picture of me without mascara!" The flash went off, blinding her. She struggled against the plastic handcuffs, gave a
small scream, and began to weep.

"Turn to your right," the woman ordered. "We have to get
a profile."

Jayne had never been good on directions. Still sobbing,
she turned meekly to the left. She had been under arrest for
less than an hour, and already they'd broken her.

The holding cell was a bright white cube, but Jayne was
too blinded by her own tears to see anything. She heard a
horrible, gut-wrenching clank as the iron door closed behind her, and every speck of claustrophobia she'd ever
stored up came rushing into her head, making her feel dizzy
and short of breath.

"Well, well, girls, look what the cat just dragged in," said
a mocking voice.

"Fresh meat," said another voice. "And scared out of her
little mind."

Jayne stumbled forward, gasping for air and waving her
arms feebly. "Don't hurt me," she pleaded. She'd seen
plenty of prison movies. She knew what happened next. The
lifers would swarm her, hold her down, and do unspeakable
things to her, after which she would be forced to work in the
laundry until all the skin fell off her hands. Only by sharp-
ening a spoon into a knife would she be able to escape, and
at the moment, she didn't even feel up to trying.

"Easy," said the first voice, no longer mocking. "Calm

down. No one's going to hurt you. You really are new at this, aren't you?"

Jayne blinked and the other occupants of the cell came into focus. There were four women imprisoned with her this evening. They ranged from maybe fifteen to forty, and they appeared to have been arrested in the middle of a Britney Spears concert. All four wore brightly colored miniskirts, formfitting cropped tank tops, and strapless bras that made their breasts jut out like shelves. Three had on heels so high that they could have repaired ceiling fans without a ladder. The fourth wore a pair of dirty red cross-trainers with frayed laces. But it was their makeup that gave them away. The women's faces were done with a professional skill that, even in her present state of abject terror, Jayne couldn't help but admire: false eyelashes perfectly positioned, lips outlined in graceful curves, cheekbones expertly emphasized. Jayne felt a relief so great it made her dizzy.

"You're actresses, aren't you?" she said eagerly.

The women laughed in a good-natured way. "No, honey," one said. "We're hos."

"Hoes?" In any other context, Jayne would have understood immediately, but she was confused and traumatized. Were these migrant workers? Is that what they were telling her? And if they were, how did they hoe things in those tight skirts?

"Although we prefer to be called 'sex workers,'" said another.

"Right," said a third, "we got no pimp. We're independent contractors."

"We're gonna form a union," said the first woman. "Just like the hos got up in San Francisco. I'm Cherry. These other girls are Bambi, Monica, and Corette."

"That's Corette with two *t*s," said the blonde, who was very tall. She stuck out a large, beautifully manicured hand. "Pleased to meet you."

For once, Jayne didn't mind being touched. She seized Corette's hand and shook it. Then she shook hands with

Cherry, who had red hair and chocolate-colored eyes, and Bambi, who if she hadn't had acne scars under her makeup, would have been a dead ringer for Michelle Yeoh.

Monica evidently was not in a cordial mood. There were several metal, traylike shelves hanging from the walls. She slouched on one of them, sullenly flaking the decals off her fingernails. The youngest of the four, she wore the red crosstrainers.

Jayne walked over to Monica and stuck out her hand. "Hi," she said warmly. As a matter of principle, she intended to be extra friendly to everyone in the cell. It might be a matter of survival.

"Hi yourself," Monica mumbled, not looking up.

"Don't pay any attention to Monica," said Cherry, who seemed to be the leader of the group. "Monica's aggrieved."

Monica darted Cherry a dark look. "I got a right to be aggrieved." She turned to Jayne. "All the others snapped up the sexy names and I got left with 'Monica.' What kind of name is that for a working girl? Everybody knows Monica Lewinsky did it for free. Would you *pay* to sleep with a woman called 'Monica'?"

"Uh, well . . ." Jayne nervously took a step back and let her hand fall to her side.

"You see!" A triumphant glint came into Monica's eyes and she tossed her head so hard her earrings jangled. "I'm right. It's a loser name. I want to change it. I want to call myself 'Honey' for professional purposes, but Bambi says that's got no class."

"We already got a reputation," Bambi said sternly. "We're known all over town as Cherry, Bambi, Monica, and Corette. You can't go around changing your professional name anytime you feel like it. Ever hear of 'brand recognition'? You don't hear about Pepsi changing its name, do you? You don't hear about McDonald's calling itself 'the Billion Sold Café.' 'Monica' is classy. It's memorable."

"You bet your ass it's memorable. Every damn day some john asks me: 'You do Bill Clinton lately?' Or 'Hey, Monica, you one of those intern girls? You got any cigars?' It isn't fair. I never should have been stuck with 'Monica' in the first place. I should have at least been the one who got 'Corette,' particularly since Corette doesn't even have real tits."

"I do too." Corette looked genuinely hurt. "I grew them myself." She ran her hand over her bosom. "My tits are as much a part of me as yours are of you."

"Corette's our little secret," Cherry said, and all the women except Monica laughed. "She's a he. The guards haven't figured that out yet, or they'd have put her in with the men."

"I'm only technically a he," Corette objected. "I don't use the he part anymore since I started taking hormones."

"It still isn't fair." Monica turned to Jayne. "Tell them it isn't fair."

Jayne opened her mouth, but nothing came out. If she sided with Monica, the others might turn on her; on the other hand, if she sided with the others, Monica might slit her throat. Monica had very long fingernails and an unstable light in her eyes that Jayne associated with aspiring starlets. Fortunately, Cherry went on talking as if Monica hadn't tried to derail the conversation.

"Corette used to belong to the Hunt Club when she was a he. You know what the Hunt Club is?"

"You mean foxhunting?"

Once again everyone but Monica laughed. "The Hunt Club is the boys from Public Health," said Corette, sitting down on one of the shelves and primly crossing her ankles. "They make the rounds of the bars tracking down the sex partners of people who've come up positive for communicable diseases that I'm now too much of a lady to mention."

"Lady, hell," Monica snarled. "You just wait until they strip-search you. Then we'll see how much of a 'lady' you are, *Mr.* I-Got-The-Best-Name-Of-All Corette." They went on trading insults, but Jayne was no longer listening. The word "strip-search" was roaring in her ears, blotting out all other sounds. With a monumental effort of will, she forced her lips to move.

"Strip-search?" she asked. "What do you mean strip-search?" And in an instant, she learned what the rest of them had known all along: that it was the weekend. And on the weekends, if someone didn't show up to bail you out, you ended up being put in a regular cell instead of a holding cell. In other words, you joined the long-term prisoners until Monday. Before they put you there, the guards stripped you, searched all your body cavities, took away your street clothes, and issued you an orange jumpsuit.

"Let me out!" Jayne screamed as soon as she understood what was about to happen to her. Running to the far side of the cell, she threw herself against the metal door. "They can't strip me! They can't! I've never done a nude scene in my life! I've always had a body double." She clenched her fists and began to pound. "Help! Let me out! Help! Somebody help me!"

The next thing she knew, Cherry had grabbed one of her wrists and Bambi had grabbed the other. Corette put her hand over Jayne's mouth, and the three women pulled her back into the cell and forced her to sit down on one of the shelves.

"Stop screaming," Monica hissed, "or you'll lose us our TV privileges."

Corette was kinder. She looked at Jayne with sympathy. "Take a deep breath, honey, and don't hyperventilate. I remember how scared I was the first time they threw me in here, but you'll get used to it." Jayne tried to yell that she'd never get used to it, but Corette's hand over her mouth was an insurmountable obstacle.

"Calm down," Cherry said. "You look like the kind of girl who has a lot of friends. Maybe one of them will come bail you out before we have to go upstairs."

Jayne shook her head and made a "no" sound.

"No friends?"

Again Jayne shook her head.

Cherry turned to Corette. "Take your hand off her mouth,

Corette, but if she screams, slap it on again." Corette removed her hand, and Jayne began to cry.

"Agents," Jayne sobbed. "Fans, lovers, directors, assistants, acquaintances, publicity handlers, studio execs, people who pretend to adore me, a mother who does her best, but no real friends except maybe Mary Lynn, who's going to hate me when she finds out I got us arrested."

"That's one of the saddest things I ever heard. It doesn't make any sense, but it's sad." Corette pulled a lacy handkerchief out of her bra and dabbed at her eyes. "All whores are romantics," she said. "And I'm no exception. What did they arrest you for?"

"Disorderly conduct, assault, and shoplifting"—Jayne sobbed—"and suspicion of being an accessory to a maniac. And all because I ate some hideous, moldy grapes!"

"What did you do? Eat them off the belly of the mayor?" Corette put her arm around Jayne's shoulder and drew her close. "Never mind. It doesn't matter. Come on, honey. Have a good cry. In my limited experience, a good cry is one of the best things about being a woman."

"I hate to cry," Jayne wailed. "It makes my nose red."

Bambi grabbed her hand and patted it. "Now, now," she said. "It's not the end of the world. Try to think about something else. For example, you haven't even told us what you do. No offense, but from the looks of that sweater, if you're a hooker, you aren't doing a booming business."

"She doesn't peddle her ass for money," Monica said. "All you have to do is look at her to see that."

"But I do," Jayne sobbed. "All my life, I've peddled my—my . . . ass. . . . I'm a—a . . . movie star."

Suddenly, except for Jayne's sobs, the room was dead silent. Corette coughed and tucked her handkerchief back in her bra. "I didn't see this coming," Corette said. "Poor little thing."

"They got her in the wrong place," said Bambi. "They should have put her under psychiatric observation. What's our judicial system coming to anyway? Letting a poor crazy girl like this spend all night without meds."

"I'm not crazy," Jayne insisted. "I'm Jayne . . . Jayne . . . Jayne—"

"Mansfield? March? Fonda?" Corette prompted.

"Cooper," Jayne finally managed to say. "I'm Jayne C-C-Cooper."

"Sure you are," Bambi said, giving Jayne's hand another pat.

"No, really I am."

"Prove it," said Monica.

Cherry, Bambi, and Corette frowned and looked uncomfortable. "Get off her back, Monica."

Instead of taking the hint, Monica walked over to the shelf Jayne was sitting on and motioned for Corette to move over. Corette moved, and Monica sat down next to Jayne and stared at her in a way that wasn't exactly friendly but not overtly hostile either. For the first time, she seemed to be taking an interest in something besides her name, and the new thing she was taking interest in was Jayne.

"Whores have great bullshit meters," she began.

" 'Sex workers,' " said Cherry.

Monica nodded and began again. "Sex workers have great bullshit meters. We working girls hear more bullshit per hour than highway patrol cops pulling over speeders. But here's the funny thing: when you say you're Jayne Cooper, my bullshit meter's not going off, which means that either it's broken, or somehow"—she paused and looked thoughtful—"somehow, crazy as it sounds, you're telling the truth. I been checking you out ever since you started going psycho on us, and I got to admit that you look sort of like Jayne Cooper on a really bad day. You even got that little black mole below your eye like she does."

Jayne was so shocked that someone was finally willing to believe her, that she stopped crying.

"So," Monica continued, "all you have to do is prove you

are who you say you are, and, hey"—she shrugged—"I'll believe you."

"How can she prove who she is?" Corette said. "How can any of us prove who we are except by our fingerprints?"

"Easy." Monica leaned back and folded her arms across her chest. "If you're Jayne Cooper, do a scene from one of your movies. Do my favorite scene: the one from *The Loves of Leonardo* where you tell that Italian painter you'll love him forever. Can you do that?"

"Of course." Jayne was delighted to be put in a situation where she could at last reassume her rightful position in the world. "We filmed twenty different versions of that scene, mostly because I kept having problems with my hair. I've said those lines so often I could say them in my sleep."

"Then go for it," Monica said.

Jayne licked her lips, smoothed her hair, and closed her eyes. She tried to imagine the set: a room in a Renaissance Italian villa, green velvet hangings, heavy carved furniture, a silver basin, pools of golden light, and handsome Leonardo da Vinci (aka Edward Surrey) on his knees by her bed, stroking her hair, which was spread out on the pillow Botticelli-style.

"My darling, my darling," she said in a soft, tremulous voice. She opened her eyes and raised one hand. Somehow she managed to make it appear wasted and frail. "Paint on. Paint on. Although I am dying of the plague, my dearest, which I caught from you. . . ."

Oh no! My love! Surrey had cried, grasping her hands. Jayne curled her hands as if they had been grasped and continued. "I shall love you . . . forever." She gave a wonderfully convincing death rattle and fell back, dead.

There was applause. When she looked up, Bambi and Cherry had tears in their eyes, and Corette was sobbing into her lace hankie as if her heart would break.

"You *are* Jayne Cooper!" Corette sniffed.

"No, she isn't," Monica said sharply. She turned to Jayne. "That stunk!"

"Stunk!" Jayne was furious.

"Jayne Cooper's a lot better actress than you are. And besides, you don't have enough hair."

"It was a wig!" Jayne yelled. "Ten pounds of fake hair!"

"Oh yeah?"

"Yeah."

They glared at each other. Finally Monica shrugged. "Okay," she said. "You win. It was a wig. But tell me this: what does Tom Cruise look like naked?"

"Monica!" Corette gasped.

"In Hollywood, girls in our profession know a lot of things. I'm not saying Tom Cruise was ever a patron of a sex-working professional, but I am saying that people who sleep with people who sleep with people talk too much, if you know what I mean."

"How the hell should I know what Tom Cruise looks like naked?" Jayne snarled. She was still furious over being told she couldn't act.

"There." Monica turned to the others. "What did I tell you? She's not the real thing. Everyone knows that Jayne Cooper used to have a thing going with Tom Cruise."

Bambi nodded. "You're right. I read about the two of them in the *Comet*." She looked disappointed.

Now that she had stopped crying, Jayne was starting to think. Anger was a wonderful stimulant. It cleared her head and made her cold, precise, and inventive. She suddenly understood what she needed to do.

"Have any of you ever met Edward Surrey?" she asked, and she knew as soon as she said his name, that if they hadn't met Eddie, they knew someone who had.

"Maybe." Bambi gave the others a warning look. "And maybe not."

"Well, if you've seen Eddie with his clothes off, then I imagine you've noticed something different about a certain very special part of him." She emphasized the words "special part" and sat back to observe their reaction.

Corette shifted uncomfortably and refused to meet Jayne's eyes. "Like what?"

Jayne didn't need any more encouragement. She told them. It was intimate, funny, obscene, and such a hot bit of gossip that the editors of the *Comet* would have hocked their grandmothers to get the rights to it. But although Cherry, Bambi, Corette, and Monica laughed until they were almost sick, they weren't surprised, because all four of them already knew.

When the girls finally came up for air, they all agreed that Jayne had to be either a sex worker herself or a movie star. Given her reaction to being tossed in jail, even Monica agreed movie star was the only real possibility.

"Call your lawyer, Miss Cooper," Bambi said. "What are you doing in this place? You got more money than God. Go post your own bail and ours too, and let some of those poor drunks in the drunk tank out while you're at it."

"I did call my lawyer," Jayne said bitterly. "But for reasons I'd rather not go into, I didn't have his private number, so I got put into the firm's phone tree, run around for five minutes, and then disconnected before I could leave a message. I wanted to call back, but the vampire with the ghastly pink-and-white cats in her hair wouldn't let me make another call."

"You only get one phone call," Cherry said.

"Not necessarily." Monica looked at Jayne thoughtfully.

Corette sighed and uncrossed her ankles like a matron about to rise and deal with an unruly child. "Monica always has to be the center of attention, Miss Cooper. Don't pay any attention to her."

Monica flaked off the last of her nail polish and continued to stare at Jayne. "If I had a name I really liked," she said, "I might just give you my call. I haven't had it yet, because I was so depressed about my stupid ass name, that I forgot to ask for it. But if you can think up a classy name for me that the others will go along with, I'll call anyone you want. I don't need to contact my attorney because I'm gonna get bailed out the same time the other girls do—

which is more or less when hell freezes over. Also I don't mind being strip-searched, since it's more or less business as usual for me."

There was a stunned silence.

"That's brilliant," Corette said.

"Brilliant, hell." Cherry turned to Monica. "You should have asked for money, you fool. You got a fairy godmother by the short hairs and you're wasting your wish."

"There are things," Monica said, "more important than money."

Jayne knew she had to move fast before Monica changed her mind. She looked at Monica's earrings and was suddenly inspired. "You could call yourself 'Ritzy'!"

Monica's face turned pink with pleasure. "'Ritzy.' I love it."

"Classy," said Bambi.

"Lovely," agreed Corette.

"Why didn't we think of that?" said Cherry.

"There's one more thing," Corette said shyly. "It's just a favor, really, since Monica—"

"Ritzy!"

"Since Ritzy has already promised to make a call for you. I was just wondering"—Corette blushed and looked at the others—"if maybe you could . . ."

Jayne saw it coming. People always asked for the same thing when they found out who she was. It didn't matter if they were international megastars with high-powered agents, or fans scrambling for autographs. "You want to be in one of my movies, right?"

"Hell no," Corette said. "I've had my run in the movies. Porn films. Great pay but lousy work conditions. No, I was just wondering if, when you got married, if you ever did get married, if you'd let the four of us be your bridesmaids." Corette grew dreamy. "I've always wanted to be a bridesmaid."

"And wear pink," Bambi said softly.

"And carry little bouquets of lilies of the valley," Cherry said with a sigh.

"I've always wanted to marry a rich man and settle down," said Ritzy. "Have babies. A nice little house or even a nice little mobile home."

My God, Jayne thought, *this is like a Jane Austen movie. They all want a rich husband, a home, babies. Family values right where you'd least expect to find them.*

"Well?" said Corette expectantly.

Jayne thought fast. She needed that phone call and she knew there was no way in hell she was ever going to get married.

"Sure," she said, shaking hands all around. "It's a deal."

Joe had just come home from the shipyard when the phone rang. He grabbed for it before it could wake up Carmen and the girls, figuring that it was one of his buddies who'd forgotten the rest of the world didn't work the swing shift.

"Hi," said an unfamiliar voice. "My name is Ritzy and I'm calling to tell you a friend of yours needs you to bail her out of jail."

"I think you have the wrong number." Joe started to hang up and was stopped by a screech from the other end of the line.

"Wait a goddamn minute! She says you live downstairs from her." Ritzy, whoever she was, started to give him directions to the jail. There was the sound of a small scuffle and muffled protests. "Damn it!" Ritzy said. "Let go. You can't—"

"Joe," a familiar voice said, "it's me, Mary Lynn. Please come get me, Joe. Deliver me from this ghastly place, I'm begging you. I found your number in the pocket of my sweater. You're my only hope. All my other numbers are on speed dial, and I don't have my cell phone and . . . Oh, my God, here comes the Hello Kitty Nazi with two guards. They're going to take away the phone. I can't talk any . . . Get away, damn it! Back off!"

There was a muffled yell and several loud thumps, and the line went dead.

Two hours later, a badly shaken Jayne sat on Mary Lynn's sofa beside Joe; she was doing yoga breathing exercises to calm down. Her hair lay flat against her skull; her nose was red; she had on no makeup; and none of that mattered, because Joe was being so nice that every time she thought about how he'd shown up and bailed her out of jail without asking any questions, she felt like weeping with gratitude.

"You're a saint," she told him between breaths. "If you hadn't come to my rescue, I might have spent the rest of my life on a chain gang surrounded by sadistic guards and attack dogs." At the thought of huge, snarling canines attacking her and ripping her panty hose, she had an almost overwhelming urge to sob. She bravely repressed it, which proved to be a mistake. The sobs turned into hiccups, which linked together in little embarrassing squeaks.

"L.A. doesn't have chain gangs." Joe patted her softly on the back as if burping a baby—something he'd had a lot of experience with, particularly when Janeira was an infant.

"It—*hic*—doesn't?" One of Mary Lynn's cats had drawn near. Jayne seized it and clutched it to her chest like a fur life preserver. She looked up through wet lashes and gave Joe a small, hopeful glance. He wondered if she had any idea how beautiful she looked. Probably not. Well, he wasn't about to tell her, because that might sound like he was coming on to her—not that he didn't want to.

"I'm sorry for making you come down to that ghastly police station in the—*hic*—middle of the night," she said, furiously stroking the cat. Joe noticed she was petting the cat in the wrong direction. He wondered if he should intervene before she got clawed.

"I was out of my mind with fear. I felt like—*hic*—Marie Antoinette in the Bastille."

"You don't owe me an apology."

"Yes—*hic*—I do. I'm always causing you trouble and then acting like you're—*hic*—paid to help me, but all that's going to change. I'm not the same woman I was before they threw me in that—*hic*—dungeon. I'm ashamed of myself. You've been so nice."

"It was nothing, really."

"Nothing? You bailed me out of—*hic*—jail, you extinguished my toaster when it went berserk, you unstopped my sink, and I didn't even say 'thank you.' I treated you like-*hic*—well, to be hideously honest, like I always treat everyone. But I can see now that I was rude and—*hic*—ungrateful and—*hic*—thoughtless. In some other historical period, I'd probably be decapitated by a man in a black mask for criminal ingratitude. My only hope is that he'd—*hic*—use a silver sword."

With an irritated hiss, the cat clawed its way free and leaped from her arms. "There!" she cried. "You see: even he knows! Cats are—*hic*—psychic. They live in another dimension where they can sense my selfish inner child, the miserable—*hic*—brat who never says 'thank you.'"

Joe tried his best not to laugh. "Don't be so hard on yourself. You thanked me for dinner, and you're saying 'thank you' now. Two out of four isn't bad. You're doing just fine."

Jayne tried to say something, but the hiccups seized her again, and the words came out in incomprehensible little squeaks.

Joe stared at her for a moment, wondering if he should tell her what he always told the girls when they got hiccups. He decided it couldn't do any harm. "Put your fingers in your ears and your thumbs in your nose and swallow three times without breathing," he suggested. Jayne obediently crammed her thumbs in her ears and pinched her nose shut. Sure enough, her hiccups stopped.

She removed her fingers and stared at him with awe. "You're a genius. This is a miracle!" Her face fell, and she stared glumly at the cat who had turned its back on her and was attempting to lick its fur into order. "I bet you think I'm a horrible nuisance. No, don't bother to deny it. There's no use being polite. Nobody really likes me when they get to know me."

"Don't talk that way." On impulse Joe put his arm around her, and when she didn't object, he drew her closer. "Carmen really likes you and so do the girls."

"Really? You're not just saying that to get on my good side?" Her face darkened. "Not that I have a good side."

"Really. Janeira and Lisa love being with you. You're funny and kind, and you have a great imagination. How many other adults can do a perfect imitation of Miss Piggy?"

"Thank you," Jayne murmured in a voice still rich with despair. "That's one of the nicest things a man has ever said to me."

Joe knew this was no time to laugh, but it was hard going. He coughed several times and cleared his throat. "Are you telling me no man has ever said you were beautiful, or kind, or sweet?"

"Beautiful, yes. But sweet? Let me put it this way: have you ever had someone roll over in bed and tell you that you reminded him of a velociraptor?"

Joe bit his lips and studied the far side of the room. "No," he said as soberly as possible. "I can't say that I have. What kind of men do you usually go out with, anyway?"

"I date handsome, self-absorbed, egotistic bastards with the morals of rutting minks—plus, a few charming blond Peter Pans with tight buns who are all in love with their own reflections. How about you?"

Joe was so surprised, he hardly knew what to say. He stared at her for a moment, trying to figure out if she was kidding, but it was clear from the expression on her face that she wasn't. "I haven't dated all that much since my wife died," he said.

"There, you see? I've done it again. I've said something that hurt you. I didn't know you were a widower. I figured you were divorced like ninety-nine percent of all the other men in L.A. I'm a public menace. I should be forced to wear a label like a pack of cigarettes. *Warning: the surgeon*

*general has determined this woman can be hazardous to
your happiness."*

She didn't know that she was sweet. She actually didn't
know. And apparently—amazing as it seemed—no one had
ever told her. Joe took her by the shoulders and gently turned
her to face him. "Listen, I know you're upset, but you don't
have to attack yourself or apologize. You can just be."

"Be what?"

"Yourself."

"Myself?" She shook her head sadly. "I don't even know
if I have a self. Ever since I was a little girl, I've had to be
other people. Oh, sure, it was fun sometimes, you know,
playing queens, mistresses, and beautiful spies. But in the
end when the lights go off and the cameras stop rolling,
you're left with nothing but a lot of prime real estate, a di-
versified portfolio, cellulite, and your own personal plastic
surgeon."

Joe looked at her in confusion. "You aren't making much
sense."

"No, I don't suppose I am."

"Are you telling me you have a multiple personality?"

"No, but I have a terrible secret."

Joe let go of her and sat back. "Okay, I'm a big boy. I can
take it. Break it to me."

"I can't."

"How bad can it be?"

"Really bad. Like the worst thing you can think of."

"You're wanted by the FBI?"

Jayne shook her head.

"You're a contract killer?"

She shook her head again.

"You have a body in the trunk of your car?"

"No."

"Well, hey, I'm running out of ideas. You aren't a guy, are
you? Because if you are, that plastic surgeon of yours
should get the Nobel prize in medicine."

"No." Despite herself, Jayne smiled.

"You know," Joe said, "having eliminated all the really bad possibilities, I think I'm going to kiss you. How would you feel about that?"

"You're actually asking?"

"Sure. Otherwise you might think it was in trade for posting your bail, and I wouldn't want you to think that because I really like you. You're smart, assertive, eccentric, and extremely creative in a slightly crazed way." He grinned. "And sexy too. Very, very sexy, even when you have a red nose and hiccups."

"You like me? You really like me? Just for who I am?" She paused. "Oh, my God, I sound like Sally Field. But you do like me for myself?"

"Who else?" He leaned forward so his lips were almost touching hers.

"Joe . . ." she said softly.

"You know, I think I'm going to take that 'Joe' for a 'yes.'"

"Joe, seriously. I'm big trouble. You don't want to kiss me."

"How about you let me be the judge of that?" he said, and leaning even closer, he gave her a long, sweet kiss. Jayne kissed him back and felt something warm run from her lips to the tips of her toes. *Whoa,* she thought. *I'm giving this a ten out of ten , maybe an eleven , maybe . . . Whoa, this guy is . . .*

Her mind paused, froze, and stopped. Lost in Joe's kisses, she forgot who she was and who she wasn't. The kisses continued, each one better than the last. A great burden lifted from her and she felt free and light, and very happy. She went back for more, and for the first time in her life, she didn't stop to wonder if the man who embraced her was only interested in her because she was bankable.

Nineteen

Mary Lynn sat at a cedar table under a green umbrella; she was drinking lemonade and staring morosely at the Esther Williams pool. She had abandoned the Elvis pool for the duration of her stay. She couldn't stand the sight of it.

The Elvis pool reminded her that Arnie didn't want to love her tender; it reminded her that she was living in Heartbreak Hotel. When she stared at the Esther Williams pool, she could imagine teams of hard-bodied swimmers in pink rubber bathing caps forming great chrysanthemums with legs for petals. In the center, Esther herself rose up from beneath the chlorinated water like Cassandra, that prophet from the *Iliad* whom no one would ever believe, the one who had had a fling with Zeus and lived to regret it. *You've screwed up,* Esther said.

"I know," Mary Lynn muttered to the imaginary swimming champion. "So what do you suggest I do about it?" As if in reply to her question, Jayne's cell phone rang. She picked it up, looked at it wearily for a moment, then punched the ON button.

"What is it this time, Jayne? Did you break a nail?"

"Love," an unfamiliarly dreamy voice replied.

Whoops, Mary Lynn thought, *someone's called the wrong number.* She was about to hang up, when the voice continued. "I'm in love with a man I haven't even slept with. At least I think I am. Can this be possible? I mean, what could be more wonderful and more ghastly? He's a welder. Me with a welder! I didn't even know what welding was until he let me play with his blowtorch. Unfortunately, those things take some getting used to. I took out every flower in the garden before I could find the Off switch."

"Jayne?"

"Ummmm?"

"Are you okay?"

"I'm fantastic. I'm free. I'm a wild thing streaming like a beam of moonlight across a—hell, I don't know—the roof of a Jeep Cherokee in some place where there's no traffic. Love is intoxicating, wonderful, like . . ."

"Heroin?"

"Now, don't get bitter. You know, even the cats sense I'm happy. Their toys arrived today, and they're leaping about like little fur Tarzans."

"Who's the lucky guy?"

"Your downstairs neighbor."

"You're kidding. You mean the guy with the two kids who lives with the older Brazilian woman? The one who makes mobiles?"

"That's the one. His name is Joe Porter, and I've never been more serious. If Eddie Surrey wanders back into my bed, take him with my blessings. I've found a new kind of man, one who doesn't wear a hair net at night. At least I don't think Joe does. As I said, I haven't actually slept with him yet."

"Jayne, I know you probably don't want to hear this right now, but you're sounding more and more like a psychiatric emergency."

But Jayne wasn't listening. She was doing a great romantic scene, improvising her own lines. If Mary Lynn wanted to listen, that was fine. If not, it didn't matter.

"I wanted to sleep with him, but he wouldn't. Can you believe that? I mean, he's not gay or anything, which, of course, was my first thought, even though there weren't any signs of it. He said the timing wasn't right. Did I feel scorned? Yes. Did I feel for a moment at least like making him sorry he was ever born? Yes. But then, he said that he couldn't do it because I was under great emotional stress, and it would be taking advantage of me. It was like Richard Gere in *Runaway Bride* in those scenes where he won't tell Julia Roberts he loves her because she's engaged to that football coach."

"Did you tell my downstairs neighbor who you really were?"

"No, that was the fantastic part. Joe was attracted to the real me, even though he thought I was a pathetically poor, dowdy little drudge of an English professor without a dime to her name."

Mary Lynn closed her eyes and counted to ten. "Jayne," she said in as friendly a voice as possible, "if you didn't tell him who you were, then what 'emotional stress' were you under?"

"Oh, I got arrested. Didn't I tell you that? I meant to tell you that first thing. Well, strictly speaking, *I* didn't get arrested. You did."

"Arrested! What for?"

"Frugivorous shoplifting. 'Frugivorous' is one of the vocabulary words you assigned your students this week. It means *fruit-eating.*"

"I know what it means, damn it! Don't try to change the subject. Are you telling me that I now have a criminal record?"

"Only a teensy little criminal record for a teensy little crime. It's nothing to get excited about. Technically, you only ate two grapes. When you come to trial, your prints aren't going to match mine. They'll have to dismiss the case. If it will make you feel better, we can even sue the LAPD."

Mary Lynn dropped the phone and put her head down on the table. "This just goes on and on, doesn't it? There's never any end to the trouble you can get into."

"I can't hear you. You're cutting out."

Mary Lynn sat up again and retrieved the phone. "Never mind. So why did you call me, except to tell me that you're in love and I'm a felon?"

"I have a favor to ask."

"Ask away. I live but to serve you."

"Joe's on vacation next week. He's invited me to go camping with him, Carmen, and his daughters. Carmen's his mother-in-law."

"You're going camping with a married man and his wife's mother? I don't think I want to know the details."

"No, no, Joe's a widower. Here's the deal: I know you're eager to get back to your own life. . . ."

Mary Lynn stared morosely at the Esther Williams pool and thought of Wendell. "Not all that eager, really."

"Good, because I was hoping that I could talk you into spending an extra week as me. Except for the prospect of getting a professional massage and eating some food that isn't floating in palm oil, I don't see any reason to come rushing back. The publicity junket for *Salome* is over, and that scandal about you and Arnie is definitely history. In fact, if you check out the front page of the *Comet*, you'll see that speculations about my sex life have been displaced by a juicy rumor about Prince William.

"So, with the worst behind us, there's nothing for you to do this week but call in Moonflower to lather you with aromatherapy oils, drink my gin, and buy yourself lots of cute clothes while I go off to the wilderness with Joe to find out if my feelings for him are real. You won't be able to use my credit cards, because I canceled them, but if you look in my jewelry box, you'll find a couple of cute little diamond bracelets you can hock. 'To hock' means *to pawn*. I learned that last night in jail from a completely fascinating sex worker named Corette."

She paused. "You know, I'm not entirely brain-dead over here. I realize what I'm feeling for Joe might not be love at all. Maybe after a couple of days, I'll decide he's a loser, Carmen's a nag, and the kids are brats. On the other hand"—her voice took on a brisk, practical tone—"even if he doesn't pan out, I'd like a chance to get into the sack with him and run him around the block. I have a strong suspicion that he has totally fabulous buns. So what do you think? Are you up to being me for a while longer?"

"Sure," Mary Lynn said. "Why not? The hours are good, and there's no heavy lifting. Plus, since Arnie walked in and saw Gino trying to hump me, I've had nothing better to do." A thought occurred to her. "Jayne, have you ever been camping?"

"Technically, no. Although, I did work in a blue silk tent for hours on end when I was playing Mary, Queen of Scots."

"Do you realize that you may be sleeping on the ground?"

There was a shocked silence on the other end of the line.

"And that there will be no hot water?"

Jayne gave a little gasp.

"Not to mention that—how shall I put this?—you won't have to be looking under any stalls for Malfredi's feet when you go to the bathroom, but you will have to be looking out for poison oak."

"What does poison oak look like?" Jayne said weakly.

"It's slick and green and has three leaves. Don't use it for toilet paper. I made that mistake once and lived to regret it."

"Will there be wild animals?"

"Possibly."

"Bears?"

"Possibly."

"Tigers?"

"I think you can relax on that one. I predict that there will be a serious shortage of tigers in the mountains of southern California. On the other hand, you should take insect repellent. The deerflies can be horrible this time of year."

"I don't know how to thank you for warning me about all this. It sounds like the script of *Predator*. But I shall soldier on. If I'm eaten by a lion or torn apart by a pack of voracious piranhas, tell my mother that—"

"You're still going?"

"Yes."

Mary Lynn sighed and watched the wind ripple the water

on the Esther Williams pool. "Then you must be in love. Nothing else can explain it."

After she finished talking to Jayne, Mary Lynn sat for a while, drinking lemonade and thinking about what she was going to do during her extra week as Jayne Cooper. One thing was certain: she intended to take Jayne up on that offer to buy cute clothes. She vaguely recalled that exclusive stores had professional shoppers, and that if you were very rich, you could tell them what you wanted and they'd pick it out for you. Maybe, since she was a famous movie star, she wouldn't even have to go to the stores. Maybe they'd bring the clothes to her. But how would she know what to buy? The last time she'd read a fashion magazine, she'd been waiting to get her wisdom teeth pulled.

She'd have to do a little research. In the world of fashion, anything was possible. For all she knew, shoulder pads and hoopskirts were going to be staging a comeback this fall. She was just sucking on the last of the ice and thinking about having her colors done, when the phone rang again.

She unfolded the phone and slapped it to her ear. "Hi," she said. "Having second thoughts?"

"Second thoughts about what?" said Clarice.

"Never mind." Jayne and Clarice often called within minutes of each other like a psychic tag team. Mary Lynn made a mental note that in the future it would be wiser not to assume which of them was on the other end of the line. "So what's up?"

"I'm calling to know if I should fatten the calf."

"The what?"

"Is my prodigal daughter going to get her disobedient little ass back here soon, or do I take out adoption papers on you?"

Mary Lynn told Clarice the latest news, minus the part about Jayne being in love with Joe. "Camping?" Clarice said. "I never would have guessed in a million years that she'd go off somewhere she can't get cable. I wish I could be there to see her face when she discovers she can't plug in her hair dryer. So you're her for another week, are you?

Well, I hope you're up to it, because I'm not going to be there to hand you hankies if something goes wrong. I'm going on a weeklong retreat with Guru Ananda Ananda Shri Joti Amrit Ananda."

"Who?"

"We call him Babaji for short." Clarice chuckled. "He's a cute little, sawed-off saint from Haridwar, India, who dispenses bliss by slapping you on the head with peacock feathers. Unconditional love, that's Babaji. Oh, and before you ask, I don't believe any of that crap about reincarnation. Although, if pressed, I sometimes tell Baba's other disciples that in my most recent past life I was Elizabeth Taylor."

"Elizabeth Taylor is still alive."

"Lord, honey," Clarice said, "I know that. You should see the look on their faces as they try to puzzle it out. In any case, the bottom line is that I'm tired of taking care of Jayne's business for her. I've spent a week doing damage control, and I'm exhausted. It's too codependent. I've had this retreat with Babaji scheduled for months; if things go to hell because she's too stubborn to come back—well, then, so be it. Babaji is only in the U.S. for two weeks and he's over eighty with a heart condition. Rumor has it, he may drop his body anytime. Besides, the better I've gotten to know you, the more convinced I've become that you're perfectly capable of handling anything short of a volcanic eruption. As much as I love Jayne, I sometimes wish she had your common sense."

Common sense! Mary Lynn thought. *What common sense? I'm about to panic like a rabbit.* She gripped the phone and took several deep breaths. "How do I get in touch with you if something goes wrong?"

"You can't. That's the point of a retreat. No cell phones, no faxes, no Palm Pilots, no pagers. Just Babaji, peacock feathers, and waves of bliss. Plus, of course, half the major players in Hollywood. The last time I went on a spiritual retreat with Babaji, I negotiated Jayne an eight-figure deal over a bowl of curried carrots."

"Clarice . . ."

"Relax. I took a look at Jayne's appointment book. For the next week, she's got nothing scheduled but an appearance before the Beverly Hills Society for the Propagation of Rare Irises. I canceled that one. With a totally blank calendar, it's not likely that there's going to be another crisis, provided you stay put and tell Lois to hold all your phone calls. I hardly need to remind you not to talk to anyone from Global while I'm off getting my karma retooled. But if Jayne calls, tell her I've determined that in her most recent past life she was a small, uncontrollable Shih Tzu." She hung up.

Mary Lynn immediately tried to call her back, but all she got was a recorded message of Hindu chanting. She waited it out, hoping for some word from Clarice at the end that might give a clue to her whereabouts, but there was nothing.

The first few hours after Clarice left were hard. Mary Lynn spent a sleepless night imagining one disaster after another, but as time passed, she gradually began to believe she had panicked for no reason. With Jayne and Clarice out of town, things were so quiet on Sunday that it was almost eerie. After wandering aimlessly around the estate—trying, and failing, to find something useful to do—she finally dug Jayne's diamond bracelets out of a velvet-lined jewelry box the size of a small suitcase. On Monday she sent Lois out to pawn them, called several exclusive shops on Rodeo Drive, and bought herself sixteen very cute little suits, sixteen pairs of matching heels, sixteen silk blouses, five evening dresses, and a whole closetful of casual clothes, including thigh-high leather boots from Spain and a jeans jacket with diamond buttons.

As she had hoped, the professional shoppers all came to her, pulling up to Jayne's front door in vans loaded with beautiful outfits. Swathing her in the latest fashions, they did alterations on the spot; no one—including Lois—blinked an eye. Evidently, buying thousands of dollars' worth of clothes was something Jayne frequently did to amuse herself when there was nothing interesting on TV.

On Tuesday morning, Mary Lynn was sitting in the liv-

ing room, absorbed in *The Loves of Cleopatra*, when Lois
appeared in the doorway.

"Miss Cooper?" Lois said, rocking nervously from one
foot to another. Lois had never been quite the same since
Mary Lynn yelled at her for admitting Arnie without an-
nouncing him. Although Mary Lynn had apologized at least
a dozen times for flying off the handle, Lois now approached her as if she were wired to explode.

"So what's up?" Mary Lynn asked. She gave Lois a big,
warm smile and got a faint, nervous little smile in return.
Lois blinked and kept rocking. She looked like a lemming
poised on the edge of a cliff. Mary Lynn toyed with the diamond buttons on her jacket, and hoped Lois wasn't about
to tell her bad news. Things had been going so smoothly.

Lois cleared her throat and paused in midrock. "The teeth
whiteners are here, Miss Cooper."

"Ah." Mary Lynn relaxed. "Right." She put down her
book and thought this over. During the last two days, a number of people had appeared at Jayne's door, none of whom
she'd admitted. Keeping Jayne in shape appeared to be like
keeping a great cathedral from falling into ruins. Apparently, half the population of greater Los Angeles was
involved in making sure her nails, hair, and skin were perfect, her body was buffed, and her hems straight. Mary
Lynn had turned away a plastic surgeon who had shown up
to discuss a face-lift and tummy tuck, canceled an appointment for dermal abrasion, sent a man who specialized in
pedicures packing, and informed Lois that anyone who
came offering liposuction should be politely, but firmly,
sent off to suck the fat from someone else's thighs.

But tooth whitening was another matter. She'd never much
liked the color of her teeth. They were, to be honest, a bit on
the yellow side. The process of whitening them was, as she
recalled, rather harmless. They would just put some sort of
plastic thing in her mouth with a gel on it, and when they took
it out, she would look like an ad for toothpaste. She spent a
moment imagining herself with gleaming white teeth and was

tempted. If there was any downside to getting her teeth whitened, she couldn't see it. Besides, Jayne's cell phone hadn't rung in nearly three days, and she was getting bored.

"Great," she said. "Let them come in."

Lois blinked and looked surprised. Perhaps she thought "Miss Cooper" had decided to become a hermit. A few moments later, Mary Lynn heard footsteps approaching. She froze at the sound. There was something . . . terribly familiar about them. All at once, she realized what it was.

"Lois!" she cried. But it was too late. The second the "teeth whiteners" walked into the room, she knew she'd been had. He was tall, blond, and looked—as Jayne had so accurately noted—as if he had never held down a steady job in his life. The woman was young, athletic, and had abs of steel.

"Hi, Mary Lynn," the man said. "Nice place you got here. Real nice place." He turned to the woman with him. "Check out that carpet, Sandy. Classy. Whew. As the poet said. Whew."

Mary Lynn groaned. He was handsome; he was incoherent; he was Ron, her ex-husband. She thought fast. The only thing she could do was to try to convince Ron that he'd just made the biggest mistake of his life. It was possible that he wasn't absolutely sure who she was.

She stared at him blankly, as if she hadn't spent some of the best years of her life picking up his dirty socks. Then she slowly put down her book and gave him her most Jayne-like glare: the one that made directors and producers long to spend the rest of their lives in the Australian outback making documentaries for the Nature Channel.

"Are you speaking to me?" she said in the tone of voice she sometimes used on William Hestene when he went psycho. She noticed that Ron was wearing running shorts and a sleeveless T-shirt that read: REBIRTHING, ONE BREATH AT A TIME. Did Sandy have to listen to those tapes about moving down the vaginal canal? She hoped so.

"It's no good." Ron grinned at her and winked. "Hey, Chicken Little, I'd know you in the dark."

Despite her attempt to look as if she'd never seen him before, Mary Lynn flinched. "Chicken Little"—often shortened
to "CL"—had been Ron's pet name for her. Her pet name for
him, she was ashamed to recall, had been "Mr. Rooster." Actually, it hadn't been her pet name for all of him, just a part
that she'd rather not think about at the moment.

"Who's Chicken Little?" asked Sandy.

Fortunately, Ron ignored Sandy's question, which wasn't
surprising. Ron lived on Planet Ron, a cozy little place
where listening to other people was optional as long as there
was cold beer in the refrigerator. He looked Mary Lynn up
and down as if trying to figure out how much her Coors-
buying potential had increased since the last time they'd met
face-to-face.

"Nice try, CL, but it's no use. I knew the minute I saw
that cute little bare ass of yours in the *Comet* that somehow you'd struck it rich, but I went over to your place
anyway to check it out. And there she was—Jayne Cooper
herself, with a little mole below her left eye, and her super
perky tits. She didn't recognize me, of course." He winked
at Mary Lynn. "Whew, as the poet says. Whew." He grew
thoughtful. "I wasn't surprised. Hey, I always thought you
looked a little bit like Jayne Cooper with love handles."

Mary Lynn grabbed the cell phone. "You're a total
stranger. I've never met you before and have no idea what
you're talking about." Love handles! She did not have love
handles! "I'm calling security. If both of you aren't off this
property in sixty seconds, I'll have you thrown off."

"I wouldn't do that, CL."

"Security!" Mary Lynn barked into the phone. "Living
room, stat."

"Cards are against you, CL. Never bet when the cards are
against you. If I'd followed that advice, I'd still have my
Harley. You see, you got a secret. Whew, what a secret. As
the poet says—"

"What fucking poet?" Mary Lynn yelled. "What poet,
you raving gerbil!"

Securely inhabiting Planet Ron, he didn't even pause. "As the poet says, when you got a secret this big, you don't want to go pissing off someone who might go around telling people about it. Hey, suppose Sandy and I called up the *Comet* and told them to go over to your place and find out why Jayne Cooper decided to live in a dump with no dishwasher." He turned to Sandy. "When CL and I were married, I always had to do the dishes. Whew. Very negative experience. Totally screwed up my biorhythms."

Mary Lynn saw that it was no use. "Liar!" she yelled. "You never washed a single dish!"

There was a brief silence while they stared at each other. Then Mary Lynn picked up the phone and punched the redial button. "Security? Cancel. Versace."

"Versace" was Jayne's private code word that meant everything was okay. Which, Mary Lynn thought grimly, it certainly wasn't. She slammed the phone back down on the table and glared at Ron. It was her own glare this time. He knew it well.

"You're blackmailing me, you devious little creep. If I'd known who you were, you'd never have gotten past the front gate. Teeth whiteners! Damn it, I forgot your father was a dentist!"

"Whew, CL. Strong words." Ron turned to Sandy. "Did I say anything about blackmail?"

"Whatever," Sandy said like some kind of steroid-enhanced Delphic oracle.

Ron turned back to Mary Lynn. "Hey, have you met Sandy?"

"Not formally," Mary Lynn said through gritted teeth. "Although, I believe I once found her panty hose in our bed."

Sandy nodded, and her cute little hairdo fluttered around her ears. "Kewl," she said cheerfully. Evidently, she was an inhabitant of Planet Sandy, which meant she and Ron were perfectly matched. "Ron's told me a whole lot about you."

"I bet he has."

Sandy grew pensive. "Like, I thought you'd be younger."

"I've aged a lot in the last few minutes."

"Yeah, well, you know, like, you should jog or something. You're really out of shape, and, like, you're getting to that age where you can't take the pounds off. How old are you, anyway? Forty?"

"Thirty. And thank you for sharing, you little home-wrecking, anorectic adolescent."

Sandy looked as if she were trying to figure out if this was a compliment or not. Mary Lynn repressed a strong urge to yell at her, and turned to Ron. "Let's get it over with," she said. "How much do you want?"

Ron smiled. "CL, CL, what a silly question. You know me. I want"—he turned to Sandy—"What did I say I wanted, Bunzie?"

Bunzie! He called her "Bunzie"!

Bunzie stuck her little pink tongue between her teeth and thought it over. "I think you said you wanted every dime."

"Right." Ron turned back to Mary Lynn. "Every dime."

"No!" Mary Lynn rose to her feet. "I supported you the whole time we were married. I've been paying you spousal support for months. When you left, you cleaned out our apartment and our bank account. You took the blender, the stereo, the queen-size sheets, the car, both electric tooth-brushes, and the art deco bookends my parents gave us when we got married. You even took a bag of cat kibble."

"Hey"—Ron shrugged—"no problem. I never opened the kibble. I'll give it back."

"It's stale!" Mary Lynn yelled. Like all conversations with Ron, this one was going nowhere. "I'm not feeding my cats stale kibble!"

"Whoa," Sandy said to Ron. "Is your ex always into, like, the rage thing?"

"Oh, go jog off a cliff," Mary Lynn snarled. She turned back to Ron. "If you're *not* blackmailing me, why should I give you a cent?"

"I have needs."

"We're divorced, Ron. The judge gave me a piece of paper that says your needs are no longer my problem."

"Like, you don't get it," Sandy said. "Like, Ron has debts. Like, if he doesn't get some money soon, they're going to, like, cap him."

"Cap him?" For one crazy moment, Mary Lynn thought she meant someone was going to put a hat on Ron's head. Then she got it. She turned to Ron. "You've been gambling again and lost, right? You owe money to the Mob."

Ron nodded. "To Sandy's uncle."

"How much?"

"Fifty thousand. And hey, CL, like the poet said, if you don't want to share, I guess I'll have to, well, whew, 'blackmail' is an ugly word, but . . ."

"Uncle Rick is totally into the capping thing." Sandy shrugged. "Go figure. Who knew? Is he going to give his own niece's boyfriend a break? I don't think so. I mean this is, like, totally not kewl."

"Miss Cooper?"

Mary Lynn looked up and again saw Lois standing in the doorway. Had Lois heard any of this? Evidently not.

"What is it, Lois?"

"One of Mr. Laughton's assistants just called."

"Bert Laughton? The director of *Salome*?"

"Yes, Miss Cooper. I told him you weren't taking phone calls, so he left a message." Lois looked from Ron to Sandy as if wondering why they weren't in the process of putting whitening gel on Mary Lynn's teeth. "He said it was urgent."

Mary Lynn decided that whatever the message was, it would be a bad idea to share it. She asked Lois to go into the next room where she could talk to her in private. Then she turned to Ron and Sandy.

"I'll be right back. Meanwhile, stay where you are and try to resist the urge to steal the silver."

"Kewl," said Sandy, who possessed a vocabulary remarkably lacking in adjectives.

"Do you have any beer?" Ron asked Lois. He stared at

the silver frames around Jayne's pictures as if calculating
how much he could get for them. "Whew. Like the poet
said: I could really use a couple of cold ones right now."

A few seconds later, Mary Lynn was in possession of the
message left by Bert Laughton's assistant. The message,
which Lois had written neatly on a piece of Jayne's personal
stationery, was simple, and straight to the point:

"Please tell Miss Cooper that, due to technical problems,
Mr. Laughton needs to reshoot scene 104 of *Salome* on the
Global lot Thursday morning. Miss Cooper's makeup call
is at six A.M."

Twenty

It was noon, and so hot the boulders shone like glass. Overhead, in a sky the color of Leonardo DiCaprio's eyes, a hawk was gliding in great swooping circles, looking for some small, furry creature to munch on.

Jayne plodded wearily up the trail, keeping a wary eye out for movie-star-eating mountain lions, rattlesnakes, and large, unidentifiable, possibly poisonous insects. Up ahead, Lisa and Janeira were hopping from rock to rock like little mountain goats, giggling and laughing as if there weren't a thousand-foot drop-off to their left and a million tons of rock with major landslide potential to their right. Carmen—who should have been yelling at them to come back before they fell and broke their necks—strolled casually after them, listening to samba tapes on her Walkman.

Giving a moan of despair, Jayne threw down her pack and fell in a heap beside it. "How does Carmen do it?" she gasped. "She must be fifty-five at least."

"Sixty-one," said Joe, who had politely fallen back to keep Jayne company. He sat down beside her and watched Carmen deftly samba around a fallen log. "Don't worry about her. She can outhike all of us." He reached for his canteen, unscrewed the cap, and offered it to Jayne. "Here, have a drink. You look like you could use one."

"Please tell me you've got iced gin and tonic in there."

"Nope, just water."

Jayne sighed, took the canteen, drank, and wiped the

sweat off her forehead with the sleeve of the oversize denim shirt Joe had loaned her. Camping. It had sounded so innocent. No one had bothered to tell her the trail went straight up the side of the mountain. In the back of her brain, a very bad band kept playing "My Heart Will Go On." Maybe she was getting delirious. Perhaps she should have brought along a tank of oxygen. She vaguely remembered that people sometimes died of altitude sickness.

"How high are we?" She pulled off her hat and began to fan herself with it.

"About three thousand feet."

That was disappointing. Even she knew that you didn't get altitude sick at three thousand feet. She'd hoped for something more dramatic. "How much farther is it to the campground?"

"We only started out five minutes ago. If you look down, you can still see our car parked at the trailhead."

"My God." Jayne put her hat back on and took another gulp of water. "It seems like we've been scaling this mountain for hours. I feel like we're trapped in those scenes from *Predator* where Arnold Schwarzenegger stumbles through the jungle; only, instead of invisible, homicidal, trophy-taking aliens, we've got ninety-degree heat and deerflies."

"Want to go back?"

She thought it over. The prospect of returning to civilization was tempting, but she hated to give in so easily. Joe would be disappointed in her, and he looked so strong and manly in his T-shirt. She felt a wave of sexual desire. Such great eyes, such well-developed biceps, such a large vocabulary . . . shit, she was actually starting to think like an English professor. She had to get a grip on herself.

"I'm fine," she said briskly as she mentally stripped him to the buff, knocked him over on his back, and threw herself on top of him. "Actually, I'm having a wonderful time in a ghastly sort of way." She waved at the landscape. "This is all so amazingly primitive. You know, like *Cast Away*. I mean, knowing I could be consumed by a rabid bear, or plunge screaming to my death, or develop Lyme disease, makes every moment intensely thrilling."

Joe chuckled. "I'm glad you're having fun." As they started to get to their feet, he reached out to retrieve her pack. "Hey, this weighs a ton. What the heck are you carrying in here?"

Jayne took the pack, unzipped it, and peered inside. "Just the bare necessities: a hairbrush, a bottle of moisturizer, a couple of tubes of lipstick, a can of Raid. . . ."

"Raid?"

"For the tarantulas. Rubber boots."

"It's probably not going to rain until November."

She pulled out the boots and examined them. "They're not for rain. They're for snakes. I'm pretty sure snakes can't bite through rubber." She continued to rummage. "Let me see. What else? Two bars of"—she inspected the labels—"jasmine-scented soap, which I suppose I might call a gift from a friend since I more or less loathe jasmine. A bottle of shampoo, a bottle of cream rinse, a bottle of setting gel, a couple of tubes of cheap mascara, powder, foundation, an eyelash curler, which"—she held up the eyelash curler and clicked it—"is somewhat the worse for wear. An economy-size can of Food Barn talcum powder, a small mirror to start fires and signal for help, a pack of matches from the Smoke House, which appears to specialize in a dish called surf and turf, toothpaste, and of course this." She pulled out a large serrated bread knife.

"What's that for?"

"Bears or rabid squirrels, whichever attacks first."

"Right." Joe cleared his throat and developed a sudden interest in something just over her left shoulder. "Is that all?"

"Pretty much. Except for this." Jayne dug into the bottom of the pack and fished out a large plastic case.

"What's that?"

"Hot Curls."

"Hot Curls?"

She opened the case and displayed plastic curlers parked in neat rows. "For my hair."

"Electric?"

"Why, yes. Is that a problem?"

"Not if you have a kite with a wire string, a thunderstorm, and a handy little twenty-eight-pound item called a portable inverter that converts DC to AC. Otherwise, I'd say you're not going to have much use for those."

"I thought you said we were going to a campground. You know, with a convenience store, showers, maybe a small pool."

"There's only a clearing and a fire ring. We'll be getting our water out of the stream and hauling it up the slope in a collapsible bucket."

Jayne repressed an urge to wail. "Are you telling me there's no electricity?"

"Not a bit."

She looked at the curlers sadly. "Then how am I going to do my hair?"

"You don't have to do your hair. It looks great just the way it is."

Jayne pulled out the mirror, contemplated her own image, and frowned. "You must be joking. I'm seeing sweaty, stringy, and windblown here. I'm seeing a rapidly deteriorating situation." She snapped the mirror closed. "If I go on like this, I'll stagger out of the wilderness looking like a cross between Marge Simpson and Bigfoot."

Joe laughed. "The girls would be thrilled. They're big fans of *The Simpsons*." He picked up one of the tubes of lipstick, tossed it in the air, and caught it. "Seriously, you don't have to wear any of this stuff. You look great the way nature made you."

"Great? I look like I should be on my knees saying, '*Fashion Emergency,* please help me.'"

"You're a beautiful woman. You don't need makeup."

Jayne looked at him with shocked delight. "Tell me again I'm beautiful."

"You're beautiful."

"No, I mean say: You're beautiful without makeup."

"You're beautiful without makeup."

Jayne tried to remember the last time she had gone outside her own house without wearing lipstick. She must have been eleven, perhaps twelve. "How many times would you be willing to say that?"

"As many times as you like." He picked up her pack. "Look, why don't I take most of this stuff back to the car? Your pack's so heavy, I wouldn't put it on a mule. We're only walking in about eight miles. If you discover you can't live without setting gel, I'll walk back out and get it for you. Come on. What do you say? Pick one lipstick; dump the Hot Curls; lose the rubber boots."

This was real life: up close, personal, in the raw. This was living without a net. Jayne felt the wilderness humming around her like a giant mosquito closing in for the kill. Would she let it suck her dry? No. Joe was right. Her pack was too heavy. Surely, a woman who was tough enough to go head-to-head with Carleton Winters over residuals was tough enough to survive for a week on one tube of lipstick. Had the pioneer women worn mascara? No. Had Joan of Arc used moisturizing cream? Not the Joan of Arc she'd played in *The Loves of Joan of Arc*, but the real Joan of Arc, the one who had talked to God and got herself burned for witchcraft? No, and no again.

She closed her eyes so she could no longer see the pack that contained her last link to a world that included emergency comb-outs, therapists, iced gin, and manicures. "Take it," she said in the tone of voice she usually reserved for films in which she died for love.

"That's the spirit." Joe bent down and gave her a long kiss that left her breathless. "Live on the edge," he whispered. He kissed her again. "Be a wild woman. Who knows? You might like it."

To her surprise, Jayne discovered that living without mascara wasn't so bad after all. With a half-empty pack, she was able to hike with renewed energy. She even found enough spare breath to sing to ward off bears. For several hours, she strolled beside Joe, admiring the intensely blue sky and the wildflowers, and listening with pleasure to flocks of small, yellow-breasted birds that seemed to have nothing better to do than sing their heads off. And she began to think: *Hey, this outdoor stuff isn't half bad.*

Although she frequently felt as if she had become a character in a postapocalyptic action-adventure film, her enthusiasm did not falter when they reached the campsite. She pitched in gamely: collecting wood, hauling water, and making up silly stories about Teletubbies, which sent the girls into hopeless giggles. Dinner was cheese, crackers, and freeze-dried chicken stew, which she ate like a good sport. Afterward, she helped Joe and Carmen wash the dishes with some kind of insanely pure organic soap that smelled like peppermint. Then she toasted marshmallows over the fire with an expertise that brought cries of admiration from Janeira and Lisa, and went on to make s'mores like a pro. Once or twice, as darkness fell, she and Joe even had an opportunity to sneak behind a bush and exchange a few quick kisses, which promised good things for tomorrow.

Then, just as she was congratulating herself on showing true grit, Carmen led her to her bed. Jayne stared in disbelief at the miserably thin foam pad that was apparently intended to separate her body from the earth.

"You're kidding," she said.

"You be very comfortable." Carmen smiled and fluffed up the sleeping bag. "Cozy, *sim?*"

Cozy? Hello? What did Carmen usually sleep on? A bed of nails? Jayne poked at the foam with the toe of her boot and tried to calculate the possibility of calling a helicopter and getting herself flown out to a five-star hotel. Of course, she couldn't call because she didn't have a cell phone, and even if she had, cell phones didn't work up here. With a sigh of resignation, she crawled into the sleeping bag, zipped it up around her like a baggy girdle, and lay down—only to sit up with a small screech.

"What's wrong?" Joe whispered. He was only lying about three feet away, but since Carmen and the girls were well within earshot, there was clearly going to be no midnight commuting.

"Rock," she moaned, rubbing her skull.

"You hit your head on a rock?"

"Uh-huh."

"Try using your pack as a pillow."

Jayne put her pack under her head, which wasn't much of an improvement. She shut her eyes and started to count sheep, then changed her mind and started to review her stock portfolio. She had just reached her Small Cap funds, when she felt Joe reach out and take her hand.

"Sleep tight," he said, giving it a squeeze.

The old Jayne would have said something sarcastic, but the wilderness had already gotten to her. Much as she hated to admit it, there was something about being in the mountains that was better than tranquilizers. She lay back and allowed herself to feel the sweetness of the moment: no planes, no phones, only the soft swish of the pines and a man beside her who certainly liked her and maybe even loved her just for being herself. She squeezed his hand in return. "Sweet dreams," she said, and meant it.

About an hour later, Joe, Carmen, and the girls were startled by a piercing scream. Thinking Jayne had been attacked, Joe catapulted out of his sleeping bag and leaped to his feet, only to find her well, alive, and continuing to shriek. He knelt down beside her, gathered her in his arms, and held her.

"What's wrong?" he asked.

"A thing!" she cried. "A giant thing! I woke up and there it was, inches from my face." She shuddered and buried her face in his shoulder. "My God, it was horrible. It was like something out of *Alien*!"

"Try to calm down. Try to tell me what it looked like. Was it a bear?"

"No!"

"Is she dying?" Lisa asked.

"Hush," said Carmen. "She's fine."

"I'm not fine," Jayne yelled. "I was nearly eaten by a twenty-pound rat with hideous yellow teeth and nasty beady little eyes. The damn thing was standing beside my head, looking at me like I was an appetizer!"

"It's okay," Joe said soothingly. "I think from your description that you saw a possum."

"Possum?"

"Did it have a furry body and a naked tail?"

"Yes, damn it. Are possums carnivorous?"

"They eat roots and insects. This one was probably just curious. You don't have any food in your pack, do you?"

"Only a little chocolate." Jayne was beginning to feel foolish. A possum. Right. She'd seen them in zoos. The only fact she could remember about the damn beasts was that the females carried their young in pouches.

Joe dug into Jayne's bag, took out the chocolate, unwrapped it, and tossed it into the stream. "Can't have this around," he explained. "It might attract something serious next time."

"Like what?"

"Like bears."

"Bears!" Jayne screamed. She was beginning to bitterly regret that she had ever been persuaded to give up her knife. "What are we? A free lunch!"

"It's no problem," Joe said. "If you don't have any food near the place you're sleeping, then . . ."

He never managed to finish the sentence. Taking up the cry of "Bears! Bears!" the girls had dissolved into hysterics. "We want to go home!"

The sound of the girls sobbing sobered Jayne like a bucket of cold water. She hadn't meant to frighten them. "It's okay," she called. "Everything is okay." She turned to Joe. "We can't go back, can we?"

"Not in the dark."

"Is it really safe? I mean, are the bears really not likely to eat us?"

"As far as I know, no one's been eaten by a bear around here in the past hundred years."

"Could we sleep closer together?"

"Sure, if it will make you feel better."

Five minutes later, Jayne was sleeping with Lisa curled up under her left arm and Janeira snuggled against her back. Carmen lay inches away, already snoring softly; Joe was stretched out at their feet like a large guard dog.

Several hours passed. Somewhere deep in the forest, the possums found other things to terrorize, and the bears did whatever bears did when they weren't acting in nature specials. In the sky, great constellations of brilliant stars rolled west through air clear as glass, and satellites spun overhead like klieg lights.

Just before dawn, Jayne woke with an urgent need to pee. Slipping out of her sleeping bag, she quietly stepped over Lisa and Carmen, grabbed one of the flashlights, and made her way to the edge of the clearing, where she bent down and promptly tumbled backward into a large bush.

"Damn it to hell!" she snarled. She scrambled to her feet, retrieved the flashlight, and was just about to pick up where she'd left off, when she noticed that the bush she had tumbled into had slick green leaves that came in bunches of three.

"Gramma says you should hang on to a tree trunk next time," Janeira told a wet, shivering, blue-lipped Jayne.

"Thanks," Jayne said through chattering teeth. "I'll keep that in mind." She was standing in the stream, in water so cold it probably could have been marketed as a birth control device. Carmen stood behind her, scrubbing her furiously with peppermint soap and sand, an odd combination that provided instantaneous aromatherapy and dermal abrasion. Mixed with the smell of peppermint was the smell of coffee, which suggested that Joe, who had remained discreetly behind, was preparing breakfast.

"Gramma wants to know if you ever had poison oak before."

"No, I've never even seen it."

"She says maybe then you won't get it."

Jayne turned her head, arched her back, and contemplated her own rear end with a certain amount of nostalgia. She'd never realized before how much she'd taken it for granted.

Having survived a concussion, poison oak, and a giant carnivorous rat, Jayne spent most of the morning in camp recovering her equilibrium while the others hiked. Since there was no television and no prospect of doing even the most primitive shopping, she took a long nap. Afterward, in a fit of near-terminal boredom, she gave herself a makeshift pedicure using the scissors on Joe's Swiss Army knife and put her hair up in curlers that she had cleverly constructed from twigs.

By the time the others returned for a lunch of peanut butter and crackers, her hair was dry and fluffy, her toenails were clipped to perfection, and she was ready for a bit of adventure—provided it didn't involve poisonous snakes or large animals. Sensing her mood, Joe offered to take her fishing, and when she accepted, he led her upstream, where he unfolded an ingenious canvas bag that contained lines, reels, hooks, two collapsible poles, and an assortment of cute little objects made out of shiny metal and feathers, which, he explained, were supposed to resemble flies.

"Are you saying that fish are fooled by these things?" Jayne extracted a large pink-and-green knot of what appeared to be hair that had been shaved off the head of a punk rocker. She held it up and jingled the hooks together. "They must be pretty dumb."

"Let's hope so, or we'll be eating freeze-dried chicken stew again for dinner tonight." Joe pulled out a piece of laminated paper and pinned it to her shirt, and then pinned one to his own. "These are our fishing licenses. We have to wear them in case a game warden comes along. There's a fine for fishing without one. Ever fished before?"

"Yes," Jayne said, not adding that her one "fishing" experience had consisted in sitting on a French count's yacht, sipping gin and tonic while he reeled in dozens of gigantic fish with a line suitable for tying up an ocean liner. She'd felt sorry for the fish and had broken up with the count a few days later when he insisted she admire his prize-winning stuffed marlin.

Joe assembled the poles, then put his arms around her waist and began to show her how to cast. She felt the heat of his body on her back, the prickle of his chin against her head. He smelled like peppermint soap and wood smoke. For a moment, she was so overcome with the sense of being next to him that she almost swooned like some nineteenth-century heroine in a tight corset.

"You cast like this," Joe said. "First you . . ."

She couldn't take it any longer. Wheeling around, she threw her arms around him. "Try 'First you kiss me,'" she said. Joe dropped the pole and grabbed her.

"Right," he said in a hoarse whisper. "First I kiss you." He kissed her long and hard, long and soft, and several other ways she wasn't completely familiar with, all of which were delicious. She closed her eyes and saw the shadows of the pine trees playing across her lids. She felt light and happy and very, very randy. It was an odd sensation. She wasn't particularly calculating about sex, but she usually had a sense of performing: enjoying herself, but ready for a re-take. But as Joe kissed her, the invisible cameras stopped rolling, and she forgot about everything but the soft circles he was making in her mouth with his tongue.

"Whew," she said when they finally disengaged.

"The nice thing about the outdoors," he whispered, "is that there's a lot of privacy." He put his arm around her waist and they walked to a grassy place beside the stream. They sat down and he began kissing her again.

"I like you," he whispered. "I like you very much." He

pulled the pins out of her hair and let it fall to her shoulders. Then he buried his face in it. "Your hair smells sweet, like summer." He wound her hair around his hands, then covered her mouth with it and kissed her through the strands. He felt the weight of her breasts against his chest, the curve of her waist, the incredible smoothness of her skin. He wanted her so much he could hardly speak. "Let's take a long time," he whispered. "A long, long time."

She must have agreed, because the next thing he knew they were undressing each other. When they were naked, he spread their clothing on the grass and they lay on top of it and embraced. His body was firm and lean, his arms powerful, but he held her very carefully. When at last he came into her, he rocked her back and forth until she laughed, and moaned, and cried out with joy. Then he came with a cry and fell beside her.

For a long time, they lay side by side looking up at the sky through the branches of the pines. Jayne rested her head on his shoulder and watched a few small clouds blow toward L.A. and a whole world that now seemed very far away. She had never made love outside before and had had no idea that the sky could be so blue and peaceful. After a while, Joe turned and faced her. Once again he took her in his arms and drew her toward him.

"I hope this doesn't ruin anything," he said gently, "but I think I love you."

Jayne, who had done hundreds of love scenes, was at a loss for words. Reaching out, she gently stroked his eyelids and lips with the tips of her fingers.

"Life," she said softly, "is nothing at all like the movies, is it?" He didn't understand, of course, but it really didn't matter, because he understood about love, and that was all that counted.

Twenty-one

Back in Los Angeles, the sun was shining, the humidity was low, the temperature was in the 70s, and the air was so clear you could see the tops of the buildings without using a periscope. In Venice, the sea breezes were wafting lazily in from the channel islands, and flocks of gulls were riding the thermal currents above Ocean Front Walk with their wings spread like sails.

Arnie Levine sat on a wooden bench under a palm tree; he was ignoring the skateboarders, the fire breathers, and the psychedelic orange-and-red trash cans. In his hands, he held the latest issue of the *Comet,* which he was reading with the kind of grim pleasure usually associated with reading obituaries. Once again he had discovered he was yesterday's news. Not that he minded. In fact, it was a big relief. Today the editors of the *Comet* had devoted the entire front page to a hot affair between Prince William and a young ballerina, complete with separate photographs of the two placed so they appeared to be gazing at each other with unbridled lust.

Arnie sighed and turned the page. He felt sorry for the poor motherless kid, but maybe when you were a prince, you got used to people publishing lies about you. He quickly skimmed a story on page 2 about aliens using pets as spies (IS YOUR DOG WATCHING YOU?), and a piece on page 4 about a woman in Thailand who had recently been arrested for torturing shrimp on a hot plate (SHE LAUGHED AND

MOCKED THEM, SAID POLICE). He was searching for the Jayne
Cooper story, and having become a daily reader of the
Comet, he knew if he kept on long enough, he'd find it. As
far as he could tell, the *Comet* hadn't published an issue in
the past decade without at least one story about Jayne.

A few days ago, he had had the dubious pleasure of reading a statement she had supposedly made to the press about
how much she appreciated him slugging Malfredi, followed
by her impassioned plea for more laws to protect the privacy of celebrities. Claiming that the photos of her and
Arnie having sex had been faked, she vowed to sue the
Comet; all of which the *Comet* noted with glee, since every
time Jayne Cooper sued them, their readership soared to
new heights.

Arnie read every word of the shrimp abuse story, trying
to delay the moment when he'd once again be forced to look
at a photo of Jayne and learn what she had supposedly been
doing since he'd walked in and discovered her rolling
around on the floor with some guy who looked like an extra
from *The Godfather*. Following her through the tabloids
was becoming an obsession he wasn't proud of. He knew if
he had an ounce of self-respect, he'd throw the damn paper
in the trash and get on with his life. There were support
groups in L.A. for everything from weight loss to freeway
phobia. Maybe he should start one for poor, sensitive
schmucks who had slept with famous movie stars who
didn't give a damn about them.

Reluctantly he turned to page 5, and gave a small moan.
This was the worst yet. There was Jayne, smiling the way
she had smiled just after they finished making love—only
it wasn't good old Arnie Levine she was smiling at: it was
a photo of Edward Surrey. According to the article, Jayne
had just announced her engagement to the British actor.

Arnie felt a knot in his stomach that sent him scrambling
for the Pepto-Bismol tablets in his pocket. He popped two
in his mouth and chewed them as he read on. According to

the *Comet*, Jayne had called Surrey "the love of my life." Was that possible?

Maybe yes, maybe no. Surrey, it seemed, was already married. His wife had expressed her surprise at the news ("I'll wring his scrawny little neck," says Glenda Surrey), and Surrey himself had issued a hasty statement through his publicity agent claiming that he and Jayne Cooper had never had anything more than a "purely professional relationship."

Arnie closed the newspaper, closed his eyes, and swallowed the last bits of Pepto-Bismol. The stuff tasted like peppermint chalk. His stomach heaved, and he felt like crying. He had had his moment, and it was over. He was never going to know anything about Jayne's life that hadn't been written by the same bunch of slimeballs who had claimed only yesterday that Elvis had been an ambassador from Mars. If he had an ounce of self-respect, he'd never buy another issue of the *Comet*.

He was just trying to calculate how much longer he had to stay in L.A. when he felt someone sit down beside him. Opening his eyes, he saw that a woman in a black raincoat, black scarf, and oversize sunglasses had joined him on the bench. The hair that poked out from under her scarf had been coiled into platinum-blond dreadlocks, and she appeared to be wearing a pair of dark blue ski gloves with white racing stripes. What else she might have been wearing was not immediately apparent since the raincoat pretty much made her look like a duffel bag full of laundry.

Bag lady, he thought. *Well, good.* He was happy to share his bench with her. Misery did indeed love company. Maybe he'd give her a few bucks and make her day.

"Arnie," the woman said.

Arnie froze as if he'd been poleaxed. He knew that voice. No, it couldn't possibly be. He must be hallucinating.

"Arnie, please. I know you're mad at me, but I've got to talk to you."

"Jayne?"

She glanced around warily, then turned toward him and

lowered her glasses an inch or so, so he could see her face. Arnie made a small choking noise and dropped his copy of the *Comet*.

"Jayne, it is you!"

"It's me."

"What are you doing here? Where's your limo? Your bodyguards? Your new boyfriend? Why aren't you off at some in place like Patrick's Roadhouse, sharing an omelette with George Clooney?"

"Arnie . . ."

He closed his eyes again. "Oh, God, just go away," he said. "Go back and screw Edward Surrey and Tom Cruise until their eyeballs fall out, and let a poor playwright live in peace."

She reached out and touched him on the shoulder. "Arnie, please, I'm begging you: don't send me away. I need your help."

He opened his eyes. She was still there. Worst of all, now that he could see her face, she still looked beautiful to him despite the stupid kerchief and the big coat. "How could I help you?" he said through clenched teeth. "What do I have that you can't buy?"

"Arnie, I need a friend right now, and you're the closest thing I have to one. I'm not asking you to forgive me. I'm just asking you to give me a chance to explain."

"Hey," he said, "no explanation necessary. The whole scene is burned on my brain. In fact, I've started writing a new play about it called *Lady Chatterley Does Hollywood*. I keep thinking it was too bad I didn't get my heart stomped on in Texas by Debbie Reynolds. *Debbie Does Dallas* was one of the big porno hits of all time."

She flinched. "I don't deserve that," she said.

Arnie saw that he had hurt her and was immediately sorry. He had spent days fantasizing about getting even, and now that he had the chance, he found he didn't want to.

"I'm sorry," he said. "It's just that I'm still hurting. Look, why don't you tell me why you're here? I figured you'd forgotten all about me. If you need some help, maybe I can do something for you. I can't imagine what that would be, unless you need some last-minute rewrites; but go ahead, ask."

"Not here." She put her glasses back on and looked around in a hunted way that made him feel sorry for her. He knew that when he started feeling sorry for a woman, his instinct for self-preservation always went out the window, but he couldn't help himself.

She turned to him again and lowered her glasses. "We've got to go somewhere the damn photographers can't find us. I think I've eluded them so far. You wouldn't believe what I went through to get here." She gave him the ghost of a smile. "The paparazzi camp outside Jayne's house in a big pack like wolves. They're there twenty-four hours a day. I knew I couldn't just walk out and not expect them to follow me, so I rooted around in Jayne's closet and found this outfit. . . ."

Alarm bells rang in Arnie's head. She was talking about herself in the third person. The last woman he'd known who'd done that had ended up emptying his entire bank account.

". . . then I put on the weirdest wig she had, sneaked out when Lois wasn't looking, disabled the security system using Jayne's secret code, and climbed the fence by the Esther Williams pool. It was like a jailbreak." She put on her glasses and did the 360-degree stare again. "Where can we go to talk that's private?"

Arnie knew of only one place where the paparazzi wouldn't be likely to find them. *Okay,* he thought, *I'm doomed.* Reaching into his pocket, he took out two more Pepto-Bismol tablets and popped them into his mouth; he wished they were Prozac.

"How about my place?" he said.

Twenty minutes later, Mary Lynn sat in Arnie's desk chair. Since there was no other chair in the room, Arnie was forced to sit on his bed. Not wanting a repeat of the last time they'd been alone together, he sat on the very edge, trying to look as much as possible like a man who had absolutely no interest in sex.

"Okay, Jayne," he said in what he hoped was a somewhat friendly, but not too friendly, voice. "What's up?"

Now that they were finally alone, Mary Lynn had no idea how to begin. She looked around the room, thinking how happy she'd been in it only a few days ago. Up until now, she'd still treasured a faint hope that she'd somehow be able to work things out with Arnie; but now, face-to-face with him, she realized that was unlikely. This relationship, if you could even call it that, was going to end exactly like the rest of her relationships had ended: badly. Some women got to have nice boyfriends who later became nice husbands. Others got a lifetime of the Romance Channel and Lean Cuisine.

She decided that there was nothing to do but tell him the truth and get it over with. "I'm not who you think I am," she said.

"Oh," said Arnie, looking at her warily.

"I'm not Jayne Cooper."

His wariness changed to pity. "Jayne, I think you need professional help. You're clearly having a—"

"Nervous breakdown? No, I'm not, Arnie. I'm telling you the truth. I'm not Jayne Cooper. I tried to tell you that the last time we saw each other, but you didn't listen. I don't blame you. I probably wouldn't have listened either if I'd found you on the floor with another woman. Jayne Cooper is paying me one hundred fifty thousand dollars to impersonate her for a couple of weeks while she lives my life. She's doing research for a film. We . . . Well, crazy as it sounds, we traded identities. I look sort of like her, not to anyone who knows her intimately, but with enough makeup and the right hairdo, I can pass. It's like that Mark Twain novel."

"The Prince and the Pauper?" Arnie said in a tone of voice that gave no hint of what he was thinking.

"Exactly. The one where the little prince and the poor boy switch roles. Only, instead of a little prince, we have a famous movie star and me."

"So if you're not Jayne Cooper, who are you?"

"Mary Lynn McLellan."

"I see. And what do you do, Mary Lynn?"

"I teach composition part-time at Coast Side Community College. Also, I work at the Food Barn as a checkout clerk, or at least I did until Jayne got me fired."

Arnie stood up. "God, Jayne, this is such bullshit. I don't know what you're up to, but I'd appreciate it if you'd leave right now."

"Arnie," Mary Lynn cried, "please sit down! At least give me a chance. I can prove I am who I say I am."

"Yeah, and I can prove I'm Edward Surrey, who I hear you've been bonking in addition to the guy you wrestle with."

"I'm an English professor; I have a master's degree from UC Santa Cruz. Check me out. You're a well-educated guy. Ask me things no movie star would know. I bet you majored in English. I can sense it the way salmon can sense the stream they spawned in." She paused. "Excuse me. Bad choice of metaphor. But go ahead. Ask me questions only a bona fide English professor could answer."

Arnie sat down and glared at her. "Okay," he said. "You want to play *Celebrity Jeopardy*, Jayne; we'll play *Celebrity Jeopardy*." He paused and then leaned forward and got in her face.

"What's blank verse?"

"Unrhymed iambic pentameter. Too easy. Try again."

"Synecdoche?"

"A figure of speech that substitutes the part for the whole, as when we ask someone to 'lend a hand' or speak of 'a hundred head of cattle.'"

"Very good." Arnie was both surprised and impressed. "How about this one: What do Coll, Gill, Gib, Daw, Mak, Mary, and Angel have in common?"

Mary Lynn tried to remember and drew a blank.

"So, 'Mary Lynn,' nothing comes to mind, does it?" Arnie stood up again. "Game over. You lose."

"Wait," she cried. "I think I've got it! Of course! They're the characters in the *Second Shepherd's Play*. It's one of the finest examples in English of a medieval mystery play, written sometime in the fifteenth century, as I recall." She looked down at her hands and thought for a moment. "Mak is sometimes seen as a precursor of Shakespeare's Falstaff." She looked up and saw that Arnie was staring at her open-mouthed.

"God help me," he said. "I think you're telling the truth. I know that play by heart. I directed it when I was in high school. It was the reason I fell in love with the theater. Jayne Cooper would never have recognized the names of those characters in a million years." He walked slowly back to the bed and sat down again.

"So you believe me?"

"Yes." There was a long silence while they stared at each other as if they'd never met, which, Mary Lynn thought, was pretty much the case. She kept hoping he'd say more, but he didn't. "Arnie," she said when she could stand the silence no longer, "you know what this means, don't you?"

"I guess it means that I slept with someone before I knew her name. A personal first for me."

Mary Lynn turned bright red. "Well, yes. I guess it does mean that. But it also means that, now that you believe me, our positions are reversed." She bit her lower lip and looked at him anxiously. "I'm going to have to throw myself on your mercy. I can't do anything for you. I'm not a megastar. I don't have any more power in Hollywood than you do, probably a whole lot less. If you were going out with Jayne Cooper because you thought she could help your scriptwriting career, I'll understand if you ask me to leave now. But if by any chance you think you could be friends with a comp instructor named Mary Lynn McLellan, I could really use some help."

"I don't give a damn about having a career as a scriptwriter," Arnie said, still looking at her as if she had recently arrived from outer space. "All I want to do is finish the rewrite of *Star Whale*, cash the check, and get back to New York. I've got a play in preproduction. Live theater— real actors—a play I wrote and care about, which no studio execs in Armani suits can make me change." He paused, looked at her for a few seconds, and then shook his head. "I don't know what to say. Mary Lynn, is it?"

She nodded.

"You're absolutely sure about that? You're not going to suddenly tell me you're named Angela, or Brie, or Moon Unit?"

"I was named after my two aunts: Mary and Lynn. Aunt Mary has three kids and spends her time putting on bake sales to raise money for the Methodist mission schools in Korea. Aunt Lynn became a doctor, which made her the first real career woman in our family. She's in general practice in Bakersfield. They're my father's sisters."

"Great. Now that we've got you born and named, let's move on from there." Arnie reached out, grabbed a pillow, slapped it against the wall, and leaned back against it. "I want to know who you are and how you managed to get yourself into this mess. I suspect it's a long story, but at this point, I've got nothing but time. Oh yeah. And one more thing: if you lie to me, you're out the door. I once had a girl-friend who was a compulsive liar, and it's not an experience I care to repeat."

Mary Lynn didn't know exactly where to begin, so she just started in the middle and worked her way back and forth. She spoke for a long time, telling him everything from the moment she met Jayne at the Food Barn to the mo-ment Ron walked in and demanded hush money.

As she spoke, the grim expression gradually left Arnie's face. Having already believed the impossible, he found that he had no choice but to believe the rest. Of course, she had a big advantage: he wanted to believe her. By the time she finished, he realized that he liked her even better than he had when he thought she was Jayne. He gave a silent moan. God had clearly created him to be a doormat for women.

One thing was certain: she was right when she said she needed a friend. She was in big trouble, and Arnie Levine had never been able resist an appeal from a beautiful woman. Taking a deep breath, he committed his soul to whatever god looked out for suckers.

"I think I can help you," he said. The look of surprised delight on her face was his reward. He let himself bask in it for a second before he continued. "What was the name of Sandy's uncle again? The one who owns an interest in that casino in Vegas?"

"Rick."

"Rick what?"

Mary Lynn frowned. "Good question. I'm not sure. Sandy's last name is Spoletto. I know that because once when I noticed that Ron was making a lot of toll calls, I used a reverse phone directory to figure out who he was talking to. I knew he was having an affair, but for a while I wasn't sure with which gender. Sandy had her name listed as 'S. B. Spoletto,' which sounds like a guy. But then I went back over our MasterCard statements and realized he'd been using the Internet to order thong underwear on the sly."

"Rick Spoletto. The name doesn't mean anything to me, but I think I might know someone who might know him."

"I think he's a mobster. Do you know mobsters?"

Arnie grinned for the first time in days. "Hey," he said, "I was born in New Jersey. Seriously, I have a connection that might do you some good. I used to live on Mulberry Street in a part of Manhattan called Little Italy. One night just before Thanksgiving, I was coming home and there was this old lady walking down the sidewalk ahead of me. It was sleeting, very nasty. She slipped on some ice and took a tumble. I ran over to help her up, and just as I bent down, some junkie kicked me in the teeth and stole her purse. Result: I hail a cab and the two of us end up in the emergency room. Me with a split lip, her apparently having a heart attack. They take her right away because she's eighty and has chest pains. But since I only have a split lip, I get put so far down the triage line that I figure I'll probably get seen by a doctor about the time someone discovers a cure for cancer.

"I'm just about to go home and put an ice pack on my face, when this guy walks up to me and asks me if I'm the guy who saved his grandmother's life. I tell him yes, and the next thing I know, he's pumping my hand and telling me he owes me a favor. If I ever need one, I should just ask. I say it was nothing, but he keeps on thanking me and insists on handing me a card that says: 'Mark Ryman, Attorney-At-Law.' Since I figure it never hurts to know a lawyer who owes you a favor, I stick the card in my pocket.

"Two weeks later, I see Ryman again, but on the front page of the *Times*. Turns out he's a lawyer for some big-time Mafioso who's on trial for something—I forget what, maybe corrupting police officers without a permit."

Mary Lynn stared at him as if waiting for him to go on. "And?" she said.

"And what?"

"That's a great story, but I don't see how you knowing some Mafia lawyer in New York is going to help me out here in California."

Arnie reached out and patted her hand. The touch of her skin was electric. He swallowed hard, and gave what he hoped sounded like a casual laugh. "You really are from Bakersfield, aren't you? Hey, not to worry. Even here in Hollywood, everything's done by connections. Back East, it's even more that way. Those boys throw a wide net. Here's what I'll do: I'll call Ryman and remind him that I'm the guy who kept his grandmother from freezing to death on the sidewalk. I can practically guarantee that Ryman will know someone who knows Rick Spoletto. I'll ask Ryman to ask Spoletto if there's any way Spoletto can get Ron off your back. By the way, what's Ron's last name?"

"Ronald Morgan McDonald."

"Ronald McDonald? You're kidding."

"I wish I were. Believe me, the guy hasn't been a Happy

Meal. Still"—she looked thoughtful—"I wouldn't want him killed or anything, or even maimed. I mean, I suppose I wouldn't mind if he suffered a little. Nothing physically painful, just psychological terror. I owe him that in memory of Mr. Dickens."

"Mr. who?"

"My late cat." She stood up. "Arnie, I don't know how to thank you. You're a real friend." She offered him her hand. "I may not have any connections with the Mob, but if you ever need a paper edited or a sentence diagrammed, all you have to do is call."

Arnie rose, took her hand, and shook it in as brotherly a way as he could manage. "Good-bye," he said. "Go home and I'll call you if I get any results."

"Thanks again."

"You're welcome, Mary Lynn."

At the sound of her real name, Mary Lynn suddenly sat down on the edge of the bed and began to sob. "Oh, this is so stupid," she said. "It's so damn idiotic. Here we are shaking hands like strangers, and all I want to do is kiss you, and I know I've alienated you forever, and I certainly don't deserve for you to want to kiss me or even ever want to see me again; and you're such a great guy, and you're being so nice; and, oh, damn it all to hell, relationships never work out for me. Clearly, I'm going to spend the rest of my life living like the only spare zebra on Noah's ark. . . ."

Kiss her? She was asking him to kiss her? That was all he had been wanting to do for the last hour. He sat down beside her and gathered her in his arms.

"There, there," he said. "It's all going to be okay."

She looked up at him with tear-streaked cheeks. "No, it *really* isn't," she said. "I've been a beast to you."

He took her chin and tilted her face up to his. "I like beasts." He wiped away some of her tears and kissed her on the forehead and then on the lips. "Umm. Yes, a beast all right, but a very tasty beast."

She smiled wanly. "Arnie, I'm really, really sorry."

"Hush," he said, kissing her a third time. "You never need to apologize again." He paused and then smiled. "But don't keep changing your name on me, okay? I don't think I could take it a second time, my dear"—he kissed her on the tip of her nose—"Mary Lynn."

Twenty-two

Silver candelabras marched down the center of the long mahogany table in Jayne's formal dining room like a line of showgirls. The flames flickered off the silver frames of Jayne's photos and danced across the gold rims of her Rosenthal china. There were tiny quivering lights in the blades of the heavy silver knives, bent lights in the bowls of the soup spoons, and hundreds of twinkling stars in the wide diamond collar that circled Mary Lynn's neck. More light poured from the diamond bracelets on her wrists and the diamond rings on her fingers. Even the tight, low-cut, white silk dress she was wearing glowed faintly in the candlelight with a shimmering phosphorescence that made her breasts look like a pair of pale jellyfish fighting their way to the surface.

Candlelight was definitely a girl's best friend. It hid so much while pretending to show everything. Mary Lynn decided that if she got out of this dinner party alive—and the prospects were looking good—she'd start having dinner by candlelight more often. She picked up her fork, took a bite of boned quail, and allowed herself to imagine that Arnie was sitting across the table from her instead of a middle-aged mobster named Ricardo Spoletto.

"There are over twenty thousand varieties of dahlias," Spoletto was saying. "They come in every color except blue."

"Ah," Mary Lynn replied in what she hoped was a tone

that indicated fascinated interest. Having dinner with Spo-letto had been the price he had demanded for making sure Ron never bothered her again. Although, of course, he had no idea it was Mary Lynn he was helping, and Mary Lynn hoped to God he never found out. The only thing Spoletto was more crazy about than dahlia breeding was Jayne. Ac-cording to Ryman, Arnie's Mafia lawyer contact, Spoletto had seen every one of Jayne's films a dozen times.

In fact, he had so much respect for Jayne that when Ryman had told him the dinner deal didn't include sex, Spoletto had warned Ryman to watch his mouth. Jayne Cooper was an artist. He'd said he wouldn't dream of mak-ing a pass at her.

So far, Spoletto appeared to be keeping his promise—un-less you counted boring a person to death as a technical foul. Mary Lynn would never have dreamed in a million years that she could be on the verge of falling asleep while listening to a man who might have her kidnapped, shot, and permanently encased in concrete if he discovered she wasn't who she was pretending to be.

"A lot of the most interesting work with dahlias is being done in Poland," Spoletto said. He smiled at Mary Lynn and took a sip of wine.

"Mr. Spoletto, I can't imagine anything in the world more fascinating than dahlias. Tell me more." That was a tactic stolen directly from an article in a women's magazine that she had once bought when she was feeling particularly des-perate. The article had been entitled: HOW TO MAKE MEN THINK YOU'RE A GREAT CONVERSATIONALIST. Rule one had been: "Get them to talk about themselves."

Spoletto's smile broadened. Obviously, he was pleased. On the other hand, he hardly needed encouragement, since he had been talking about himself all night. In an instant, he was off and running again. Mary Lynn gazed at him with a frozen smile of absolutely rapt delight and wondered when the hell this interminable dinner would be over.

Surprisingly, by the time they were spooning up crème

brûlée and sipping coffee from Jayne's tiny, shell-like cups, she had, against her will, developed a wary respect for him. He might have bored her to the edge of distraction, but he hadn't once mentioned Ron, tried to bargain with her, talked business, or put her on the spot.

After they finished dessert, he left—just as he'd arrived—with no fuss. Mary Lynn watched his bodyguards lumber after him and pause to check out his limo for bombs. As Spoletto got in, he gave her a friendly wave. Still smiling, she waved back.

She waited until the front gates had closed behind him before she wiped the smile off her face and breathed a sigh of relief. Whatever he really did for a living (and she didn't like to think about that too much), Ricardo Spoletto had been a perfect gentleman.

Back inside, she took off the diamonds, draped the silk dress over the special rack where Jayne put everything that needed dry cleaning, scrubbed Jayne's beauty mark off her cheek, climbed into jeans and an oversize T-shirt, poured herself another glass of wine, and waited. Half an hour later, the phone rang.

"Success!" Arnie cried triumphantly. "Ryman just called. Spoletto was on his cell phone before he was halfway down your driveway. Apparently, you charmed the socks off the guy. He loved having dinner with you. He says you're a great conversationalist and a real lady."

Mary Lynn closed her eyes and breathed a small prayer of thanks. "What about Ron?"

"That's the best news of all. Not only is Spoletto going through with his part of the agreement, he liked you so much, he's going to add some extras. First, he's going to forgive Ron his gambling debts; which, by the way, only amounted to about eight thousand, which Spoletto calls 'chicken feed.' Second, he's getting Ron banned from the gaming tables at all legally licensed casinos and probably all the illegal ones too. And third—get this—he's giving Ron a job."

"A job? Ron? What's he going to do: lie around on a couch in his underwear and watch TV for a living?"

"Close. Spoletto is hiring him to monitor the security cameras at a little casino called the Lucky Dog. It's out in the middle of the desert, about a hundred miles from anything remotely resembling civilization. Apparently, it caters to the patrons of a nearby salt flat where they hold weekly stock car races. But that's not all."

"There's more?"

"You bet there's more." Arnie paused dramatically. "Spoletto is insisting Ron and Sandy get married."

"No way!"

"Way. In fact, as we speak, I believe the two of them are on their way to Vegas to a complimentary, no-holds-barred ceremony in the Little Chapel of the Desert, complete with bridesmaids, organ music, and free flowers."

"What if Ron refuses or Sandy comes to her senses in time?"

"Not to worry. They have a big incentive to do exactly what Spoletto tells them to do, even if it means that they have to spend the rest of their lives drinking warm beer and watching second-rate stock cars kick up salt."

"But what if Ron and his little jogging buddy decide to tell Spoletto who I really am?"

"Not a chance. They wouldn't dare. Ron didn't just owe Spoletto money. It went way beyond that. Evidently, Spoletto's boys caught him trying to cheat. Sandy was in on it too. She was feeding him the cards. According to Ryman, who gave me the whole story, Spoletto was furious when he found out. The Mob doesn't take kindly to cheating, and I suspect that if Ron hadn't been dating Sandy, she would be in a convent in Sicily, and he would have already been sleeping with the coyotes somewhere between here and Vegas. But thanks to you, they lucked out. Spoletto has apparently told Ron that if Ron makes an honest woman out of Sandy, he'll forget about the cheating. He's also told both of them that he never wants to hear 'Jayne Cooper' from their lips again."

"So if Ron tries to persuade him that the Jayne Cooper he had dinner with was really a nobody named Mary Lynn McLellan, what happens?"

"You don't want to know. Let's just say that Sandy would probably end up a very young widow."

Mary Lynn gave a yell of triumph and slammed her fist in the air. "Arnie, get over here! I want to celebrate. I just realized that spousal support ends when the spouse remarries. That means I won't have to send Ron half my take-home pay anymore. We'll drink champagne. We'll—"

"I'm coming right over," Arnie said, "but we better hold off on the champagne. Tomorrow's Thursday and you have to get up early. Didn't you tell me your makeup call was at six—"

"Thursday!" she shrieked. "*Salome*! The retakes! Oh, my God, how could I have forgotten!"

"I was totally in denial." Mary Lynn stared anxiously at the script of *Salome*. It had arrived last night by messenger in a plain, three-hole-punch cardboard cover with a small pink Post-it peeking out from scene 104; so far, she hadn't even looked at it.

Walking over to the sideboard, she poured herself a cup of coffee, retreated to the other side of the room, and stared at the script from afar. The damn thing looked a lot smaller from this angle. It was comforting to think that if she walked out, it would disappear altogether.

Arnie picked up the script and carried it over to her. "Come on," he said, settling down on the couch beside her. "At least take a look at your lines." He was being kind, encouraging, and upbeat. He had offered to do whatever it took to get her ready for tomorrow; he might as well have offered to teach her how to tap-dance on a tightrope over a pit of alligators.

"I can't do this." She took a slug of coffee, looked at the

script, and took another slug. "Remember Pandora's box? Seriously, Arnie, don't even open it."

"You can do it."

"No, I can't."

"Sweetheart, Jayne has a contract."

Ordinarily hearing Arnie call her "sweetheart" would have made her smile, but the word had no effect, except to send her deeper into gloom and coffee. The batch Lois had brewed was so strong you could stand a spoon in it. Maybe if she chugged enough, she'd fly into thousands of small, unidentifiable pieces.

"The studio," Arnie continued, "has spent tens of thousands of dollars to re-create the interior of Herod's palace so they can do the retakes without shipping everyone back to that godforsaken desert. A delay of even a day will cost them a lot of money. If you don't show up at six tomorrow morning prepared to say your lines, an entire firm of lawyers is going to descend on you. They'll discover you aren't Jayne, and you'll be seeing your face on the front page of a lot more credible places than the *Comet*. Come on. Give it a try."

He opened the script and turned to the pink Post-it. "See? It's only a few words."

Mary Lynn shuddered, finished her coffee, and rose to get herself another cup. "I'm not an actor, Arnie."

"Sure you are. Everyone can act at least a little. I've coached plenty of actors with less talent than you. You acted well enough to convince me you were Jayne. And all teaching involves performing. If you count your students, you've stood up in front of audiences hundreds of times."

"This is different." She sat down and stared at the script as if it were a very large, very poisonous snake. "The last time I was on stage was when I played Bunny Number One in my kindergarten Easter play. I took one look at the audience, panicked completely, forgot my lines, and froze in midhop. No one could get me to move. My mother had to come up and carry me off the stage. My ears broke off. I lost my tail. It was one of the most humiliating moments of my entire life."

"This is a film. There's not going to be a live audience. The set will probably be closed, which means that the only people who will be watching will be the director, his assistants, and the crew. You don't have to remember your lines. They'll write them on cards for you. A lot of film stars can't remember lines. Marilyn Monroe was famous for it. If you screw up, they can do retakes. Did you know it took something like eighty-three retakes for Marilyn to get through one line in *Some Like It Hot*? When Billy Wilder told her not to worry, she said, 'Worry about what?'"

Mary Lynn set down her coffee cup and repressed an urge to wail. "I appreciate the encouragement—I really do—but the bottom line here is that I'm totally terrified. Could you please put your arm around me?"

He moved over and put his arm around her. "There," he said, "is that better?"

She gave him a weak smile. "Yeah, now I'm terrified but warm. Damn it, why can't I get hold of Jayne or Clarice! Why did the two of them have to pick this week, of all weeks, to skip town?"

"Try to calm down."

"I am trying."

"Come on. Give it a go. What do you have to lose?"

"What if Bert Laughton realizes I'm not Jayne? He's worked with her on four films. He must know every inch of her body."

"According to the notes that came with the script, you're going to be wearing a black wig, heavy makeup, kohl around both eyes, and about ten pounds of strategically placed fringe."

"I'm going to look like Bubbles the Raccoon."

"Bubbles who?"

"Never mind. Just a desperate attempt at humor that only Clarice would appreciate." She closed her eyes. When she opened them, the script was still there. "Oh, hell," she said. "You're right. I don't have any choice. Give me the damn thing. But I'm warning you: you may be responsible for encouraging the worst acting since Bo Derek danced topless in *Bolero*."

Arnie handed her the script. She bent over it. Apparently, Jayne had only one line. Good. Maybe she could actually get through it. She read further and then slammed the script closed with a moan. "No. It's totally hopeless. Did you read those directions? They're insane. I might as well make a run for it while I still have a chance. How much is a one-way ticket to Tierra del Fuego?"

Arnie reached out and began to massage the back of her neck. "Relax. I swear, this will be a piece of cake. It's nothing. Believe me, I'm a director and know all about stage fright. You've got nothing to worry about." He retrieved the script and opened it again. "See, it says here that all you have to do is look sadly at John the Baptist's head, put the platter on the table without dumping the thing on the floor, look regretful, and say—"

"It's not going to be a real head, right?"

"Of course not. Fake blood all the way. So you put it down on the table and you say: 'My love, my love, how could I have done this to you?' Then if possible you cry. If not, they stop the cameras, come up, and put some fake tears in your eyes."

"This must be one of the worst movies ever made. How could anyone with an ounce of brains believe Salome was in love with John the Baptist? She was a teenager; her mother made her ask for John's head because John had said her mother's marriage to Herod's brother wasn't valid. I know. I looked the whole story up on-line in a thing called 'Your Personal Cyber Bible.'"

"In this version, Salome has the hots for John. You have to remember this is a Jayne Cooper film. Jayne always has the hots for the lovers she kills. It's sort of her signature. Now try again."

Mary Lynn picked up the script. " 'My love . . .' " she read aloud, and then stopped.

"What's wrong?" Arnie said.

"How does a person look regretful about a stuffed head on a fake silver platter?"

"You need to try to feel the emotion from the inside. It's called 'method acting.' "

"I know what it's called. I've read about it; I've even written seminar papers on it; but damned if I can do it. I'm torn between laughing hysterically and shrieking for help. If I'm this upset tonight, what am I going to be like tomorrow?" She threw the script down again. "Who writes this garbage, anyway?"

"The scriptwriter got two million for *Salome*. You—or rather Jayne—got twenty-four million."

"That's obscene."

"That's Hollywood."

Mary Lynn grabbed her coffee cup and finished off what was left. There was a moment of silence, broken only by the ticking of the antique clock on the sideboard. Finally she spoke. "Do you know why they want to do this retake, Arnie? I was curious, so I had Lois call Bert Laughton. Of course, she didn't talk to him directly. Apparently, no one ever gets to talk to anyone directly in Hollywood. Mr. Laughton's assistant told Lois they were doing retakes because the light wasn't right. But Lois is smart. She didn't buy it. She called a friend of hers whose sole mission in life is to bring Laughton coffee with nonfat milk in it, and found out that Laughton had been saying Jayne didn't look 're-gretful' enough. It seems what he actually said was: 'Jayne Cooper looks about as sorry as a bitch on ice.' Lois was so upset by that comment that I had to give her one of Jayne's tranquilizers before she'd tell me. I think she expected me to behead her."

Arnie picked up the script and once again handed it to Mary Lynn. "From the top, please."

"If Jayne can't do it, how can I?"

"You're a better actress than Jayne. At least you would be if you had more experience and self-confidence. Your face is more mobile. It conveys real emotions."

"I really appreciate you lying to me. I know it isn't true, but it helps."

"I'm not lying. Trust me. I'm a professional. Come on. Go for it."

Mary Lynn accepted the script and opened it to scene 104. "'My love, my love . . .'" she read. She paused again and decided that the best way to look regretful was to think about the last time she'd taken a hot cookie sheet out of the oven without using a mitt. "'. . . how could I have done this to you?'" She stopped with a sharp intake of breath.

"Great!" Arnie said. "You're even crying. See, I told you you could act!"

"I'm not acting," Mary Lynn grabbed a Kleenex out of Jayne's gold-plated tissue dispenser and dabbed at her eyes. "I'm scared out of my mind."

Arnie had been overly optimistic. The set wasn't closed. Because the studio was in the middle of the publicity campaign for *Salome*, they had invited an audience of distributors and media people to watch the retakes.

"Quiet on the set!" yelled the assistant director.

The audience fell silent. Every face turned in Mary Lynn's direction.

"Roll film."

"Rolling."

"Sound."

"Sound rolling."

A production assistant scuttled forward and slapped a pair of clapboards in front of Mary Lynn's face. Mary Lynn jumped as if she'd been shot.

"*Salome,* scene one-oh-four, take one," the clapboard operator yelled.

Mary Lynn stared at the camera. The expression on her

face was that of a suicidal deer about to run out onto an eight-lane interstate. On her head, she wore a wig so heavy it made her neck ache. Makeup would have been dripping off her face, except that it was waterproof and glued down with powder. In her arms she carried a silver platter with a severed head on it. She envied the head, which had nothing to do but sit there like a pot roast.

"Action!" cried Bert Laughton.

According to Arnie, the word "action" was her signal to walk forward, put the head on the table, and say her line. Okay, okay, she could do this. How hard could it be? Ten steps. Twelve words. All she had to do was look "regretful." Well, at least that shouldn't be hard.

"Action!" Laughton cried again.

Mary Lynn tried to take a step forward, but her feet wouldn't move. She looked at the audience and opened her mouth, but nothing came out.

"Jayne, sweetheart," Bert said, "you need to move now."

She remained frozen. It was Bunny Number One all over again.

"Jayne? Is there some problem?"

Somehow she managed to nod.

"Cut!" he said.

"*Salome*, scene one-oh-four, take two."

"Action!"

Mary Lynn took a step forward, stepped on the fringe of her costume, and fell flat on her face. The platter flew out of her hands and went clattering across the floor. When she looked up, John's head was nowhere in sight. It took her a moment to realize that it had rolled into a group of reporters who were staring at it with a mixture of alarm and curiosity.

"Cut!" yelled Laughton.

Two production assistants helped Jayne to her feet. Another retrieved the head and put it back on the platter.

"Jayne, sweetheart," Laughton said, "let's try that again."

"*Salome,* scene one-oh-four, take three."

"Action!"

"My love, my love—"

"Cut!"

"Jayne, sweetheart, you're supposed to put the head on the table before you say the line."

"*Salome*, scene one-oh-four, take four."

"Action. Good. Good. That's it. The head on the table, sweetheart. Great, great. Gently, sweetheart. Gently! Wonderful! Now the look of regret."

"My love, my love, how did—"

"Cut! Would someone please make Miss Cooper a cue card?"

"*Salome*, scene one-oh-four, take twelve."

"Action. Good. Wonderful, sweetheart. We're almost there. The platter, the table. Great. You're doing just fine. Now the look of regret. Wonderful. Oscar material. Now the line."

"My love, my live—"

"Cut! Just read the cue card, sweetheart. Bruce, will you please hold the cue card up so Miss Cooper can see it? Tony, throw some more light on it. Good."

"*Salome,* scene one-oh-four, take fifteen."

"Action! Okay, Jayne, start off slowly. That's it. You're sad. Great. Stare at the platter sadly as you make the cross. Don't worry about your fringe. It's too short for you to step on now. And don't worry about the head. It's anchored. Come on. That's it, sweetheart. Perfect. Platter on table. Find your light. Great. Amazing. No one can do it like you. Now the look of regret. Fabulous. Now the line, sweetheart. There's the cue card. Just read it, sweetheart. Don't worry about feeling. We'll postdub it. Come on. Pause. Now speak."

"My love, my love. How could I have done this to. . ." It was no use. She couldn't go on. She'd never get through that damn line if she lived to be a hundred. She took one last, desperate look at the cue card, gave up, and began to sob uncontrollably.

Laughton stared at her in stunned silence and motioned for the cameras to keep rolling. For a good twenty seconds, she stood there crying real tears. This was the most amazing performance Jayne had ever given. He hadn't known she had it in her. He hoped to God they had a usable close-up of her face.

"You broke down?" Arnie said.

"Totally. In front of the distributors and everything."

"And they thought you were acting?"

"Apparently. Laughton ordered one of his assistants to bring me a robe and a glass of water; then he told me I'd just given him the most moving expression of grief he'd seen in thirty years of directing. He shook my hand and said it was an honor to work with me and that this movie was going to win Jayne an Oscar. I suspect he's being overly optimistic, but apparently most of the audience were wiping their eyes as they left. I wouldn't know, because I was too busy having hysterics."

"How do you feel now?"

Mary Lynn snuggled closer to Arnie and put her head on his shoulder. Jayne's satin sheets felt even better, now that he was sharing them. "I'm just glad it's over."

Arnie turned and ran his hand over her breasts, lightly teasing her nipples to attention. Mary Lynn drew him close with a soft murmur. They'd made love half a dozen times in the last three days, and each time had been better than the last.

"Do you have any idea how beautiful you are?" he whispered.

Arnie always said the right thing. Also, she thought, as he moved down between her legs and began to gently lick the inside of her thighs, he had a great imagination. She should have dated a playwright years ago.

Arnie continued to trace the outlines of her thighs with his tongue. She was just approaching that lovely state of mind when her body went on automatic and her brain switched off entirely, when there was a knock on the door. She and Arnie both froze, sat up, and looked at each other in disbelief.

"My God." Mary Lynn brushed her hair out of her eyes and tugged the sheet up around her chin. "That can't be Lois. She'd never dare interrupt Jayne at a time like this."

"Maybe there's been some kind of emergency."

"Like what?" Mary Lynn threw him a lusty look and then surrendered to the inevitable. "Come on in," she said.

It was Lois. She entered the room with a slightly dazed expression on her face. She was in her pajamas. In her hand she held what appeared to be her toothbrush. "Miss Cooper," she said, "I'm really sorry to interrupt you, but I think you need to come to the phone."

"Who died?"

"No one." Lois looked at Arnie and went bright red. Then she looked at Mary Lynn and went so white Mary Lynn thought she was going to keel over on the rug. She opened her mouth, closed it, opened it, and tried again. "There's a man," she said.

"Easy, Lois," Mary Lynn said in what she hoped was a kindly but firm voice. "What man are we talking about here?"

"A man named Trevor Wild. Mr. Wild says he's the president of the International Association of Film Distributors."

"And how did Mr. Wild get my phone number, Lois? My very private phone number that not even God Himself could get without a federal warrant?"

"Mr. Winters gave it to him, Miss Cooper."

"Carleton Winters?"

Lois nodded.

"Why, Lois?"

"Because Mr. Wild called to say that you've . . ." She froze.

"What, Lois? I've what?"

"Won an award!" Lois shrieked, losing all semblance of self-control. "An important international award! Oh, Miss Cooper, I'm so happy for you!"

Twenty-three

Jayne came back from the mountains so relaxed that she forgot to curl her eyelashes for a full twenty-four hours. Living close to nature had been a conversion experience. She adored the wilderness and had every intention of returning someday, preferably armed with Mace and a lightweight flamethrower suitable for taking out poison oak.

On Saturday, Carmen took the girls to the park, and she and Joe spent the afternoon in bed making love until they were so exhausted they could hardly stumble downstairs to eat dinner. After Lisa and Janeira fell asleep, they went back to Jayne's apartment, curled up in each other's arms, and drifted off into a sweet, dreamless sleep.

Near dawn Jayne woke to find Joe still lying next to her. She raised herself on one elbow and studied the careless curl of dark hair that hung over his forehead, his high cheekbones, the smile lines at the corners of his mouth. Everything about him felt so right. Did she really love him? That wasn't a question she was prepared to answer at four A.M. Snuggling back down, she planted her cold feet on his warm legs and went back to sleep.

By the time she woke for a second time, he had gone downstairs to make breakfast for the girls. She lay in bed for a while, petting the cats and enjoying the scent of freshly brewed coffee and cinnamon buns. Again the question came to her, nibbling at her peace: did she really love Joe, and if she did, what was she going to do with him when she went back to her real life?

After breakfast he went out to buy some supplies for his mobiles. He'd been gone for less than five minutes, when Carmen called and invited her downstairs for a *cafezinho* and a chat.

"You good Joe," Carmen said as soon as they filled their coffee cups and took their seats at the kitchen table.

Jayne spent a moment trying to puzzle this out. "Do you mean I'm good *for* Joe, or that I should be good *to* Joe. I need a preposition here."

"You need be good *to* Joe." Carmen took a sip of coffee and gave her a stern but friendly look. "Joe real lonely since Claudia do this." She did an interesting imitation of someone dying, which forced Jayne to bite her lips to keep from laughing. This was clearly not the time or the place. "Not good Joe sleep alone."

"I'm totally with you on that. He's too great a guy, plus he's a fantastic foot warmer. Was there anything else you wanted to tell me?"

"Sim." Carmen paused. "Girls need a mama."

"Mama?"

"Mmmm," Carmen said, looking at her thoughtfully.

Jayne coughed and cleared her throat. "You don't have me in mind for this job, do you?"

"Mmmm," Carmen said.

"Look, I hate to pop your bubble, but I don't think I'm ready to mother a four-year-old and five-year-old without some fairly intense therapy."

"You like kids?"

Jayne sat back and thought it over. "Frankly, kids have always reminded me of midget starlets trying to break in to the big time. They make noise; they mess things up; they throw tantrums; they always upstage you. On the other hand, Lisa and Janeira are exceptional." She picked up her cup, took a sip of coffee, and nearly choked to death. "What the hell's in here?"

"Cachaça."

"Liquor?"

Carmen nodded. "You like?"

"It's only ten in the morning. Are you trying to get me drunk?"

"You betcha. So you like Janeira and Lisa?"

Jayne gingerly took another sip. "Well, to be perfectly honest, I do seem to have developed a strong attachment to them."

"A what?"

Jayne set down her cup. "Okay, I'll come clean. Unnerving as it is to contemplate: I really like them. They've got a great sense of humor. They do a lot of hugging. They're bright; they're cute. They've definitely worked their way into my heart in a fashion I never thought possible. But let's get real here. Do you have any idea what a rotten mother I'd be? It would be Joan Crawford and *Mommie Dearest* all the way. I'm completely selfish. I have hysterics when I get a blemish the size of a pinhead. By the time they were thirteen, they'd hate me. I'd have to hire a poison taster to sample my orange juice." She took a sip of the spiked coffee. Had she lost her mind? She was talking as if she were actually entertaining the idea of marrying Joe and mothering his girls.

Carmen smiled. "Good."

"Good? Didn't you understand a thing I said?" She pointed at her chest. "Me not good mama. Me like creature from *Alien.*"

"So you love Lisa and Janeira?" Carmen persisted.

"Yes, damn it. Now can we just drop the subject?"

Carmen's smile grew broader. "You be great mother." She reached out and patted Jayne on the stomach. "You and Joe have own babies. You love them too."

Jayne suppressed a strong urge to get up and bolt for the door. "Babies? Carmen, let me try again: Motherhood terrifies me. I'm totally unqualified. I probably couldn't get a permit to raise hamsters."

Carmen reached for the coffeepot and refilled Jayne's cup. "Don't worry," she said. "All mamas feel scared at first. You gonna do just fine."

Jayne finished her coffee and left as soon as possible, but it seemed there was to be no escape. As soon as she walked into the living room, Lisa and Janeira threw themselves on her like tiny, adoring pit bulls.

"Come play Run Bunny Run!" they cried. "Come swing with us at the playground or tell us a story!"

Lisa waved a small puppet at Jayne; it was probably a squirrel but might have been a scrawny teddy bear with the ears chewed off. "Barney likes you."

"Barney's a purple dinosaur," Janeira said. "Everyone knows that."

"Not this Barney." Lisa gently pushed Jayne down on the couch, scrambled up in her lap, and threw her arms around Jayne's neck. "I love you," she said, making kissy noises.

"Me too," said Janeira, climbing up after her and settling herself on Jayne's other knee.

Lisa put the puppet to Jayne's lips. "Barney loves you too."

Jayne sat there, not knowing what to do next. She felt like the victim of a conspiracy. She enjoyed holding the girls in her lap. She liked their little heads, their trusting faces, their tiny hands. Was she insane? What had she gotten herself into? Maybe she really did have a brain tumor.

Her heart sped up and she began to hyperventilate. This was becoming a full-fledged panic attack. Fortunately, she was a veteran of panic attacks and knew exactly what to do. Seizing a small cushion, she unzipped the cover, stuck her head in it, and began to rebreathe her own CO_2.

"What are you doing?" Lisa asked.

"Playing hide-and-seek," Jayne snapped. "What does it look like?" Gradually she grew calmer. Taking her head out of the cloth bag, she gave each of the girls a hug and a kiss, picked them up, and deposited them gently on the rug. She felt a kind of hollow sickness in her chest. These poor kids had no idea she was soon scheduled to walk out of their lives forever.

"Bye," Lisa said.

"Bye," said Janeira.

Jayne tried to say good-bye, but the word stuck in her throat. With a squeak of anguish, she grabbed for the cushion cover and plunged her head into it again.

Safely back in Mary Lynn's apartment, she stood in front of the full-length mirror in the bedroom and stared at herself in disbelief. Conservatively speaking, she had probably spent 15 percent of all her waking hours examining her own reflection, but this time was different. She felt as if she'd just been handed the starring role in another remake of *Invasion of the Body Snatchers*. Who was this woman who was feeling so many strange new emotions?

"Get a grip," she commanded this new Jayne, who had been issued without her permission. "You should never have gotten involved with them in the first place. This was all meant to be temporary." Usually, when she told herself to get a grip, it worked; this time it didn't. She just went on loving Joe and Carmen and the kids, and she didn't seem to be able to do a damn thing about it.

Choking back a wail of misery, she walked into the living room. She had to call Mary Lynn immediately. If she stayed any longer, she might not be able to leave; and instead of becoming the next Meryl Streep, she'd end up spending the rest of her life sitting on a plaid couch playing Run Bunny Run. Horribly enough, the Run Bunny Run option had a certain appeal. She clearly needed crisis counseling, long-term therapy, strong drugs, and maybe a complete brain transplant.

She picked up the receiver, but there was no dial tone. This was the last straw. Suppressing an impulse to stuff the phone in the oven and bake it at 500 degrees until it melted, she slammed down the receiver. There was no use putting off the inevitable. She'd have to use a pay phone.

She dumped the last of Mary Lynn's piggy bank change into her pocket and went over to the window to see if the coast was clear. Joe was still nowhere in sight, but the girls were swinging on the swings in the little park across the street. She decided to leave by the back gate so they wouldn't see her. Great. Now she was cheating on a four-year-old and a five-year-old. This was worse than having an affair with a married man.

A few minutes later, she was out of the building and heading toward the nearest bar with an expression on her face that made people step aside to avoid her. The market around the corner was closer, but she wouldn't have gone back to that den of rotten grapes if she'd been bleeding to death.

Outside the bar was a newspaper vending machine that sold the *Comet*. Jayne noticed that her name was once again in the headlines, but she didn't stop to read the article. They were probably claiming they'd caught her having sex with Big Bird.

She went inside and walked up to the bar. "Phone," she said.

"What?" said the bartender. He was a youngish guy with a pierced eyebrow and a row of rings in his upper lip that made him look like he needed a shower curtain.

"The phone. I want to know where the phone is."

"It's right over there, honey. Beside the rest rooms."

Jayne put both hands on the bar and leaned into his face. "I don't like to be called 'honey' by strange men, you pathetic little twerp. I find it demeaning." She reached out and took two quarters out of a beer mug marked *Tips*. "You got any problem with this?" she said, flaunting the quarters in his face.

The kid turned pale and backed away from the bar. The rings on his upper lip trembled. "No, ma'am," he said.

"That's better." Jayne gave him one more glare for good measure and stomped over to the phone to make her call.

*   *   *

Arnie and Mary Lynn were having a late breakfast when the phone rang. Mary Lynn grabbed for it so fast, she knocked over a rack of toast. "Jayne!" she cried. "Tell me it's you! Tell me you're back!"

"I'm back. Listen, I'm in a perfectly ghastly state of mind. Bleak doesn't begin to describe it. I feel crazed, like I might be capable of consuming small animals without cooking them. Bottom line: the party's over. I've decided to call it quits and come home."

"Thank God. You have to get here as fast as possible."

"What's the rush?"

"You have to get ready for the ceremony."

"Ceremony? What ceremony?"

"Haven't you seen *Variety*?"

"No, I've been too busy turning into Marge Simpson."

"You're getting an award!"

"Don't tell me I actually have to be present to win."

There was a stunned silence on the other end of the line. "Well, sure. I mean, I thought you'd be thrilled."

"Who's giving it to me? No, don't spoil the fun: let me guess. It's one of my fan clubs and they want to give me a bronze plaque with 'Paint On, Paint On. I Shall Love You Forever' engraved on it. I have forty-three of those things rattling around the house somewhere: one in Finnish, one in Hungarian, and seven in Japanese. But I suppose I'll have to show up. To tell the truth, I'd rather just come home, lie in bed, drink gin, and think up new ways to sue the *Comet*."

"No, no, you've got it all wrong. You're going to want to go to this ceremony. You're getting the Kleinhaus Award for Outstanding Achievement from the International Association of Film Distributors."

Jayne made a small gasping noise and clutched at the phone. "I'm actually winning the Kleinhaus!"

"Well, to be strictly honest, the president of the association said that, even though you'd made the short list, they were originally planning to give the award to another actor, but he got arrested on drug charges on Friday night. The nominating committee was at their wits' end, because the ceremony had been planned months ago, people were flying in from all over the world, and it was too late to recall the invitations. Then they had the wonderful idea of giving the award to you. Mr. Wild said no one deserves the Kleinhaus more. He said, and I quote: 'Miss Cooper, no one has done more than you for the film industry, and it's time your contributions were recognized. We'd be honored to have you accept.'"

"The Kleinhaus! I can't believe it. This is fabulous news!" Jayne suddenly felt a lot better. Praise was as good as Prozac any day. "Tell me you accepted."

"Sure. I snapped it up so fast Wild didn't know what hit him. At first I was all modesty and dignity. Then I remembered I was supposed to be you. By the time I hung up, he was actually apologizing that the association hadn't honored you years ago."

"So it's a sure thing?"

"Absolutely in the bag. The IAFD has already announced it to the press. Go buy a copy of *Variety*. Your name's splashed all over the front page, plus there's a full-page spread on you in the Sunday section of the *Times*. They're going to give you a gold-plated statue of Melpomene, the Muse of tragedy."

Jayne turned, leaned up against the wall, and smiled so spontaneously and warmly that the man on the nearest bar stool lost his balance and dropped a full mug of beer in his lap. A big award from an international organization. She didn't care if she was second choice. She didn't even care that, although the association claimed the Kleinhaus was for acting, they always gave the award to a star who'd made them a lot of money. She'd always wanted recognition. Her first doll had been a miniature Oscar, but the real one had never materialized. At the moment, the only trophies on her mantel were from the Malibu Society for the Propagation of Rare Iris.

"What am I winning for? *The Loves of Leonardo? The Loves of Joan of Arc? Queen of Scots?*"

"All those, plus, uh . . . *Salome.*"

"Salome? Are you sure?"

"Positive."

There was a dead silence while Jayne tried to wrap her mind around this. "That's positively demented. What could they be thinking? Even I know it's not my best film. It hasn't even been released yet."

"Uh, Jayne . . ."

"Yes."

"A lot has happened since you left on that camping trip."

"Like what?"

"Like retakes."

"Retakes?" Jayne turned back to face the wall. Her voice dropped to a low hiss. "Are you telling me Bert Laughton had the gall to put you up in front of a camera and let you reshoot one of *my* scenes?"

"Yes. I'm afraid he did. How mad are you?"

"Tell me what happened, and then I'll tell you."

"I broke down and started crying and made a complete ass of myself. There were a lot of reporters and distributors in the audience. They all thought I was acting, but I wasn't. Wild and a couple other members of the nominating committee were there. He said my performance was what finally tipped the scales."

"You didn't actually act?"

"Of course not. I don't even know how."

"Does Bert suspect it wasn't me up there?"

"No, I swear. He had no idea."

Jayne thought this over for a while. "Okay," she said, "then I forgive you. As long as you didn't really act, it doesn't count. I mean, you didn't actually win me an award for acting by outacting me; you just sort of accidentally snagged it for me by going hysterical. But don't let it happen again."

"I'd rather be dragged to my death by wild horses."

"That could be arranged. Seriously, I suppose I should thank you. What time is the ceremony?"

"One-thirty. It's a fancy lunch. Roast beef in a pastry shell, tiramisu—"

"Never mind the menu. Just call a cab and send it to your apartment. I'll be back there in ten minutes. And while you're at it, tell Lois to lay out my Ungaro linen pant suit; not the heather and umber one, the one in raspberry and pink that comes with the silk-lined jacket. I'll also be wanting my leaf-embroidered tank top and my Cartier locket. Never mind the shoes, I'll pick those out myself. Then give Vlad a call. He's on my speed dial, button six. After that, call Nine-one-one Manicure. My nails look like claws." She paused. "Did I remember to say 'please'?"

"No, but I don't blame you."

"Please," Jayne said. "See, I *have* changed. I'm a better person than I used to be, so these two weeks haven't been a waste, after all."

It was hard to feel totally guilty, miserable, and torn apart by tragic inner conflicts, when you were about to slip into a luscious raspberry-pink pantsuit and be handed a gold statue. By the time Jayne approached Mary Lynn's apartment building, she felt confident enough to walk past Lisa and Janeira and give them a friendly wave instead of sneaking in by the back door.

After the ceremony, maybe she'd come back and spend a few more days with them impersonating Mary Lynn while she figured out a way to explain things to Joe. There was no use panicking. The only thing she had to decide in the next few hours was whether to wear raspberry-red heels with ankle straps to match her pantsuit or gold heels to match the statue.

The girls were so busy swinging that they didn't see her at first. She waved at them again. "Hi," she called.

"Hi," yelled Janeira, catching sight of her and standing up on her swing to wave back.

"Hi, hi!" cried Lisa, imitating her older sister.

There was a moment when everything was just fine;

when they were all waving and smiling. Then Lisa let go of the chains on the sides of the swing, and all at once she was plunging toward the ground, a small wheeling bit of pink that collided with the seat of the swing and hit the sand with a sickening thud. For a second, Jayne froze, waiting for her to scream; but she just lay there.

"Lisa!" Jayne ran into the playground and knelt beside her. "Are you okay?"

"Lisa's dead!" Janeira wailed. "The swing hit her and she's dead!"

"No, she's not! Don't say that! She's just knocked the air out of her lungs!" Jayne scooped Lisa up and held her. "Come on, honey," she said. "Wake up!" Lisa's eyes opened and she began to scream. There was a gash in her forehead where the swing had hit, and it was bleeding like crazy. Forgetting that she always fainted at the sight of blood, Jayne ripped off her sweater, slapped it against Lisa's forehead, and pushed. In seconds it was soaked.

"Go get Carmen! Tell her Lisa fell and cut her head! What are you waiting for? Run! And for God's sake, look both ways before you cross the street!" As Janeira bolted off to get her grandmother, Jayne hugged Lisa closer and tried to soothe her. "Lisa, baby," she said. "Lisa, honey, hush. It's okay. I'm here."

Jayne looked toward the apartment building and saw the cab that was supposed to take her home pulling up to the curb. This was definitely a no-brainer. She got a tighter grip on Lisa, struggled to her feet, and ran.

"Take me to the nearest hospital!" she yelled to the driver. She jerked open the door and climbed inside. "My daughter's been hurt!"

"She's gonna bleed all over my upholstery," the driver objected.

Jayne gave him the look that had made strong men check into rehab facilities. "Don't fuck with me," she said. "Just drive."

Twenty-four

Mary Lynn and Arnie sat in Jayne's dressing room worrying. Jayne's raspberry pantsuit hung on a padded hanger. Her leaf-embroidered tank top had been freshly pressed. Lois had laid out underwear, panty hose, and six pairs of shoes, plus two Power Bars in case all the excitement gave Jayne low blood sugar. She had even called the hotel where the ceremony was being held and ordered Diet Coke and gin and tonic with organic limes. Everything was ready for Jayne to sweep in and accept her award—except Jayne herself.

Mary Lynn stared at the clock on the dresser. "Where the hell is she?" she asked Arnie for the third time in less than fifteen minutes. "She said she'd be here in half an hour. What are we going to do if she doesn't appear in time to drive to the ceremony? Do you think she's been in a wreck?"

"I doubt it." Arnie took a drink of water and jiggled the glass so the cubes clinked against the side. "I just listened to the traffic report for the fifth time. There isn't a wreck or a jackknifed big rig anywhere between here and San Diego."

Mary Lynn got up, walked over to the clock, picked it up, and shook it to see if it was still running. "Well, if she's not in a wreck, what's happened to her?" She checked her watch and frowned. "I can't let her mess up our career by pulling a no-show."

Arnie put down his glass so fast, water sloshed onto the carpet. "Did I just hear you say *our* career?"

"Right."

"Care to elaborate?"

Mary Lynn shrugged. "It's hard to explain. I've been Jayne for two weeks. I feel as if I understand her at a very deep level. Call it friendship, compassion, identification . . ."

"Or call it 'demonic possession.'"

"That too. In any event, the bottom line is: I can't let her insult every major film distributor in the world by blowing off this award ceremony. If she doesn't show up by one, I'm driving over there and accepting the Kleinhaus for her. I'm good at being her. Maybe even better at being her than she is. So what do you think? Will she thank me and give me another bonus, or will she kill me and bury me in a shallow grave?"

"I'd go for the shallow grave."

Mary Lynn looked out the window, and then she looked at Jayne's pantsuit and shoes. She weighed Jayne's anger against the wrath of the distributors. "I think it's a risk worth taking. I can't figure out if Jayne will be angry or grateful, but I pretty much hit bottom when I tossed John the Baptist's head around like a basketball in front of all those reporters, so I'm going to go by my gut feelings. Jayne no longer scares me. Public speaking no longer scares me. Making a fool of myself no longer scares me."

She opened the top drawer of the dresser, selected a bittersweet cognac truffle, peeled off the gold foil, and popped it into her mouth. "In the last two weeks, I've come to the conclusion that life is too short to do anything except make love, take risks, and eat chocolate."

At twelve Vlad arrived. Mary Lynn sat quietly while he combed out her hair and the manicurist from 911 did her nails. Outwardly she was calm, but inside she was preparing to be Jayne. Things were spiraling seriously out of control. Jayne was still nowhere in sight. Out in the driveway, the limo that was supposed to take her to the ceremony was waiting.

At 1:05 P.M., Mary Lynn slipped into Jayne's pants and zipped the zipper. The hotel where the ceremony was to be held was in Century City on the Avenue of the Stars. Even if they left immediately, they would be nearly an hour late. She stood in front of the mirror and stared at herself, looking for something that might give her away, but there was nothing. The pants fit her like a second skin. She had lost weight. Her butt was fabulous. She looked more like Jayne than ever.

Arnie slipped his arms around her waist. "You look great."

Mary Lynn gave him her best Jayne Cooper smile. "Of course, darling. You wouldn't expect me to accept my award looking ghastly, would you?"

"It's eerie how much you sound like her."

"The question is: shall I be the nice Jayne, the rude Jayne, the humble Jayne, or the imperious Jayne?"

"How about the nice, rude, humble, imperious Jayne?"

Mary Lynn plucked Jayne's jacket off the rack and slipped into it. "Sounds like a winner," she said.

At 1:15 P.M. Mary Lynn adjusted the Cartier locket so it fell directly between her breasts, walked over to the sideboard, and poured herself and Arnie two Diet Cokes. "To my last performance as Jayne Cooper," she said. "Wish me luck."

"Break a leg," Arnie said.

They clinked glasses, drank their Cokes, and then walked downstairs and got into the limo.

If Clarice hadn't been off at the ashram making sure she didn't spend her next life as a fruit fly, she would have been proud. Mary Lynn arrived at the hotel just late enough to make a first-class movie-star entrance. The walkway between the curb and the front door was lined with security guards and waist-high, portable metal fences. Thanks to all the publicity, Jayne's fans had flocked to the scene, and as the cameras clicked and the flashes strobed, they shrieked and cheered and pushed forward trying to get autographs.

At the door, Mary Lynn impulsively turned around and blew them kisses.

"Aren't you overdoing it a little?" Arnie whispered.

"These are my fans. Of course it would be nice if they groveled a bit more, but still"—she blew more kisses—"I like to make them happy."

Inside, the staff of the hotel had rolled out a strip of red carpet. Mary Lynn suddenly came to an abrupt halt and stared at it in her most Jayne-like way.

"Rose petals?" she said.

The manager of the hotel froze, hand outstretched.

"Rose petals, Miss Cooper?"

Mary Lynn sighed. It was a sigh that conveyed many things, patience, disappointment, and just a hint of bitterness. "I had so hoped there would be rose petals for me to walk on," she said sweetly. Arnie moaned and gave her a sharp dig in the ribs. He was starting to regret the day he had decided to teach her about method acting.

The ceremony was being held in the courtyard under half a dozen tall palm trees. There were about fifty tables, round, covered with white linen, and set with heavy flatware and black china. Each table also sported a small candle lantern surrounded by a wreath of white and pink roses and a discreetly numbered card so the guests could find their places. To emphasize the fact that this was a very classy event, the numbers had been done in Gothic script, and each card was stamped with the crest of the association: a tasteful line drawing of Melpomene, who appeared to be tossing a laurel wreath over her head like a basketball.

"Miss Cooper!" said an elderly man with a strong English accent. "I'm Trevor Wild of TMW Film International. What a pleasure to meet you."

"Trevor Wild." Mary Lynn lingered over each syllable of the man's name as if it were honey. She licked her lips and smiled at Wild, instantly reducing him to a mass of lusting protoplasm. "This is my good friend, Arnie Levine, the famous playwright."

Wild shot Arnie an intensely competitive glance that implied he would be happy to duel him at any time. Clearly, he had seen those photos of Arnie and Mary Lynn in the *Comet*. "A pleasure," he said stiffly.

"It's such a warm day," Mary Lynn said sweetly.

"Warm," Wild echoed as if he had gone brain-dead, which, as far as Arnie could tell, was the case.

Mary Lynn gave Wild another smile and wiggled out of her jacket. "Could you hold this for me, darling?" she said, handing it to Wild. Wild took the jacket and stared at it as if he had never seen one before. Then he looked at Mary Lynn, who stood before him in a tank top so tight it appeared to have been welded to her body. Over each of her nipples was a tiny gold leaf. Every time she took a breath, the leaves appeared to stir in the wind.

Wild opened his mouth, shut it, and opened it again. "Table," he gasped.

"Table?" Mary Lynn said brightly, blowing a bit more breeze through the leaves.

"I believe he wants to show us to our table," Arnie said. If Wild hadn't been nearly seventy, bald, out of shape, and clearly not Mary Lynn's type, Arnie might have been jealous; at the moment, he was primarily concerned that the man didn't have a heart attack.

Wild nodded and made a small choking sound th[at] might have been interpreted as "Right" or "Yes." The[n] suddenly laughed. "We always feed our victims first[,"] cried. He stared at Mary Lynn as if hoping for som[e] of reaction.

"That was a joke? Right?"

Wild nodded.

"Work on it," she told him.

On the other side of town, Jayne sat on Joe's couch; she was cradling Lisa in her arms and watching television with the sound off. On the screen, her own face smiled back at her. The Jayne on the screen was dressed in velvet and lace; her hair was wound in graceful coils, and a starched ruff surrounded her face like one of those paper frills that cooks stuck on turkey legs. The Jayne on the couch tried to imagine telling Joe that the woman in the ruff was her; then she tried to imagine not telling him. Neither plan seemed workable.

She turned her thoughts to the Kleinhaus Award. If Joe didn't show up soon, the whole ceremony would be over. Did you have to be present to win? She looked down at Lisa and gave a small sigh of regret. At the moment, getting the Kleinhaus seemed both terribly important and completely irrelevant. The Jayne on the TV screen would have cheerfully ripped out the lungs of anyone who stood between her and the award; but the woman on the couch was just glad that the child in her arms had finally fallen asleep.

Jayne pulled Lisa closer. There was definitely something about holding a sick child that made a person less ambitious. She wondered why no one had ever bothered to tell her this. Had Clarice known?

She was just reaching for the remote when she heard ͏a car pull up out front. She clicked off the TV, took a ͏and silently repeated her mantra. It was sup-͏m" but it came out "damn!" In a few ͏ing to have to have a conversation ͏efinitely didn't want to have. She ͏convinced Carmen to take Janeira to ͏unch on the pretense that Lisa needed ͏y they were here on the couch with her,

chatting and laughing and making any really intimate
conversation impossible.

Joe's key turned in the lock and the door swung open.
Suddenly he was standing before her, against a background
of light so bright he seemed like a shadow.

"Hi," he said, "I'm sorry I'm late. I had to drive all over
town to find the right kind of paint for . . ."

He stopped talking and inhaled sharply. Jayne knew he
had just spotted the bandage on Lisa's head and the pink
cast on her arm. Dropping his shopping bags on the floor,
he rushed toward the couch. A ball of anxiety moved from
Jayne's stomach to her throat. Every mobile he had ever
made seemed to clang together inside her chest.

"What happened to Lisa?"

Jayne put a finger to her lips and struggled to her feet.
She held Lisa out to him, a tiny bundle of slightly broken
little girl. It would have made a great sentimental scene,
but for once, Jayne didn't see an important moment in
her life as a series of close-ups and two shots. The pro-
jector inside her head was unplugged. The movie that
always starred Jayne Cooper was no longer running. All
she felt was anxiety that Joe would wake Lisa up. He must
have been feeling the same, because he took Lisa carefully so as not to wake her. Together they went to the girls'
room. Joe settled Lisa in her bed and gave her a kiss on
the forehead. Jayne arranged the covers around her and
gave her another kiss. Then they retreated to the living
room to talk.

"Lisa's okay," she told him as soon as they were out of
earshot. "She fell off a swing and hit her head and broke her
arm, but it's nothing serious. The cut on her forehead bled
a lot, and they had to put in a few stitches, but she doesn't
have a concussion. The break in her arm is about as minor
as they come."

"Are you sure?" Joe looked sick with worry. This was
something Jayne could sympathize with. She had felt the
same way herself until about an hour ago.

"Absolutely sure." She picked up a sheet of paper, pretended to consult it, then handed it to him. She appeared calm, but she was so nervous she could hardly speak. As soon as Joe read the medical report, he would start to ask questions.

She cleared her throat. "Here's the whole story on her starting from the moment I got her past that demon of a triage nurse. They X-rayed her; they gave her neurological tests; they even let her pick out the color of her cast. Right now, there's not much we can do except let her heal. Dr. Beardsley says we can't give her any pain medication for the next forty-eight hours because of the head injury."

Joe studied the report. "Who's Dr. Beardsley? Her regular pediatrician is Dr. Guftason."

Jayne licked her lips, which had suddenly gone dry. *Go on!* she commanded herself. She went on. "Beardsley's the best neurologist in L.A. You can definitely rely on his diagnosis. He's consulted on several famous cases: Michael J. Fox, Christopher Reeve . . ."

"Christopher Reeve?" Joe put down the report and stared at her.

"Plus, I got Dr. Callen to look at Lisa's arm. Callen's an orthopedist—she specializes in sports medicine. Patches up the Dodgers and Lakers on a regular basis. Global keeps her on retainer for the stuntmen. She confirms that Lisa's break is minimal and should heal fast. She'll be doing an ongoing evaluation of how the bone is healing. The cast should be on for six to eight weeks."

"I don't understand. You say you took Lisa to the hospital?"

"Cedars-Sinai." Jayne forced herself to meet his eyes. "I had a teensy bit of trouble with the cabdriver, but nothing I couldn't handle."

"You called in specialists?"

"Yes. I tried to get in touch with you first, but you don't have a cell phone or a pager, and I could hardly let Lisa be examined by residents who hadn't had any sleep for thirty-six hours."

He read the report again and shook his head. "But I don't understand how you could get these doctors to see her. When I took Janeira in for an earache, we had to sit in the emergency ward for three hours, not to mention that my health insurance doesn't cover second opinions."

Jayne took another deep breath. "Forget the money. I paid for everything. It was the least I could do for Lisa, poor little thing. Frankly, I was frantic. I'd have paid a lot more."

Joe appeared stunned. He stared at the report again, but seemed unable to focus on it. "Thank you. You're absolutely sure she's okay?"

"Positive."

He looked relieved and confused, which under the circumstances made perfect sense. "Thanks again. Of course, I'll pay you back. How much did it cost . . .?"

"Eight thousand dollars, more or less, including Callen."

He gasped.

"But there's no need to repay me," she added hastily. "It's nothing, really. I just called my lawyer and had him messenger over a cashier's check. I hadn't wanted to risk letting him know where I was, but an emergency is an emergency; besides, I figured there wasn't much chance anyone would be looking for me in a room full of middle-aged men with chest pains." Her eyes narrowed. "It's a disgrace that hospitals want money up front to treat little girls with broken arms. I may just have to buy one and run it my way."

Joe sat down next to her, put the report on the coffee table, and took her hand. "I can never thank you enough for taking such good care of Lisa," he said quietly, "but I don't understand a word you're saying. Eight thousand dollars? Cashier's checks? Lawyers? Doctors who treat the Lakers and movie stars? What did you do? Win the lottery? Seriously, are you sure you're okay? Frankly, you sound like the one who fell and hit her head."

Now it was Jayne's turn to grow pale and silent. The moment had arrived. She had known they were going to have to have this conversation ever since the camping trip, ever since the lovemaking beside the river and the lovemaking afterward, and because of the way Joe made her feel when she was around him. She had known she couldn't go on being dishonest with him, but she had hoped to find a better time to tell him the truth. Lisa's accident had forced the issue. When she told him who she really was, would she lose him? Would he be furious at her for having lied?

She thought about all those famous men she'd dated and tossed aside like outtakes from a film that never got edited. Joe was different. Her fame would mean nothing to him. Before he was old enough to vote, he had sat across the dinner table from half the famous artists in the world. Her money would mean nothing to him. He had come from a rich family and walked away from their money without a backward glance.

He was that rarest of all species: an honest man. And if there was going to be any hope of being with him in the future, she was going to have to be an honest woman. She couldn't weasel her way around this problem. She was going to have to tell him the truth.

She cleared her throat. "Joe," she said, "do you remember I told you that I had a secret?"

He nodded and pressed her hand encouragingly. "Sure, I remember."

"Do you want to know what it is?"

"Only if you want to tell me."

"I don't want to tell you."

"Then don't."

"But I have to."

"Then tell me."

Jayne opened her mouth and nothing came out.

"Come on," he said, squeezing her hand again. "How bad can it be?"

"That's exactly what you said last time." She took a deep breath. "Okay, okay, I can do this." She removed her hand from his and sat up very straight. "Joe, I'm about to tell you something that may make you walk out of the room and never speak to me again." She paused. Like all of her pauses, it was dramatic and perfectly timed. Even when she wasn't acting, she couldn't help herself. "I'm not . . . me."

"What do you mean you're not you?"

Jayne managed a very nervous smile. "Well, I am me, of course, but not the me you think I am. I'm not a professor. I'm in the . . . entertainment business."

Joe looked at her with concern. "Are you trying to tell me you're a stripper? Because if you are, I don't care. Let's get something straight here: I love you for who you are, not for what you do. I love you because you're warmhearted, smart, affectionate, and good to my girls, and sexy as all get-out, and—"

She interrupted him. "Joe, it's worse than that. I'm not a stripper. I'm an actress."

"An actress? Why, that's not a bad thing. Where do you act? At the Taper?"

"No, not the Taper or any other theater. I act in films." She didn't want to continue, but there was no help for it. "Actually, I'm a famous movie star." She gave a nervous, desperate laugh. "Look at me, Joe. Really look at me. I know you've spent the last few years in Brazil, and you've probably never seen any of my films, but doesn't my face look familiar now that I've told you?"

He looked at her, and she met his gaze bravely, trying not to flinch. She watched as he took in the blond hair she had returned to its original color using Carmen's mustache bleach, her cornflower-blue eyes no longer hidden by clunky glasses, her gently curved lips, her perfect nose, her small chin, her flawless skin, and all the other things that had made her rich and famous, and which at the moment she could have gladly done without. Suddenly a look of astonishment spread over his face. When he spoke, he was no longer smiling. "This is crazy," he said. "You look like . . ." He seemed unable to continue.

"Jayne Cooper?"

He nodded.

"That's who I am, Joe: Jayne Cooper." And with a feeling of dread beyond dread, she began to explain how she had switched lives with Mary Lynn.

Joe let her talk for a long time without saying a word. When she ran out of explanations, and excuses, and apologies—when she was absolutely sure she had blown it forever and that he would never want to see her again—she stopped talking, sat back, and waited. There was a silence so deep she could hear the refrigerator humming in the kitchen. Joe still didn't speak. He just sat there, looking at her face as if searching for the woman she had pretended to be: that ordinary woman who made bad coffee, fell into poison oak, and played Run Bunny Run with his girls.

Finally she couldn't take it any longer. *I'm going to cry,* she thought. *If I don't get out of here immediately, I'm going to make an absolute fool of myself.* She cleared her throat. "Well," she said briskly, "that's that. Now you know." The only thing she could do was walk away while she still had some dignity left. She started to rise to her feet, but he caught her by the wrist and gently pulled her back down beside him.

"Jayne?" he said awkwardly, as if trying out the name.

"Yes." She could feel the tears burning in her eyes. She tried for a bright, phony smile, but she could tell he wasn't buying it. "That's 'Jayne' with a *y*, Joe."

"With a *y* or without, Jayne's always been . . ." He leaned toward her.

"Always been what?"

". . . one of my favorite names."

She stared at him in amazement. He was smiling. He wasn't telling her to leave. Could it be possible that he wasn't angry?

He drew her closer. "Jayne," he repeated. "I suppose I could get used to it."

"Then you believe me?"

"Carmen said it was you."

"What!"

"She said you were Jayne Cooper that first evening. I'd forgotten, but when you told me to look at you, I suddenly remembered. Carmen claimed you were a princess in disguise. I didn't believe her. I told her she'd been watching too much TV. I should have listened. Carmen is almost always right. Jayne Cooper. The movie star. Yes, it's a totally crazy story, but I believe you. Am I shocked? Yes. But not as shocked as I might have been if Carmen hadn't warned me."

Suddenly he leaned forward and kissed her. Everything else he had to say was contained in that kiss: forgiveness for her deception, love, even the fact that he really didn't care what she did for a living. He only had one question: one he asked between that first kiss and the ones that followed. "Do you love me, Jayne?"

"Yes."

"Really, truly?"

"Really, truly, and maybe even"—she hesitated, realizing she'd never said the word before and meant it—"forever."

Joe smiled. He put his hand under her chin and tilted her face to his. "You know," he said, " 'maybe even forever' is about as good as it gets these days." Jayne felt a wave of relief so great she could have wept. Suddenly she knew—as clearly as she'd ever known anything—that whatever happened from now on, they'd work it out together. *I'm finally listening to my heart instead of my head,* she thought. And she was amazed.

After they kissed some more, she explained that she had to leave, but that she'd come back as soon as she could. She told him about the ceremony, how she'd been on her way to it when Lisa fell, how she really wanted to accept the Kleinhaus Award in person. After having confessed who she was, that part was easy. Joe took the news of the award in stride. He couldn't go with her because he had to stay and take care of Lisa, but he congratulated her and wished her luck.

"I think I'm going to have to get used to seeing you up on stages," he said; then he took her in his arms, brushed her hair out of her eyes, and gave her one more kiss for the road.

Twenty-five

About the time Mary Lynn was eating the last of her *filet de boeuf en croute* and making conversation with a small, compact German film distributor named Gisela, Jayne finally arrived to collect her award. Jayne looked as good as a person could look who had spent the last three hours at a hospital getting a cast put on the arm of a four-year-old, and whose choice of outfits had been limited to either a navy blue polyester suit, a slightly soiled white miniskirt, or a Go Everywhere black dress from TravelSmith.

She had had enough experience with public events to realize that she needed to go around to the back entrance of the hotel.

"I'm Jayne Cooper," she announced as she attempted to sweep past the security guards.

One of the guards quickly stepped in front of her and blocked the doorway. "Sorry," he said. "Invited guests only."

"Did you hear what I just said? I'm Jayne Cooper. They're giving this award to me. Now if you'll just step out of the way . . ."

The guard looked at his companion and rolled his eyes. "They just keep coming out of the woodwork, don't they?" He turned to Jayne. "Listen, whoever you are, why don't you just go home, relax, and take your meds?"

Jayne was annoyed. She hadn't anticipated that the security guards would be too stupid to recognize her. She pointed to her face. "Look. Recognize this? It's on a bill-

board on Sunset Boulevard. Jayne Cooper? Famous movie
star? Is that ringing any bells?" She had a distinct feeling of
déjà vu. How many times in one afternoon did a person
have to point to her own face? "Good. Now suppose you
just step out of my way before I call your boss and get you
fired." She tried to execute a quick end run around the
guard, but he reached out and blocked her.

"I feel sorry for you," he said. "Of all the nuts who've
tried to get in today, you're the most pathetic. About an hour
ago, a big guy came at us like an NFL quarterback, tackled
Matt, and almost knocked me over like a bowling pin. We
had to call the cops for backup. Then there was the little
Italian with all the cameras who tried to bribe us."

"Get out of my way!" Jayne snarled. "I'm late, and you're
making me later."

The security guard didn't even blink. He was used to
being snarled at on an hourly basis. "Sorry. You're not en-
tering the hotel. You aren't Jayne Cooper. Jayne Cooper is
sitting at the head table eating"—he looked at his companion—"What's Miss Cooper eating right now, Matt?"

The other guard listened to his earphone for a moment.
"Dessert," he said.

Jayne retreated, fuming. Heads would definitely roll.
Meanwhile, she needed to get into the hotel, find Mary Lynn,
and change places with her as discreetly as possible. If there
was no way to make the switch without going public, then
she'd give the editors of the *Comet* the best story they'd had
since Prince Charles called himself a tampon. After everything she'd gone through, there was no way in hell she wasn't
going to accept the Kleinhaus Award in person. Carleton Winters could sue her until he was blue in the face.

She began to walk around the building, searching for another entrance, but there didn't seem to be any that weren't
heavily guarded. The hotel was a giant fortress of concrete
and glass, shaped—more or less—like a drawing pencil
with a blunted tip. Unlike the nearby Century Plaza, it offered its guests no balconies. Up on the fifteenth floor, there

was an open window, but a lot of good that was going to
do her unless she grew wings.

As she was craning her neck to see if there were any open
windows closer to ground level, she suddenly felt something strike her shins. Losing her balance, she fell forward
and hit the concrete with an unpleasant thud. She sat up, un-
hurt but dazed. It took her a second to realize she had
tripped over an orange rubber cone.

She got to her feet, brushed off the skirt of her dress, and
gave the cone a kick that sent it skittering down the sidewalk. What the hell was the hotel management doing
leaving cones around where people could trip over them?
Hadn't they ever heard of personal-injury suits? Her stockings had runs in them, there was dirt on the palms of her
hands; she had broken two fingernails. At this rate, she was
going to be the first bag lady ever to accept the Golden
Melpomene.

She wiped her hands on her skirt and started to walk on,
only to discover that she had also broken off one of her
heels. Jerking off her shoe, she limped over to a large metal
scaffold, sat down, and tried to gather her wits. Somehow
she must have blundered into a construction zone.

Or had she? The longer she looked, the less it appeared
as if any construction was going on. There was no dust, no
chopped-up concrete, no yellow tape or nasty-looking
holes; there was only the scaffold and the cones. She examined the scaffold more closely. It was an odd affair: built
like a big metal birdcage on three sides with an open side
that faced the building. Inside were red plastic buckets,
squeegees on long poles, and bottles labeled WINDOW-
WASHING FLUID. On the left was a metal post with three
buttons that read: UP, DOWN, and STOP.

Jayne leaned back and inspected the top of the scaffold.
The whole contraption was on tracks. Suddenly she understood what she was looking at. It was an elevator, a
mechanical scaffolding elevator designed for washing win-

dows. And fifteen floors straight above her was the open window.

This was a no-brainer. She kicked off her remaining shoe, scrambled into the cage, and pressed the UP button. There was a deep humming sound, and the elevator slowly began to rise up the side of the building. For a few seconds, she floated above the city like the angel she had always meant to be someday. Then she reached the fifteenth floor, pushed the STOP button, and stepped triumphantly through the open window into the dark hotel room.

Unfortunately, she miscalculated. The window was not at floor level. With a small shriek, she fell the last foot or so, landing on top of a man. The man was on top of a woman, the woman was flat on her back in a king-size bed, and they were both naked.

There was a moment of screaming and thrashing when everyone got tied up in the sheets. Somehow Jayne managed to extract herself. Rolling out of the bed, she stood up and faced the couple, who where still screaming.

"Who the hell are you!" the man demanded.

Jayne gave him a warm smile. "Room service," she said.

Down in the courtyard, Trevor Wild had almost finished reading the speech he had spent the last month and a half writing. So far, it had been a modest success. The audience had laughed in all the right places and applauded where appropriate; even Miss Cooper had looked pleased in ways that made Wild want to pound the RESET button on his pacemaker.

"And now," he said, "comes the moment we've all been waiting for. On behalf of the International Association of Film Distributors, it is my great pleasure to present the Golden Melpomene for Excellence in Acting to . . ."

There were only two more words left, but he never got to say them. Suddenly there was a scuffle at the back of the room, followed by the sound of breaking glass. A woman in a short black dress darted between the tables and headed toward the podium, yelling something incomprehensible. Behind her ran two security guards in hot pursuit. Depending on their countries of origin, the members of the association either threw themselves to the ground to avoid gunfire or stood on their chairs to get a better view. Being British, Wild didn't move a muscle.

"Mary Lynn!" the woman yelled. "It's me! Ja—" One guard seized her from the right as another seized her from the left. As Trevor Wild watched in dismay, the poor demented woman grabbed a tablecloth, sending crystal and china cascading to the floor. Wriggling loose, she attempted to kick the nearest guard in the testes. Fortunately, she missed. To Wild's relief, the guards got hold of her again and began to bear her off, kicking, screaming, and scratching like a Bengal tiger.

As she passed the Russians, a distributor named Boris Kamisky reached out and deftly stuffed a napkin in her mouth. There was a sudden silence, followed by a series of infuriated grunts and snorts.

Wild stepped back up to the microphone. "Ladies and gentlemen," he said, "I'm terribly sorry. We seem to have had an unfortunate incident with one of Miss Cooper's fans. If you'll all please resume your seats—"

"Wait!" a voice commanded. Wild turned and found Miss Cooper approaching the podium. What was she doing? She was supposed to remain seated until he presented her with the statue.

She took the microphone out of his hand and racked up the volume. *"Let that woman go!"* she commanded. The sound of her voice boomed off the tiled walls of the courtyard. Startled, the security guards came to a stop.

"Let her go!" she repeated. *"That's Jayne Cooper!"* She turned to Wild. "She really is Jayne Cooper. I'm an impostor. Make them let go of her right now."

Wild stared at Miss Cooper in horror. Apparently, she had decided to use the occasion of the award ceremony to go barking mad.

"Now!" Mary Lynn snarled. She had spent two weeks

being Jayne and was very, very good at it. Wild shuddered, took the microphone from her, and cleared his throat.

"Let . . ." Realizing he was still at full volume, he turned down the microphone. "Let that woman go, please." The guards released Jayne, who pulled the napkin out of her mouth and glared at them like a feral cat.

Mary Lynn took the microphone out of Wild's hand again, and stood for a moment facing the audience. The courtyard was so silent you could hear the palm fronds clicking together. "Jayne," she said, "come on up here and get your award."

Jayne smoothed the wrinkles out of her dress, fluffed her hair, and gave the security guards a triumphant smile. She walked past the stunned distributors, climbed the steps that led to the platform, and stopped.

Mary Lynn held the microphone out to her. "Go for it," she said.

Two weeks ago, Jayne would simply have taken the microphone, but a lot had changed since the afternoon she walked into the Food Barn and found Mary Lynn. Slipping her arm around Mary Lynn's waist, she led her to the podium. As the two women stepped into the light, a gasp went up from the crowd. One wore an inexpensive black dress, the other wore a designer pantsuit the color of raspberry sorbet; one had neatly coiffed hair, the other had messy hair and a small smudge on her nose. Otherwise, they were virtually identical.

"Ladies and gentlemen," Jayne said, "you're probably wondering who's the real Jayne Cooper. I am." She paused, looked at Mary Lynn, and smiled. "I'm deeply honored to be here this afternoon, but before you give me the Golden Melpomene, I'd like you to meet Mary Lynn McLellan, my stand-in and"—she gave Mary Lynn a hug—"the best friend I've ever had."

Twenty-six

One year later

Jayne Cooper's wedding was going to be the most exclusive wedding in Hollywood history. In fact, if Jayne had anything to say about it, her wedding wasn't going down in history at all. The ultrasecret ceremony was being held in the ashram of Clarice's guru, Ananda Ananda Shri Joti Amrit Ananda. Located between Santa Barbara and Esalen, Babaji's ashram sat on a wide shelf of solid granite two hundred feet above some of the wickedest currents on the West Coast. On three sides, the gardens, cottages, pools, and meditation halls were enclosed by a twelve-foot fence concealed by a hedge of pink and white oleanders. The western side of the property looked straight out over the Pacific into some of the most spectacular sunsets east of Hawaii.

Jayne had issued all the invitations either in person or using an encrypted landline phone so secure that in a pinch it could have been used to trade atomic secrets. So far, her privacy had remained inviolate, which meant that there were no reporters trampling each other outside the gate, no crowds of star-crazed fans, and no paparazzi crouched in the eucalyptus trees that shaded the tables set up for the wedding breakfast. Not even the editors of the *Comet*—who were definitely going to commit seppuku when they learned Jayne had been secretly married—had gotten wind of the event.

Despite the fact that this was Babaji's turf, Joe's parents

had insisted on a Christian ceremony. Joe had agreed and, for once, Jayne had given in gracefully. Babaji had given permission for a Presbyterian minister to marry the couple in the ashram rose garden. Suddenly, for the first time since Joe dropped out of Harvard Law School, he found himself on speaking terms with his parents.

Paul and Audrey Porter had known some of the most famous artists of the twentieth century, so they weren't particularly impressed that their youngest son was marrying a movie star. But they weren't getting any younger, and they had two grandchildren they had never met, and one on the way. Joe had recently had two very successful shows of his kinetic sculptures, which hadn't hurt either. Plus, Jayne could be extremely charming when she put her mind to it; so charming, in fact, that, ten minutes after meeting her for the first time, Joe's father had decided that she was the daughter he had always wanted.

In short, all differences had been put aside, and as Jayne stood in the rose garden beside Joe reciting her vows, she looked exactly as a bride should look: radiantly happy and totally in love. No one needed to ask why she and Joe had finally decided to get married after a year of living together. Not only did they clearly adore each other, Jayne's white maternity wedding gown was a blossom of white lace on the brick path.

Mary Lynn stood directly behind her, holding a small bouquet of lilies of the valley. A lot of things had changed since she and Jayne had gone public in front of the International Association of Film Distributors. The publicity had been fierce, and for a while, Mary Lynn had been unable to go out of her apartment without photographers following her like a pack of Border collies. Gradually the flap had died down. She'd done her best not to look like Jayne, and except for occasional offers to work as a celebrity impersonator, life had pretty much returned to normal, except that she now had plenty of money and no longer cut her own hair.

At the end of the spring semester, Coast Side Community

College had finally offered her a full-time teaching job, but she'd turned them down. In late June, she had rented a U-Haul, packed up the cats, and moved to New York to join Arnie, who, sustained by the proceeds from *Star Whale*, was writing the wonderful, serious, quirky, off-Broadway plays he had been born to write.

After she settled in, she gradually discovered that she really did have a talent for acting. In the last few months, she had begun to have a modest career in the theater, although she still hadn't decided whether or not to pursue it. She and Arnie would be celebrating their first anniversary about the time Jayne and Joe became parents; recently she'd been thinking that they needed to take a serious look at the possibility of having children before they were so old they'd have to use their Social Security checks to send the kids to college.

The wedding ceremony was short and simple. Besides Joe's parents and Babaji, the only other guest was Carmen. Clarice was there, of course, but since she was giving Jayne away, she was in the wedding party. Lisa and Janeira, now big girls of five and six, didn't count, because Jayne had assigned them the job of looking impossibly cute and spreading rose petals on the path that led to the altar. The bridesmaids didn't count as guests either. They stood behind Mary Lynn, dressed in pink satin and holding their own bouquets of lilies of the valley; they looked as dreamy and romantic as four young women could look. Technically, Jayne had informed Mary Lynn, the tallest bridesmaid was a man, but since she called herself Corette and walked as if she'd been born wearing heels, no one except Carmen had managed to figure this out.

It was a beautiful day, sunny and full of promise. The ceremony ended, as all good wedding ceremonies do: the bride and groom gave each other a kiss; the minister shook their hands and congratulated them; Jayne exchanged another round of kisses with her mother, Mary Lynn, Carmen, her new in-laws, all four bridesmaids, and the girls; then everyone adjourned to the other side of the garden for breakfast.

Alcohol was forbidden at the ashram, but everyone was too happy to miss the champagne. They poured sparkling apple juice into the crystal wineglasses, and Joe's father rose to toast the newly married couple.

"In the wedding ceremony," he said, "the minister begins by saying, 'Dearly beloved.' This morning, dearly beloved, we have come here to . . ."

It sounded pretty good for a wedding speech given by the father of the groom, but how it would have ended, only Joe's father knew. Just as he got to the words "here to," a sound like the roaring of a giant eggbeater blotted out his words. The seabirds scattered screaming, and everyone watched in horror as a large helicopter rose slowly over the edge of the cliff and hovered above the wedding party, kicking up dust and scattering napkins.

Jayne looked up and saw a telephoto lens pointed straight at her face. With a shriek, she picked up the skirt of her wedding dress and bolted awkwardly toward the meditation hall.

The next morning, every newspaper in America—except the *Washington Post* and the *New York Times*—carried Antonio Malfredi's famous photo of a very pregnant Jayne Cooper attempting to escape. The *Comet* ran a five-page photo essay entitled NO MERCY FOR THE RUNAWAY BRIDE: Jayne in a black raincoat, black scarf, and dark glasses, with Joe at her elbow hurrying toward the garage where the limo was parked; the limo passing through the front gate as Jayne attempted to escape on her honeymoon through a crowd of reporters and fans who swarmed the car, forcing it to stop; a harried, weeping, near-hysterical Jayne rolling down one of the tinted windows of the limo and begging the media to let her and her husband-of-half-an-hour have a little privacy. It was almost forty minutes before the highway patrol arrived, dispersed the crowd, and cleared the road; then the limo was finally able to start moving again.

* * *

By noon everything at the ashram had been back to normal. The altar had been transformed into a simple oak garden bench. Babaji's disciples had picked up all the napkins, swept the rose petals off the path, packed away the collapsible tables, gathered up the remains of the wedding breakfast and fed them to the seabirds.

By the time a white van pulled out of the garage, there was no one left to notice. The disciples were all in the meditation hall chanting prayers to Krishna. The reporters had headed back to the city to write their stories. The photographers were sitting in front of their computers Photoshopping tears onto Jayne Cooper's cheeks, and Antonio Malfredi was involved in a shouting match with the firm that had rented him the helicopter for a set sum and was now demanding overtime for the pilot.

The white van drove slowly out the service entrance of the ashram. It had a cracked windshield, a rusty tailpipe, and no hubcaps. At the wheel sat a workman in a stocking cap. To his right sat a gray-haired woman dressed in a faded sari. She looked as if she might be his mother. The woman's head was covered with one end of her sari, and she slumped over in the seat, with her eyes on the floor.

For a quarter of an hour, they drove down the coastal highway until they came to a dirt road that led into the National Wilderness. If you followed this road, you would eventually come to another road that led to the interstate that ran along the eastern side of the Coastal Range, but few people bothered. There were no towns, no improved campsites: only dust, hundreds of switchbacks, and potholes the size of dishpans.

The van continued chugging up the steep grade for another half an hour. Finally the woman straightened up and looked around. Tossing the end of the sari off her head, she shook the flour out of her hair and sneezed. The sunlight that shone through the dusty windshield revealed the triumphant, smiling face of Jayne Cooper.

It had been an easy switch: Jayne and Joe had simply

walked into the garage, where Mary Lynn had been waiting. Mary Lynn had tied a pillow around her middle, put on Jayne's black scarf, dark glasses, and raincoat, then climbed into the limo.

Jayne laughed wickedly at the thought of the paparazzi snapping photos of Mary Lynn. Then she reached over, snatched the stocking cap off Joe's head, and gave him a kiss.

"Pull over, honey," she said. "It worked. Those ghastly photographers will probably follow Mary Lynn all the way to the airport before they figure it out."

Ten minutes later, anyone who had happened by would have seen an apparently empty van parked in a pull-out behind a screen of pine trees. The van had originally been designed for camping. It might have been old and battered, but the seats still converted into a bed very easily.

Grab These
Kensington Mysteries

__**Blowing Smoke** by Barbara Block	1-57566-723-1	**$5.99US/$7.99CAN**
__**Dead In The Water** by Carola Dunn	1-57566-756-8	**$5.99US/$7.99CAN**
__**The Confession** by Mary R. Rinehart	1-57566-672-3	**$5.99US/$7.99CAN**
__**Witness For The Defense** by Jonnie Jacobs	1-57566-828-9	**$6.99US/$8.99CAN**
__**Mad As The Dickens** by Toni L. Kelner	1-57566-839-4	**$5.99US/$7.99CAN**
__**Stabbing Stephanie** by Evan Marshall	1-57566-729-0	**$5.99US/$7.99CAN**
__**Shooter's Point** by Gary Phillips	1-57566-745-2	**$5.99US/$7.99CAN**

Call toll free **1-888-345-BOOK** to order by phone or use this coupon
to order by mail.
Name_____
Address_____
City _____State_____Zip_____
Please send me the books I have checked above.
I am enclosing $_____
Plus postage and handling* $_____
Sales Tax (in New York and Tennessee only) $_____
Total amount enclosed $_____
*Add $2.50 for the first book and $.50 for each additional book.
Send check or money order (no cash or CODs) to: **Kensington Publishing
Corp., 850 Third Avenue, 16th Floor, New York, NY 10022**
Prices and numbers subject to change without notice. All orders subject to
availability.
Check out our website at **www.kensingtonbooks.com**.

Mischief, Murder, &
Mayheim – Grab These
Kensington Mysteries

GET YOUR HANDS ON THE
MARY ROBERTS RINEHART
MYSTERY COLLECTION